Wolfbane

Wolfbane Series: Book 1

Celia Hart

Celia Hart
AUTHOR

Celia Hart LLC

WOLFBANE
WOLFBANE SERIES: BOOK 1
by Celia Hart

Copyright © 2022 by Celia Hart

All rights reserved.

This is a work of fiction. Names, characters, organizations, places, events, media, and incidents are either products of the author's imagination or are used fictitiously. No portion of this book may be reproduced, stored in a retrieval system, or transmitted in any form or by any means, electronic, mechanical, photocopying, recording, or otherwise, without written permission from the author, except as permitted by US copyright law.

Edited by Corbeaux Editorial Service
Cover design by Emily's World of Design
Chapter heading artwork by Studio Saturno

ISBN: 979-8-9864024-0-6

The unauthorized reproduction or distribution of copyrighted work is illegal. Criminal copyright infringement, including infringement without monetary gain, is investigated by the FBI and is punishable by fines and federal imprisonment.

Content Warning

These content notes are made available here so readers can inform themselves, if they want to. Some readers might consider these "spoilers." If you don't like spoilers, look away. You've been warned.

- **Bad language**: strong and frequent, including slurs
- **Sex**: several fully described and explicit sex scenes, including cunnilingus and fellatio
- **Violence**: some graphic violence
- **Other**: death, depression, domestic abuse, homophobia, panic attacks, pregnancy

If you'd like more information on any of the above content notes prior to reading, please reach out (celia.hart.author@gmail.com) and I will be happy to elaborate so that you may make a fully informed decision before choosing to turn the page!

For Jen and Amanda, who believed in me and this story.

Chapter 1

*** *Two years ago* ***

Jasmine

Rules. I was good at following rules. Rules like always bring home report cards with a vertical line of As; go to temple to worship the Moon Goddess, Artemis, every week; prepare dinner for the family on weeknights; help keep the house clean. My parents had lots of rules, and I followed them, the number one being: never ever date anyone who isn't your mate.

I liked rules. They kept my life simple. If I followed the rules, my parents would be pleased, and I'd be rewarded with future success and happiness. At least that was what I believed for a long time. Looking back, I could pinpoint the day my feelings began to change—exactly a month before my eighteenth birthday.

It was one of those perfect days at the end of August where the sun didn't scorch you, and the breeze was cool on your skin. Engrossed in a book, I had lost track of time when the loud drumming of a woodpecker broke my concentration, and I realized—*shit!*—I was late meeting my best friend, Lucy.

Wasting no time, I hopped on my bike and sped through the woods to meet her at what was dubbed the "party lake," where we had made plans to decorate for her boyfriend Luke's goodbye party happening later that night. I was in good shape, so pedaling quickly wasn't a problem.

The scent of damp wood, pine sap, and decomposing leaves surrounded me as I pedaled through the lush Vermont forest—thick with trees, ferns, and pine needles littering the ground. Years of traveling these paths had made me confident in my ability to dodge rocks and tree roots on the uneven terrain. Maybe too confident.

Changing gears, I pushed my legs harder, racing downhill along a path through the woods. I was well on my way when suddenly I lost balance, my bike shaking underneath me. I stretched my leg out to steady myself, only to step on a slippery leaf on a rock, and—*shit, that hurt!* My ankle contorted all wrong, bent sideways, crushed by the weight of my body.

I crawled out from under my bicycle and stood, hobbling a bit, searing pain shooting up my leg.

Damn, I must have fractured my ankle.

I picked up my bike and limped beside it to get to my destination. I wasn't going anywhere fast now. My ankle would take a good few hours to heal, possibly the whole night depending on the severity of the fracture. I'd have to live with the pain until then.

A twig snapped nearby. Instinctively, my head turned in that direction, taking my attention from the throbbing pain pulsing up my leg. That was when I saw him. Well, I didn't see his face exactly, because it was partially obscured by a branch and a ray of sunlight directly in front of me, but I couldn't have concentrated on his face at that moment anyway. Without even realizing it, I stopped dead in my tracks. I lost all sense of my surroundings, time—I could only stare at this tanned Greek god standing before me. My gaze slowly made its way down his body, from his broad shoulders and picture-perfect pecs to his six-pack abs.

Oh my Goddess! I was completely in awe. My gaze continued down his rock-hard stomach to where his body made a chiseled V, directing my attention farther south, a place my eyes had never gone before.

Shit, it was hot! Where had the breeze gone? My whole body was overheating, revealing feelings I'd never felt before. My stomach quivered, flames engulfed my skin, and a tingling sensation sparked between my thighs. My injured ankle was now long forgotten as I stared at the golden-brown Greek statue that had come to life before me.

He ducked his head under the tree branch, coming forward, blocking out the rays of the sun. And when he looked up, our gazes locked; my lips parted.

"Oh my Goddess!" I actually said it out loud, yet it had a different meaning this time. I instantly recognized that it was Luke! Lucy's boyfriend. I had been ogling my best friend's boyfriend! Both our faces reddened in recognition. And just like that, Luke quickly shifted. He was a huge wolf with gray, black, and brown fur on top and white fur on his bottom half. I was stunned and beyond embarrassed. Before I had a chance to look away in shame, he glanced at me for a moment, then used his mouth to pick up his shorts from the ground and broke into a run, heading back through the woods from where I had come.

After spending the day helping Lucy string up lights, streamers, and balloons into trees by the party lake, we now stood together admiring our work. The small gleaming bulbs contrasted against the dark forest created the ambience of an enchanted forest hideout with fairies twinkling above us.

"Thanks for your help today." Lucy threw her arms around me. "Goddess, I'm so heartbroken about Luke leaving. But at least we put together a pretty awesome party for him, right?" My cheeks burned at the mention of his name, recalling what I'd seen earlier that day. The reminder evoked a fluttering in my stomach and a pang of guilt for having unintentionally lusted after my best friend's boyfriend.

"How'd you get away with it anyway?" I asked, pushing the image from my mind. "Don't they normally have warriors patrolling the area, especially with all the recent safety concerns?"

"I talked to Luke's dad, and he agreed to turn a blind eye to tonight's party. There are perks to him being the beta's son!" Lucy gave one of her winning smiles. Above all things, Lucy was beautiful, with a supermodel stature, long blonde hair, and sapphire eyes. And she was persuasive—very, very persuasive—and not someone that took no for an answer.

Lucy was always getting away with things—for example, dating. She was the only person my age that openly had a boyfriend. Our pack was very religious, and we were all taught from a young age to wait for our mate, a gift granted to us by the Moon Goddess, a person we'd innately be able to sense beginning at dusk on our eighteenth birthday. So long as our mate was also of age. Dating anyone other than your mate was looked down upon, but Lucy didn't care. She was convinced that she and Luke were mates anyway. While Luke was nineteen and old enough to recognize his mate now, Lucy was still seventeen like me, so they had yet to confirm the bond.

Luke arrived at his party not long after we did. After greeting his buddies, he made his way toward Lucy and me. Lucy jumped into his arms, pulling his face against hers, zealously kissing him. Although I tried to look away, for the most part, I caught a glimpse of Lucy gently biting down on his bottom lip just as they separated. The scene in front of me awakened the feelings from earlier that day—my body overheated, and my breathing turned erratic. Before I could stop myself, I was imagining what his solid muscles would feel like under my fingertips.

No! I pushed the thoughts from my mind. Girls like me didn't have thoughts like the ones going through my head right then! I didn't date or even think about dating anyone that wasn't my mate. Especially not when the person in question was my best friend's boyfriend!

After they pulled apart, their eyes fell on me awkwardly staring back at the two of them. Luke gave me a big smile and said, "Glad you could make it tonight, Jasmine."

I smiled back at him, hoping he couldn't tell I was blushing in the dark.

"How about I go get you ladies something to drink?" he asked.

"Yesss!" Lucy cheered.

"Sure, I'll have a Coke, thank y—"

Lucy cut me off and said, "Don't listen to PJ. Get us some real drinks and fill them to the top!"

PJ was my nickname, which was short for "Perfect Jasmine." My classmates came up with it years ago as a taunt for being a religious, straitlaced, perfect student. Lucy was the only person I tolerated using it. I found her use of the nickname a bit ironic considering she was the perfect one, being so magazine gorgeous with a charming and sociable personality to match.

Luke came back with red plastic cups filled to the brim and handed one to each of us. Lucy stared at me, beckoning me with her head to take a sip. I sighed and tipped my cup back. I wasn't a big drinker, but Lucy always convinced me to at parties. Before long, a large group of friends from school had joined us, and everyone was starting to let loose. I was thankful for the buzz that came on as it helped distract me from how awkward I felt in Luke's presence.

The late-August full moon was glowing above the lake, making the water sparkle. At least a hundred werewolves from our pack had come to say goodbye to Luke and a few of his fellow warriors who would be leaving on a mission the next day. It was a mix of older high schoolers, such as Lucy and me, and young warriors who trained and patrolled with Luke and his friends. Our pack was a community of about forty-five hundred werewolves located deep in the woods of northern Vermont, where humans didn't normally venture, a heavily forested area surrounded by mountains.

As the party progressed, people began jumping into the water, some coming out of the woods shifted into their wolf form. Lucy and the others ran toward the shoreline to join everyone in the festivities. Because my ankle still wasn't 100 percent, I decided to hang back and chill out on a blanket by the bonfire. Getting comfortable, I pulled my long, dark hair into a ponytail and stretched my toned legs out in front of me.

A red cup appeared over my left shoulder. I could smell his cologne. I glanced over my shoulder at him and smiled sheepishly.

"Jasmine, you've been nursing the same quarter of a cup all night," Luke said as he gently shook the cup for me to take it.

My mouth agape, I took the cup and replied, "No, I haven't!"

He laughed. "I know, I'm just kidding." He sat down on the blanket next to me. "I saw the way you wobbled over here." Damn, he smelled so good. It was almost intoxicating—a musky, sensual fragrance.

"Oh, stop!" I said, "I'm having a rough day." I stared down at my ankle that was still a little swollen and flinched at the sight of it.

Clearly noticing the look on my face, Luke asked, "What's wrong?"

"Oh, nothing."

He pressed. "Tell me."

"It's not a big deal. I think I fractured my ankle earlier, but it's almost healed now."

"Which one?" he asked, looking down my bare legs. The shorts I'd worn suddenly felt much more revealing and inviting than previously. "Oh, never mind, I see it. It looks pretty swollen." He moved down the blanket to get a closer look and gently touched my ankle, his touch more intimate than it normally would have been. A soothing sensation radiated from his hand. "If it doesn't feel better by tomorrow, definitely drop by the clinic to have it looked at." He slid back up the blanket to sit down next to me and looked at me seriously. "Anyway, the reason I came over is to talk about what happened earlier today in the woods."

My face burned, recalling vividly what had happened earlier that day, trying my best not to visualize it while he was right in front of me, thankfully clothed!

Luke continued, "Don't feel bad about it. I'm not embarrassed, and I didn't say anything to Lucy." He put his hand on my knee, shaking it a little and then retracting. I felt the soothing sensation again as he touched me.

"Thanks, I didn't say anything to Lucy either," I replied, relieved that we were mutually agreeing to just forget about it. His scent filled my nose. Trying to decipher the fragrance, I could almost sense notes of cedarwood and maybe amber. For the past few months, I'd noticed that he'd been wearing the most divine cologne.

"We're always taking our clothes off to shift during warrior training, so I'm used to it by now." He gave me a reassuring smile. While it was true that nudity wasn't a taboo in werewolf culture, there were still more timid ones, like me, that preferred to shift away from others.

Desperate to change the topic of conversation, I asked, "How do you feel about becoming the beta soon?"

Luke relaxed and spread his long legs out on the blanket, leaning back on his hands. "I mean, I've been training for the job forever, so it just feels natural at this point. I was supposed to take title from my dad after graduating from high school last year. But because of the whole battle and everything that happened, it's been put off until the alpha heir gets back from college in a couple years, and we'll both succeed our fathers then."

We all remembered the battle that happened three years ago. Our pack, the Midnight Maple Pack, had been called in to defend our ally in Quebec, the Lune Nordique Pack, against one of their enemies, the Bois

Sombre Pack, who had waged war on them. The battle lasted at least a week, and we lost many of our warriors. Our pack was still affected by the loss, as it had happened so recently, and many people's children, mates, and parents had never returned.

Luke continued, "I was too young to go to battle back then, but the Bois Sombre Pack is still a threat, so that's why I'm heading up north with some of the other guys to keep an eye on things for now. I'm actually pretty surprised my dad was okay with this party happening tonight with everything going on."

"Do you think they might attack us?"

Luke considered my question, looking out into the distance, appearing as if he were deep in thought, and finally replied, "We shouldn't worry about that tonight. Let's talk about something less heavy! Like, how long did it take you to put up all these decorations? They look great!"

"Thanks," I replied, relaxing into the conversation, and feeling hopeful that things wouldn't be awkward between us. "It took us a few hours. It was all Lucy's vision—I just followed her directions. She's great at throwing parties. I'm really more of a nerd and normally prefer to be at home with a good book."

"I'm kind of a nerd too, to be honest." He gave a coy smile. "What're you currently reading?"

"I just started a book called *The Disasters*. It's really good so far!"

"You're into sci-fi?" Luke raised his eyebrows at me. "I read that book a few months ago. I didn't think you were into that kind of stuff."

"Yeah, I really enjoy sci-fi," I replied.

"Cool!" He smiled. "I never admit this to anyone, but I actually love my name because of *Star Wars*. I grew up watching it with my dad, and I used to pretend I was Luke Skywalker as a kid." He chuckled. "Okay, I told you something embarrassing about me. Now you have to tell me something about you."

"Okay, okay." I laughed. "I never tell anyone my favorite sandwich because people think it's really weird. But I have a guilty pleasure for peanut butter, bacon, and banana sandwiches."

"Seriously?" Luke stared at me wide-eyed.

"I know, it's really weird." I put my hands on my face in mock embarrassment.

"No, it's just crazy because it's my favorite sandwich too. I've never met anyone else that eats them."

I laughed. "Wow, that's a crazy coincidence. I don't even remember how I came up with it, but I've been eating it for years."

We fell into easy conversation while lively music played in the background, contrasted by the cheerful clamor and howls of partygoers. I'd never really spent any time one-on-one with Luke before but found that we avoided awkward pauses and never stopped having something to talk about. I regretted never being more friendly with him now that I knew we had so much in common.

Luke moved closer to me, and I took a sip from the cup he had brought over. And then... *was he*? It seemed like he was smelling my neck. I looked over at him and he smiled. He did have a really nice smile that lit up his whole face. He was really quite attractive, with deeply tanned skin, faint freckles dotting his nose, and long lashes that surrounded his vibrant brown eyes.

Being so close to him now, his scent overpowered my senses, filling my nostrils with the most intoxicating and salacious fragrance. As his hand casually touched me in conversation, a relaxed feeling came over my body. The feeling stretched through me, mixing with my buzz. We, again, moved closer, something within us drawing us to each other, his face now only inches from mine. As he spoke, moving his full, rosy lips, I had an illicit thought—I wanted to feel his mouth against mine.

"Hey, guys! Come on, let's go dance with everyone!" Lucy stirred me from my thoughts, coming over half-dressed, her jeans missing from the lower half of her body, and her underwear exposed. I shook the thoughts from my head, realizing that I was about to commit the ultimate crime against my best friend. But I couldn't control how I felt—it was at that moment that something rose up from deep within me, a raw desire—I wished that I had been the one that had met Luke first.

Chapter 2

*** *Present Day* ***

Jasmine

After I spent the last hour putting together dinner that consisted of crispy, oven-baked chicken thighs, twice-baked potatoes, and a garden salad, my parents and I sat down to an early meal. We always ate early on Sundays so that we'd make it in time for the weekly temple service that started at six thirty in the evening. As I was cutting into my chicken, my dad looked over at me and asked, "So, Jasmine, have you given any more thought to your college major?"

It was mid-June, and I had just completed my freshman year of college a month earlier. Although I was quite clearly an adult now, my parents still treated me the same way they had in high school—micromanaging my life.

"Honey, she's going into biochemistry as we did of course!" my mom jumped in before I could reply. "Then she can work at the pharmaceutical lab just like us. I mean, clearly, there aren't many career options around here, so this would be perfect for a smart girl like Jasmine."

"Is that what you're planning to do, Jasmine?" My dad looked at me.

"We already talked about this," I replied, annoyed by the repetitive conversation. "I'd have to move onto campus if I go into biochemistry because it requires taking lab classes."

"That's okay, right? It's been years now since, well, you know," my mom said. She hated the topic just as much as I did. She couldn't stand anything that made anyone in our family anything less than perfect.

"Yeah," I agreed. "I'll think about it." Don't get me wrong, I would have loved to live on campus during the school year. My parents still treated me like a kid, never allowing me to do anything. I honestly thought my dad would never even allow me to get my driver's license! After begging him for almost three years, he finally agreed to it after I graduated from high school. I was now actively saving to buy a car. Hopefully, that would give me some of the freedom I was currently lacking in my life!

The problem with going to school in person was that we lived in the middle of nowhere northern Vermont, not far from the Canadian border, so I would have to move onto campus. That would require me to be incessantly vigilant at keeping up the ruse of being human, something that wasn't always possible for me; something I felt so ashamed about but couldn't control. Most other werewolves had no problem blending in with human society, and many werewolves went away to human colleges. But I had a flaw. Yes, it had been a couple of years since it'd been an issue. Maybe if I could go another year, I'd finally feel comfortable enough to move onto campus and follow in my parents' footsteps.

For now, it was better that I just stayed a remote student. Yes, it sucked—I was still under my parents' thumbs as an adult. But it just wasn't worth the risk.

Werewolves generally preferred to live in sparsely populated regions, and we naturally felt at ease in the cold weather. There were even more werewolf packs up in isolated parts of Canada and Alaska. In fact, my mom's original pack was in Alaska, although we rarely saw that part of the family—we'd only ever visited them a few times and they never came here. I was much closer with my paternal grandparents since they lived down the street from us and always watched me growing up.

My parents met in college, and, upon graduating, moved back here to my dad's pack to work at a pharmaceutical research lab owned by the neighboring Autumn Moon Pack. To afford the upkeep, most packs ran large, lucrative businesses. Our pack's business was the only casino in the state, which was a popular tourist destination for humans, especially during fall foliage and ski season. It was located about twenty miles away, near a human town.

We ate quietly until my mom spoke again. "So, I heard tonight's service should be more interesting than usual!"

"Why's that?" my dad asked.

"I heard Alpha James will finally be announcing the transition of title to his son."

"About time!" my dad exclaimed. "Alpha James is getting up there in age. What's he now, sixty-five-ish? I think I was around two when he and Beta Alfred took title from their fathers. The whole pack is getting weak now."

"What was he supposed to do—give his title to one of his illegitimate pups?" My mom snickered. "He's only got the one legitimate son otherwise."

"We don't actually know if the rumors are true," my dad responded.

"Oh, please. I've heard so many stories around the pack about his mistresses that were banished. It's common with alphas. They don't want any issues with their title passing to their legitimate heirs. Easy fix, right?"

"I'm just glad the transition is finally happening. That last battle our pack fought had way too many casualties. I could see passing title in your late forties, max. But sixties? That's just asking for a hostile takeover by another pack. I can't understand why he let his son go away to college for four years. Anything could have happened during that time. We need a young, strong alpha to keep the pack in good shape."

After we finished eating, we all piled into my parents' Tesla SUV to head to the temple service. Because we lived so far out in the forest, it was impractical to have any car except an SUV or truck. Our home was located on the outskirts of the territory, closer to the border, which was heavily patrolled by warrior werewolves. The main entrance, which connected our pack to the outside world, was gated to keep intruders and humans out. Not that humans ever really made it out this far into the deep Vermont woods. If a human did happen to stumble across our pack, it could easily be explained away as being a private, gated community or commune.

We drove into the downtown area of the pack, where the temple, schools, library, and some shops were located. I worked at the bakery café with Lucy and had picked up full-time hours during the summer in order to speed up the accumulation of funds for my future car.

When we arrived at temple, the pews were fuller than usual. My family took our normal seats, toward the front. Temple services were held twice a week—on Sunday evenings and Monday mornings. Most people only attended on Sundays. However, my family always also attended on Monday, the lunar sabbath. The alpha and beta families similarly attended both services as part of their obligations in leading the pack.

After we completed our regular chants and meditations, led by the temple priest, Alpha James took his place at the podium in front of the congregation with his mate, the luna of the pack. He looked good for a man in his midsixties—you could easily tell that he had been devastatingly handsome in his youth. Even at his age, he still had a thick head of black hair that had only partially grayed, and it was clear that he kept up with his training regimen. Even his face had barely sagged through the years with just moderate wrinkles lining his face, crow's feet surrounding his most prominent feature: the most enchanting blue eyes. When he made eye contact, it was as if they were piercing through you, right into your soul.

The congregation was silent as he began to speak. "Good evening, my pack family, Midnight Maple Pack. Thank you to everyone for joining me tonight for another beautiful service put together by our talented priest, Bernard. As usual, his sermon was thought-provoking and profound." He nodded at the priest who smiled back at him.

Alpha James continued, "Earlier this week, I asked Bernard if I could have a few minutes tonight to make an announcement to the pack. Looking around and seeing how many have joined us, I can see that word travels fast! I am sure you're all just as anxious as I am to celebrate the good news that I will be revealing tonight. It is with great pride that my mate, Luna Sienna, and I announce that our son, Blake, recently graduated with his business degree from the werewolf-led Grey Wolf University in Siberia. With this update comes even better news that he will be returning later this week and will spend the remainder of the summer preparing to become your new leader.

"I invite everyone in the pack to witness the passing of the alpha title to Blake on the evening of the autumnal equinox." He paused for effect as everyone clapped and cheered. Once everyone calmed down, he continued speaking. "While I am overjoyed to finally watch the son I raised and trained for this moment succeed me, it is also a bittersweet event for me. While unorthodox to reign for so long, it has afforded me the opportunity to get to know and become close to many pack families over the years. I had the privilege to witness many young pups turn into strong warriors who trained and battled alongside me during the past four decades. I feel the same pride that my late father, grandfather, and great-grandfather did as they led this pack and watched families thrive in this community.

"The alpha ceremony will be held in our outdoor stadium. Afterward, we plan to have a fair to celebrate, with a traditional pack run at midnight. We will be emailing additional information in the coming days. I look forward to all of you joining my son and me for this momentous event."

After the alpha completed his speech, the entire congregation erupted into another round of applause. Alpha James then stepped down from the podium and went to go mingle with families after the service. Many people went over to pat him on the back and congratulate him on his upcoming retirement. My parents, of course, rushed over as they were always anxious to have good standing within the pack.

A few days later, Lucy got a group of us together for a day trip outside the pack to Sand Bar State Park, a large beach along a river that runs between Vermont and New York. Lucy's older brothers, Jack and Kyle, helped us load beach chairs and coolers into their SUVs. Two of our friends from high school, Emma and Madison, arrived with large containers of food.

Upon witnessing the excitement in the driveway, Lucy's younger brothers, Mark and Neil, had complained they were being left out, and her mom forced us to let them tag along too. Lucy's father was a pack warrior, and his sons were all following in his footsteps. Jack and Kyle were already full-time warriors, and her younger brothers would be joining them as soon as they graduated from high school. As you can imagine, Lucy's family portraits all looked like pages ripped straight out of a Swedish catalog—all tall, blond, and toned.

Once the cars were packed up, Emma, Madison, Lucy, and I, along with Lucy's younger brothers, divided ourselves up among the two cars to drive down. We were soon outside the gates of the pack and on our way. The drive to the beach took about forty-five minutes since we lived a fair bit north. After we arrived, we brought everything out and set up our sitting area near a grill on the beach. Being werewolves, we had much bigger appetites than the average human, so having an abundance of food available was necessary. Jack and Kyle had packed a cooler full of meats to grill, Emma had made potato salad, Madison had made her famous baked beans, and Lucy and I had baked a huge batch of cookies and brownies the night before.

Lucy, Madison, Emma, and I unfolded a portable table and began setting it up to lay everything out while Jack and Kyle cleaned the grill and began the charcoal chimney starter. Mark and Neil wasted no time stripping down to their bathing suits and running into the water.

As Kyle started throwing meat on the grill, Emma kept distracting him, brushing up against him. After being all over each other for months beforehand, Kyle and Emma realized they were mates after Emma turned eighteen, which explained the strong attraction they had before confirming the mate bond. They were now planning to move into a house together after getting married later in the summer.

"Gross! Get a room!" Lucy shouted at the two of them, making a gagging face. Lucy had a difficult time hiding her bitterness about the situation presumably since things had turned out differently for her and Luke. After planning a big trip for her eighteenth birthday to visit Luke in Quebec, she was devastated to learn they weren't fated to each other. And despite the blow, they continued seeing each other anyway, against everyone's better advice.

Once the grill was going and we all sat down, a well-built man in a fitted black T-shirt and swim shorts approached the group. He was very imposing—I couldn't help but notice him as he walked toward us from the parking lot—his swagger and air of confidence commanded my attention. The first thing I noticed was his size. He was easily taller than everyone in attendance, which was saying something considering Lucy's whole family could be mistaken for a basketball team, and his brawny arms made it clear he was dedicated to the gym. Lucy, Emma, Madison, and I all gawked at his ripped body as he approached us. As he got closer, I noticed how striking he was with the beginnings of a five o'clock shadow covering his prominent jaw and thick, dark hair that fell casually over his sunglasses. To be honest, I didn't even know men this hot actually existed outside of book covers for bodice rippers. He was so sexy that I suddenly understood what made women lose all inhibitions and forget about the Moon Goddess.

Jack got up from his beach chair and waved the hot guy over. He quickened his pace and strode directly over to our group. "Hey, man! You made it! Wasn't sure if you would!" Jack patted the hot mystery man. After the two of them shook hands and patted each other on the back, they turned in our direction.

The four of us women sat there with our mouths hanging open. "Ladies, you might not remember this handsome fella, but this is Blake, our soon-to-be alpha," Jack introduced him to us. I had almost forgotten that Jack had been close friends with the future alpha in high school. Jack never let Lucy or me hang around his friends when we were younger, and Blake had left when I was only fifteen. I barely remembered him. I definitely didn't recall him being this ridiculously hot.

Blake pushed his sunglasses onto his head and came over to give a firm handshake to each one of us as we introduced ourselves.

"Damn, Blake, you've gotten hot!" Lucy exclaimed, taking his hand.

"You're looking quite well yourself, Lucy," he replied. Madison and Emma both pushed forward to meet him. Kyle put his arm around Emma, pulling her toward him after she shook hands with Blake.

He approached me and I instantly noticed that his eyes were a piercing shade of blue, the same as his father's. I could barely get the words out as I told him my name. He stared deeply into my eyes as we shook hands, something I'd only ever witnessed confident older men do up until now. He repeated my name back to me.

"Jasmine, very nice to meet you," he said, winking at me. His stare lingered for a moment. I felt like a silly little girl in his presence.

Lucy pulled out two very large water bottles and some plastic cups. "I made us all some juice." She winked. She poured some of her cocktail for each person. "Be careful, it's really strong!"

I was initially planning to just drink water, but being in such an imposing man's presence brought out my self-consciousness. I couldn't help but suddenly wish I were cooler and prettier than I was, all my insecurities coming forward. It didn't help that Blake was not only ridiculously good-looking, but he was also essentially the prince of the pack. Once he became alpha, he'd be the equivalent of a king—the most powerful person in the pack and responsible for all the laws and consequences.

I did my best to position myself in my beach chair so my stomach rolls wouldn't form from slouching forward. I sat up straight and flexed my abdominal muscles, putting all the hours at the gym to good use. I was thankful for the drink to calm my nerves, trying to hold it in a sophisticated way. Lucy wasn't kidding—this drink was strong. I drank it faster than I had initially intended and began to feel a bit light-headed and floaty, my head moving more quickly than my eyesight as I glanced around.

As if reading my thoughts, Kyle exclaimed, "Damn, Luce, what did you put in this?"

"Just an old secret recipe I have. Like Mom says, nothing like alcohol to liven things up!" She laughed. She refilled all our drinks and then we began making our plates of food as the meat was finished being grilled. Blake handed me a plate, nodding at me. Goddess, he was so hot. I took less than usual, not wanting to overeat and become bloated. After we finished eating, Lucy refilled all our drinks again. Blake and Jack sat down in the chairs next to mine, deep in conversation. I could sense his presence next to me as I tried to focus my attention on the conversation I was having with Madison, who was seated on the other side of me. I normally controlled myself more than this, but my nerves had caused me to drink a lot more than I was intending. While werewolves did have a much higher alcohol tolerance than humans, it was quickly becoming clear that I was overdoing it. It didn't help that Lucy consistently filled my cup to the top, always eager to get me drunk.

After we cleaned up a bit, everyone stripped down to their bathing suits and Lucy led us into the water. As I got up to follow, pulling my shorts off, the world seemed to spin around me, and I lost my balance. I was about to fall over when Blake caught me, wrapping his arm against my back to steady me. I stared up at him, my eyes wide, speechless at the situation and in disbelief that the future alpha was holding me.

"Lightweight, I see." He smirked.

My face burned hot.

"Or maybe you're just so taken with me that you can't help but faint in my presence."

Holy shit, this guy was cocky! I was so drunk I couldn't even think of a comeback. I knew this was one of those times I'd think of a comeback hours later and hate myself for not coming up with it when it was needed.

"Come on, you can hang on to me. Just don't act too obvious so we don't get arrested for drinking in public and, in your case, underage drinking."

He led me into the water, which was cold, but warm enough for those with werewolf blood. And alcohol blood, as in my case. I couldn't help but notice his jacked body now that he had removed his shirt, his broad shoulders, large traps, and wide chest on display. My eyes trailed down his body, landing on his rock-hard abs, each muscle projecting against the deep grooves etched in his skin. His swim shorts sat low on his hips, revealing the well-defined V-cuts on his lower abdomen. Damn, he had an amazing body—he could have been a fitness model.

He had me get on his back while we waded in the water. I gripped his shoulders, which were extremely broad and hard. He leaned forward and pulled my legs around him. Holy shit, my entire body was pressed against his. I could feel my boobs pushed against his muscular back. This was definitely more intimate than I'd ever been with anyone of the opposite sex. My heart was racing, and I was a bit light-headed. But it also felt kind of nice, an energy pulsing through my veins, a greedy indulgence in feeling his skin against mine. If I were sober, I'd be dying of nervousness right now. I was very thankful for the alcohol because it almost made me feel relaxed lying against his back, my arms draped over his massive shoulders and his hands gripping my thighs.

The thoughts, *Holy shit! This guy is hot! And ripped! And the future alpha!* Repeated themselves in my head. It was surreal that this was actually happening.

Breaking my internal panic, Blake glanced back toward me and said, "So, Jasmine, tell me about yourself."

"Me?" I asked, completely blanking on anything I could possibly tell him about myself.

"Your name is Jasmine, right?"

I started giggling, the buzz overtaking me. "Yes, Jasmine, that's me!"

"Ok, well you still remember your name, so that's good." He chuckled. I could feel his body shake against mine. "How old are you, Jasmine?"

I stammered, "Twenty, no, nineteen, but I'll be twenty soon! What about you?"

He gave another small chuckle and replied, "Twenty-three." He moved us closer to the shore, and let me off his back. Turning so he was facing me, he took my hand in his, a very intimate gesture, his large hand engulfing my small one. His palms were calloused—he must have worked a lot with his hands, or I realized, pumped a lot of iron. The water came about to my waist. He gazed at me intensely—or maybe it was just his eyes were so piercing that it felt intense.

"I'm an only child," I blurted out. Why did I just say that?

He smirked at me, moving closer.

"It's just me and my dictator parents." My voice trailed.

"I have one of those too." His eyes seemed to soften.

"Your eyes," I said.

"My eyes?" He squinted at me, appearing to be intently focused on me, as if he was struggling to read my mind.

"They're beautiful," I replied.

Goddess, did I just tell the hottest guy I've ever met he has beautiful eyes? The filter that normally kept my every thought from being verbalized was clearly not functioning at all whatsoever right now.

"All of you is beautiful." *Did I just say that too?*

If I didn't know better, I'd say he suddenly looked a little sad. The corners of his eyebrows and mouth drooped slightly. If we hadn't been making such intense eye contact with each other, I would never have even noticed. His free hand tucked a piece of hair behind my ear.

"Hey, Blake, catch!" Kyle called to him, throwing a ball his way. Blake turned to catch the ball and then threw it back to one of Lucy's other brothers. I began to move my feet, losing my balance again just as Blake turned back toward me. I fell forward and he caught me against his body, grabbing my sides to steady me, his large hands touching my bare skin. My body burned from the compromising position I'd gotten myself into, my whole upper body pressed against his torso, my head pushed up against his muscular chest.

"Shit, I drank way too much," I said, pushing myself off Blake and standing back up. I couldn't believe I just did that. He looked down at me, taking my hand again.

"Hey, you're fucked up just like me." He softly chuckled. I stared at him, wondering what that could possibly mean. It seemed like he was lost in thought. He looked back down at me and continued speaking. "But don't worry, unlike me, you'll be okay tomorrow. I better stay here with you and make sure you don't drown. It's my duty to protect the lives of all pack members after all."

"You're going to be the alpha. Alpha Blake!" I blurted out. What was wrong with me?

The corners of his mouth turned upward. "Yes, that's true."

"Do you want to be the alpha?" I asked.

"I don't really have much of a choice, but I heard you can get some prime pussy as an alpha." He smirked.

I couldn't believe how vulgarly he was speaking. I glared at him and responded, "I guess that means you're not saving yourself for your mate."

He suddenly had a pained expression on his face and looked at me very seriously. "My mate's dead."

The water turned icy as a chill crept up my back, instantly some of my buzz wore off. Taken aback, I replied, "Wow, I'm really sorry. That's horrible." I felt like I should say more than that, so I continued, "If you ever want to talk about it more, I'm a good listener." I squeezed his hand.

"Thanks, I appreciate it, Jasmine. You seem like a nice girl. You probably shouldn't be talking to someone like me."

I stared at him, wondering what he meant. "Why not?"

"There's a lot you don't know about me." His eyes suddenly looked dark, ominous, dangerous, startling me.

Chapter 3

Jasmine

A few days after the beach trip, I entered the café in our downtown area to start my shift. I was on the early shift that day, so I had to be there at five in the morning to clean and prep everything. I always started by wiping down all the tables and counters and sweeping the floor. Even though this had already been done the evening prior. Valerie, the owner, was very obsessive about cleanliness, which I appreciated. I then went to brew the drip coffees. Valerie was busy pulling everything out of the oven and into the displays. She had arrived even earlier than me. Valerie almost never took a day off and often worked twelve-hour shifts. She was very curvy with curly red hair and a fiery personality to match. She never took crap from anyone.

As all the different coffees were brewing, I went to open the register. At six, we switched the sign to Open. When I had first started the job, I thought I'd never learn everything, but now I was an expert at all the different types of espresso drinks—cappuccino, latte, Americano, macchiato, mocha, flat white, etc. Even though Lucy had been working here longer than me, she still got the drinks confused sometimes. She mostly helped with decorating cakes and making dough for all the different pastries anyway, since that was her true passion. She was basically Valerie's protégé and always helped her whenever someone ordered an elaborate cake, especially for weddings.

We normally had busy mornings during the week as most pack members would stop by the café on their way to work. I pretty much had everyone's orders memorized. During the school year, when it would slow after the morning rush, Valerie didn't mind if I studied while I stood next to the register.

Lucy came in at seven forty-five for her shift. Valerie glared at her, looking at her watch. "Fifteen minutes late today! At least it's better than yesterday!"

Lucy put her hands up and ran into the back to drop all of her stuff and put on her apron. She then rushed to take her place at the register so that I could help Valerie put together all of the drink orders that were coming through. The morning rush normally lasted from seven thirty until ten. Lucy loved working the registers because she would flirt with every single male that came in, no matter their age. Valerie believed that's why she has so many regulars, and one of the reasons she put up with Lucy's terrible punctuality.

"Oh, hello, George! You're looking good in that suit today! The usual Americano and chocolate chip muffin for you this morning?" I heard Lucy from the register. I just rolled my eyes at her nonsense. As it got closer to nine, I heard her say, "Hello there, Mr. Alpha! Damn, you're looking fine today!"

I turned around to Blake standing at her register, ready to place an order. My stomach fluttered in response. He smiled at Lucy and said, "As I do every day. Just a large black coffee, please."

Lucy rang it in and moved on to the next customer to take their order. I ran to grab the ticket and make his order, then I went over to hand it to him.

He looked straight into my soul with his piercing blue eyes and said, "Thanks, Jasmine. Nice to see you," then he turned and walked out the door.

I left work at one thirty, when my shift ended. I decided to go for a bike ride around the pack territory instead of going home. After riding around aimlessly for about an hour, I rode out to the lake at the outskirts of the pack and found a shady place to sit under a tree where someone had left their towel behind. I shook it out and sat down on it, staring out at the glistening water, the sun's rays reflecting off it. It was so peaceful that I decided to pull out my cell phone to read a book on it, leaning my body against a large tree trunk. I became so immersed in the book that I lost track of time.

It had to have been over two hours that passed when a huge wolf with brown fur that was so dark it almost looked black came sprinting out of the woods and shocked me. I sniffed the air and realized the wolf smelled just like Blake. He looked at me for a minute and then mindlinked me, *"Mind if I borrow your towel?"* Although I knew we could communicate telepathically with other pack members when in our wolf forms, it still caught me off guard—his imposing presence completely threw me off my game.

I blinked a few times and came back to reality, realizing I was sitting on a towel. Speechless, I stood up to hand it to him. He took it with his mouth and ran into the woods, emerging a minute later with it slung around his hips.

"Thanks, I didn't want to be the one to corrupt you." He smirked.

I couldn't help but stare at his broad shoulders, muscular arms, and well-chiseled chest and abs as he approached. Damn, he had an amazing body.

He sat down next to me and asked, "So, what are you doing out here?"

I took a seat next to him, baffled by his sudden appearance, and replied, "I was riding my bike around the pack territory and ended up here. It was so relaxing by the water, I decided to stay and read a book."

"Do you come here often?" he asked, holding my gaze. Goddess, he had the most mesmerizing eyes.

"No, not really. But I didn't feel like going back home yet and this was a good place to be alone."

"I know the feeling." He looked at me sincerely.

"What brings you out here?"

"I like to run through the forest in my wolf form. I wasn't planning on stopping here but then I saw you and thought it looked secluded enough that I could work my charm on you and get in your pants."

I widened my eyes, not knowing how to respond.

He chuckled. "Don't worry, I'm joking! Anyway, one of the first rules of being alpha is don't screw around with pack members. Just makes things really messy!"

I began to relax. "What are some other rules of being alpha?"

"Well, let's see, make sure you walk around shirtless as much as possible so that your abs can be admired, and don't think I didn't catch you looking"—he winked at me—"and don't let drunk girls embarrass themselves falling over at the beach."

I glared at him. He smirked and continued, "Also, it's probably best if you're not naked when you hang out with that now-sober girl at a different beach, especially if your first rule is don't screw around with pack members."

"You wish," I replied.

"Oh please, if I took this towel off, I bet you one hundred bucks you couldn't resist me. Trust me, the alpha genetics don't end at my abs." He smiled mischievously.

"Well, you're not my mate, and my rule is no screwing around with anyone that isn't your mate," I replied earnestly, annoyed that he believed I would just fall at his feet.

"Wait, so are you a virgin then?"

My cheeks burned at his question. I nodded my head, not able to speak the answer.

He kept looking at me. "Wait, seriously? Have you really never done anything with anyone that isn't your mate?"

"No, I haven't." I could tell that I was completely red, the skin on my body burning. Why did I have to blush so easily?

He stared at me for a while, his piercing blue eyes not blinking. Finally, he asked, "Have you ever kissed anyone?"

"No."

"Wow, I can't believe I've met a unicorn in the flesh. You're actually completely saving yourself for your mate? I didn't think anyone did that anymore."

"I'm not the only one!"

"Well, I definitely haven't met many others like you. And most that I have were still in high school."

"I follow the scriptures of Artemis. Anyway, my parents would never let me date anyone that wasn't my mate, and I still live with them."

"What they don't know can't hurt them. Also, it makes things kind of exciting when you have to sneak around." He smiled and seemed to zone out as if he were remembering something.

Suddenly, I felt my phone vibrate. I looked down to see my mom was texting me, asking me where I was.

Oh, shit! I had totally lost track of time. I quickly texted her back to let her know I was on my way home. "Shit, sorry, I have to go home. I didn't realize how late it was."

"No worries, it was nice to hang out with you for a little while. Maybe we can do it again sometime. Next time, I'll have some clothes on, but only if you want."

I laughed, waved goodbye to him, and turned to go. As soon as I was about to toss my leg over my bike to pedal away, he called out to me. "Hey!"

"Yeah?" I turned back to look at him curiously.

"Did you want your towel back?" he asked as he stepped toward me, his thumbs hitched inside the top of it, as if he was about to remove it.

"Oh." I felt my face burn in reaction. "It's not mine."

He nodded, a twinkle in his eye. I turned back toward my bike and immediately left, speeding back toward my house. I wasn't sure what to make of our meeting. It was so hard to read him. But something about him made me feel comfortable while simultaneously putting me on edge.

Chapter 4

Jasmine

The following weekend, Lucy invited me to attend a friends-and-family plated-dessert experience at her culinary school to celebrate the end of the school year. She had to be there early to set up, so she took the family car. In turn, I borrowed my parents' Tesla SUV and drove down with her mom, Ivy. Because we lived in the middle of nowhere, it took us an hour and a half to get to her school. She had told me how long the drive was before, but I couldn't believe how far she commuted now that I'd actually done it myself!

We parked and entered the school, following the sound of people until we found where tables were set up with white tablecloths and desserts displayed. As soon as we walked in, Lucy spotted us and came over wearing a white jacket and hat, her eyes lighting up, greeting us both with hugs.

I looked around and saw that everyone had put out intricately designed dessert plates. They looked more like art than food. I'd only ever seen desserts like this a few times in my life.

"Come right this way," Lucy said, leading her mom and me to a table. "These are my creations." She smiled, reminding me of a little kid showing off a painting she did in pre-school.

I looked down at the table and I was in awe. "Wow, these are amazing!" On display were mini-cakes that she had clearly spent copious time detailing until they were perfect. She had put out three options—what looked like a chocolate cake detailed with swirls and whipped cream with chocolate spirals and raspberries on top, a very fancy-looking strawberry shortcake, and what appeared to be crème brûlée plated with mini-macarons and various berries.

"Try all of them." She looked at us eagerly. I took the chocolate cake first, grabbing a spoon off the table. It almost looked too beautiful to eat.

"Wow, this is so good!" I gasped after taking a bite. I mean, I'd always known Lucy was a good baker, but something about a dessert being so pretty made it seem like it wouldn't taste as good. I quickly finished it and Lucy took my plate from me, handing me the next cake. Her mom, similarly, praised Lucy, which made her glow.

Before long, more people began coming in. Lucy's face lit up as different people approached her table to try her desserts. I'd never seen her look so passionate about anything before, besides maybe Luke. Later on, she took Ivy and me around and introduced us to her classmates while we sampled all of their creations as well. Others had done a nice job but—maybe I was biased—Lucy's were definitely better. It was like you could taste the passion as you bit into her desserts. By the time we'd walked around to everyone's tables, I was starting to feel nauseous and bloated from all the sweets I'd eaten. "I really need to go for a run after this," I said to Lucy, clutching my stomach. Lucy laughed and rubbed her stomach in agreement.

Signaling the end of the event, the chef quieted everyone and made an announcement that he had two awards to hand out. The first award was for perfect attendance, which went to one of Lucy's classmates.

"The second award is for our student of the year. This year's award goes to Lucy Owen. Congratulations, Lucy!" Everyone clapped as she went up to collect her certificate. She rejoined Ivy and me at her table, a huge smile on her face.

After everyone filed out, she began cleaning up. Ivy and I offered to help, but she turned us away and said, "No, it's fine. It'll only take me a few minutes, and I'll be right out." We left the room and found a bench to sit on and wait for her. She came out about a half hour later.

Once Lucy joined us, the three of us walked down the street to a café to wash down the desserts we'd just stuffed ourselves with, enjoying the nice weather. While Lucy's mom went up to the register to place the order, Lucy and I grabbed a small table by the window.

"Thanks so much for coming today. It means a lot to me!" Lucy said, a wide smile on her face.

"No problem," I replied. "Your desserts were really good."

"It's nice being the customers for once," she said, leaning back in her chair and looking relaxed. We normally worked at the café back home on Saturdays, but Valerie had given us the day off for Lucy's showcase.

"Congrats again on getting the student of the year award," I said.

"I know, can you believe it?"

"You always had it in you. You just needed to find something you actually enjoyed studying," I replied, feeling pride that Lucy had finally found her calling after years of trying to motivate her to care about school.

"Thanks, Jaz. You've always been a really good friend to me." She sighed, looking troubled.

"Is everything okay?"

She looked at me seriously and said, "It's just that things are going so well right now. I'm doing good in school, Luke's coming home at the end of the summer, and Valerie's finally trusting me to decorate wedding cakes without supervision. I just keep feeling like disaster's around the corner." She suddenly looked very vulnerable, a side of herself Lucy didn't often show.

"You should just enjoy the feeling and not worry. My grandma used to say worrying means you suffer twice." As I said this, I realized how lame the advice was. If stressing out were a sport, I would be an Olympic champion. I can't recall a time in my life when school didn't bring me constant, overwhelming anxiety.

"Yeah, you're right," she replied, but didn't look convinced. Her mom joined us, and Lucy went back to being her old bubbly self.

"Any plans for this weekend, girls?" Lucy's mom asked.

"I'm trying to convince Jasmine to go to a party Emma got invited to! But she's using the old *you know how my parents are* excuse," Lucy playfully whined.

Ivy laughed and said, "Jasmine, your parents need to lighten up! These are some of the best years of your life and you can never get them back! Once you find your mate, it's all diaper changes and feeding schedules. After I realized Lucy's father was my mate, we couldn't keep our hands off each other and just popped one pup out after another!"

"Mom, stop!" Lucy shrieked.

Lucy's mom laughed and continued, "We used to throw tons of parties when I was growing up. It was much easier back then because they didn't patrol the party lake as much. Tons of sex at those parties too. Nothing like alcohol and a dark forest to encourage naughty behavior!"

"Oh my Goddess, Mom! We definitely don't need to know this!" Lucy started to look a little green. I was on the edge of my seat, wanting to hear more. My parents never told me stories about growing up in their respective packs, and we never talked about sex in my house. They made it seem like no one ever dated when they were growing up. I was riveted by the information Ivy was revealing, especially knowing that my dad had graduated in the same class as her—although I'd prefer not to imagine him as one of the people that was having sex at those parties. Ick!

"Just make sure you use protection." Ivy gave us both a severe stare. "It's okay to not be careful with your mate, but it definitely complicates things if you already have a pup once you meet them."

"Wow, could you imagine if that really did happen?" I asked, horrified at the idea of it.

"Well, yeah, I know someone. Poor girl," Ivy replied.

"Who?" I asked, curious to know.

Ivy hesitated, but then replied, "Oh, just a girl I went to high school with. We lost touch."

"What happened to her?" I was dying to know the story now.

After a beat, Ivy replied, "Well, I had a friend named Katie growing up who had a pup with someone who wasn't her mate, and the father left her after he found his true mate. Then, to rub salt in the wound, *her* true mate rejected her after he realized she'd had someone else's pup. Things were a little more traditional twenty or so years ago."

"What happened to Katie?" I asked.

"I tried to be there for her and support her while everyone else in the pack shunned her. But, after I started having my own pups, it was very difficult. She stayed about four or five years after her son was born, but it became very hard once the father of her son had a pup with his own mate, and she had to witness the two of them raise their pup all while ignoring her existence. Her parents found a new pack to accept them out in the Midwest, and they all moved there together. She wrote me a letter, not long after, to inform me that she told her new pack that her mate had died."

"Did she ever find another mate?" This story was piquing my curiosity.

"Actually, I don't know! We lost touch." She looked pensive. "Maybe I should look her up on Facebook! Everything's on the internet these days. Much harder to hide your past!"

After we finished our coffees, Lucy and I drove to my house so we could go for a run in our wolf forms to burn off some of the desserts. My house was on the outskirts of the pack, so my backyard was very forested. We walked a few yards in until we found a place to leave our clothes and shifted into our wolves.

Lucy's wolf emulated her, with a tall, elegant build, thick, golden cream fur, and blue eyes. She only glanced my way for a moment before we made a break for it, savoring the freedom of running through nature, succumbing to our animal brains. My paws blissfully bounced off the dirt path as tall trees surrounded us, the shadows of their sun-dappled leaves and pines flickering along the ground. The wind whipped through our fur while we dodged roots and branches, hopping over fallen tree trunks. The scent of wet wood, moss, and skunk cabbage filled my nostrils, delighting me in this form—the great outdoors enveloping me in all its glory. After some time, we stopped at a brook to take a break. I lapped at the water heartily, parched from the run. Once Lucy and I were both satiated, we stood side by side, staring down at our reflections in the water. My wolf's bright amber eyes stared back at me, surrounded by brown fur, tipped in black, especially at the ears. The brown, thick fur turned white as it disappeared into my underside. It wasn't often I looked at myself in this form, and the image never failed to mesmerize me.

Lucy interrupted my observation with a mindlink. *"Well, some good news is that I spoke with Luke on the phone last night, and he agrees with me that if we don't find our mates within the next two years then we should become chosen mates."*

"Why two years? That seems a bit arbitrary," I replied, finding myself annoyed by the topic of conversation she'd chosen. Lucy and I had spent a year discussing, ad nauseam, the notion of taking Luke as a chosen mate. She knew my stance on the matter—it was completely disrespectful to the Moon Goddess to reject a fated mate for a chosen one.

"Because we love each other, and we don't want to wait any longer to be together. Plus, at twenty-one I'll be old enough to drink at my own wedding.

I tried to convince him that we should just go ahead and move in together as soon as he comes back, but he told me that we need to wait. I asked how long, and he originally said until I'm at least thirty, but I talked him down."

A dull pain stirred within me, as if my inner wolf were aching, a feeling that had become familiar every time I conversed about Luke with Lucy. Although I hadn't seen him in almost two years, I had a hard time forgetting him, and to this day held an unexpected longing for him.

I couldn't even say for sure what it was about him that I coveted. Was it because he was the first man that I ever had a carnal attraction to? Was it how much we seemed to have in common? I knew my crush on him was silly bordering on crazy, but no matter what I did, I couldn't seem to push him from my mind. And it didn't help that he was Lucy's favorite topic of discussion.

"But what if you meet your true mate and realize you're meant to be with them?" I asked, trying a different approach with Lucy, hoping she'd see how foolish she was being.

"I can't imagine that happening. There's just no way. The way I feel about him I will never feel about anyone else. The Moon Goddess made a huge mistake when she didn't fate us to each other. Either way, it's almost archaic, the whole idea of it—like an arranged marriage. We should be allowed to choose who we love. Why does some invisible person get to decide for us?"

"The Moon Goddess doesn't make mistakes! There's a reason she mated you to someone else." I was quickly becoming exasperated by this conversation and my need to explain the obvious to Lucy.

"Look, I know you're really religious but I'm not, and anyway, I can feel he's meant to be my chosen mate. We love each other. Plus, he's amazing in bed!"

I cringed internally at her statement, envisioning the two of them in the act with their perfect bodies, both of which I'd, unfortunately, seen in the buff, and was now able to conjure a full visual. I tried to wipe it from my mind as I blurted, *"I hope you're at least using protection! You just heard the story your mom told us about Katie."*

"Calm down, PJ! We're using condoms. If this place wasn't so backward and the clinic didn't refuse to prescribe it, spouting nonsense about interfering with the Moon Goddess's will, I'd go on birth control. I've thought about going to a human clinic to get it but, anyway, who cares if I get pregnant. We're going to be chosen mates anyway. This would just speed things along."

I started to feel nauseous imagining Lucy getting pregnant with Luke's pup. Although they had been dating for almost four years now and were clearly in love, it felt wrong. It was wrong. She was fated to someone else. Luke was fated to someone else. Then, I thought something that I couldn't even admit to myself that I thought—Luke could be fated to me. I instantly pushed the idea from my mind, not knowing where it came from.

But I did know where it came from. It was all because of that one day before he left, a month before my eighteenth birthday. After that one day, I suddenly didn't want him to be with anyone else, as irrational as it all seemed. I realized, with horror, that I wanted him to be with me. But there was nothing I could do without being a terrible friend and, quite frankly, seeming crazy. Lucy had been with him for four years and he clearly loved her, not me. Out of every unmated male in the entire pack, I had to develop a crush on my best friend's boyfriend. But, as much as I tried, I couldn't forget the feeling I had as we sat next to each other that one fateful night—the overwhelming feeling that he should be mine.

I couldn't bear to talk about Luke anymore and decided to change the subject. *"So, what do you think of Blake?"*

"I saw the two of you getting hot and heavy at the beach last week! Maybe you should hook up with him! It would be good for you!"

"Hook up with the future alpha!? First of all, I'm not hooking up with anyone until I meet my mate. And second of all, what makes you think the future alpha would want to hook up with me?"

"Because he's an unmated man and you're cute! He was clearly enjoying you all over his body at the beach. There's nothing wrong with having a little fun before you settle down. Just don't tell your parents." She paused and appeared lost in thought for a moment, then continued, "Besides, this would be great! You and I are best friends and Luke is Blake's future beta! We could go on double dates!"

"What? That's ridiculous! Blake and I are not happening. Anyway, I'm pretty sure he's not looking for a girlfriend right now."

"Who said anything about being his girlfriend? You should just hook up with him for now, until you find your mate."

"Oh my Goddess, Lucy. If I didn't make it clear, I am no way, no how either dating or hooking up with Blake. First of all, I am saving myself for my mate, and second of all, Blake is the friggin' future alpha who can have anyone, so why would he waste his time on me?"

"He just came back from Siberia and that place can't be much fun. He's probably desperate to get his dick wet."

"You did not just say that!"

"You're such a prude! Come on, that guy is hot. If I didn't love Luke, I'd be lining up to wet his dick myself. If you don't feel the same way you're either blind or a lesbian. And I know you're not a lesbian because you were obsessed with Taylor Lautner for a while."

I wasn't blind either.

After spending some more time in the forest, we finally made our way back to our clothes and shifted back to our human forms. Once I got inside, I offered to make dinner. This was something my parents expected me to do on the days they worked, but I usually helped my mom on the weekends too because I knew it was helpful to her and I also enjoyed cooking.

I put on music and danced around the kitchen as I cooked. I may have also spent a little time fantasizing about Blake. What? I didn't intend to actually act on any of my fantasies, but Lucy was not wrong. He was very hot. And mysterious. Although, there was also a part of him that seemed dark and ominous that I wasn't sure about.

Chapter 5

Blake

My father and I were, once again, in a heated argument. He always played the nice, fatherly Santa-type in front of the pack but, behind closed doors, he terrorized my mother and me. I wouldn't be surprised if his goal in life was to do as much psychological damage to me as possible before his ultimate death. There were days I considered killing him myself. It was common in some packs for an alpha son to kill his father to assume the alpha title, especially when it wasn't handed over peacefully, but I had yet to be driven to that point. He was still my father, as much as I hated him, and I wasn't in any rush to assume his title. I had been eager five years ago, ready for the power, but things changed...

"I compromised and let you have your fun for four years," my father raged.

"You think Siberia is fun?"

"I don't give a shit if it is or isn't. It is your duty as my heir to assume the title of alpha, and I'm not allowing you to put it off any longer. The pack is becoming weaker as time goes by."

"For years I was too weak and an embarrassment to you. Suddenly you need me to strengthen the pack?"

"I know I don't need to remind you about what happened five years ago. More pack members died than in any other battle this pack has ever fought, and it will only be worse next time." He knew this was my soft spot, but he took the opportunity to push it anyway. I glared at him. He continued, "Whatever you may think of me, I care about this pack. My great-grandfather built this pack out of nothing, and I will do whatever the fuck I need to in order to assure that the lineage continues. End of discussion!"

With that, he stormed out of the room. At least these days he resisted the urge to throw heavy objects at me. He had noticeably aged in the four years I was gone, his wrath and impulses not quite to the level I remembered.

I decided to go for a run. It was hot outside, but I was so worked up that I barely noticed. I walked out of the packhouse, where my family lived, and into the woods. After walking a few yards in, I stripped myself naked, and threw my clothes onto a tree stump. I then shifted into my wolf form. My bones transformed, my skin stretched to accommodate the changeover, fur tingled as it sprouted from my body. The pads of my massive paws fell against the pine needles scattered along the ground. I scratched my razor-sharp claws through the dirt, getting used to the new form I was in, the wind ruffling my fur. I had come to appreciate being in my wolf form—everything was simpler. The animal part of my brain took control and practically the only things that mattered were food, water, and sleep.

I'd first grown fond of this form after I began shifting at the age of twelve. While my father had always been a dick, he really came down hard on me once I was able to turn into a wolf. While my classmates mostly only trained at school, my father would force me to train for countless additional hours every week. I vividly recalled sweltering summers during my middle school years where my father would push me to complete various exercises in brutal heat, hitting me with a tree branch if I was too slow, denying me water, yelling in my face if I didn't complete tasks to his standards. There were times I'd fall over and throw up, pushed to my limit, only to be rewarded with my father kicking me. "Get the fuck up, Blake! There's no time to throw up when you're in battle!" He'd pile weights on top of me, forcing me to do push-ups until I couldn't lift myself off the ground anymore. "Fucking weak. You're an embarrassment as an alpha." The only way I could stop the trauma from overtaking me was to shift and run deep into the woods, far from home. I sometimes wished I could just live as a wolf. But I couldn't let my father see he got to me.

And there was a sick part of me that couldn't stand the idea of failure. I couldn't help but strive to finally please him. This desire for his approval always pulled me back, forcing me to try that much harder, only to endure the abuse all over again. The harder I worked, the more abusive he became, the goalpost always just out of my reach. I was nothing more than a sad puppy that kept getting kicked by his owner, only to come back and eagerly beg for love and praise that would never be offered.

After four years away, the area had changed. My previous favorite spot was now overtaken by humans. What had previously been, clearly, an unpopular hiking trail to visit had gotten trendy with a new resort built nearby. It was now summer and hiking trails in Vermont were littered with humans. I ran deep into the forest to find a new place to go and be by myself.

After running for an hour or so, I found a mountain to climb in an area that didn't have any hiking trail nearby, so I knew I'd avoid humans. I climbed until I reached the summit. The sun was beginning to set, so I lay down on the rocky peak and looked down upon everything below, admiring the pinks and oranges that painted themselves across the sky. While I was perpetually agitated and in a state of rage within, the peaceful surroundings helped quiet the storm. Once it became dark, I made my way back home, feeling calmer now. I shifted back to my human form and redressed myself before going back into the packhouse.

I found my mom inside, still in her scrubs, having clearly just finished a shift. She was one of the pack doctors and had met my father after finishing her medical residency training and returning to the pack. She hugged me and kissed my forehead as I entered. She was proof that not all mates are created equal and sometimes the Moon Goddess has a sick sense of humor. My mom mostly worked in pediatrics, healing and caring for young pups. She never raised her voice and strived to make my father and me happy however she could. In return, my father berated and cheated on her throughout the entirety of their marriage. While his philandering had calmed down with age, I still had memories burned into me of spying on her crying alone after she discovered his latest transgression.

She was the main reason my father allowed me to go away to college for four years. I had been ready to take the position of alpha after finishing high school. But, after Ria died, I couldn't do it. My mom convinced my father to allow me to go away for a few years. After months of fighting matches between my father and me, he finally agreed to let me go to the only werewolf university in the world, Grey Wolf University, because he knew I'd be able to keep up with my training there.

He wasn't wrong about that. Training in Siberia may as well have been synonymous with torture. In the first week I arrived, they required us to begin building tolerance to wolfsbane, werewolves' kryptonite. We began by ingesting a small vial at first. I wanted to pass out, but they forced us to run five kilometers in our human form, being too weak to shift into our wolf forms anyway, before they let us rest. Over time, we began receiving regular injections and were forced to train while our insides burned. We got used to coughing up blood. It was not uncommon for a student to get up in the middle of class to crouch over the trash can and spit blood from his mouth.

In our first year, they purposely paired us up with fourth-year students during training to break us in and toughen us up. One time, several of my ribs were broken and I had to spend three days in recovery while they healed, my healing abilities weakened by the wolfsbane fed into my system regularly. During our third year, we had to spend a week in the dead of winter surviving in our wolf form, hunting for food and finding shelter in the tundra of Siberia, as if we were actual wolves.

In our fourth year, we visited neighboring packs to be trained in torture. They'd lead us down into their cells where they'd be jailing a perp for who knows what. Sometimes the pack needed information and we were forced to torture the perp until they would be begging for their death and gave up the information that was needed. Sometimes it was just an innocent rogue that had accidentally stepped over a pack's border, their only crime that of being in the wrong place at the wrong time. They were then barbarically cut into pieces for no good reason, just so we could become desensitized. I recalled, vividly, chopping limbs from their bodies as they thrashed against the restraints placed on them, crying and begging for death, their eyes terrorized, pleading.

What the professors didn't know was that my father had already been teaching me the art of torture from the time I turned ten years old. While others vomited or passed out, and later paid for it, I was cold and calculating as if I were a psychopath. They didn't even have to break me in—I had already come prepared, wielding a sword confidently, chopping through flesh and bone with ease. I had been forced to observe my father use the same techniques they taught for almost a decade. I ended up getting a five in torture, the equivalent of an A in Russia.

Chapter 6

Jasmine

In early July, my parents and I were sitting together at the Monday-morning service. It was a small crowd that day—only the totally devout along with the alpha and beta families. I was having trouble concentrating during the meditations and kept sneaking looks at Blake while everyone else's eyes were closed. Suddenly, Blake opened his eyes and looked up at me, catching me staring. He gave me a quick wink and then closed his eyes again.

Was I developing a crush on Blake? How basic, having a crush on both the alpha and the beta. Could I be any more of a cliché?

After the service, I excused myself to go to the bathroom while my parents mingled with the congregation, as usual. It seemed like they came here more for the gossip than the actual service. When exiting the bathroom, I almost crashed into Blake, eliciting a gasp from me.

"We meet again!" he exclaimed, smiling widely.

"Hi, Blake," I replied, not knowing what else to say, smiling back at him. He did have a really nice smile. It was a nice change to the broody appearance he had on the first day we met.

"Hey, want to go do something fun after this is over? I've been stuck in the packhouse with my father all week and I'm literally about to kill him. I need to get out. We can leave right now," he said, grabbing my arm, trying to pull me away with him.

"No, we can't! My parents can't see me leaving with you." I panicked, shoving his hand off me. He stopped walking and turned to look at me, frowning. Suddenly, an idea came to me. "If you want, I can meet you after they drop me at home and leave for work."

Blake grinned. "Why don't I come pick you up? Here, give me your phone and I'll enter my number. You can text me your address when you're ready."

I looked around to make sure no one was watching and handed him my phone so he could enter his information. After he returned it, I strolled back over to my parents, baffled by what had just happened. My parents were deep in conversation, gossiping with another couple who also came to every service. My dad finally checked the time and nudged my mom to go so that they wouldn't be late. They dropped me at home before heading off to work. I ran into the house and watched out the window as they disappeared down the road. When I was sure they were gone for good, I pulled out my phone and scrolled through my contacts to find Blake had entered his name as *Blake Sexy AF*. I rolled my eyes. Goddess, this guy was so full of himself.

I opened a text message and entered my address, then waited on my doorstep. A black Jeep Wrangler pulled up into my driveway about ten minutes later.

He got out of the car and opened the passenger side door for me. When I approached, he reached out his muscular arm and ushered me into my seat.

"Wow, so chivalrous!" I lauded.

"Good breeding," he responded as he shut the door.

When he got into the driver's seat he looked me up and down and said, "I hope you enjoy hiking."

"I do."

"I know a good place we can go where there aren't any humans around, and there is a pond near the base of the mountain where we can cool off after."

"Should I have packed my bathing suit?"

"Maybe part of my plan was to make sure you didn't." He smirked as he backed out of the driveway.

We drove about a half hour before he pulled over on the side of the road. This was clearly not a tourist location. We were on a rural road with no cars or buildings in sight. The forest on either side was thick with trees, without any clear path or trail to enter.

He swung a backpack over his shoulders and led me into the woods until we reached the base of a mountain. "It's not a difficult hike. I've done it in both my wolf and human forms before." We began our ascent. He was right, it wasn't too difficult. I was easily able to keep pace with him. It only took about an hour to reach the summit.

We sat down once we reached the top and he opened his backpack. "Here, I brought snacks and water." I took a granola bar and water bottle from him, and he opened a package of beef jerky for himself. We sat next to each other and stared out over the view of the wilderness. There was something majestic about the Vermont outdoors—it was so thick with nature—maple, pine, and birch trees spread for miles, rising and falling against rocky hills and mountains.

"So, why couldn't we be seen together by your parents?" he asked, looking at me curiously.

"I told you, I'm not allowed to hang around any males."

"You said you couldn't date. I didn't know male friends were also against the rules."

"My parents are super strict and religious. I'm not allowed to be around unmated males until I find my mate. Even then, I'm pretty sure they'll lock me in the house until we're married."

He laughed heartily. "Why don't they just buy you a chastity belt?"

"I'm surprised they haven't yet!" I joined in with his laughter.

"So, I take it you don't have one on now, and nothing would stop you from having your way with me on this mountain?" He smiled mischievously, moving closer to me. "You're already rebelling by spending time with someone of the opposite sex." He took my chin in his hand and held my gaze, whispering, "Why not take it a step further? What do you say, want me to be your sneaky link?"

I was suddenly extremely hot and anxious. He pushed a piece of hair behind my ear. Instead of dropping his hand, he allowed his fingers to brush against my ear and then slowly skimmed the back of his fingers against the side of my face. The gesture was very intimate, and my skin was sensitive to his touch, practically tingling with each movement of his hand. My heart beat feverishly against my chest and my breathing turned heavy. He continued tracing down my neck and along my collarbone. I couldn't decide whether I should push him off or let him keep going, probably enjoying what he was doing far too much. He finally allowed his hand to drop. We sat there like that for what seemed like an hour but was probably only seconds, looking into each other's eyes, his blue eyes glowing in the sunlight, focused intently on me.

He eventually turned away from me and went back to eating his beef jerky, as if we hadn't just shared a heated moment. I took a sip from my water bottle, suddenly feeling parched.

He turned to me and asked, "So you are planning on only kissing one man your entire life?"

"Is there something wrong with that?" I asked defensively.

"Just seems kind of boring."

"It doesn't seem boring to me." As I said it, I wasn't sure if I liked the idea as much as I had thought my whole life. My stomach trembled as I imagined what it might be like to disregard all my prior convictions and kiss Blake. I couldn't help but focus on his lips—they were quite alluring, rosy with a full bottom lip. I envisioned them being both firm and gentle, wagering he knew how to use them too.

"What if you don't meet your mate anytime soon? What if you're still mateless at thirty?" he asked, distracting me from my thoughts.

"I never gave it much thought," I replied. We sat in silence for a minute. Then I asked, "What about you? Was your first kiss with your mate?"

"Nah, I was a horny bastard in high school. Being the future alpha definitely has its advantages in that area."

"What happened to not screwing around with pack members?"

"Let's just say I learned that lesson the hard way."

I looked at him curiously, wanting to know more about him. "If you don't mind me asking, when did you meet your mate?" He seemed to hesitate, letting out a deep breath. "It's okay, you don't have to tell me if you don't want to," I said, realizing that maybe I'd overstepped a boundary.

"Not long after I turned eighteen," he replied suddenly. "She was two years older than me, and I'd always known her, but we'd never hung out, so I didn't know much more about her than her name. She was a warrior. She was extremely tough and beautiful. I used to call her my Amazon woman. We locked eyes during training one day, and a realization came over me that we were mates." He looked out into the distance as he told me this story.

"What was her name?"

After a beat he said, "Ria."

"Are you afraid you won't find another mate?"

"No, I'm not interested in finding another mate."

"Don't you want an heir?"

"I didn't say I wouldn't fuck anyone else." He turned and smiled at me, but I could see there was a bit of sadness behind his eyes. "Anyway, what's this? Twenty questions?"

"I'm just curious about you," I responded quietly, realizing I had definitely asked too much, and this was a touchy subject for him.

"Enough about me, why don't you tell me more about you. What do you do for fun?"

Not able to think of anything interesting to tell Blake, I replied, "I'm pretty boring. I mostly just work and go to school. I'm also part of the temple choir."

"You're right, that's pretty boring."

I chuckled and continued, "Like I said, my parents are really controlling. They basically have me on a tight leash."

"What would happen if you just stopped doing what your parents said and started making your own decisions?"

"I'm pretty sure they would kill me. My mom can be pretty scary when she's angry."

"Good thing she doesn't know you're alone with a dead sexy man in the middle of the woods. And good thing I have the alpha aura, so if she goes after anyone, it will be you rather than me." He started laughing. "Either way, I haven't given up on getting you out of your clothes today, and it's starting to get really hot, so I think I'm getting closer to my goal. Let's hike down to the water I was telling you about earlier."

He led me down a different path this time. It took about another hour to get down to the bottom. He was not wrong. The sun was beating down on us.

By the time I reached the water, I was ready to jump in. He started peeling off his clothes until he was only wearing his boxer briefs, his muscular body on full display. My breath hitched as I tried hard not to stare while the sun reflected off his broad shoulders and bare torso. Damn, he was so jacked and sexy. Before I could lose myself in my gawking, he sprinted to the water on his bared, muscular legs and jumped in.

"The water feels great! Come on in! I know you want to!"

I had an internal argument with myself. It was ridiculously hot, and, logically, underwear wasn't much different than a bathing suit. Thank Goddess I had chosen dark-colored underwear this morning. The devil over my shoulder won this time. I gestured for him to turn around. He rolled his eyes but still did it. Once his back was to me, I stripped down out of my jeans and T-shirt until I was standing in my dark purple underwear and black bra. I then started walking into the water. He turned around and I glared at him. He got the hint and turned back around. He wasn't wrong, the water did feel very refreshing after roasting under the sun all that time. I kept going until I was close to Blake, submerged practically to my shoulders.

"Ok, I'm in," I said, and he turned so he was facing me.

"Looks like my plan worked. I got you down to your underwear now. I wonder how much more I can convince you to take off. And don't lie, I know you're dying to sneak a peek at the below-the-belt alpha genetics that I mentioned last time." He winked at me.

"You're so arrogant."

"I call it confident. I can't help it if I'm fucking gorgeous and well hung and I know it."

We spent the remainder of the afternoon swimming and then lay out on a blanket that Blake had brought in his backpack. I was feeling more comfortable about being in a state of undress around him now. Our bodies were turned facing each other, just inches apart.

His eyes scanned my entire body, then he looked in my eyes and said, "You know, you have a really nice body." While this normally would have made me feel exposed, I instead felt sexy and desired, elated by his attention, as his eyes trained themselves on me.

He then reached out and began tracing the contour of my face as we continued to look into each other's eyes. My chin jutted forward in reaction, and my breathing shallowed as he moved his fingers slowly down under my chin and onto my neck. I was simultaneously nervous and soothed by how intimate his touch was as my heart raced in my chest. He brushed his fingertips against my shoulder and all the way down my arm, goosebumps trailing. I closed my eyes, relishing in the moment we were sharing, so close together. He skimmed his fingers so gently on my skin he was barely touching it, but my senses were so roused that the light touch shivered through my body, warming my thighs.

The cool breeze skimmed my wet skin, causing my nipples to harden under my bra. He must have noticed because he began slowly running his fingers up the center of my torso, provoking me to flex my core in reaction. His hand moved under one of my breasts and then lightly over my nipple, now erect and tingling with desire. I gasped quietly, succumbing to his caress, loving the feeling of his hands on my body. Realization hit that I didn't even care that what we were doing was completely wrong. I was ready to surrender myself to him if he kept going.

He abruptly stopped, lifting himself up onto his elbow, and said, "We should go. It's getting late." My eyes shot open in shock, and while a part of me may have been relieved that things hadn't progressed further, I couldn't even say that with conviction. If I were being completely honest with myself, I was disappointed that he hadn't continued what he had started.

I grabbed for my phone and noted it was already almost four o'clock. I had to get home to start dinner but almost didn't care. I wanted him to keep going. My body needed him to keep going. He stood up to get dressed. I followed his lead and did the same. I observed the contours of his back muscles when he slid his shirt on, feeling a strong sense of desire for him, tempted to touch his hard body.

We hiked back to the car, where he opened the door for me again. He drove me home just in time to get dinner started. But the hunger I felt inside me was not for food.

Chapter 7

Lucy

It was well into summer and hot as hell. We didn't have central AC in our house, so we relied on window air-conditioning units. It also didn't help that our gas oven was old and baked the entire kitchen every time I went to use it. Today I was making cookies to put in a care package for Luke—something I had done weekly for two years. I chose today to bake because it was my day off but was now regretting my choice as I unstuck the front of my shirt from my wet body. We were in the midst of a heatwave, and I felt as if I had just showered, sweat dripping down my face and back.

I, with all my brothers, still lived at home. There were seven of us living in a small, old four-bedroom house. My parents had five kids that they had to support on just my dad's modest warrior salary. That's why everything we had was old and in need of updating. Our windows were drafty, and many of the tiles in the bathroom and kitchen were cracked and in need of repair.

I was the middle child and the odd one out. While my four brothers all took directly after my father with their athleticism, I feigned period cramps to get out of training at school. However, being the only girl did have one perk—I was the only person in the house that got my own bedroom, a place I could be alone in a chaotic household.

My brothers were all constantly competing against each other and playing sports games with my dad. When I was younger, I tried to fit in and find my place in the family but eventually gave up. Now it was easier to tell myself that I just wanted to do my own thing than to admit that I felt left out.

When I was thirteen, soon after I had shifted for the first time, my mom took me to the casino in town to see a show to celebrate the occasion. I was already 5'7" at that age, taller than every girl in my class. We had both dressed up and my mom had helped me do my hair, so it looked really nice. We were walking through the resort part of the hotel, since I wasn't allowed in the casino, when somebody stopped us. A man told us he worked for a modeling agency and he thought I had potential. After being the forgotten one for so long, I was excited for someone to finally notice me. My mom was polite and took his card.

I begged my mom for weeks to call him. I had already started imagining myself in magazines and on billboards. Maybe I could even move from the middle of nowhere to New York City. But my mom refused and finally sat down to tell me that, because we were werewolves, we could never do anything that could make us famous. It was too risky because it could expose our entire pack. I was devastated and cried myself to sleep for weeks. That was the first time being a werewolf felt like a curse.

By the time I turned fifteen, I had gotten even taller and developed breasts. My face became more defined with high cheekbones. I started to realize that men noticed and liked me. They loved my attention. If I received a bad grade on a test, I could talk to my male teacher, laugh at his jokes, and touch his arm. Suddenly my D became a B. While my best friend Jasmine breezed through school, I just found I couldn't concentrate. When teachers would explain something, I would find my thoughts drifting to more interesting things like boys and school gossip.

Jasmine would constantly try to help me and motivate me to study, but it was honestly just easier to engage in a little harmless flirting.

I came to relish my power. Wherever I went, people would just *give* me things. If I was ordering a sandwich at our local sub shop, a man would appear out of thin air and offer to pay for my meal. Or the cashier would just hand me a cookie or brownie I didn't order. Boys at school would bring in gifts and leave them on my desk. When I'd go to the mall with my friends, cashiers would just offer me discounts on whatever I was buying, deducting an extra 10 or 15 percent off with a wink for no specific reason. One time my mom asked me to stop by the grocery store to grab something she needed. As I was walking back, a warrior took my bag from me and helped me carry it all the way home. Jack wasn't very happy about that one.

A couple months after the grocery incident, I spoke to Luke for the first time. I had known the future alpha, Blake, for a long time, him being friends with my older brother, Jack. But he was much older than me, and my brother never let me hang around him and his friends. However, the future beta was closer to my age. I'd always known of him, since our school was small, but our paths never crossed.

However, that all changed one night during my sophomore year when I'd been invited to a high school party. Someone's parents had gone out of town and the party was being held in their house. It was conveniently located in the outskirts of the pack territory where the neighboring houses weren't so close to each other, not far from where Jasmine lived. I'd forced Jasmine to go with me, and she grudgingly agreed to stay for a couple of hours until she had to be home for curfew. I constantly tried to get her to let loose—she was always so stressed about this or that. I thought if she finally let her hair down maybe she'd relax and not take everything so seriously.

The night started out rough. The party had begun early, and we got there when many people were already drunk. I'd taken Jasmine into the kitchen, and she refused to drink anything alcoholic.

"Why'd you even come, PJ, if you weren't planning to have any fun?" one of the girls in our class, Alyssa, slurred at her.

"I don't need to drink to have fun," Jasmine replied swiftly.

"I thought all you did was study." Alyssa snickered. "Go home, this is for fun people."

"Shouldn't you be at temple or something anyway?" Tina, a junior that I'd known to get around, chimed in.

"Shouldn't you be sucking someone's dick right now?" I snapped back at her.

"Too bad you can't Photoshop your ugly personality, Lucy." Alyssa laughed.

"Where'd you get that one, some internet meme?" I responded. "Goddess, even my little brothers can come up with more creative insults than that one." Alyssa glared at me, scrunching her face. I laughed at how ridiculous she looked and said, "Don't do that or your face will get stuck like that. On second thought, it's a huge improvement over how you normally look so maybe you should." I grabbed a hard seltzer out of a bucket of ice and took Jasmine's arm to take her out of the kitchen.

"They're right, I shouldn't have come," Jasmine said to me as I opened my can.

"No, they're not right," I replied. "They're just haters. Alyssa tries so fucking hard to beat you at everything. It's embarrassing because you don't even notice she's in competition with you."

"What?" Jasmine looked at me.

"You should hear her bitching in the bathroom about you every time you do better than her at something. With how much she talks about you, you'd think she's in love with you." I laughed.

Some guys from our class showed up and came over to talk to us. We hung out with them as a group for a couple of hours until Jasmine had to go home.

"Are you sure you can't stay?" Jeremy, one of the shyer guys in our class, asked Jasmine.

"No, you know how my parents are." She shrugged, pulling on her coat.

"I can walk you home," he offered.

"No, it's better that you don't. I can't be seen hanging out with guys and I only live a couple streets over anyway," she said, turning away from him to leave. I walked with Jasmine to the door to say bye to her, then turned back toward the party.

It was well into fall, and the air had the crisp smell of winter. I made my way into the backyard where a bunch of senior guys were sitting around a firepit to keep warm. That's when I spotted him. He was easily taller and more muscular than all of the other guys at the party. I wanted him, and I would do whatever I had to in order to have him.

Although it was cold, I shimmied outside in just the dress I was wearing, hoping the alcohol I drank would keep me warm long enough for my plan to begin working. "Hello, guys! Damn, it's cold out here. Do you mind if I warm up with all of you?"

They all quickly moved to make room for me. I sat down next to Luke, the future beta, my ultimate challenge. He didn't seem too enthused with me at first. However, just like with all males, it didn't take long for me to captivate his attention. I played the damsel in distress, I touched his muscles telling him how big his arms were, I asked him about himself, focusing all of my attention on him. Before the night was over, I was wearing his jacket and had my tongue in his mouth. Before the week was over, I was his girlfriend.

While my parents had never really been impressed by much that I did, they were definitely impressed that I had managed to catch the eye of the future beta of the pack. It wasn't long before my parents fell just as much in love with him as I had. Not only was he the future beta, but he was also polite, smart, articulate, and handsome. I had never met someone so perfect before in my life. He made me want to be a better version of myself.

Not long before he left for his mission in Quebec, he told me he loved me, and we agreed to continue our relationship long-distance. I went almost every month to visit him, cherishing the time we were able to spend together. Most of the time was spent cuddled up in his bed, far away from the judgment of our parents and the pack. My parents were always lecturing me, telling me not to get too serious or attached to Luke, not understanding how perfect we were for each other. And the pack was—well, the pack was just a bunch of pearl clutchers. Outside the pack, it was normal to date. I couldn't understand why we were stuck in the year 1952. Anyway, I knew he had to be my mate. Why else would we have fallen so hard for each other?

And that was when being a werewolf devastated me for the second time. We all know we're mated to someone that the Moon Goddess chooses for us. It seemed romantic when I was younger, like love at first sight and finding the other half of you. But that was before I realized that it could also break my heart.

I planned an elaborate trip to visit Luke for my eighteenth birthday. Three months earlier, my friend Emma had turned eighteen and realized that my brother Kyle was her mate after months of grossing me out with their constant hooking up. While my brother and friend becoming mates was initially shocking, it made me feel hopeful about my own relationship and that it could happen for me too. In the same way that Emma and Kyle were attracted to each other long prior to knowing they were mates, I was sure it was the same for Luke and me. In honor of the occasion, Luke booked a luxurious hotel room in Quebec City for the weekend. He made a reservation for a fancy dinner at a steak restaurant at eight o'clock, so we would be dining just as dusk hit on my birthday on April 23.

I planned to lose my virginity and allow him to mark me that night, after we knew for sure that we were mates. The act of marking each other by sinking our canines into each other's necks after having sex would solidify our mate bond. Only death would be able to sever it. That was something I had been looking forward to for years, and I was anxious to finally be bonded to Luke forever.

The dinner started perfectly. They brought out a bottle of champagne to celebrate my eighteenth birthday. Growing up modestly, I had never been to such a beautiful and fancy restaurant. We were seated next to a window, able to look over the entire city, the lights glimmering across the landscape of buildings. We ordered appetizers, dinner, and side dishes, Luke encouraging me to order anything I wanted. By the time dessert was served, I was feeling drunk and jubilant in how perfect the night had been when a horrifying thought came to me. I looked at my phone to see it was well past dusk, and I had not had any overwhelming feeling come over me that Luke was my mate.

I sat there, feeling as if the whole world was moving around me while a hole formed in my chest. I normally loved chocolate cake but found I'd completely lost my appetite and just pushed it around on my plate.

Luke suddenly looked alarmed. "Lucy, what's wrong? You look like you've just seen a ghost." At his words tears fell down my cheeks, and I was unable to stop them once they started. He then looked at his watch, coming to the same realization I had moments earlier. "Don't worry, Lucy, I still love you." He took my hand. I began wiping at my tears with my napkin, embarrassed that I was causing a scene at the restaurant.

He then signaled for the check so we could go back to the hotel. He held my hand as we walked in silence. The perfect night ruined, two and a half perfect years leading to a devastating night—a bucket of freezing cold water poured over me by Artemis. I could just hear her in my head—*Gotcha!* When we got back into the hotel room, I kicked my shoes off and sat down on the bed. Luke sat down next to me and held me against his chest as I sobbed. How could Artemis have promised someone so perfect to someone else? And I knew, deep down, it was because I was not good enough for him. My family was poor, people regularly gossiped about me, I shunned our religion, my grades were only passable because I flirted to get them, and I would never make even a half-decent warrior. What good would I be to a beta? I was not like my best friend Jasmine who was perfect at everything—I just got by. When Luke came into my life, I finally felt special for once, believing I could be the perfect beta mate and mother one day, and now even that was taken from me.

We eventually fell into the bed together, snuggled against each other. As I burrowed my head into Luke's chest, he said to me, "I'm happy just lying here with you. I know we'd planned for more tonight, but we don't have to go any further. I'm happy just spending time with you, Lucy."

I looked up at him, feeling tears forming in my eyes again. "You don't want to have sex with me anymore?"

"I do want to. I've been waiting for years until you were ready. I just assumed since we're not mates you wouldn't want to anymore, and I wanted you to know I respect whatever you want."

"But why does it matter what the Moon Goddess decides? Why can't we just choose to be mates? Why should the fact that we're not fated to each other change anything? We can still decide our own fates. You should still mark me!" I said very boldly, my sadness replaced by anger.

Luke looked at me miserably. "No, Lucy, I can't mark you."

"Why not?" I cried, incensed about the whole situation.

He kissed my head and replied, "Because we're fated to others. You have a mate somewhere out there that the Moon Goddess has gifted to you. Once you find him, it will all make sense. You can't just throw that away. I won't allow it. You deserve to meet him and be happy."

"But I'm happy with you."

"I know. But we're still young and we have time to meet our mates."

"Please don't break up with me," I cried as tears began spilling down my face again.

"I won't, not tonight." He kissed me.

"Not tonight?!" I pushed him off me, screaming, sitting up. "What the fuck does that mean?!"

He sat up as well and looked down at his lap, clenching and unclenching his fists, not responding, not looking up. My heart dropped. Was he really considering breaking up with me? My perfect boyfriend that I couldn't imagine my life without was actually considering ending our relationship, taking away the entire future I'd imagined with him. I could almost feel my heart physically tearing into two. I couldn't believe that it could actually be over.

"Do you not love me anymore?" I practically whispered, the most vulnerable I'd ever been in my life.

He suddenly looked up, his light brown eyes staring deeply into mine. "Of course I still love you."

"Then how can you just throw away everything we have together?" I was practically screaming.

"I don't want to, Lucy. I'm just trying to do the right thing. I believed as much as you did that you were my mate, and that's why I fell so hard for you. Trust me, I'm just as surprised and upset about this as you are. But now we know the truth."

"What can be truer than how we feel for each other?" Fresh tears spilled down my cheeks.

Luke pulled me back against him, kissing the side of my head, trailing kisses down my face until our mouths found each other. The kiss deepened as I slipped my tongue in his mouth, eager to be close to him, desperate to feel his skin against mine, wanting to believe he loved me as much as I loved him. Before I knew it, our kissing had progressed and his mouth moved down to my chin and then to my neck and chest. He unzipped my dress. I pulled it over my head revealing the red lingerie set I had worn just for the occasion.

"You're so beautiful," he said as I lay back and he kissed down to my breasts, unclipping my bra, and slipping it off my arms. He removed his own shirt, revealing his broad shoulders and sculpted chest and abs. I ran my hand down his abdomen as I watched a bulge appear in his pants.

He lowered his head back down toward my body and sucked gently on each nipple as he fondled my breasts. I moaned and he kissed slowly down my stomach and over the top of my thong. I was becoming very wet between my legs, a desperate pulsing emerging. I stroked the nape of his neck, eager for him to go further.

He finally removed my panties and began kissing me up my inner thighs, teasing me. I moaned more loudly, encouraging him to go further. He eventually slipped his tongue between my legs, and quickly found that sweet spot, flicking his tongue against my clitoris. A loud moan escaped my lips as pleasure radiated from where he brushed his tongue against me.

I put my hand on his head, stopping him. "Luke, I want you. I want to have sex with you."

"Are you sure?" He looked at me.

"Yes," I replied. I was ready. I loved him and wanted to feel him inside me. I undid his belt buckle. He removed his pants and underwear, allowing his erection to spring free. I watched as he pulled a condom from the pocket of his pants and rolled it onto himself. He lowered himself back onto me and began kissing me again, the taste of me on his tongue, which aroused me further.

As he kissed me, he moved his cock against my opening, rubbing it, heightening my desire, my desperation, to finally feel him inside me. "I love you," he said as he entered me, forcing my insides to stretch to fit himself within me, a tear escaping my eye from the pain. "Are you okay?" he asked.

"Yes, it's okay," I replied. He began moving slowly, and pleasure from the movement mixed with the pain from being stretched to accommodate him. He increased the speed of his movement and used his thumb to rub my clitoris, the ember inside me building to a full fire, heating and galvanizing my whole body. I dug my fingers into his back as he moved against me, relishing all of the sensations of the two of us together.

He sped up, and rubbed my clit harder, until I was trembling under him, feeling an intense orgasm blaze across my entire body. He let out his own deep growl, signaling that he had come, and collapsed on top of me. After catching his breath, he lifted himself onto his forearms and looked me in the eyes, smiling, and kissed my head. He then got up and walked to the bathroom to clean himself up. A bliss spread throughout me as I reflected on the moment we had just shared. When he came back into the bed, we snuggled up against each other until we fell asleep, and I knew I'd never let him go.

Chapter 8

Jasmine

About a week after Blake and I went hiking, I was working with Lucy. I had opened that morning. And I was working a shorter shift than normal. It was just after nine and the rush had slowed. I was looking forward to leaving in an hour when my replacement, a new hire named Reena, would be taking my place. Lucy was on her cell phone and put it down next to mine as a customer entered.

She quickly took his order, and I ran to go make it. After I handed him his drink, I looked to see the screen of my cell phone flash. I was about to reach for it, but something caught Lucy's eye and she grabbed for it first.

"Ooooh! Who's this *Blake Sexy AF*? Is that Alpha Blake?" Her eyes darted up at me. *Shit*, I forgot to change his name in my phone. "And here I was thinking you're a lost cause!"

"What do you mean by that?"

"I mean, you're such a prude. I don't mean any offense by that, but damn, I guess I had you all wrong! *Blake Sexy AF*! And here he is texting you and I had no idea you ever even talked to him after that day at the beach!"

"We don't normally talk."

"How'd you get his number then? How come you didn't tell me he gave you his number?" She narrowed her eyes at me.

"I forgot I had it," I replied, annoyed that Lucy had my phone. I wanted to see what Blake was texting me. I hadn't heard from him since that day we went hiking, causing me to feel anxious all week, desperately trying to busy myself with other things to stop thinking about him. My heart was racing, eager to know why he was finally contacting me again.

"But you didn't answer my first question. How'd you get his number? When did this happen?"

I knew I couldn't avoid it, so I confessed. "He gave it to me at temple one day, after the service, so I could text him my address. He wanted to hang out with me that day, but we had to wait until my parents left."

"What! You've been sneaking around, and I had no idea? So, what happened?" Lucy pushed my shoulder, her eyes wide.

"Well, he took me to a mountain, and we hiked. Then we talked," I replied, trying to make it seem like not a big deal.

"What else happened?" she asked loudly, her eyes bugging out.

"Nothing. We just talked and went home," I replied quietly, hinting to keep her voice down.

She didn't look convinced. "Are you sure you're not hiding anything from me? That man is fucking hot as hell. I can't believe you didn't do more than that. If I were you and alone with him, I'm pretty sure I'd give up my virginity right there and then, birth control be damned."

"No, nothing else happened, I swear. We just talked and that's it. There's not more to the story."

"Okay, I'll believe you for now. But if anything else happens, you better tell me right away. I've been waiting for years for your wild side to come out! I knew it was hiding somewhere inside you!"

"There's no wild side."

"So, what does the text say then?" She already knew my password and punched it in. She read the text out loud. "Let's go swimming again today, this time no underwear, winky face." Her eyes narrowed at me. "What does that mean? You went swimming in your *underwear*? It sounds like you may have left some details out of your story."

"Why are you reading my personal text messages?" I screamed at her, annoyed at her antics.

"Because you're clearly not telling me the whole story, so I have to find out other ways. So come on, let it out, tell me what you're hiding."

I knew there was no way out of it now. "Okay, well, we hiked down to a pond and went swimming in our underwear. Then we lay out on a blanket that he brought. But that's it, nothing else happened. We didn't kiss or anything else." Although, I supposed silently, we may have skipped first base and almost gone straight to second, but Lucy didn't need to know that. I couldn't even admit this was all happening to myself, let alone to Lucy. Especially after I'd made such a big deal to her about how Blake and I were never happening. Okay, I did really enjoy the feel of his hands on my body. Even thinking about it now was giving me a warm feeling and butterflies in my stomach. But then there was another part of me that felt shame that I had wavered on my morals, given in to Blake's touch, and enjoyed it far too much.

She then started a speech-to-text while she held me back with her free hand. "We don't need no pond, I'm already wet and ready for you, period, my work shift ends at ten."

"What are you doing?" I tackled her, grabbing my phone to see that her text was already sent.

Shit, shit, shit.

I watched as three dots appeared, indicating he was typing back, and a new text appeared on the screen.

Blake Sexy AF: *Good, I'm thirsty.*

I looked up at her with daggers in my eyes. How could she think that what she had done was okay?

At exactly ten, his Jeep parallel parked in front of the café. With a huge smile on her face, Lucy rushed to open the door. I followed right behind her. I couldn't lie, he looked delectable wearing aviator sunglasses and a thin T-shirt that showed the outlines of all his well-sculpted muscles.

Lucy pulled me out of the café with her, undid the strings to my apron, pulling it off me, and pushed me toward him. "Now, have fun! And Jaz, you better share every last detail when I call you tonight. I want a firsthand account of what it's like to sleep with an alpha." She gave Blake a quick wink before she shut the door.

"Sounds like I have an audience now, so I better make it really good." He elbowed me playfully.

I slapped his arm. "Don't listen to her."

Once we were both seated in his car, he leaned over to me. "I know Lucy was the one that sent that text, but I want to know if it's true." He leaned toward me and began rubbing his hand on the inside of my thigh, inching it under the skirt I was wearing. His fingers traveled north, until they were tracing the hem of my panties. My heart raced and my breathing shallowed. My whole body was becoming aroused, a hot shiver expanding from my inner thighs to the rest of my body. My legs tingled, the apex of them throbbing, desperate for him to keep going. I slapped his hand away, my brain finally catching up with my hormones. Damn that felt good, but no! It was wrong. He withdrew his hand and put his car into reverse. "I intend to find out."

"Keep dreaming!" I replied, not wanting him to know how much I just enjoyed that.

He drove to and parked in the same area as last time, immediately exiting the car and coming around to my side. Upon opening my door for me, he held his hand out to help me down. He grabbed his backpack from the back seat and led me to the base of the mountain so we could hike to the top. Once we got to the summit, he spread the blanket out for us to sit down and pulled out some sandwiches.

"I put a little more effort into lunch today." He grinned and handed me a ham and cheese sandwich and a water bottle. We sat in silence, eating our sandwiches, looking over the landscape of trees below, a carpet of green forest, with openings for bodies of water. I spotted the pond where we had gone swimming below, the sun reflecting off it, giving it a glass-like appearance. The view was spectacular, and I could see why Blake liked coming here.

"Do you bring all your girls here?" I asked, suddenly wondering if I was just one of the many girls he was hanging out with, especially after his revelation of how he was in high school.

"No, I've never brought anyone else here before. I only recently discovered this place. Why, would you be jealous?" He had a twinkle in his eye.

"What, no!" I exclaimed. "I was just curious about who else you hang out with. Do you bring the others somewhere else?"

He looked at me, tilting his head. "There are no others."

"Oh, I just assumed. . ." I let my voice trail off.

"No, I'm not ready to get back out there yet. But something about you feels safe." He looked at me earnestly, making my heart stop. The way he said it made me believe he was being sincere. We sat there, just looking at each other.

I broke the silence. "I'd like to know more about Ria."

He sighed. "It's hard to talk about her. Losing a mate is one of the most painful things that ever happens to a werewolf. I didn't understand it until it happened to me. It still hurts like it just happened yesterday." He looked at me with pain in his eyes.

On impulse and moved by his demeanor, I went to hug him, and he wrapped his large arms around me, placing his head on top of mine. His scent and body heat enveloped me as I listened to his deep breathing, suddenly feeling an affection for him. After several minutes of sitting like that he pulled away and looked out into the distance.

"She was killed in the battle five years ago. An enemy ripped her heart out in front of me. He may as well have ripped mine out while he was at it. I tore that motherfucker to shreds. If only I had done it sooner." He turned back to me, and his eyes had a dark, almost evil appearance.

I squeezed his hand and he closed his eyes, taking a deep breath. He opened them again and asked, "Did I play the part of the vulnerable man with a hard shell well? Do I get rewarded with some titty fondling now?" He smirked, but I noted that his eyes still looked pained. He wasn't playing a part at all.

I punched his arm. Damn, his muscles were hard. I wasn't expecting his arm to be that stiff.

"Well, it was worth a try anyway," he said, turning back toward the view and taking a sip from his water bottle.

Recognizing the punch was probably a bit too harsh after what he had revealed, I turned to him and said, "I'm really sorry, Blake, about Ria. That's really awful. I can't even imagine." When he didn't turn back to look at me, I touched his arm gently, wondering if I should do more to offer my condolences and wishing I knew how to comfort him more. It obviously couldn't be easy to lose your mate.

He shrugged. "Let's talk about something else. What are you studying in school?"

"I haven't picked a major yet. But I probably should soon. I was thinking about biochemistry like my parents."

"Your dictator parents?"

I laughed. "I forgot I called them that."

"Seems fitting. It appears they actually do dictate every single thing you do. And you don't even try to rebel."

"That's not true!" I exclaimed, but realized he might be right as I said it.

"Really?" he asked. "You've rebelled before?"

"Of course I have!" I replied.

"Somehow I don't believe you." He smiled at me, an amused look on his face.

"Are you calling me a liar?"

"Okay, tell me then—when have you rebelled?"

I pondered and said, "I'm rebelling right now by being here with you!"

"And we may as well just be back at the pack sitting around at the library with how innocent this get-together is. Besides, your parents don't even know this is happening, so it may as well have never happened." I frowned and he continued, "So my point still stands that your parents dictate everything you do."

"There have been other times too!"

"So you're not just a goody-two-shoes, perfect daughter that's saving herself for her mate?" There was a glint in his eyes.

"I can be rebellious!" I exclaimed.

"Prove it."

I crossed my arms. "I don't have to prove anything to you."

"You're the one that's telling me you can be rebellious. But I don't see any proof. So, I'm just going to assume you're being disingenuous."

I scoffed. "Well, there's nothing wrong with being a good, moral person."

"So, which are you then? Good, moral person or rebel?"

"I'm both," I replied, smiling, not even sure what point I was trying to prove anymore. All I knew was that I didn't want Blake to win this argument.

"No, you're not," he shot back. "You don't have a rebellious bone in your body."

"Yes, I do!" I retorted. "I can be very rebellious!"

"Fine, prove it then."

"How do you want me to prove it to you?"

"Let me feel you up." He smirked.

I glared at him, irritated and fired up by the argument. How dare he call me a Goody Two-shoes? He barely even knew me. I could be fun and exciting. "Fine!" I shouted, giving in.

"What? Really?" he asked, his eyes wide. He began inching closer to me.

"Not so fast, I'm setting a timer on my phone! You get one minute, that's it!" I knew I had to set boundaries, or this could get out of hand. I'd just give him one minute to touch my boobs and then, done and done, we'd settle it.

"I'm being timed?" He furrowed his brows.

"Yes, you get one minute as proof I'm capable of rebelling, but that's it!"

"No, I want five!"

"Fine, I'll compromise and give you three!" I typed three minutes into the timer on my phone and put it where we could both see it. "Ready, set, go," I pressed the timer to start.

He instantly got on his knees and positioned himself in front of me. My breath hitched in nervousness as he towered over me and brought his hands toward my body. I sat back on my hands while he grazed his fingers along the sides of my lower ribcage and slid them up my body until his thumbs were touching the sides of my breasts. Then he brought his mouth to my neck, slowly kissing his way down to my chest, moving his lips farther south between my breasts, pulling the neckline of my shirt lower with his chin. I was about to stop him, thinking this was not at all what I imagined he would do, but his lips on my skin felt too good, too heavenly. My whole body burned hot with desire as his mouth grazed the valley between my breasts. My fingers and toes tingled with the satisfaction of a forbidden desire being fulfilled as his mouth entered such a guarded part of my body, the stubble on his jaw sensually brushing against my sensitive skin.

He traced his thumbs along the sides of my breasts gently, a new, thrilling sensation materializing within me. As I leaned back, giving in to his touch, he supported me with his hands and lowered me down until I was lying flat on my back, and he was hovering above me. He quickly glanced in my eyes and switched strategies, moving his face lower down my body, untucking my shirt, kissing up my stomach and pulling my shirt up as he did.

A very weak part of me thought I should stop him, but found I was powerless against how good his lips felt grazing my skin, bringing butterflies to my stomach. He continued kissing up the center of my torso, lifting my shirt until my bra was completely uncovered. His lips trailed one of my breasts while he used his thumb to pull down the top of my bra until my nipple was fully exposed. He moved his mouth to suck on it, flicking his tongue against it, provoking it to harden in his mouth.

If I wasn't wet before, I definitely was now. My whole body desired him. He switched to the other nipple, both my breasts completely bare and revealed to him, making me feel as if I were simultaneously in heaven and hell, giving in to my most illicit desires, in complete ecstasy. A moan escaped my lips as the timer went off. I suddenly regretted my decision to limit this to three minutes. Even five would have been too short.

Blake instantly sat up and looked down at me. "Now, what do I need to do to do the same thing but on the bottom half of your body? I'd prefer more than three minutes, but I can work fast if I have to." He smiled mischievously at me.

"You're pushing your luck now," I responded, sitting up, pulling my bra back over my nipples, and pulling my shirt down. It'd be lying to say I wasn't tempted by his suggestion, now being so worked up. But I couldn't let him know that—I could barely even admit it to myself.

"Okay, maybe it won't happen today, but I know it will. You enjoyed those three minutes more than you're going to admit. I heard you moan.

If I'd had five minutes like I'd asked for, you'd be begging me to remove your skirt."

"In your dreams," I snapped back, not wanting him to know how much I enjoyed it and how badly I wanted him to continue.

"I know I'm in your dreams too. I wish I could know what I'm doing to you in them."

"Goddess, you're so conceited!"

He laughed and then stood up, giving me his hand to help me up. "Come on, we should go before it gets too late. I have pack business to take care of this afternoon." After helping me up, he packed the blanket back into his backpack and slung it over his shoulders. We hiked back to his car so he could drive me home.

When he dropped me off, he leaned over before I got out of his car and said, "Sweet dreams tonight. Make sure you text me everything I'm doing to you in them so I can make them come true next time." He winked at me and brushed my hair behind my ear.

The sensations from earlier flooded back, gathering and pulsing between my legs. Damn, I could feel how wet I was, wondering if the thin layer of my panties would be enough to shield my wetness from Blake's car seat. His eyes were staring into mine, hypnotizing me. No! Must not be hypnotized!

"Not happening," I replied, opening the door and getting out. I felt torn. What happened today was amazing, heavenly. I didn't know that someone's mouth on your nipples could feel so incredible. But it couldn't keep happening. As much as my whole body desired Blake, I knew it was wrong. No, I needed to stay away from him! But could I?

Chapter 9

Jasmine

A week went by, and I hadn't heard from Blake since the last time we went hiking. Lucy had called me that night begging me to tell her all the details, but I just told her that we hiked and talked. She obviously didn't believe me, but I wasn't ready to start spilling all the details of what had happened yet. The whole thing felt like a dream, and I didn't know how to make sense of it.

We were at work, and during a lull, she leaned over to me. "How's *Blake Sexy AF* doing?"

"I haven't talked to him."

"I don't believe you."

"I'm not lying. I haven't heard from him since last time."

"Why don't you text him and ask him to hang out?"

"Because I don't want to." In reality, I did want to, but I was too ashamed to actually do it, and ashamed of myself for wanting to. I didn't want to seem eager and was still determined to not allow things to advance any further than they had.

"You're definitely lying about that. I don't think there's a warm-blooded woman on this earth that wouldn't want to hang out with him. I'm pretty sure he could even turn a lesbian straight."

"Well, then I guess I must be cold-blooded. Maybe I'm a weregator."

At that moment, a customer came in. I was thankful for the interruption forcing the end of the conversation. Lucy went to the register as additional customers came in and a line started to form again. I busied myself preparing all the orders.

I was working the late shift that day, so I would be leaving at four. After breakfast time was over, Lucy went out back to prep dough and decorate cakes with Valerie while I ran the register. She sometimes jumped in during lunchtime if it got busy, but I could usually handle it by myself. Today wasn't too bad, so she stayed in the back with Valerie. Since Lucy opened, she left at one thirty.

I went around the café to wipe down tables and sweep the floor after Lucy left. My thoughts drifted to Blake. When I was with him, I started to question my convictions, principles I thought I would never waver on. Truth be told, I'd never been tested prior to then. I'd always just concentrated on studying and extracurricular activities. Sure, I hung out with people at school and went to parties when Lucy dragged me to them. But our school was small, meaning I'd grown up with the people I spent my days with, which didn't leave much room for temptation.

What was I doing now? None of my thoughts were making any sense. I had always vowed I'd save myself completely for my mate. I had never even had a real crush on anyone before, knowing we were all promised a mate by the Moon Goddess. It just seemed a waste of time to become attached to someone only to then break up with them once I found my mate. It also wasn't worth fighting with my parents for something that was so futile.

But now I was wavering. Something was changing inside me. As much as I pretended that I didn't care if Blake ever texted me again, I began to hope he would. I hated to admit to myself how much he'd gotten to me. When several days went by without hearing from him, all my insecurities began to come forward. Did he ever think about me? I thought about him way more than I could even admit to myself. I hated the idea of being more into him than he was into me, especially since I hadn't even wanted to start this *thing* between us in the first place. My life was great before he came along—simple. As long as I did everything I was supposed to, everything would fall into place. But Blake was complicating things.

After I finished my shift, I went outside where my grandparents had come to pick me up to bring me home. I jumped into their car and greeted them both as my grandfather began driving toward where we lived. They lived down the street from us and often picked me up from work, then stayed for dinner.

My grandma said from the passenger seat, "How was work today, Jazzy?"

"It was good. Not too busy."

"Very good," she replied.

"So, has your mate come into the café yet?" my grandfather asked. Since I turned eighteen, he was constantly asking if I'd met my mate yet.

"Not yet."

"I hope you've been saving yourself, Jasmine! Male werewolves don't like an impure woman," my grandfather exclaimed, catching me off guard.

My grandma interjected before I could say anything, "Of course our Jasmine has been saving herself! You think she's some sort of floozy?"

"You just never know these days! Back in our day, women all behaved properly. But times are changing!" my grandfather replied.

"And you think our little Jasmine is out there being improper? She's a good girl. We raised her well. She knows to wait for the Moon Goddess's gift."

"I don't think she's being improper. I'm just making sure she knows to be chaste in case it hasn't been clear. I don't want her mate to reject her because she's not pure."

"Of course our little Jazzy's chaste! She's a very good girl and her mate will be lucky to have her."

I couldn't believe that my grandparents were arguing about my sex life, or lack thereof. I felt so gross about their argument. I was also disgusted by the idea that someone would reject their mate for being "impure" as if they were some damaged goods. Why would I want to be with someone who felt that way about women—that their primary value was their virginity? While I'd always wanted to save myself because I thought it would be special to lose my virginity to my mate, I started to question my logic. There was more to me than whether or not my hymen was intact.

Chapter 10

Blake

It was now late July, and I was, once again, with my father and Beta Alfred in the packhouse office. We had spent the morning going over the pack budget with the pack accountant and office manager. My father was still mostly handling the casino along with the casino managers, which was where most of the funding for the pack came from. However, I would soon oversee the distribution of the funds that flowed down from the casino to different areas of the pack such as road repair, snow removal, security, school, temple, and housing subsidies.

After lunch, my father, Beta Alfred, and I sat together in the office at the packhouse, situated around the desk on a conference call with Luke and Alpha Antoine from the Lune Nordique Pack. These phone calls were becoming a weekly occurrence.

We were all concerned about Alpha Édouard, who led the Bois Sombre Pack in Quebec. He was a crazy motherfucker and was known for being sadistic and unhinged. He made my father look like a straight-up saint. Years ago, he was mated to the sister of Alpha Antoine from the Lune Nordique Pack, our ally and his neighboring pack. She went to live with him willingly, falling in love with him due to the mate bond, unaware of how abusive he was until it was too late. One time he punched her so hard that she miscarried. Another time, he almost killed her. Even with the enhanced healing abilities of werewolves, she was in the clinic for almost a week before she gained enough strength to walk again. This went on for many years.

When Alpha Antoine and his father found out what was happening, they stole her and her pups back. Alpha Édouard didn't take this well and declared war. Because we were their allies, our pack traveled north to help defend Alpha Antoine's pack. By that time, I had already assumed my new role as a full-time warrior and future alpha, so I, too, went to fight my first battle. However, our pack had grown weak due to my father's age, something we hadn't truly thought would be a problem as we believed it more an old wives' tale than anything. But it quickly became clear how much strength a pack gathers from its alpha as we watched many of our warriors drop one by one, life slipping from their bodies, including Ria's. My Ria. My Ria, who had been right beside me as I witnessed her heart be ripped from her chest, an image that haunted my nightmares, perpetually waking me in the dead of night. While witnessing my father slice limbs off bodies as a kid had been traumatizing, it was nothing compared to this.

We were, fortunately, able to kill off most of Alpha Édouard's family and they finally retreated. However, there were rumors that he wanted revenge, hence the need for the constant monitoring of his pack.

"Good afternoon, Luke, Alpha Antoine. This is Alpha James, Beta Alfred, and Blake here." My father spoke loudly into the conference phone.

"Bonjour, hi, everyone," Alpha Antoine responded in a French Canadian accent.

"Good afternoon," Luke repeated.

"Let's hope this is a short meeting. There's no news from Midnight Maple Pack today." My dad spoke again. "Anything from either you, Alpha Antoine, or you, Luke?"

Alpha Antoine replied first. "It's still the same from the Lune Nordique Pack. We hear the same rumors that the Bois Sombre Pack has not given up and has been growing their pack. I am sorry again that your pack is involved in our dispute. Alpha Édouard has not given up on reclaiming my sister Sofia and her puppies, and I refuse to return them to that *fils de pute*."

"Your pack is one of our oldest and best allies from the time my great-grandfather started this pack, so we will continue to support you, Alpha Antoine. Anything from you, Luke?" my father asked.

"We have some news from our end. We've witnessed alphas of other packs meeting with Alpha Édouard on neutral land. We believe Alpha Édouard may be constructing alliances with other packs. After speaking with a source at a neighboring pack, it was confirmed that he wants revenge after our pack slaughtered all the males of his family."

"He deserves every death in his family. I am only sorry that I have not killed him yet. Blake, was it not you that killed his brother?" Alpha Antoine asked.

"His brother killed my mate," I replied angrily.

"I am sorry about that, Blake. My condolences. We're indebted to your pack and will be at your beck and call should it become necessary," Alpha Antoine responded.

"Thank you, Alpha Antoine. We will let you know. Please keep us informed if you hear any additional rumors," my father said.

"I will, absolutely." With that we said our goodbyes and ended the call.

"Do you have any thoughts, Al?" My dad looked at Beta Alfred.

"With Luke coming home at the end of the summer to take the beta title, I was thinking it would be best if I replace him as head of investigations in Quebec. Luke has done a very good job and will be a great beta here. My mate has been itching to go away for a while after dedicating our lives to the pack for so many years, so I think it will be a nice change of scenery for us."

"Yes, I think that's a good idea," my father agreed.

"For now, I will start assigning some of the new warrior recruits to the rotation for deployment to the north. That'll be good experience for them, and the more warriors we have trained in investigations, the better for our pack."

"Yes, yes, very good," my father agreed. He always seemed to be a bit more agreeable in his beta's presence.

On Sunday night, I attended the weekly service with my family. I noticed Jasmine sitting with her parents and felt a longing to see her again. I'd been busy training for the alpha role with my father, so I didn't have time to focus on my social life. Seeing her in person, however, brought feelings to the surface I didn't quite realize I had. She had a warmth to her that made me feel safe. When I spent time with her, I was surprised to find that I began to feel like the old version of myself again. It had been years since I'd been able to smile and joke around, but something about her brought that part of me out again. I felt rewarded as she became less shy and opened up more to me each time we met. I wanted to know her, and I realized, I wanted her to know me too. The thing was, she *could* know me. With most people, there were topics I found physically impossible to discuss, but I was somehow able to broach those same topics with her. Plus, I loved seeing all her reactions to my teasing.

And, I can't lie, she had a really nice, toned, athletic body that I may have fantasized about once or twice, or, well, more times than I cared to admit. Damn, I loved a strong woman. It may not be for everyone, but sinewy women had always been my type. I could feel myself going hard now at my thoughts. Her physique was clearly not only a genetic gift but one she had sculpted through years of physical work. I didn't fail to notice her muscular legs, well-defined abs, and incredible ass that had seen more than just a couple squats in its day. And, Goddess, her breasts—she had the most beautiful, perky breasts that were so responsive to my touch. I was determined to discover every last bit of her body. Now that I had a taste, I wanted to savor all of it.

After the service was over, I kept my eyes on her to see if I could catch her away from her parents. I saw them being stopped by a couple I knew to be her grandparents and another elderly couple. Once they were deep in conversation, I watched as Jasmine snuck away and headed toward the bathroom. Bingo!

I waited for her to come out, the same as I had last time. After I waited a couple minutes, she finally exited, her eyes widening once she noticed me standing in front of her.

"This is the second time I almost bumped into you coming out of the bathroom. I'm starting to think this isn't a coincidence."

"Maybe it's just meant to be, and the Moon Goddess keeps putting us in each other's paths," I deadpanned.

"That's a bit less believable, but okay, I'll go along with it," Jasmine responded, an amused look on her face. I could see she was straining not to smile, her amber eyes twinkling. Did I mention how beautiful her eyes were? They were so unique. I'd been with a lot of women, and hers had to be the nicest eyes I'd ever peered into.

"So, when can I see you again? We have unfinished business."

"Can you elaborate on what business you speak of?"

"I told you I intend to find out whether the text that was sent to me is true or not. I won't give up until my curiosity is fully satisfied."

Her cheeks reddened and she retorted, "Then you'll be curious the rest of your life."

"I think you and I both know that's not true. You and I also both know that you enjoyed last time, even if you'll never admit it," I replied, turned on by the thought. Feeling my blood rush south, I shifted a bit so my thoughts wouldn't reveal themselves physically, pushing the vision from my mind. "What time are you free tomorrow?"

"I'll be busy all day," she replied curtly, crossing her arms. I couldn't tell if she was playing with me or if there was something unwelcoming in her response.

"What are you so busy doing?" I tried to draw more information out of her.

"I have to work," she responded, keeping her arms crossed.

"And when do you get out?" I tried again.

"It'll be too late to do anything. I'll be there until four."

"Then I'll see you tomorrow in front of the café when you get out. You know what my car looks like." I waited for her response. When she didn't say anything, her arms still crossed, staring at me with her mouth open, I leaned forward and quietly teased, "You didn't do your homework. I thought you were a better student than that."

"What?" She furrowed her brows in confusion.

"You were supposed to text me all of your dreams." I smirked. "But don't worry, I'm pretty creative and can just work with my own." I winked at her. "Trust me. They're good and you won't be disappointed."

She blushed and opened and closed her mouth like a fish. I couldn't help but smile at how cute she looked, perhaps looking forward to the next day a little too much.

Chapter 11

Jasmine

I knew, logically, I should say no. I knew I should reject the far-too-smug alpha. But something inside me wouldn't allow me to do it. I had been feeling a yearning blossom within me. I loved how he broke down all my barriers and made me feel desired. After being Perfect Jasmine for so many years, it was energizing to do something so rebellious and wrong for once in my life.

That was why, without argument, I found myself at the front of the café, looking forward to the evening. I had told my parents I would be eating dinner with friends that night so they wouldn't expect me at home. As soon as I exited work, I spotted his Jeep parked across the street and walked over. He opened the passenger door for me and helped me in.

Once he hopped into the driver's seat, he turned to me. "I don't want you to feel uncomfortable, but I'd like to invite you over to the packhouse. The parents are out of town on pack business and the staff doesn't work on Mondays, so we'll be the only ones there and won't be disturbed." I furrowed my brows and he continued, "I promise I'd never do anything against your will. I just want to spend some time with you." Then he added, bringing his face closer to mine, "But I also can't guarantee you'll be able to resist my pheromones while in close, intimate quarters with me."

"You do realize you previously took me into the middle of the woods where no one would have heard me scream."

"That's true, but I don't want you to think my only intention is to get in your pants. It's one of my top intentions, but not the only one."

"So much for not screwing around with pack members."

"Eh, rules are made to be broken. I have a feeling you wouldn't slash my tires at least."

"Is that something that's happened?"

He chuckled then replied, "It's not really funny. I feel kind of bad about it now. But I had been seeing someone prior to meeting Ria, and I sort of ghosted her heartlessly." I narrowed my eyes at him. He continued, "I was only eighteen and pretty dumb. I'd be more tactful today. Anyway, she obviously didn't take it well. After slashing my tires, she ran after me with a baseball bat at school asking why I didn't love her."

"Holy shit! Where is she now?"

"She met her mate when she turned eighteen and she's married with a pup now."

"That's good, I guess. Who are all these girls that you were hooking up with in high school anyway? I think Lucy's the only girl I knew who had a boyfriend. Well, Emma was with Kyle, too, but they ended up being mates."

"Everyone hooks up, just no one talks about it."

"Not everyone!"

"Well, apparently not you."

I glared at him, and he smiled, lightly shaking my shoulder.

"Anyway, getting back on topic, seeing as you seem fairly sane, I'd like to invite you over my place. As long as you feel comfortable, of course."

"Why would I feel uncomfortable?"

He looked at me for a moment and then said, "Well, you shouldn't with me because I'd never do anything you don't want me to do, but wow, you're too trusting."

I considered Blake and felt like I could trust him. "I'd like to see the packhouse. I've never been inside."

"Okay, great! Buckle up!" Blake reversed out of the parking space and sped toward the packhouse.

I could tell that Blake was softening and opening up more as I spent time with him. He also seemed much less dark and distant than the first time I'd met him, as if his icy shell was slowly thawing. I, likewise, found myself warming up to him and feeling more comfortable in his presence. He was now feeling more like a friend than a hot, mysterious alpha.

After we parked in the packhouse driveway, I went to open the door to get out of the car, but he got there in time to help me down. I tried to slap away his hand and said, "You know, I am capable of getting in and out of cars myself."

"My mom raised me better than that. Now come on, let's go inside." He took my hand and led me into the packhouse. The front door opened to a marble hallway with a grand staircase that led to the second floor. I looked up to see there was also a third floor above. He walked me around the first floor, which was set up in an open floor plan.

He started at the back and showed me the spacious living room with a generously sized wood-burning fireplace contained in stones that traveled up to the vaulted ceiling, large, plush brown leather couch and chairs, and a sliding glass door that led to a patio and garden in the backyard. Afterward, we walked through the dining room, with a huge table that could probably fit at least twenty people, and kitchen, which was hidden behind a door and contained a smaller kitchen table. He then showed me the offices—one was for the office manager and accountant to share, and one was for the alpha and beta to share, with two large desks on opposite walls that faced the center of the office, with chairs between the desks for visitors. Finally, he took me down into the basement, which had a laundry room and a separate break area for the staff that worked in the packhouse throughout the week.

Afterward, he brought me up to the second floor. "This is the beta floor, where the beta family lives." He showed me where they had a small family room and the common bathroom. He then led me up to the third floor. "And this is the alpha floor. I'm planning to renovate it once my parents move out since it needs some updating, but I'll show you around." He showed me the alpha family room, which was directly above the beta one, and the common bathroom.

He led me down the hall and stopped at different doors, one at a time. "My dad uses this bedroom as a second, private office." He opened the next door. "My mom uses this room as her own office and guest bedroom." After closing the door, he led me to the next room. "This room is mostly for storage but also doubles as a guest room."

He took my hand, skipped one bedroom, and led me to the final bedroom—his parents' bedroom where they had a large walk-in closet, en suite bathroom, and a balcony that overlooked the back garden.

"Wow, this is really nice!" I exclaimed.

"This will be my bedroom soon, after they move out. I'm planning to get a contractor in to modernize things, especially the bathroom. It'll be nice having my own private bathroom, not that I ever really shared the common one, considering I'm the only other person on this floor."

He took me out of their room, closing the door, and led me back to the room that he had initially skipped. He opened the door, letting me in, "And this is where you'll forget how to walk tonight if things going according to plan." He smirked.

"Not happening," I replied.

He smiled mischievously and asked, "Nothing happening at all, or just not the bit where you forget how to walk? Just trying to figure out my boundaries."

"What happened last time is definitely not happening again, so don't get any ideas! I proved my point, so that's all you're getting."

"Ok, second base is out of the question, got it." He gave a small, playful chuckle.

I walked in and looked around. He had a desk in the corner that was cluttered with different papers and things, a decent-sized closet, and a large window with a view of the town. After allowing me some time to look around, he gestured at the bed and said, "Anyway, sit down and relax."

I went to sit down on his bed, which I noticed was a full size. He sat down next to me, on my left, and turned to face me. As if he read my mind he continued, "I'm planning to get a king-size bed after I move into my parents' room. But, hey, that just means we'll have to get really close for now." He winked at me, moving closer.

"What was it like growing up in the packhouse?" I asked, wanting to learn more about him.

"It was interesting. I'm glad I had the beta family downstairs. My dad was an asshole growing up, so I'd go downstairs to get away from him. I'd usually hide in Luke's bedroom. He was a really good friend to me growing up."

At the sound of Luke's name, I felt something ping within my chest, bringing him to the forefront of my mind. Suddenly I was imagining being in Luke's bedroom instead, the thought somehow appealing.

I blinked a few times and pushed Luke from my mind, thinking how inappropriate it was to be thinking about him at that moment. As much as I kept trying to forget him, he always pushed himself back to the forefront of my consciousness, my old crush returning. I turned back to Blake and asked, "What about your mom?"

"My mom's the best. She's the most kind-hearted woman you'll ever meet. I am so lucky to have her." He beamed as his whole demeanor changed and his face lit up. I was seeing a new side of him—a much softer side—warming me toward him.

He asked, "What about your parents? What are they like?"

I sighed and replied, "Well, they're very straitlaced and religious. They met while attending college for biochemistry. I don't think they've ever done anything remotely rebellious, and I'm pretty sure that if they knew I was here they would lock me in my room and never let me leave. I'm too scared to find out what they would do if I don't graduate with a 4.0 GPA."

Blake brushed my hair behind my ear as I spoke and looked intently into my eyes, concentrating on what I was telling him.

I continued, "One time, in middle school, I brought home a test with a ninety-five, and my mom asked me why I didn't get a hundred and forced me to spend more hours studying for the next one. Since they both work, I spent a lot of time with my grandparents when I was younger. But they're honestly not much better. The other day, my grandfather started questioning my virtue!"

"Like if you're a virgin? Your grandfather asked you that?"

"Yes, it was so disturbing! He started telling me that no one wants an impure mate!"

"Damn, that's pretty messed up. He's definitely stuck in a different era," Blake responded.

"So, what do men think when they find out that their mate has been with others?" I asked him, curious what his thoughts were on the matter as a male.

"It didn't bother me one bit. It would be hypocritical if it did, considering I don't exactly have the best track record." He chuckled. "I know there are some guys that are weird about it, but I don't think there's anyone that wouldn't ultimately accept their mate. It's really hard not to once you realize who your mate is. It's like a gravitational pull toward the other person. I can't even imagine ever having rejected my mate. Once

I met her, I wanted to be with her all the time, and likely would have accepted any horrible thing about her, even if she told me that she was a drug addict and career criminal. Either way, I think most guys these days know that women aren't just sitting around waiting to meet them, especially if they find their mates later in life."

I pondered what he said, making me more curious. I turned to him and asked, "What was it like when you met your mate? Was it love at first sight?"

He looked back at me, and held my gaze, not answering right away. After some time, he replied, "I don't know that it was love. But it was definitely a strong attraction. The love came over time, as we got to know each other."

"Oh, I see."

"Do you feel more comfortable letting me deflower you now—now that you know your mate won't reject you for a little popped cherry?" He had a mischievous smile on his face. "If anything, your mate should be the scared one. Once you let me have my way with you, I will ruin you for all others, and no one else will compare. You'll be the one rejecting them."

Blake then put his right hand on my left knee and slowly moved it between my legs, a hot shiver subsequently running up my body. As he brushed his hand up and down my inner thigh, I started to feel aroused, the skin of my legs tingling as he trailed his fingers along it, the apex of my inner thighs wet and prickling with desire. My whole body warmed, and my breathing turned erratic. He lay down on the bed, pulling me down with him.

"Don't worry, I won't do anything. I just want to lie with you," he said softly, his voice gravelly.

I turned toward him. He was smiling, his hair falling into his eyes. I boldly brushed it out of his face. He put his hand on the side of my thigh, allowing it to slide up my leg, until his palm was resting on my hip bone with his fingers wrapped against the top of my ass. He inched his body closer to me until our bodies were touching, my face against his chest. I could feel something hard pressing against the front of me. I realized, with mortification, that it was his erection.

We lay like that for at least ten minutes, just listening to each other breathe, the sound of his heartbeat against my ear. My whole body was alive and burning lying with him, my nipples tense against his torso.

He inched away from me and pulled my chin up with his hand, so I was looking into his eyes. "I'd like to kiss you. Can I?" he asked.

I had an internal debate with myself, again. There was nothing more I wanted at that moment than to feel his rosy lips against mine, my whole body begging for it. But something was stopping me. I felt sinful at the idea—I'd always imagined my first kiss to be with my mate. Once I kissed someone else, that was it. I could never redo my first kiss again.

After deliberating for what seemed like forever, I finally sat up and asked, "What are you doing with me? You could probably get your needs met by so many other women instead of wasting your time with me for something that may or may not happen. I know you're not looking for anything long-term because I'll eventually meet my mate and leave you."

His eyes softened as he similarly sat up, his mesmerizing blue eyes trained on me. "Well, besides the fact that wolves love the hunt, there's something about you. I can't explain it. I just feel comfortable with you, like we could be friends." He gave me a soft smile and continued, "I like that there's no pressure for a relationship and this is only good for as long as you haven't met your mate yet. It makes it fun, knowing that I only have an unknown and limited amount of time to enjoy you. And I can't lie, you have a mesmerizing ass. I have a feeling you didn't get a B in training at school."

"I have never gotten anything less than an A."

"Let me guess—they tried to recruit you as a warrior."

"Yes, they did, but my parents wouldn't let me be one. Too many muscular, naked men running around." I giggled.

His eyes grew dark, appearing lustful as he stared into my eyes. "Fighters have always been my type."

"Kiss me," I said, almost in a trance.

He moved his face toward mine slowly. One of his hands went to the back of my head, weaving into my hair, and the other held my chin gently. He paused when we were just centimeters apart, the anticipation of the moment growing with each millisecond that passed. I closed my eyes, and before I could comprehend what was happening, his mouth was on mine. He kissed me gently at first, then more forcefully with each subsequent kiss. I kissed him back, nothing had ever felt so natural before. He nibbled on my bottom lip, prompting my lips to part. I inhaled as he slipped his tongue into my mouth. I felt like I had fallen into a happily drunken dream, perceptive of Blake's desire as he hungrily kissed me as though he had been starving and I was his first meal. My whole body was on fire with arousal as my tongue twined with his.

He gradually lowered me back onto the bed as we kissed and moved his body on top of mine, fervently kissing me back. I put my hands on his chest, feeling his sculpted body under my palms, and moved them up to his face, my fingertips tracing his well-defined jaw as it moved against my mouth. We rolled until we were side by side again, and he moved his hands to my ass pushing me harder against him until we couldn't possibly be any closer, a craving for him possessed my body.

Blake finally pulled away and balanced himself on his forearm, looking down at me. "Are you sure you've never done this before?"

"Never."

"Damn, I guess you really are just good at everything."

I chuckled nervously. "My nickname in school was PJ."

"PJ?"

I blushed and replied, "It stands for Perfect Jasmine. It's what people used to call me in school."

"Seems fitting. I'd love to see what else you're good at." He smiled mischievously.

"I have a feeling you don't mean academically." I swallowed.

"No, I couldn't care less about your academic achievements." He began kissing me again. Lust overtook my entire body as I gave in to my desires, greedily kissing him back.

We eventually fell into a cuddle, his arms wrapped tightly around me. I couldn't help but feel both nervous and relaxed simultaneously. I'd never been in such an intimate position with anyone before, in a man's bed. The sensations he brought out within my body overwhelmed me—like a very pleasurable form of anxiety. I inhaled his scent, never wanting to forget a single detail of this moment and how both blissful and restless I felt lying next to Blake.

He eventually ordered delivery from the pack pizza and sub shop, and we moved downstairs to the couch to watch a movie together while we shared a pizza. After we were done eating, he wrapped his arm around me, and I snuggled into him, realizing I fit perfectly against him. When it was time to go, I was gloomy, longing to stay with him. He dropped me off down the street so my parents wouldn't see his car, kissing me again before we finally said good night.

Chapter 12

Jasmine

Emma and Kyle were married on a Saturday morning in mid-August. They had a small ceremony in the pack temple and invited their family and friends for an early-afternoon celebration in the backyard of Kyle's parents' house. Lucy made the wedding cake and desserts, and I helped Madison and Emma's sisters decorate for the event. They had a tent with picnic tables set up and caterers to serve barbecue for the event. There were about fifty people crowded in the backyard.

I grabbed a lemonade and went to stand by Lucy who was hovering near the dessert table, likely keeping watch over her masterpiece. Madison came over to mingle with us, followed by the bride herself. We fell into easy conversation and laughter, and Kyle kept sneaking by and rubbing himself against Emma.

"Close quarters out here!" He'd laugh as he'd pretend to be trying to sneak by her to grab a cookie from the dessert table.

"Kyle, you need to stop coming over here and stealing all the cookies!" Lucy glared at him.

"Hey, they were made for me!"

"Leave them for the other guests! And stop grabbing for Emma's cookie in front of me!"

"Best cookie I ever tasted." He winked at Emma.

"Get out of here! And stay away!" Lucy pushed him out of the vicinity of the dessert table. She turned to Emma. "Goddess, I don't need think about my brother eating your cookie!"

"Mmm, he is really good at eating my cookie." Emma had a silly smile on her face.

"Oh my Goddess! That's so gross! I don't need to know that!"

"It's not like you're not giving your own cookie away!" she shot back at Lucy.

Lucy smiled and whispered loud enough so we could all hear, "To be honest, I'm not sure how Luke doesn't have diabetes yet with how much he ate my cookie last time I visited him."

I wanted to vomit. I'd been doing my best to avoid speaking with Lucy about her sexcapades with Luke, always finding other subjects to bring up. To this day, there was still something within me that panged with sorrow every time I thought about Luke being with Lucy. Unfortunately, this was one of Lucy's favorite subjects, and once she found herself an audience, she couldn't help giving detailed explanations of all the positions they'd been in and graphic descriptions of Luke's naked body.

I excused myself to go to the bathroom while she told Emma and Madison the gory details. I tried to stay in the bathroom for as long as possible, but unfortunately this wasn't easy in a house full of so many people. After only a few minutes, Lucy's younger brother Mark was banging on the door to be let in.

When I returned to the party, I was relieved to see the subject had changed. They were now playing matchmaker with Madison.

"Kyle and Lucy's cousin, Tom, is really cute!" Emma said to Madison, nodding her head in his direction.

"Ooh, he is cute!" Madison agreed. "But I can't. My whole family would skewer me. My cousin Tracy was caught just holding hands with some guy that wasn't her mate recently and it became a whole thing. Like everyone's been talking about it for weeks."

Madison, like me, was planning to save herself for her mate. But she did once say that if she didn't find her mate by twenty-five, she'd lose her virginity then. I never put much thought into how long I'd be willing to wait. I only hoped the Moon Goddess wouldn't make me wait until I was almost forty like she did to the current alpha. But then my thoughts drifted back to Blake, and I silently questioned, once again, whether I really wanted to wait anymore.

A few hours later, Emma and Kyle jumped into Kyle's SUV, which had been decorated during the party with window paint, streamers, and tin cans attached to the bumper. We watched as they drove away for their honeymoon.

I helped Lucy's family clean up after the guests left, and I called my parents to see if they could pick me up to bring me home. At around six that evening, the doorbell rang, and Ivy went to answer it. My dad was standing at the door. I gathered everything to leave as Ivy spoke with him. "Nice to see you, Drew."

"Evening, Ivy."

"You and Miriam raised a great girl. Such a pity she doesn't have any siblings."

I looked up and noticed that my dad was giving her a death glare. "We'll be on our way. Come on, Jasmine!"

She kept speaking before he could turn around. "Oh, Drew, before I forget to tell you! Someone started a Facebook group for our high school class. I'll be sure to send you an invite!"

"I don't use Facebook," he responded immediately and turned his back to her, walking to the car, clearly expecting me to follow. I ran after him and jumped into the passenger seat. We drove home in silence, my dad clearly in a bad mood. He was quiet during dinner too. I could tell he was lost in thought. What Ivy said seemed pretty innocuous, but I began to question if there was something I missed. Ivy and my dad never had much interaction, but every time they did it was weird, as if Ivy was mad at him for something. I always assumed she just didn't like how strict they were with me, but I now wondered if it was something else.

I couldn't ask my parents, because they were never open with me about anything. We lived in a world of don't ask, don't tell. As much as Lucy's mom annoyed her, I knew Lucy could go to her mom about anything and she would be understanding and nonjudgmental. I wouldn't be surprised if Lucy told her mom about her sex life. I think even if I were married with a pup on the way, with my parents I'd still act as if it was by immaculate conception.

When female werewolves shifted for the first time, it coincided with their first period. When it was time for us to shift, it would happen during a full moon, and then we would menstruate not long after. I remember being embarrassed to tell my parents that I had shifted into a wolf for the first time at thirteen because then they'd know that my first period would be coming. I couldn't stand the idea of them knowing, especially my dad.

After dinner, I helped my mom load the dishwasher and then went up to my room. I was watching Netflix and almost asleep when I felt my phone vibrate next to me.

Blake Sexy AF: *Feels lonely in my bed without you*

I stared at the text for a minute. I hadn't spoken with Blake in a few weeks, so the text came out of the blue. Of course, it wasn't like I hadn't thought of him during all that time. After being so intimate and sharing my first kiss with him, I thought there was something between us. It stung when he didn't contact me again right away. I couldn't help but wonder if I was the only one that felt a connection and he had moved on. The thought troubled me. I couldn't help but wonder if he'd gotten bored with me after I finally kissed him. Even though he'd made me feel special, I still couldn't push the thought away that there were plenty of other girls who would have no problem giving him what he wanted. The thought sickened me.

Then I'd remind myself that it was fruitless to even have these thoughts and become so involved with him, knowing our time together would be cut short by me eventually meeting my mate. I kept pushing him out of my mind, forcing myself not to think about him. Even so, I couldn't shake the urge to see him again, to kiss him again.

I looked at the text again and my stomach flipped. While I was inexperienced, I did watch TV and read books. I replied, *Is this a booty call?*

I watched as three dots appeared, him typing back.

> ***Blake Sexy AF***: *If you're offering, I accept*
> ***Me***: *You know my rules, and my rules aren't made to be broken*
> ***Blake Sexy AF***: *Really? I'll remind you of that next time your nipples are in my mouth*
> ***Me***: *I told you that was a one time thing!*
> ***Blake Sexy AF***: *And you loved it*
> ***Me***: *I tolerated it*
> ***Blake Sexy AF***: *Haha you're so funny. The way you kissed me, that's not how you kiss someone you tolerate*
> ***Me***: *Oh, my memory's faint. When was that?*
> ***Blake Sexy AF***: *If that wasn't memorable enough for you, next time will be. I love a challenge*
> ***Blake Sexy AF***: *When's your day off this week? We can go hiking again*
> ***Me***: *Wednesday*
> ***Blake Sexy AF***: *Be ready at 10 to go*

I looked at the text thread again, my heart beating against my chest, the desire to see him again overwhelming me. I was on the brink of breaking all my rules, and I couldn't even bring myself to care.

Chapter 13

Jasmine

On Wednesday I was ready at ten. This time I wore my bathing suit underneath a T-shirt and shorts, prepared that he'd want to go swimming, seeing as the weather was predicted to be hot. I didn't want to seem too eager. At least if I wore my bathing suit, it wouldn't appear I was determined to strip down to my underwear for him. I watched as his black Jeep pulled into my driveway, and I stepped outside to greet him. My anxiety about not hearing from him for two weeks instantly disappeared. As soon as I approached his car, he came over and kissed me on the cheek.

"I missed you," he said, leading me to the passenger door. "Sorry I haven't been in touch. This alpha shit's taking over my entire life."

I looked at him in shock. He missed me? My heart pulsed in my chest. Had he been wanting to see me as much as I'd been wanting to see him?

He opened the door for me and helped me in, then hopped into the driver's seat. When we were both settled, he pulled out of the driveway, not wasting any time to speed out of the pack entrance and toward what was now becoming our secret place.

During our drive, he glanced over my way and said, "It's nice finally getting out of the packhouse." He had a smile on his face. "You're definitely better company than my dad. Much better looking too."

After we arrived and exited the car, we were greeted by hot and sticky air which was only exacerbated by the forceful rays emitted by the sun. Blake grabbed his backpack from the back seat and said, "I think we can agree to skip the hike today and go straight to the water." He took my hand and led me down to the pond. My heart swelled at the gesture. Blake was acting much more affectionate today than he ever had previously, pleasantly surprising me.

He found a shady spot by a tree, pulled the blanket out of his backpack, and laid it out on the beach, which was more dirt and rocks than sand. I sat down on the blanket as he stripped himself of his clothes, leaving only his boxer briefs on as before. I had almost forgotten how jacked he was, his pecs prominent on his chest, atop what was really more of an eight-pack than a six-pack, but who could really count when taking in the fine piece of art that was Blake's body? Goddess, he was hot. I watched the movement of his well-defined muscles as the sun's rays reflected off his chest and shoulders, not able to tear my eyes away.

"Enjoying the show?" he asked as he sat down next to me. I blushed, realizing I had been staring. "It's okay, I worked hard for this body. Nice to have an audience every once in a while, so I'm not the only one appreciating it. Now, what do I need to do for my own show?"

"Do I look like a stripper?" I scoffed.

He smiled and replied, "You would make a great stripper. I'd love to see that ass of yours going up and down a stripper pole. Fuck, I'd bring hundred-dollar bills for that show and make it rain. You'd make very good money—men love that innocent look you have."

"I see you're familiar with strip clubs." I rolled my eyes.

"Not much else to do in Siberia."

"Is that what you did for four years."

"Not the only, but probably one of the more enjoyable things I did."

I replied, sarcastically, "Four years is a lot of rain. Hmm, maybe I should reconsider."

Blake laughed. "Oooh, look at you now." He grabbed my legs and pulled them apart, tugging me toward him so he was seated between my thighs. He pulled my face toward his and began kissing my ear, increasing my heart rate, arousing me. His tongue trailed the outline of my ear, and he lightly bit down on my earlobe. He continued kissing me down my neck, and my breathing turned heavy. His lips moved down my neck, to my chest, and then up to my chin. I moaned in response, my whole body alive and warm with desire, my thighs tingling.

My eyes locked with his half-opened and lustful eyes. I felt a mix of desire and unease, my heart racing. He grabbed my ass and pulled me up against his body, his erection pushing up against the front of me. Before I knew it, he had his mouth on mine, or maybe it was my mouth on his. I couldn't decide which of us was more desperate to feel their lips on the other as I ran my hands through his thick head of hair. I became bold, biting his bottom lip as his hands tightened their grip on me.

I moved my hands lower, wrapping them around him so they were resting on the back of his shoulders, feeling how massive they were under my small hands. For several minutes, we were lost in each other, our bodies pressed together, our tongues intertwined.

Suddenly and unexpectedly, he lifted me off his lap and plopped me down on the blanket as if I were weightless and said, "I need to cool off before I lose control."

I watched as he got up and walked to the water, his erection prominent with only the thin cloth of his underwear protecting his modesty.

I removed my T-shirt and shorts, revealing the bikini I had worn, and followed him into the pond, feeling the need to cool off myself. He turned to watch me as I walked into the water.

"I see you wore a bathing suit this time."

"It's more appropriate."

"Appropriate when in public. We're alone though—no reason not to just strip everything off and properly feel our bodies against each other."

"You wish."

"Yes, it is what I wish, very much. I'd love to touch and kiss every inch of your body if you'd let me. I know you're still working through your religious upbringing, and I'm going to respect that. But just the fact that you haven't once said no to seeing me means that you want the same thing. What else are you doing with an extremely horny, mateless man, an alpha one at that? We're not known for denying our impulses." He came closer to me and put his hands on my arms, sliding them down to my hands until he was holding them in between us. My pulse quickened, wondering the same thing myself, taking his speech to heart. "Just stop acting like we don't both want the same thing."

I suddenly felt very vulnerable. "Is that all you want from me?" I asked, afraid to know the truth.

His eyes softened, and he came closer to me. He looked at me for a few moments and said, "If I'm being honest, then no. I like you as a friend too." He pushed a hair behind my ear. "I feel comfortable around you. Some of the stuff I told you, I haven't been able to talk to anyone else about. I enjoy spending time with you. And, this might be wishful thinking, but I hope after you meet your mate, we can remain friends."

I wasn't sure how I expected Blake to answer the question, but it definitely wasn't like that. I felt my heart melt, an intense feeling within my chest. I stared at him, realizing my mouth was hanging open. I was about to close it when Blake closed the space between us, putting his mouth back on mine. It was more intense this time, a feeling unearthing itself that I'd never experienced before—a deep affection for Blake.

He then moved his hands behind me and grabbed my ass, picking me up as if I weighed nothing. My legs wrapped around his waist and my arms around his shoulders. He carried me deeper until the water was just below our shoulders. Lust overtook my whole my body as Blake's lips explored all my exposed skin—my lips, trailing my jaw, on my neck—then returning to my mouth.

When we pulled apart, we looked into each other's eyes as he smiled at me. Suddenly, and without warning, he pushed me up out of the water and launched my entire body backward, so I fell back and plunged into the water. I quickly raised my head into the air to see Blake laughing heartily, as if he were a little kid. I glared at him as he began swimming toward me. I splashed him and moved backward, continuing to splash him as he tried to get closer. He finally caught me and picked me up, and in turn, I screamed and slapped him on his chest.

He carried me out of the water and lowered me onto the blanket where his lips immediately crashed against mine, compelling me to give in and forgive him. I immediately brought my hands to the sides of his face, his stubble bristly against my palms, and pulled him closer. I was desperate with need—need to taste his lips, need to twine my tongue with his, need to feel his teeth graze my bottom lip. I fell back onto the blanket and his body followed until he was hovering over me. He brushed his free hand through my hair while his lips moved down my jaw, onto my neck and then my chest, leaving a trail of kisses.

I moved my hands to his massive biceps as he kissed down to one of my breasts and untied the top of my bikini, letting the triangles of my top fall against my stomach. He glanced up at me for a moment, his piercing blue eyes locking with mine, and I couldn't help but feel sexy, seductive, and alive. The top half of my body was completely exposed to him, and the look he gave me was one of pure, carnal need. I'd never been so turned on. The whole area between my thighs was hot and throbbing with desire.

He lowered his head back down toward my chest and blew gently on one of my wet nipples, which instantly hardened in response. He then brought his lips onto it and sucked gently while his tongue coaxed every last bit of pleasure out. My back arched and my head rolled back in response, a throaty moan following. I had almost forgotten how good it felt the first time he had done this. He kissed across my chest and did the same with my other nipple as his hand engulfed the first breast he had kissed. I was now moaning shamelessly, giving in completely, not wanting him to stop. An aching between my legs provoked me to spread them apart as he moved between them.

Before long, he was kissing between my breasts, and down the center of my abdomen until his mouth was skimming the top of my bikini bottoms. He brushed his fingers along my outer thighs until he was gripping my hips, pulling me closer to him. He pushed his fingers inside my bikini bottoms and was about to pull them down when I threw my hands on top of his to stop him.

"Wait," I cried out, panicking, realizing things were advancing far too fast. I wasn't ready for this.

"Goddess, I want you so badly," he moaned.

"I can't," I breathed, sitting up. He looked at me, appearing frustrated. I suddenly felt very naked and exposed, and tied up the strings of my bikini, covering myself again. "I'm sorry." We sat there like that for what seemed like several minutes. I looked at him wondering what he was thinking. Would he be upset?

Finally, he responded, "You don't need to apologize. Let's just eat lunch and hopefully my massive boner will get the hint." I looked down to see that it appeared he had pitched a huge tent, his erection stretching his boxer briefs to the point I was surprised they hadn't ripped. "Like I said, alpha genetics." He smirked, clearly noticing I was staring.

I felt myself go red and the need to change the subject. "So, what's for lunch?"

"Salami sandwiches." He reached into his backpack to pull them out.

"I'm starting to assume the only food you know how to make is sandwiches." I chuckled.

"Your assumption would be correct. Now either enjoy what you're getting, or you make the lunch next time."

"There's nothing wrong with sandwiches. But I'd be happy to make something different for next time."

"Sounds like you enjoyed this time then, seeing as you're already committing to a next time." He winked at me. I pushed him on his shoulder and then bit into my sandwich, realizing how hungry the morning had made me.

We sat side by side as we ate in the shade, shielded from the aggressive rays of the sun. I reflected on our conversation from earlier, suddenly having a strong desire to ask Blake to elaborate on something he'd said. When we both finished our food, I spoke his name to grab his attention. "Blake?"

"Yes?" he responded.

"Earlier you said that you've told me things you haven't been able to talk to anyone else about. What did you mean by that?"

He looked out toward the pond, picking up a pebble and throwing it into the water. He didn't say anything at first, and I wondered if he had heard me. I was about to repeat my question when he finally spoke.

"When Ria died," he started and then stopped, clenching his eyes closed. I instinctively covered his hand with mine, hoping it would comfort him, realizing that he was revealing something very painful. He took a deep breath, reopening his eyes, quickly glancing at me, and then stared forward again. "I went into survival mode. I was supposed to become alpha not long after graduating from high school, but everything just went dark and I couldn't." He sighed. "That's why I went away for four years."

I moved closer to him, rubbing his back, and I could feel his body relax as I did this. He continued, "I haven't talked to anyone about what happened. You're the first person I've been able to talk to about it, to say her name to. Just saying her name is painful." His voice broke as he spoke.

"Goddess, Blake," I said, feeling deep empathy for him.

"It's not just that," he continued. "I feel like the old me when I'm around you. I didn't think I'd ever feel happy again, but being around you...," he trailed. "Well, anyway, I hope that answers your question." He turned to me, his mouth turned upwards. But I didn't fail to notice that his eyes were bloodshot, his posture drooped. I was caught by surprise. He always seemed so put together, but I now realized how little I knew about him, and how much he must have been suffering inside.

I boldly inched my face toward his, moved by Blake's confession. Sitting up on my knees to reach, I gently pecked his lips. He instantly pulled me against him and deepened the kiss. So many emotions came over me as our lips moved together, a pang in my heart, struggling to breathe from how heavy my lungs felt. It was as if he was transferring some of his pain to me and I was swallowing it, lessening the burden for him. He clung tightly to me, and I could sense deep down that Blake was never vulnerable like this with anyone else.

As much as I fought to push everything I felt for him away, he had managed to bury himself within me. I was steps from falling for Blake and, dear Goddess, I didn't know if I could stop myself from hurling myself off the cliff.

Chapter 14

Jasmine

A few days after Blake's confession, I was lying in bed late at night, absorbed in a book, when I heard a tapping on my window. *Ping.* The sound of something hitting the glass clanged. I got out of bed to see what was happening, pulled back the curtains, and looked out my window to see that Blake was outside my house winding his arm back. *Ping.* A pebble hit my window. I opened it, the warm summer air entering my room, and poked my head out to see him smiling at me and waving his hand, signaling for me to come out.

What the...?

I stepped back, wondering what I should do. An internal battle ensued within me once again, the metaphorical angel and devil over my shoulders. I'd never snuck out of my house in my life. What would my parents do if they caught me? And should I really be sneaking around with someone, let alone someone who wasn't my mate? But then, I thought, it would be exciting. So many years I'd denied myself so many things because I didn't want my parents to be disappointed in me. Maybe Blake was right—what they didn't know couldn't hurt them. Plus, I was an adult now. I shouldn't be allowing my parents to dictate my life!

Goddess, Blake is a terrible influence!

Once again, the devil won. What was it about Blake that made me just throw all caution to the wind? Seriously, what was wrong with me that I was just going along with everything he wanted me to do? I quickly changed what I was wearing and snuck downstairs quietly. My parents slept pretty soundly, so I didn't think they'd hear me. Even if they did, they'd probably think I was grabbing a glass of water or midnight snack anyway. No, my parents definitely wouldn't think I was sneaking out.

I crept out my back door through the kitchen, opening and shutting the door as quietly as possible, and made my way around the house to the front. When I got there, he was gone. I turned in circles, trying to follow his scent. Suddenly, someone grabbed my shoulders from behind and I screamed.

He quickly muffled the noise, covering my mouth with his hands. "Shhh, don't get caught," he whispered into my ear.

"You scared me!" I whispered back loudly, turning around to look at him, seeing he had a big smirk on his face.

"It was hilarious." His eyes twinkled. "Come on, let's go." He took my hand, pulling me toward my backyard.

"This is crazy!"

"It's fun though, isn't it?" He looked at me. "Anyway, you're the one who told me you're rebellious. Don't think I forgot." After a beat, he added, "I love when you rebel, by the way."

He held my hand as we snuck into the woods behind my house. As soon as we were safely in the shadows of the trees, having walked a few yards in, he pushed me up against a tree trunk and put his mouth on mine, one hand weaving into my hair and the other balanced on the tree behind me. I pushed my tongue into his mouth, savoring the taste of him as my hands slid up his back under his T-shirt.

"Mmm, I missed you," he said, pulling away for a second, and then finding my mouth again. His mouth tasted minty, like he had just brushed his teeth right before coming to meet me. I gave in to him completely, enjoying his body against mine, my hands on his muscular back, his warm skin under my fingertips. I couldn't decide if it was the night that was hot and humid or if it was my body, feeling overheated, our T-shirts both feeling damp against our bodies.

His lips moved from my mouth slowly over to my left ear, softly tickling me as he kissed along the edge of it, and then changed to nibbling gently on my earlobe. Shivers traveled up and down my body. I was completely turned on, my nipples tingling. It was like he could read my mind as he kissed down to my neck and moved his hand under my shirt, gliding up my body and finding one of my breasts, softly squeezing it. My nipple was hard against his palm, and I suddenly wished my bra wasn't shielding me from feeling the skin of his hand.

He trailed kisses up and down my neck, and I softly moaned, loving the feeling of his stubble brushing against my sensitive skin. I was completely aroused, my panties drenched, my whole body on fire, damp with sweat. I felt like I couldn't get close enough to Blake or feel enough of his kisses and touches.

"I'm rebelling tonight too, you know." He spoke into my ear, his mouth so close that his five o'clock shadow was practically tickling me. "I'm supposed to be doing rounds of the patrol stations right now. But I wanted to see you."

I looked up into his eyes as they glowed in the darkness from his night vision, like two bright blue orbs. My heart beat fervently in my chest, two feelings emerging simultaneously—a warmth from within, the temperature in my heart matching the heat of my skin, but also a panic that we shouldn't be doing this. I put my hands on his chest, pushing on him gently.

"Is everything okay?" he asked, searching my face.

"What are we doing?" I asked, feeling suddenly that this was a very important question.

"We're doing what's natural, what we both want to do."

"But it's wrong!"

"Why's it wrong? We're both single. You haven't met your mate yet. And no one has to know about this. I'm good at being sneaky." He winked.

"My mom finds out about everything that goes on in this pack."

"Well, has she found out about us yet?" he questioned, looking at me.

"No, but...," I replied, my voice trailing.

"Stop denying what you really want." He put his hands on my arms, brushing them up and down.

I pulled away. "Why do you assume I want this? Because you're the hot sexy alpha with big, huge muscles, and everyone wants you? You think everyone just naturally loves you? And it's impossible for someone to just not be interested?"

If I didn't know any better, he looked a bit stung as I said that, stepping backward. And, just like that, the look was gone, and he stepped forward again. "Really, you don't want this?" He gestured at his body. "Because I'm pretty sure you were just all over me, enjoying what was happening just as much as I was. I felt your hands under my shirt. You were ready to take it off."

"I was not!" I instantly replied.

He shook his head, a silly smile on his face.

"Why are you shaking your head like that?" I asked.

"Because you're so hot and cold. It's amusing. You definitely keep me on my toes. But I get it."

"You do?" I asked, looking up at him.

"Sure, I can relate. You told me your parents were really hard on you growing up. The thing is, it was the same for me. It's hard to stop trying to make them proud, even when no matter what you do, it's never enough." He looked away into the distance, appearing as if he were lost in thought. I squeezed his hand, once again feeling affection for Blake. He looked down at me, appearing a bit sad. "Anyway," he continued, "I should probably do some of my alpha duties tonight. I'm glad I got to see you though." He gave me a smile and leaned over to kiss my cheek. "Have a good night."

"Bye, Blake," I replied, watching him walk into the darkness of the forest. Goddess, what was I doing? As much as I knew it was completely wrong, I couldn't help the affection I felt for him.

Chapter 15

Jasmine

Later that week, I found myself deep in thought, Blake on my mind. I was tempted to text him. While I couldn't stop thinking about him, I didn't think it was a good idea to make that known. I was afraid if he knew how much he'd gotten under my skin that things would go too far with him, both emotionally and physically. Additionally, if we started spending too much time together, it was bound to be noticed and it wouldn't be long before word got back to my parents. While our pack was one of the larger ones in the area, it was still like living in a small town where everyone was in everyone else's business.

No, it was definitely better that I just tried my best to forget him. And if he also forgot about me, it was only for the better. I tried to convince myself. However, this thought made me feel miserable. As much as I tried to deny it, Blake had definitely gotten under my skin. He consumed all my thoughts. I'd become almost addicted to the sensations I felt when spending time with him. No one had ever made me feel so sexy and desirable before. I couldn't stop reliving the past few times we'd spent together, kissing each other with an insatiable hunger. I found that a smile kept creeping onto my face, making everyone question why I was in such a good mood.

I was at work with just Valerie when she approached me during some downtime. "How's it going, Jaz?"

"Pretty good, I was just about to wipe down the tables," I replied, reaching for the spray bottle of cleaner.

"Before you do that, I need to talk to you about something. I need to start planning for September. When do you go back to school and how many hours a week can you give me?"

"I'll be going back at the beginning of September. Would it be okay if I dropped down to just sixteen hours a week?"

"We can make that work. But I'll have to hire another part-timer. Do you mind posting an ad on the temple bulletin on Sunday when you go?"

"No problem." Valerie was about to turn around to go back when I stopped her. "Valerie."

"Yes, hon?"

"You were with other people before you met your mate, right?"

"Oh yeah, those were my crazy days. I wish I could go back to those." She laughed.

"What did your mate think when he met you, knowing there'd been others?"

She started laughing hysterically, "Oh my Goddess, he hated it. Werewolf packs aren't exactly known for their open-mindedness. His parents were pissed when they found out who his mate was. You can't exactly sleep around and not expect people to talk when you live in gossip central. But everyone eventually got over it and now it's all in the past. It's kind of a double standard anyway. Why can men sleep around and not have any consequences, but women are expected to remain pure?" She paused and looked as if she were pondering something, then continued, "Of course, probably best to stay away from family members. Things are still kind of awkward at family gatherings seeing as I was with his cousin at one point long before I properly met him and realized he was my mate."

I laughed. "Okay, stay away from family members. Kind of hard when you have no idea who your mate is."

She chuckled. "Why? Is there someone you have your eye on? Maybe a certain soon-to-be alpha?"

I looked at her, wide-eyed. "How'd you know?"

"You think I can't hear your conversations with Lucy from the back?" She snickered.

"Oh my Goddess, I'm going to kill Lucy for not keeping it down!"

"Hey, the man's walking, talking testosterone. Five minutes alone with him, and even I'd be spreading my legs, completely forgetting I have a mate. I don't think anyone would blame you for doing the same." She laughed.

"I can't," I choked out.

"Sure you can. The only thing holding you back are some ancient beliefs on how women should behave. It doesn't help that the current alpha's old as hell and allows the temple to dictate how things are done around here. But, anyway, if you don't want to, then don't. You need to decide what you want, and if you want to wait for your mate, there's also nothing wrong with that. I think it's romantic. But definitely don't let some bullshit propaganda used to control women stop you from doing what you want to."

"What about my parents?"

"What about your parents? You're an adult and capable of making your own decisions. Trust me, your parents weren't as innocent as you think they were when they were younger. You have to live your own life, not some life they're forcing you into."

"What do you mean about my parents not being innocent?"

"Well, in general, parents almost always hide things about their past from their children. But there are always some skeletons in the closet. Maybe one day the ones in your parents' will come out. But don't assume that they're as innocent as they say they are." Valerie had an irritated look on her face and made me wonder if she knew something that I didn't. I was about to push the issue when a customer entered the café, giving her an escape. I took my place at the register to take their order.

After my shift was over, my grandparents brought me home. For a moment, I was tempted to ask them about my parents when they were younger but then decided against it. My grandparents were really just an older version of my parents and unlikely to volunteer any information my parents wouldn't.

After we got to my parents' house, my grandma unloaded the food she had prepared from the car. She slipped it into the oven to keep it warm until my parents arrived home. My grandfather sat down on the couch and turned on the baseball game to watch. My grandma joined him and pulled out a book to read. I was about to head upstairs to spend some time alone in my room until dinner when my grandmother stopped me.

"Jasmine," she called.

"Yes?" I replied, walking toward her.

"You seem very happy lately. Did something good happen recently?" she questioned in a voice that seemed suspicious.

"No, nothing specific. I've just been in a good mood," I replied, hoping I sounded convincing.

"Usually when someone smiles like that it's because they met their mate." Both my grandmother and grandfather were now staring at me. My grandfather lowered the volume on the television.

"No, no mates over here!" I replied, my voice practically cracking, and I could feel my face going red.

"Have you perhaps met someone who isn't your mate?" My grandfather narrowed his eyes at me.

My chest contracted and a dizziness came over me. I sensed the beginning stages of a panic attack, something I used to experience more frequently but hadn't in a while. I tried to calm myself down, not wanting what was occurring inside me to be obvious. If I didn't control myself

I knew that the overwhelming sensation would force me to shift into a wolf and then my grandparents would definitely know something was up. I tried to think quickly of an excuse and finally blurted out the first thing that came to me.

"I bought a car!"

Both my grandparents looked very surprised. "What? You did? Where is it?" my grandmother asked.

"I haven't brought it home yet. We're still finalizing paperwork. I wanted to make it a surprise, but I am so happy I couldn't stop smiling about it and now you know!" I started to feel myself calm at my clever excuse.

"What kind of car is it?" my grandfather asked.

"A Jeep!" I replied, blurting out the first type of car that came to mind. Oh shit, aren't Jeeps expensive? Fuck, what was I going to do? Why did I say Jeep? Why did I say I bought a car at all?

"Really?" my grandfather asked, looking interested now. "Tell me more about this Jeep. What model is it?"

"Wrangler!" I said, recalling the name of the model that Blake drove. Oh my Goddess, I couldn't believe I just told them the same exact make and model that the future alpha drove. "It's a used one of course," I added, hoping that made the lie seem more believable.

"That café must be paying you pretty well then," my grandfather commented.

"Erm, well, I've just been saving really hard."

"That's my girl!" My grandfather smiled. It seemed they bought it. Of course, now I was on the hook for buying a used Jeep Wrangler.

After dinner, I googled *Jeep Wrangler* only to find out that, out of all Jeep models, Wranglers held their value the most, and Jeeps in general tended to hold their value from the time of purchase. What did I do? I finally texted the one person that I thought may be able to help. I pulled up *Blake Sexy AF* in my contacts and wrote, *I need your help.*

Not long after I texted him, I saw the three dots appear and his immediate response.

> **Blake Sexy AF**: Ready and willing to provide my services
> **Blake Sexy AF**: Assuming you need help getting off
> **Me**: No, that's not what I need help with!
> **Blake Sexy AF**: That's too bad, had my hopes up
> **Blake Sexy AF**: Does that mean you're servicing yourself? ;)
> **Blake Sexy AF**: Call me so I can listen in. Or you can just text me the play-by-play
> **Me**: Stop! This is serious!
> **Blake Sexy AF**: Ok how can I help?
> **Me**: I need to buy a Jeep Wrangler
> **Blake Sexy AF**: Random?
> **Me**: It's a long story… But can you please help since you have one?
> **Blake Sexy AF**: What do you need help with?
> **Me**: I don't know how to buy a car…
> **Blake Sexy AF**: Why does it have to be a Jeep Wrangler?
> **Me**: This is easier to explain not over text but I can't call you right now because my parents are home. Can we talk tomorrow? I will get out of work at 10
> **Blake Sexy AF**: My Jeep Wrangler will be waiting for you outside :)
> **Blake Sexy AF**: Maybe you'll let it park in your garage? JK see you tomorrow
> **Me**: Haha… Good night

I wrote my final text message to Blake and clutched my phone against my chest, sighing deeply, feeling torn. I kept vowing to stay away from Blake. But dear Goddess, he was like a drug and I was completely addicted. Stricken, I realized I had gone from wishing he'd forget me to running to him as soon as I needed help with something. Goddess be damned, I'd already flung myself off that cliff and was now free-falling, praying the crash wouldn't destroy me.

Chapter 16

Jasmine

Just before ten the next day, I saw his Jeep parallel park in front of the café. This time, much to my dismay, he came in to place an order. Lucy ran out from the back, flour dusting her arms and cheeks.

"Well, hello there, Mr. Alpha! I knew I smelled your scent from the kitchen!" Lucy leaned over the counter, her low-cut shirt and loosely tied apron displaying her cleavage. "Seems you're right on time for the end of my friend here's shift."

"I am indeed," he replied, smirking, looking between the two of us.

"What can I get you today?" I asked, interrupting their conversation.

"I'll get a large, black coffee and what do you drink?" Blake looked at me.

"Oh, you don't have to get me anything," I replied.

"She likes cappuccinos." Lucy pushed me out of the way. "Let me ring you in. Jaz, go make the drinks! Here, I'll throw in some of my croissants on the house as well." She pulled some out of the case and put them into a to-go bag as I began preparing the drinks, listening to their conversation, suddenly feeling a bit jealous at their interaction.

What did Blake think of Lucy? I mean, she was so tall and beautiful, I thought, contrasting her appearance to my shorter one. I wasn't exactly short, but I also didn't look like a supermodel. And Lucy was also much curvier than me, at least as far as her chest was concerned. I was only a cup size or two away from being completely flat.

"Much appreciated." He pulled out his credit card and handed it to Lucy.

"So, where are the two of you off to today?" she asked as she inserted his card into the reader.

"Apparently your friend needs to buy a car. One that's the same make and model as mine."

"Isn't that interesting. I had no idea Jasmine had saved up enough to buy a car already." She turned her head to glare at me.

I threw my hands up. "It's all very last minute! I just happened to notice I had enough money saved!"

"For a Jeep Wrangler?" Lucy questioned, crossing her arms and continuing to stare at me.

"Erm, well, I'm going to get an old, used one, that's not that expensive."

"Why a Jeep Wrangler?" She had her eyes narrowed at me.

"I'm wondering the same thing." Blake looked at me, waiting for an answer with an amused smile on his face.

"Because I told my grandparents I bought one and they're expecting me to bring it home from the dealership soon. Now my parents think I bought one as well. They were definitely a bit confused about when and how this happened, but I just made some stuff up and they seem to be convinced."

"Why did you tell your family you bought a Jeep Wrangler?" Lucy asked. Just then, a customer walked in followed by Reena, signaling the end of my shift.

"Got to go. I'll tell you later!" I replied. I handed the drinks I made to Blake, threw my apron in the dirty laundry hamper, and grabbed my purse, leaving Lucy to take the customer's order. I grabbed Blake's arm, pulling him out of the café before I was forced to give any more information.

Blake handed me back my cappuccino so he could open my door. Once we were both inside the car, he turned on the engine and rotated his head so he was facing me. "So, are you going to tell me the rest of the story?"

I laughed nervously, trying to decide how to best word what I was going to say. "Well, my grandparents kind of got on my case yesterday. They started asking me why I've been smiling so much lately and if I had met someone who's not my mate. I sort of panicked and told them I was so happy because I finally bought a car."

"And why did you tell them you bought a Jeep Wrangler?" He had an amused glint in his eyes.

"It was the first car that came to mind," I replied, starting to panic, realizing how much I'd just revealed to Blake.

"Because it's the car that your not-mate drives?"

I felt my cheeks burning, likely turning a deep shade of crimson. I was completely embarrassed about the situation, feeling extremely vulnerable, and I just exposed far too much to Blake. I started to hyperventilate and could feel the panic attack coming on again, my arms tingling as fur began to sprout out of them. Afraid I would shift in his car, damaging it in the process, I quickly opened the door and jumped onto the sidewalk, falling into a squatting position. I inhaled and exhaled deeply, trying to stave off the panic attack, willing myself to shift back into my human form from the half form I'd gotten myself stuck in before it was too late.

Suddenly, Blake's warm body surrounded me, his arms wrapped tightly around me, concern in his voice. "Are you okay? What happened?"

I forced myself to continue taking deep breaths, trying my best to take my mind off the situation as it was unfolding. Blake stroked the fur on my arm with one hand while the other stayed wrapped around me, holding me close to him. I began to calm down as he caressed me, the fur slowly disappearing. The anxiety overtaking me died down.

When the panic eased, I spoke. "Sorry, I'm prone to panic attacks. This is really embarrassing. Luckily I didn't shift this time."

"Does this happen often?" I looked up at him and saw he appeared concerned, his brows furrowed as his piercing eyes searched my face. I started to stand, and he stood with me, keeping his arm around my shoulders.

"It hasn't in a while, but they started up again yesterday," I replied. He helped me back into my seat and buckled my seatbelt for me.

Once he was seated next to me, he took my hand in his and asked, "How often do these panic attacks happen?"

"When I was younger, they happened pretty frequently. After I started shifting, I'd have to bring a change of clothes to school just in case. Usually, it was just stress with school stuff getting to me. But I haven't had them in a couple years now. My parents put me in therapy, so I learned some coping techniques, which have helped."

He kissed me on the top of my head, revealing a new side of himself. After a few moments, he asked, "What triggered this one?"

"This whole situation with us is just becoming too much for me. I can't do this." I could feel my anxiety rising again and began taking deep breaths.

"What do you mean?" he asked, his eyes trained on me.

"Things are just going too far between us. It's stressing me out."

"Going too far how?"

"We shouldn't be doing all the stuff we're doing together. You're not my mate. And now my grandparents are on my case. I'm sorry, I shouldn't have asked for your help. Oh Goddess, I think I need to get out of the car again." I felt another panic attack coming on, my lungs contracting as I began gasping for air, feeling dizzy.

I was about to undo my seatbelt when he put his hands on the sides of my face and turned my head so I was looking into his piercing blue eyes. Speaking softly, he said, "Hey, Jaz, it's okay. I'm happy to help. And we can just be friends." He ran his hand over my hair affectionately. "I know I joke around a lot with you, but I can cut back on that."

I nodded, feeling myself gradually calm down.

"I still want to get in your pants, but I'll just not vocalize it." He smiled, pausing. "As much."

I chuckled softly. He pushed a piece of hair behind my ear and smiled at me, moving his hand to my shoulder, and rubbing it gently. My chest settled and my breathing became even under his touch.

Blake continued, "Anyway, let's go buy you a car."

I sighed and replied, "That's the other problem. I don't think I have quite enough saved."

"How much do you have?"

"Just under eight thousand."

"Well, let's just go to the dealership and see what they have. I looked it up this morning and there's one about ninety miles from here that seems to have a pretty good inventory. Do you have time?"

"I just have to be home by five to make dinner."

"Okay, let's not waste any more time and go then." He entered the information into his navigation app, shifted into drive, and sped away from the pack.

After seeing what cars they had on the lot, I fell in love with a bright blue Jeep Wrangler Sport that was eleven years old with just under a hundred thousand miles on it. Once I test drove it, I didn't want to leave without it. We were able to talk the salesman who was helping us down to $15,000, but he wouldn't budge any further.

"We have some great financing options right now," he offered, looking across a small desk at us, the three of us seated in a cubicle. "We can put something together with a small monthly payment."

"No thank you, I don't think financing will work." I felt defeated and was ready to give in and make up some crazy convoluted story about why the deal with the car fell through.

"Do you mind if we talk alone for a few minutes?" Blake asked. The salesman agreed and stepped away. Then Blake turned to me. "Why don't you just finance half of it?"

"I don't have any credit," I replied. I'd never had a reason to open a credit card and my parents were paying for my college. I knew that even if they did agree to finance the car for me that it would be at a really high interest rate.

"Don't give up without even trying. Let's just see what happens first." Blake caught the dealer's eye and waved him back. "She'd like to finance half the car." The salesman smiled and handed me a form to complete. I filled in the required fields and slid it back across the desk.

We waited for at least fifteen minutes until the salesman came back. He asked, "Is there any chance you could have someone cosign for you?"

Before I could respond, Blake spoke up. "Absolutely. I'd be happy to cosign."

"Great, just fill this portion out over here." He slid the form back over to Blake. I was dumbstruck but didn't want to say anything in front of the salesman.

After he walked away again, I turned to Blake. "What are you doing? Why are you cosigning for me? This is absolutely crazy." I was baffled by how quick he was to cosign for me as if he was just lending me a couple dollars. Was he really that helpful and friendly? Or was there something in it for him as well?

"Why not?"

"Because what if I don't pay and destroy your credit?"

"First of all, I highly doubt a perfectionist such as yourself would just stop paying your bills. Second, did you forget I'm going to be the alpha soon? I have a lot more influence over you than even your parents. I could banish you from the pack if I wanted to. That would be pretty fucking dumb to screw the alpha of your pack, unless it's in a sexual context of course." He laughed. I glared at him. "Just kidding. Last joke of the day."

After another fifteen minutes the salesman came back smiling. "Mr. Wulfric, we were able to run your credit, and there won't be any issues with you as the cosigner." He then looked at me. "We have a great promotion right now where we're offering financing at only 2.5 percent interest. Ms. Dale, I only have one question for you. Are you ready to drive your new car home today?"

Chapter 17

Blake

I returned home around five thirty after spending the day with Jasmine. My father stopped me as soon as I walked through the door. "And where the hell have you been all day?" His face was red, brows furrowed.

"Out," I replied, not wanting to give any additional information.

"In case you forgot, you're going to be the alpha of this pack soon, which means you have a lot of responsibilities around here."

"And it also means I don't need to answer to anyone."

"I'm still the fucking alpha, so you will answer to me! Where the fuck were you?" he bellowed, using his alpha aura, something he hadn't used with me in years, probably since I was still in high school.

I felt my neck maneuvering to bare itself in submission, feeling forced to reply to his question. But, for the first time, I found I was easily able to override the command. I could tell that I had grown much stronger than my father and would easily be able to overpower him if it ever came down to it. I replied, "None of your fucking business!"

He gasped in shock, clearly not used to anyone being able to overcome his alpha aura. Then I decided to give him a taste of his own medicine and used the alpha aura back on him. "Now leave me alone." I watched as my father bared his own neck in submission, a pained look on his face.

I left my father, relishing in my newfound power, and walked to the kitchen where the packhouse cook was preparing dinner. I inhaled the delicious smell of pot roast and potatoes. "What time will dinner be ready?" I asked.

"In half an hour—your mom should be returning from her shift then," Connie, the cook, replied. I left the kitchen to go to my bedroom and opened my laptop to review the meeting minutes that I had requested from our office manager, Mariette. I then scrolled through the remainder of my emails, seeing what I had missed during the day. There was an email from Luke with updates on the situation with Alpha Édouard and the Bois Sombre Pack. Fortunately, there weren't any new developments in the situation at the moment. Unfortunately, there was still evidence that Alpha Édouard might be building alliances. I knew a war was inevitable. I just wondered how much longer we had to prepare.

After going through my emails, I pulled up a picture on my phone from earlier that day. I'd secretly taken it of Jasmine test-driving her new car, bliss on her face. I smiled and decided to send it to her in a text message, thinking she'd like to see it and save it as a memory. After pulling up our text thread, I typed, *Congrats again on your new ride,* and hit send. I sat back in my chair, realizing the smile was still plastered on my face without any intention of fading. Shit, what was happening? A familiar feeling flooded through me—a feeling I'd only ever felt once in my life before, with Ria.

I made an abrupt decision that I would push it away, deep into my subconscious, just like I had with everything else I didn't want to feel. The last thing I needed right now was to develop feelings for someone else. The last time still seared my insides and left me with nightmares I couldn't rid myself of. And this situation was, similarly, bound to end in pain—maybe not as bad, but pain just the same. While I no longer had a mate and was free to take a chosen one, Jasmine still had a fated mate somewhere out there and would eventually take him as her own, as she should. She was right—we needed to give each other space and cool things down. I threw my phone on my desk and exited my bedroom to go to dinner.

My parents and Luke's parents were already seated at the dining room table when I arrived. I was also surprised to see Luke's oldest sister, Peyton, with her mate, Ryan, seated at the table. She was now very pregnant with her third pup, her belly swollen against the table. "How much longer until the due date?" I asked. Luke's sisters and their families rarely joined us for meals at the packhouse these days.

"A little over a month. We're hoping she makes it to the alpha ceremony. The last pup was a couple weeks early," Ryan replied. Werewolf pregnancies normally lasted around six months.

I took a seat next to my mom who spoke next. "I checked Peyton over today, and everything is progressing very well. Pup and mom are both nice and healthy."

"Thank you again, Dr. Luna, for taking the time to look her over," Ryan said, appreciatively. He then turned to me. "She's been having some cramps, so we were worried. She's no spring chicken, and this pregnancy was very unexpected." Peyton was much older than Luke at thirty-six years old.

"Humans are having children in their forties nowadays, and werewolves are much better equipped to carry children, so there's nothing to worry about." My mom smiled at the couple.

"It will be so nice to have a baby in the family again." Luke's mother, Robin, smiled, hugging Beta Alfred. "And who knows, maybe soon our Luke and Blake will bless us with some more grandpups." She looked at my mom, joy on her face at the thought.

Despair ripped through my body. My mom took my hand, squeezing it in hers. I was grateful for my mom's reaction, allowing her to hold my hand, feeling comforted by it as if I were a kid again. Even when I was at my worst, my mom never gave up on me, always trying to push through to me. I didn't know what I would have done if it weren't for her. "Let's not rush our sons. They're going to be really busy soon, and there's plenty of time to start families," my mom said.

"Damn right!" my father roared, never being able to keep his mouth shut for too long. "We've got an emerging war on our hands. There are more important things to focus on now than mates and babies. Let's not encourage this foolishness."

"Everyone knows a mate strengthens a werewolf!" Robin replied.

"When the mate's not a distraction!" My dad looked angered at being argued with. I was surprised at Robin's boldness. She usually knew better than to get into an argument with my father. "That's enough of this talk. Let's eat." His word was always final.

Yes, mates strengthened werewolves but loss weakened them. It was a double-edged sword. That was the reason why werewolves would fight for their mates above all else and start wars over them. That was the reason why Alpha Édouard was unlikely to surrender. As long as his mate, Sofia, was alive, he would fight to the death of his entire pack to see her returned to him.

After dinner, I went back up to my bedroom where I saw a text message was waiting for me.

> **Jasmine**: Thank you so much for today! Next time lunch and the ride are on me

As much as I wanted next time to be as soon as possible, I resisted. It would be for the best if there wasn't a next time.

I ignored the text, descended the stairs, and exited the packhouse, undressing as soon as I entered the woods. Once I was stripped of the last piece of clothing, I shifted into my wolf form, succumbing to my animal brain, forcing all my human emotions deep to a place I wouldn't retrieve them.

Chapter 18

Jasmine

On the next day off from work we had together, I took Lucy for a ride in my new car. It was now nearing the end of August and Lucy's youngest brother, Neil, would be turning sixteen in a couple days. We stopped at a shopping center so Lucy could buy him a present. We were browsing different colognes at a cosmetic store when a question I'd been wondering for two years suddenly came to me.

"Lucy, what cologne does Luke wear? I hope this isn't weird, but it smells really nice and I'd never smelled it before."

Lucy tilted her head, considering me. Finally, she replied, "Luke doesn't wear cologne."

"Oh, weird, maybe it was someone else's cologne I smelled. It's been a long time since I last saw him anyway, so I'm probably just misremembering." But that didn't sit right with me. I only ever smelled it when he was around, and I couldn't forget how divine and sensual it smelled. I sniffed a few of the samples, and nothing came close to how wonderful that scent had been.

We continued shopping for the remainder of the afternoon. I let Lucy drive my car home, which I almost instantly regretted. Lucy was a terrible driver, and I was certain that the car I had just bought less than a week earlier was about to end up in a scrapyard. Luckily, we made it home unscathed. I made a mental note to never allow Lucy behind the wheel of my car again.

After dropping Lucy off, I headed home to start dinner. I loved my new car and took every opportunity to use it. I was constantly offering to run any errands for my parents and grandparents. As I was driving home, my phone rang. Seeing a call was coming in from my grandmother, I took the call via Bluetooth. "Hi, Grandma!"

"Hello, Jazzy dear. Would you like to run an errand for me?"

"Absolutely!" I replied.

"Wonderful. I'm in the middle of cooking dinner and just realized I forgot to pick up your grandfather's prescription today. Would you mind swinging by the pack clinic and bringing it over? I have some muffins to trade you."

"No problem! Be there in a few minutes!" I replied, turning to drive toward the clinic. I headed into the downtown area of the pack and drove past the packhouse where I saw Blake's Jeep parked in the driveway. It had been about a week since he'd taken me to the dealership, and seeing his car now brought the longing to see him I harbored to the forefront. I did my best to ignore it and drove directly to the clinic.

I entered the clinic to pick up my grandfather's prescription. I was surprised to find Luke's mom was working at the front desk. Granted, adult werewolves very rarely needed to go to the clinic, especially at my age, being apt at healing themselves, so I wasn't necessarily familiar with all the staff that worked here, since I wasn't a frequent visitor. My grandfather, on the other hand, was now aging and, clearly, his wolf was becoming weaker, so he wasn't able to heal himself as easily anymore.

"Good afternoon, Mrs. Hemming. I didn't know you worked here."

Robin smiled at me warmly. She had a very friendly and motherly composure to her. I recalled meeting her in the past and wishing I had a mom like her. She was the complete opposite of my cold mom. "Hi,

Jasmine. Nice to see you. With all my pups now grown and out of the packhouse, I needed something to do. Luckily, I have connections through the luna and she got me set up over here." She winked at me. "What can we do for you today?"

"I just need to pick up a prescription for my grandfather."

"Oh yes, let me go grab that for you," she said, standing up and moving to the back where all of the prescriptions were organized. After she found it, she came back to hand it to me. "There you go."

"Thank you," I replied.

"How's Lucy doing? We haven't seen much of her lately. I know it was devastating for both her and Luke when they found out they weren't mates."

I was irritated—clearly Luke's mom had no idea that Luke was still seeing Lucy and carrying on as if they'd never discovered they weren't mates. I wanted to ask how she felt about the fact that Luke was presently copulating with someone who wasn't his mate and acting as if she was. I did my best to put my feelings aside and replied, "Lucy's fine."

"Neither of them should worry. They'll both meet the people they're meant to be with soon." She smiled. "I'm hoping once my Lukey comes back to the pack he'll finally find his mate."

I nodded, not sure how to respond. After saying goodbye to Robin, I returned to my car. Once again, I started internally questioning why I had such strong feelings about Lucy and Luke's relationship, especially now that even stronger feelings had emerged for Blake. One would think that I would have forgotten a silly crush that I had two years ago by now. I hadn't seen Luke in all of that time, but his name still brought a strange yearning to the forefront. I shook my head, forcing myself to stop thinking about him, then shifted into drive to head to my grandparents' house.

I walked into their house where both my grandparents enveloped me in hugs. "How's the Jeep?" my grandfather asked.

"It's great! I love it!" I replied.

"It's a very nice-looking car," my grandfather said, looking out the front window of his house.

"Thank you," I replied, feeling pride for my new car.

"I'm proud of you, doing things the right way. Saving until you had enough to buy it outright instead of living above your means like so many people these days. That's how people get into financial trouble."

I may have left out the fact that Blake had cosigned a loan for half the car, making sure all the bills would be sent electronically to me rather than by mail. I smirked to myself thinking about how crazy that would be to explain. Sometimes I imagined telling my parents or grandparents something crazy just to see how they would react. I didn't have the balls to actually do it, but it often made me laugh to myself.

For example, while eating dinner a few weeks back, my parents asked what I had done that day, that day being the one where I had been at the pond making out with Blake. I secretly considered how they would react if I told them that I'd let the future alpha put his mouth on my bare nipples that day. I could only imagine their shocked faces and the anger that would follow. I ended up just telling them that I had gone to the library and read all day.

After my grandmother handed me the muffins that she had promised me, we said our goodbyes and I went home to start dinner. After everything was prepared and cooking, I checked my phone. I opened the text thread with Blake only to feel disappointed again. He had left my message on read and never replied. I supposed he was busy. It wasn't like we frequently spent time and texted with each other prior to that message. In fact, my message didn't require a response, so it really wasn't strange at all that he hadn't supplied one. I forced myself to stop overanalyzing and to think of something else.

Next week I'd be going back to school, and I'd finally be able to concentrate on something else. All this idle time was driving me crazy.

I had never spent so much time considering my love life. I was ready to go back to the old, practically asexual, me. The me that focused on just my obligations: school, temple choir, keeping up with a training routine, and my job.

Then, I had an epiphany—I no longer wanted to be the old me anymore. The old me was boring. This new me drove a bright blue Jeep Wrangler and thought about doing unthinkable, immoral things with a very sexy man who was not my mate.

Chapter 19

Lucy

After working a full-day shift at the end of August, I went home and spent the next few hours baking dozens of cupcakes, cookies, and brownies. I was now the designated family baker. Any time someone had a celebration, I was assigned to make all the desserts. At first, I enjoyed this appointment, feeling like I finally had a place in my family. It would bring me joy to watch as everyone ate my pastries and showered me with compliments. But, before long, it became more of an obligation than anything, my efforts forgotten just as quickly as the devoured cookies.

The next day, my mom helped me package everything up, loading it into the car so we could go to my cousins' house for a birthday party. I had dozens of cousins, all tall, blonde, and athletic. Everyone in the pack knew of the Owens—mostly positive things, but we also weren't known for being as devout and religious as others, something that could be alienating. While I was grateful that my parents weren't as strict and overbearing as Jasmine's parents, I already felt like I didn't fit in with my family—and to not fit in with the pack, well, that was just the icing on the cake, and not in a good way.

But I always smiled and held my head high. Fake it until you make it, right? So, maybe I wasn't perfect. But I could pretend I was. And if they thought I was scandalous or too much, well, I could act like they were the ones who were in the wrong. No, I was enlightened, ahead of my time. Yes, exactly!

But it still always stung deep down that I wasn't like everyone else—that I didn't really have my place. As soon as my family arrived at the party, greeting all our extended family (and there were a lot of us Owens!), everyone was already congregating in the backyard, ready to pull together teams for a sports game. Maybe football this time. I sighed and busied myself in the kitchen, unpacking all the desserts.

*** *Three and a half years ago* ***

Luke and I fell for each other fast. It started out purely physical. I mean, he was the future beta and he was hot! He was much hotter than all the other guys at our school. A lot of that had to do with the fact that he worked out far more than everyone else. While most warriors didn't begin their training until after they graduated from high school, Luke had started his junior year, in preparation for becoming the future beta.

All the girls at school would stare at me with envy as I'd hold hands with Luke, walking down the hallway and making out with him against his locker. Not only was I the only sophomore to have a senior boyfriend, but he was the friggin' beta. Pretty much everyone had a crush on him, but I was the one he chose out of everyone at school.

It was a Sunday, the day before my sixteenth birthday. My parents had invited our extended family over to celebrate my sweet sixteen, and I had invited Luke to join us. We had been dating for just over five months at this point. I was sitting with Luke on the couch when my older brother, Kyle, came over.

"Hey, Luke, we're getting teams together for baseball out back. Do you want to join?" he asked.

"Sure," he replied, standing up. I sighed. While I loved that Luke got along with my whole family, they never really included me in their games, so I'd probably end up sitting on the sidelines as usual. He surprised me by putting out his hand and saying, "You're going to play too, right?"

"I'm not any good." I frowned.

"That's okay, I'll help you." He smiled. "Come on."

They let Luke and one of my cousins pick the teams. I was further surprised when he picked me first. I'd never gotten picked first for a team in my life. Sure, I usually didn't get picked last at school because whatever guy was picking usually had a crush on me. But my family always picked me last when I agreed to play. I was literally the only person in my entire extended family that wasn't athletic.

"Why would you pick me first?" I asked him quietly so no one would hear.

"Because I believe in you," he said, smiling. "You can be good. You just need someone to show you how."

While I was waiting in line to bat, Luke handed me a spare bat and taught me how to swing. He stood behind me, helping me position the bat correctly in my hands. "Now, make sure you keep your knees slightly bent, and sink into the balls of your feet. Perfect." He stepped away. "You look great. Now take a few practice swings." He watched me as I swung, making corrections as he noticed them. "You're a quick learner. Much faster than my nephew."

"Your nephews are three and seven years old!"

"The seven-year-old's already practically a pro. But you're definitely picking it up much faster than him."

When it was my turn to bat, Luke gave me a thumbs up, smiling. He had the most amazing smile—his teeth so white, and his face like a model in a J. Crew ad. He signaled for me to keep my eye on the ball, pointing two fingers at his eyes and then at the pitcher, who was currently my oldest brother Jack. Jack pitched the ball to me, and I swung, missing.

"Strike one!" one of my cousins yelled.

"Don't worry, Luce. You've got this," Luke encouraged me. Jack pitched again, and again, I missed. I frowned, sighing. "Lucy, you can do this. I believe in you," Luke said, looking me in the eyes. "Just keep your eye on the ball."

I straightened up, getting back in the right position. Jack pitched again, and I swung, my bat connecting with the ball. I watched as it flew into the sky.

"Run, Lucy! Run!" Luke yelled, and everyone else on my team joined in. "Run!" I quickly dropped my bat and ran toward first base, my feet touching the base before the ball got there. I jumped up and down, celebrating. That was the first time I'd ever even made it to first base.

Luke was up next, and he was able to send the ball really far. I ran to second and then third. Mark was up next, and he struck out. One of my cousins went after him, and I finally made it to home base.

"Nice job, Lucy." My dad patted me on my shoulder.

Once Luke returned to home base, he gave me a huge hug and said, "See, Lucy. I knew you could do it."

After the baseball game, Luke and I went for a walk around the neighborhood, holding hands. "Why do you believe in me so much?" I asked.

He stopped and took my other hand in his, so he was holding both my hands between us. He looked in my eyes and said, "Because you're so determined at everything you put your mind to. I knew you just needed some encouragement. I think you just had it in your head that you're bad at sports, so you never even bothered to try to be good at them. It's the same in school. I know you're a smart girl. You just have it in your head that you're not for some reason. But I see how you are when you set a goal. You do everything in your power to make sure you accomplish it, and you figure it out. I've never met anyone as resourceful and persistent as you are."

I stared at him, my mouth agape. No one had ever said anything so nice and sincere to me in my life. He smiled and continued, "Honestly, I think you see yourself as just a dumb blonde sometimes. But I know you're not. Don't get me wrong, you're very beautiful, but you're also so much more than that, Lucy. I wouldn't have thought that at first. But after I got to know you, I realized how much more you are than the image you project of yourself to everyone. You are also so loyal and sweet. I see how you stick up for your friends at school without even hesitating."

I took my hands out of his and wrapped my arms around him, amazed by how highly he thought of me. He returned the hug, then put his mouth on mine, kissing me deeply. When we finally pulled apart, he said, "Lucy, I am completely crazy about you."

"You're the best thing that ever happened to me, Luke," I said, feeling deep inside how true it was. He finally made me feel like no one ever made me feel in my life—like I was valued, and I belonged.

My youngest cousins all swarmed the kitchen, fighting to grab cookies off the table.

"None for you, Lily!" My little cousin Jacob held his sister, not allowing her to take a cookie. She began crying, unable to free herself.

"Jacob, stop it! That's not nice!" I chastised him, pulling him off his little sister. "Big brothers are supposed to help their little sisters, not make their life more difficult!" I took Lily's hand and brought her to the table. "Which one do you want?" I squatted down in front of her.

"Chocolate chip," she said, shyly, sniffing back tears.

"Here you go." I smiled at her, grabbing a cookie off the table. "Don't let your brother bully you like that. You need to tell him he's being bad." She nodded and ran away.

"These cupcakes are amazing!" My friend Emma approached me, looking tan and relaxed after returning from her honeymoon. "Your mate's going to be one lucky man!"

"You mean my boyfriend?" I asked.

"I mean, sure, Luke's lucky for now. But that's not forever."

I was annoyed by her comment. Why would she say that? She knew how I felt about Luke. Why did everyone dismiss our relationship as if it were some childish infatuation? It was so demeaning! Like, how could silly Lucy know anything about life and love? "Of course it's forever!" I snapped back. "We're going to be chosen mates!"

"I know you always say that, but you can't be serious!" Emma looked at me critically. What, had she thought I was joking all this time?

"Why not?" I asked, giving her a hard stare.

"Because you have a mate out there somewhere. And Luke has one too."

"So what?"

"I don't know, Lucy. It just seems wrong. Artemis gives us all mates. I mean, look how happy Kyle and I are together. I can't imagine ever meeting anyone more perfect for me. And he's so creative in bed. Last time, he blindfolded me—"

I cut Emma off. "For the love of Artemis, stop telling me about what you do with my brother in bed! I don't need to know any of that!"

She laughed and said, "Lucy, just think about it seriously. You could be missing out on something really great by clinging on to Luke. I mean, I know he's the future beta, but titles aren't everything."

I didn't even bother responding. Sure, maybe at first it was all about the title, but that was before I really got to know him, and he really got to know me. No, we were perfect for each other, and there was nobody that would ever convince me otherwise, even if she was a fucking Goddess.

Chapter 20

Jasmine

Before I knew it, it was halfway through September. I had found myself preoccupied with school and work, and temple choir had started up again. We were now rehearsing every night of the week as we would be performing during the alpha ceremony. At work, Lucy and Valerie were busy prepping for all of the desserts and the huge cake they'd have to prepare for the occasion. The whole pack was alive with excitement for something that hadn't occurred for over forty years—the transition from one alpha to the next.

I had given up on checking my text thread with Blake. He had never responded. I was disappointed and wondered if it was something I did—was it the revelation about my panic attacks or the finality of our decision to just remain friends? Perhaps he had no desire to see me if our relationship would no longer be physical. But, I reminded myself, he did cosign a loan for me, and that isn't something that someone who wants you out of their life would do. Deciding it was for the best to not dwell on it and accept that we weren't meant to be together anyway, I did my best to shove him from my mind. But then, sometimes, late at night, I'd find myself thinking about him again, my thoughts spiraling.

One day, after working the early shift, I went down to the pack gym. As part of our obligations, all pack members were required to stay physically fit to a minimal standard in case of an attack. While warriors were trained to a much higher standard and to fight on the front lines, it was important that everyone be capable of defending themselves should it become necessary. Of course, being a perfectionist and overachiever, I always made sure that I was to the top standard. Lucy, on the other hand, was often failing physical tests and had to be put on remediation programs.

Going in the middle of the day, during the week, meant that the gym wouldn't be too crowded. I preferred this. I always felt awkward lifting weights and sweating in front of the males of the pack. Plus, when it got busy, the equipment I wanted to use often wasn't available.

Today was my leg day. After stretching and warming up, I went to the squat rack. I added all the weights I needed and began squatting. Suddenly I noticed someone in my peripheral vision and looked to my left to see Blake intently watching me.

After reracking the barbell, I removed my headphones and looked up at him as he spoke. "Damn, that's hot." He came over and began adding up all the weights I'd placed on the barbell. "Holy shit, you squat 320 pounds?" While werewolves were naturally much stronger than humans, this amount was still impressive for a female werewolf, and I knew that. "I'm about to go to your house and convince your parents to let me recruit you as a warrior."

"What are you doing here? Don't you have your own gym?" I asked, giving him attitude and knowing that the alpha, beta, and warriors all had a much nicer gym that they used, separate from the one used by the general population. I felt wary about him turning up all of a sudden after ignoring my existence for at least three weeks. But, damn, he did look hot.

No, stop thinking that! He is bad news.

"I was in here planning a new training schedule for the whole pack. We're going to have required sparring and ask that everyone see a trainer to be put on a personalized workout regimen. It's one of the first things I'm going to announce after becoming alpha."

"Is that what you've been up to?"

"It's one of the things. To be honest, I've been really busy. There's a lot going on. I don't want to worry you but the situation with our enemy pack's not looking good right now." I noticed he wasn't making eye contact with me.

"Is that why I haven't heard from you for weeks now?" I asked, hoping I didn't sound accusatory. The last thing I wanted was for him to think I was sitting at home pining for him. It stung so much that, in reality, that was exactly what I'd pathetically been doing. Ugh, I was so ashamed of myself!

"It's one of the reasons. I also thought you might want some space."

My stomach dropped at his response. That's exactly what someone said when they, themselves, wanted space. Was I like his crazy ex-girlfriend that he just ghosted and expected not to slash his tires in frustration? Shit, now I was sounding like a crazy ex-girlfriend in my mind. Goddess, what was happening to me? I was the one who had said our relationship was too much for me, so maybe he really was just doing what I'd asked.

After mulling everything over in my mind, I finally replied, "Oh, okay." I didn't know what else to say. I had no claim to him, and he had no obligations to me. Although, logically, I knew that was true, I couldn't help the sting I felt that Blake had decided to distance himself from me and was now showing up as if he didn't do anything out of the ordinary. Then, I reminded myself, he wasn't my mate and I needed to just get over him.

We held each other's gaze for at least a minute. Finally, Blake spoke again. "How's your new car?"

"It's good. Thanks again for your help. My family bought the whole thing, so that was good." I forced myself to smile.

He smiled back at me, his eyes softening. "I'm sorry I haven't been in contact. I'll be really busy for the next week with the lead-up to the alpha ceremony and Luke coming back to town. But maybe after the dust settles, I can take you up on your offer for lunch and a ride in your new car."

"I don't know. School's been really busy lately," I replied, thinking I shouldn't be so quick to just accept his offer. Why did he think it was okay to make me feel like I was so special to him and then just fall off the face of the earth? But I couldn't help desperately wanting to give in as he stood there, his thin T-shirt revealing his sculpted body and his icy blue eyes peering into mine. Goddess, what was wrong with me? Why did he have to be so hot? Maybe if he was just average-looking this wouldn't be so difficult.

He seemed as if he was about to speak again, half opening his mouth, but he didn't, closing it. I wondered what he wanted to say. After shaking his head, he finally said, "It was really nice to see you. I've got to go though." He touched me on my shoulder, then turned on his heel to walk away.

"See you," I called back. He put his hand up in a wave, not turning back around. I, once again, felt confused by him, which had now grown to becoming frustrated with him and frustrated with myself for letting him get to me like this. He affected me far too much for someone who wasn't even my mate.

Blake

After weeks of shoving Jasmine from my mind, she had hurled herself back into it. I hadn't expected to be so excited to see her at the gym. Seeing her made me realize how much I had missed her. And, damn. I knew she was fit, but I had no idea that she could squat so much weight. Thinking about it made my cock rock-hard. I loved a tough woman. And now that I knew she could pump iron like a warrior, I was a goner.

I wanted to stay longer and had an overwhelming desire to kiss her again. Hell, I'd love to have stayed and worked out with her. But there was just too much going on. The alpha ceremony was less than a week away, and Luke was due back home later today.

I had just exited the gym and was striding toward my car when someone stopped me.

"Blake!" she yelled, forcing me to turn my head. I felt a blistering pain in my chest as the person calling my name approached me. My hands turned into fists, digging what little nails I had into my palms, staving off the impulse to run that was coursing through my body at that moment. I watched helplessly as the figure moved closer to me—Ria's older sister, BB.

Everyone called her by her initials, short for Belinda Baker. While there were certain physical differences between the two of them, such as Ria having been much taller and more fit, and BB choosing to straighten her hair while Ria had always embraced her lion's mane of curls, their faces were very similar. Looking at BB now, I was forced to confront a ghost that, to this day, haunted me almost every waking moment, and the sleeping ones as well.

I nodded at BB, not sure I could trust myself to speak without breaking apart, a stabbing pain in my chest, certain my lungs might collapse.

"Blake." BB spoke my name again, more quietly since she was standing right in front of me. "How are you doing? It's been a long time since we've seen you."

"Fine," I replied. The fewer words the better. I took a deep breath, trying my best to act normal.

"You should go see my parents. I know they'd like to see you. They have Ria's engagement ring, and they want to return it to you. They've been waiting for you to come back."

"I don't want it," I replied, probably more curtly than I meant it to be.

"At least go see them." BB looked at me, pleading with her eyes, touching my forearm.

I sighed, knowing I couldn't avoid it forever. It was difficult enough to avoid her father, considering he was a senior warrior. Soon I'd have no choice but to interact regularly with him.

"We all miss her." She spoke again. "My mom hasn't been the same since we lost her. I think it would help if you went and saw her."

I nodded.

"I'll text you so we can plan something," BB said, likely knowing she wasn't going to get many more words out of me. She put her arms around me, hugging me, and then walked away, heading into the gym. As soon as she disappeared inside, I sprinted toward my car, driving it to the outskirts of the pack. I jumped out and ran into the woods, feeling my eyes burning, forcing myself to hold on until I could shift into my wolf.

*** *Five years ago* ***

It was the perfect June day—not too hot and partly cloudy with a slight breeze. To celebrate our engagement, I'd planned a trip for Ria and me to spend the weekend of the summer solstice in Kennebunkport, Maine, days after I graduated from high school. We'd driven over four hours and checked in the evening prior.

The early morning was spent jogging the beach, taking in the East Coast sunrise. After returning to the hotel to freshen up and eat breakfast, we were now strolling hand in hand in the crowded Dock Square shopping area. Ria was wearing a very short, strappy sundress, showing off her toned, brown thighs, making it difficult not to imagine being between them, which intensified my anticipation for that evening. My mate had bewitched me—I'd never felt this way in my life. I was head over heels, on cloud nine, fallen hook, line, and sinker.

After having some lobster rolls for lunch, we made our way to a shop that rented kayaks. They brought us down to a boat launch and left us to spend the remainder of the afternoon in the water.

Ria instantly took off in her kayak, looking back at me and yelling, "Come on, Blake, let's see if those arms are good for anything other than flexing in front of the mirror!"

I paddled out toward her. As soon as I caught up, I said, "They're good for other things too."

"Really, like what?"

"You already forgot this morning in the shower? Pretty sure you didn't get in that position without me holding you up." I smirked.

"My legs were doing most of the work. I just let you think you were doing something so your ego wouldn't get hurt."

I smiled. "You do have very strong and flexible legs. I've been staring at them all day. I think you wore that dress on purpose."

"You think I wore a dress just so you can act like a creep and stare at my legs all day?"

"You do love to tease me," I said, maneuvering my boat so it was next to hers, and putting my hand out. She took my hand and looked at me, smiling. I pulled her hand up to my mouth and kissed it. Then we spent some time wading in the water. We eventually began paddling again, taking in the scenery from the water.

When we returned to shore, it was already evening. We made our way to a restaurant overlooking the water, retiring to our hotel room afterward. As soon as we got inside, I closed the space between us and moved my hands to her legs, caressing them and reaching for the hem of her dress, ready to remove it.

"No!" she said, moving away from me.

"No?" I moved back toward her.

"No!" she said again, a glint in her eyes.

"Are you trying to torture me?" I looked at her.

"What's the big bad alpha wolf going to do about it?" She smiled.

"Torture you back." I began tickling her. She was very ticklish. She laughed and shrieked, falling back in the bed. I followed, climbing in after her.

"Stop! Stop! Stop!" She was gasping for air through her laughter. I stopped and she sat up.

"Okay, I'll try a different tactic," I said, moving behind her and putting my hands on her upper back. I kissed her neck while I rubbed her bare shoulders. She relaxed and laid her back against the front of my body. I could feel my erection digging into her back, desperate to have her.

"Put that thing away!" she yelled.

"Sorry, no can do. It's too big." I smirked.

"It's not that impressive," she huffed.

"Really? Now you're making me jealous. When have you seen a more impressive one?"

"I saw one in a porn."

"What's a nice girl like you doing watching porn?" I asked pulling back so I could kiss her across the shoulders, pushing the straps of her dress off as I did.

"What, is it only for quote, unquote, 'bad girls'?"

"It's not for girls who won't let me take their dress off."

"You're just jealous because the porn satisfied me more than you do."

"Is that a challenge? Because you know I love a challenge."

"In that case, yes. Let's see if the big bad alpha wolf can fuck me as good as a porn star," she teased.

I smiled and instantly grabbed her to flip her onto her back. "I can fuck better."

After we were panting and catching our breath, she snuggled up against me. I wrapped my arms around her, holding her close to my body, inhaling the fragrance of her shampoo mixed with her intoxicating scent. I loved her hair. It was so wild, like her—curls that had a life of their own.

She looked up at me and I stared back at her. "Blake," she said, looking vulnerable.

"Yes?" I replied, my heart swelling at how sweet she looked.

"I'm scared."

"Why?" I kissed her forehead.

"Do you think we'll really have to go to war?"

I closed my eyes and nodded.

"I know I've been training for this for two years now, but I've never been to battle before."

"You'll do great. You're so great during practice, my Amazon woman." I smiled at her. "Just stick close to me when we go. I'll always protect you."

She nodded.

"Just think about the future," I continued. "Soon I'll officially be alpha and then we can finally get married and mark each other. And you'll move into the packhouse with me, where we'll be able to wake up together every single day. And go to bed together every single night—probably the part I'm looking forward to the most."

"I love you, Blake." She sighed.

"I love you too, Ria. You're perfect, even when you're being a pain in the ass." I beamed, kissing her, not able to imagine ever living without her now that I had finally met her—my perfect mate.

After running in the woods for several hours, I finally made my way back to my car. I knew my father would be pissed. He had given me a shit ton of stuff to work on before the big welcome-home dinner for Luke that night, and I'd neglected all of it. Once I had access to my cell phone again and was able to check the time, I realized that I had run for longer than I thought.

I drove back to the packhouse, and saw the group of cars parked in the lot. I pulled up next to my father's car and made my way inside. Everyone stared at me as soon as I walked into the dining room. I looked around at Luke's entire family and my parents. I could see my dad was pissed, his face was red as he glared at me, not daring to say anything.

"Blake, come sit." My mom summoned me over, pulling out a chair next to her, conveniently also next to my father who was sitting at the head of the table.

Luke got up, and I went over to greet him. "Hey, man, welcome home," I said, shaking his hand and patting his back.

"Welcome home to you too." He smiled.

I took my seat next to my parents, and my father glared at me. I did my best to ignore his silent hissy fit as I took some food to put on my plate.

"One week until the big day. How does it feel, Blake and Luke?" Beta Alfred asked.

"It feels great," I replied. "I'll finally be the one in charge around here." I could feel my dad growing angrier, and something about it felt really satisfying.

"I think we're ready," Luke replied.

"Yes, you absolutely are." Luke's mom smiled. "I'm so proud of you boys." She started dabbing a tissue to her eyes.

Chapter 21

Luke

After I returned home, I was thrown right back into pack life and training. Blake and I followed the same training schedule as the warriors. Most warriors had to train ten to thirty-two hours and patrol eight to forty hours a week, depending on their seniority and rank. Because we were to become the alpha and beta, Blake and I were exempt from patrol duty. However, that didn't mean a single day off for either of us. We were forced to sit with our fathers in the packhouse office, getting the last bit of wisdom crammed into us before the alpha ceremony took place in just days.

Alpha James was eager to retire and move out of the packhouse—thank Goddess for that. He had always been a brute and showed no sign of changing in his old age. It would be nice to finally be able to work or eat dinner without listening to his appalling and vulgar opinions. I have no idea how my dad put up with him all those years. My dad was a nice, decent guy. When I'd asked him about it in the past, he had said that Alpha James wasn't always so bad. He had actually been okay in the early years. But after his father died and he had to shoulder the responsibility of alpha alone, he began to change. After he met his luna, he softened, and my dad thought she'd be good for him. But it was short-lived, and after a few years, he was right back to his dickish self.

The bell sounded, signaling the end of the current day's training. I had spent the late afternoon sparring with several different warriors outdoors. Luckily, the weather had begun to cool as we were well into September now. During the summer, there were days that training was almost unbearable. While toweling myself down, I looked over toward the bleachers where Lucy was sitting in a light blue dress with a picnic basket next to her. Reliable, sweet, and eager Lucy. With her long legs, voluminous blond hair, and button nose, she was easily the most beautiful girl in the entire pack. She had enchanted me from the time I first met her.

Once everyone had left the field, I climbed the bleachers and took a seat next to her. She turned to whisper in my ear. "I brought you dinner. Oh, and I'm not wearing any panties."

I instantly felt myself go hard. After being apart for two years, we were now sneaking around to go at it every free moment. I couldn't get enough of her. She was always finding creative ways to surprise me.

I traced my fingers up her thigh, under the skirt of her dress, to see if she was telling the truth, curiosity getting the best of me. She definitely wasn't lying.

"How am I supposed to eat dinner now that you've got me so worked up?"

"We should go somewhere more private," she whispered and started nibbling on my ear.

"Okay, but you need to stop doing that, baby, and give me a second. I can't be walking around with a tent in my shorts."

After I calmed down and was able to stand up, she took the basket in one hand, my hand in other, and led me into the forest. We walked about a hundred yards in until she climbed onto a large rock, sitting herself down and spreading her legs. "I've always wanted to have sex outdoors."

I instantly dropped to my knees and pushed my head between her legs, smelling her sweet scent. I slowly kissed her up each inner thigh until I made it to the center of her pussy, sucking all of her in, eventually switching to my tongue, trying to put pressure on all the right spots. I didn't even care that my knees were pressed against small stones and pine needles on the ground. I could hear her soft moans from up above, and I didn't think I could ever tire of hearing that sound. The louder she moaned the more it motivated me to keep going, enthusiastically flicking my tongue against her clit. Before long, her legs were trembling, and she was pulling at my hair.

Goddess, I love when she goes crazy like this.

I lapped my tongue against her even more fervently until she let out a loud moan. I reveled in the taste and sensation of her coming against my mouth, thinking there was nothing better in the world than knowing I had made her come undone like that.

I stood up and kissed her, drawing her tongue out with my own, tracing the outline of her face with my fingers as I deepened the kiss. After a minute, she stopped me and said, "Your turn, baby," and spread her legs even farther than earlier.

She didn't have to ask twice. I pulled a condom out of my wallet, dropped my shorts, and buried my cock in her. *This girl drove me absolutely crazy.* I put my hands under the skirt of her dress and grabbed her tight little ass as I plunged my cock as deep as it would go, hitting her cervix, but she didn't stop me. In fact, she encouraged me to keep going as she dug her fingers into my back, moaning, "Harder, Luke, harder."

I growled in response and went deeper and harder, savoring the feeling of being inside her. I brought my thumb to her clit, rubbing it gently at first, which she rewarded with loud moans. I kissed her neck as she continued moaning, provoking me to rub harder and thrust more vigorously. I didn't know how long I'd be able to hold on as I slid in and out of her, her pussy so warm and wet, the building pressure in my dick driving me to the edge.

"I'm about to come," she whimpered.

I pounded against her even more forcefully, if that was possible, until she began shaking, screaming, "Luke, Luke, oh Goddess, Luke." My name on her lips tipped me over the edge, as I came at the same time as she did, riding out my orgasm while she shook against my body, throwing her head back and screaming into the forest.

Afterward, we stayed still for a minute panting, me still inside her, holding her against me. We finally broke free and she pulled some napkins out of the picnic basket so I could clean myself up and wrap up the used condom.

She pulled out a picnic blanket that she dropped to the ground and began putting out the food she had brought. She had made some fried chicken that still tasted good even though it wasn't hot anymore, coleslaw, and chocolate cupcakes for dessert. She really was the perfect little housewife. I could imagine a life with her, coming home to her every night, eating her cooking and desserts. My family even loved her family. And with a total of seven siblings between the two of us, our pups would have an abundance of cousins to play with.

I smiled at her between bites. "I love you, Lucy."

"I love you too, Luke. I don't ever want to be without you." She laid her head on my shoulder. I put my free arm around her, but I suddenly started to worry. It had always been at the back of my mind that she wasn't my mate, but when she said that, realization once again struck that I couldn't promise her anything. As much as I loved and cared for her now, would I still feel the same way once I finally met my true mate? Was it worth rejecting a fated mate for a chosen one? While I felt very strongly about Lucy, maybe I'd feel even more strongly about my true mate, the new feeling overpowering the one I had now.

Alternatively, Lucy could meet her mate first and leave me for him. My heart sank at the thought. While I'd rather Lucy hurt me than for me to hurt her, I started to consider whether I'd taken things too far. In fact, I knew I had, and I was now playing with fire. While Lucy's parents were aware we were still seeing each other, I had failed to mention the fact that we'd never broken up to my own, deciding to only break the news once I'd made my final decision on whether to take Lucy as a chosen mate. While my parents weren't strict about dating like most parents in the pack were, I knew there was an expectation that I'd end up with my fated mate once I met her. But my parents had always been understanding—I'm sure if I decided on a chosen one instead that they'd ultimately understand. I just didn't want to bother them with the thoughts floating around in my head until I'd made a concrete decision.

I don't think either of our parents knew exactly how deeply we felt for each other. They had always assumed we were casually dating with the intent to break up once we met our mates—no harm, no foul. But now I wasn't sure if things were so clear-cut. We were in so deep now that I knew only pain lay ahead, either for us or for our mates.

Chapter 22

Jasmine

On Sunday night, my parents and I were seated farther back than usual at the temple service, having gotten there later than normal that day. Partway through, the priest welcomed Luke back to the pack and invited Luke and Blake to join him at the front where they helped him lead a chant. It had been two years since I'd seen Luke in person. He had filled out and was much more muscular now than I had remembered. However, he still had that pretty boy, movie star handsome face, contrasted to Blake's much more mature appearance.

I looked between the two of them, wondering which one I preferred. They were both good-looking in their own ways. However, thinking about Luke made my chest ache. I was still very attracted to him and felt something drawing me to him, as if I should go stand beside him. While I had a steady, ceaseless longing throughout the years, it was somehow more powerful now that I was seeing him in person. My heart raced in my chest while my stomach did somersaults. I chanted the prayer loudly to overcompensate for suddenly forgetting how to breathe normally. Fighting the feeling of being desperately drawn to Luke, I averted my eyes. For the rest of the service, I did my best to ignore the existence of both Luke and Blake.

Blake

It was a Sunday night, and I was seated at temple with my parents. The only representation from the beta family this week was Luke, since his parents had traveled up to Quebec to address some issues. They were planning to return in time for the alpha ceremony in a few short days. He had been smiling all day since his girlfriend left after breakfast that morning, clearly having taken advantage of his parents being out of town. When we met with my dad in the afternoon to go over more pack logistics, his mind was elsewhere, as if he was daydreaming. I was envious of his good spirits. I hadn't felt the way Luke appeared in years now.

Luke and I used to be much closer. Besides Luke's sisters, who were already teenagers by the time we could walk and talk, we were the only kids that lived in the packhouse growing up. Consequently, we grew up like brothers, often spending the night in each other's rooms and talking until dawn. He was always there for me when my father went into one of his rages. He'd let me hide in his room, knowing my father would never dare to terrorize his beta's pup. His dad was often there for me too, warning my mom and me to leave when my father was in one of his moods.

After my father began forcing me to witness him torturing prisoners in our cells at the age of ten, I began having nightmares. I couldn't push the image of my father cutting off their arms, legs, and testicles from my head. When I'd wake up petrified, in a cold sweat, I could always count on Luke to let me crash in his room, being too terrified to go into my parents'. He didn't even mind when I sometimes slept in the same bed as him.

But after Ria was killed in battle, things changed. Although I was always open with Luke, I found myself closing off even to him. I had heard that losing a mate can drive a werewolf into madness, and I now understood. My one saving grace was that we had never marked each other. My parents had convinced me to wait until we were officially married to go along with the traditions of the temple, especially being an alpha. We were planning to wed not long after I assumed the alpha title, anxious to finally mark each other. Unfortunately, that day never came. Fortunately, I had listened to my parents and avoided the worst of despair, a pain reserved for someone marked by their mate.

My father was eager to continue with the alpha ceremony. He became enraged when I told him I couldn't do it. We fought for months. Beta Alfred tried to take my side, which enraged my father even more. My mom finally desperately begged him to let me mourn my loss. While he never treated my mom well, he did always have a soft spot for her, since she was his mate. He finally agreed to let me take time away from the pack under one circumstance, and that was to attend the Grey Wolf University, which was notorious for producing some of the strongest and most brutal alphas in the world. Having no other choice, I took that option, starting school a year after the worst day of my life.

The four years I spent there were excruciating and bleak. But they were also like therapy. The physical pain and torture allowed me to feel something when otherwise I was numb. It distracted me from my thoughts and memories. I was able to run on instinct alone, where the only objective everyday was survival. I preferred the training to the academics.

After the service ended, I stood with Luke and made small talk. I noticed Jasmine standing with her parents, her back turned to us, giving me a perfect view of her ass. I turned back to Luke to say something only to notice that he was staring at the same place I had just turned away from. I suddenly felt possessive, not liking one bit that my friend was staring at Jasmine's ass. I wanted to call him out on it but didn't want to do it in a way that would make my feelings obvious.

Before I realized what I was saying, I said, "Now that's the kind of ass you just want to grab and shove your dick into." I have no idea what had possessed me to say something like that, and I instantly regretted it.

Luke turned to me with an intense glare and his nostrils flared. "What the fuck, man? Why are you talking about Jasmine like that?"

I was ashamed of my comment. I didn't know where it came from or how I could have said something like that. If I were in my wolf form, I'd be whimpering with my tail between my legs. After deliberating on what I could possibly say to follow something like that, I responded, "You're right, man. What I said was really uncool."

"You just sounded exactly like your dad." He was right. I clenched my fists, disgusted with myself.

After the service, we went back to the packhouse to sit down for dinner at the kitchen table. Connie had Sundays and Mondays off, so my mom fried up some bacon and put out ingredients to make sandwiches for my father, Luke, herself, and me. Luke grabbed a banana out of the fruit bowl to make his weird favorite sandwich. I, myself, preferred something meaty like roast beef.

"So, Luke, I heard you'll be leading some of the training sessions at the elementary school in the fall." My mom looked over at Luke.

"That's right. I've volunteered to lead training for the young pups in the mornings before lunch, and I'll be taking college courses in the afternoon twice a week, managing beta duties the rest of the week. Then I'll be doing my own training in the evenings, three times a week."

"Sounds like a busy schedule. Any time left to spend with your girlfriend?"

Luke eyes shot up, wide open, his mouth agape, practically gasping. Clearly his girlfriend was not something he was open about.

My father cut in. "He doesn't need time for girlfriends. They're just distractions. He should be focusing on the pack until the Moon Goddess brings him a mate. Even then, the pack is his first priority as beta. No, sir, you shouldn't be wasting your time wining and dining some bitch that isn't even a mate. Just get what you need from her and get back to work."

I could feel Luke's anger. His jaw was stiff and he had his hands balled up tightly into fists next to his plate. Luke knew it wasn't worth fighting with my father, but I could tell it was taking everything in him not to shift into his wolf form and tear my dad into shreds. I felt even worse for what I had said earlier this evening.

"Now, honey! We're not going to war yet. Luke has been a very good beta-in-training, even with his girlfriend. He's clearly very dedicated with his full schedule." My mom tried to de-escalate the situation but had to tread carefully because one wrong word and it would set my father off.

"War could happen at any moment. Werewolves are not known for being peaceful. I've been leading this pack for over forty years now, so I think I know a thing or two about pack leadership priorities. Your own son has let this pack get weak with his distractions. I let you manipulate me into letting him find himself or whatever shit he went to do. But I'm done with these games. Leading a pack is life or death. If our leadership doesn't have their priorities straight, you may as well kiss this packhouse, your clinic, the pack schools, everything goodbye! There are packs out there that wouldn't hesitate to burn all our homes to the ground, kill all our men, and rape all our women, from old geezers to young little pups. I've seen it with my own eyes. My own great-grandfather built this pack after his original pack was eradicated by a rival pack."

We ate in silence after my father's speech. I was used to my father's aggressive and vulgar personality, and Luke was too, to a certain extent. But he was usually a bit tamer when his beta was here. While no one could completely control my father, Beta Alfred's presence reeled him in most of the time, but not always.

After I helped my mom load the dishwasher, I went up to Luke's room and knocked on his door. He opened the door and let me in.

"Do you mind if I sit?" I asked.

"Sure," he pulled out his desk chair and sat down on his bed, which I noticed was made even though the packhouse housekeepers had Sundays and Mondays off. I looked around, and noticed that his room was really tidy, which was the complete opposite of mine. While the housekeepers helped, I had clutter everywhere normally.

"Look, I'm really sorry about my father. What he said was really disrespectful."

"Hey, it's ok. I know your father. I think you forget I grew up in the same packhouse as you. While you've been away for four years, I've been putting up with his running commentary." He smiled.

"Right, but it still doesn't make it right."

"You don't have to apologize for your dad."

"Maybe I don't, but I was also really disrespectful earlier. And I don't want to be like my father."

"Don't be so hard on yourself. You've been through a lot, and sometimes we all say things without thinking. But I'm going to call you out when you do." He lightly punched my arm.

"So, what's the deal with your girlfriend. She's not your mate, right?" I asked, changing the subject.

"No," he replied, looking uncomfortable. "Can you keep it on the DL? I kind of made my parents believe we broke up after we found out we weren't mates." He rubbed his neck. "I didn't think your mom noticed us."

"How long have you been together now?"

"Four years. We met a couple months after you left for Siberia."

"That's a long time. You must have it really bad for her."

He sighed. "I love her." His whole body glowed as he smiled. "I don't know what I'll do once I meet my mate. How do you end a long-term relationship with someone you love for a stranger? Maybe you can tell me. What was it like when you met Ria?" He paused. "You don't have to talk about it if you don't want to."

Did I want to talk about it? No, every part of me rejected the idea, knowing it would be practically impossible. But I seemed to be healing lately, didn't I? Maybe I could. I wanted to rekindle the close relationship Luke and I used to have, so I decided to attempt the conversation.

"The moment I saw her after I turned eighteen, I just knew. Even though she was practically a stranger to me at that point, I had a feeling come over me like she was made just for me—like the Moon Goddess had put her on this earth just for me—as if I'd been walking around my whole life just half a person and I'd discovered my missing puzzle piece. After we realized we were mates, we couldn't keep our hands off each other. She used to sneak out of her parents' house and climb into my window at night."

I paused, feeling tears threatening to spill over. "Sorry, man, I have to go," I said, and walked out of Luke's room not waiting for him to say anything, out of the packhouse, and into the forest. I tore the clothes off my body, not even caring to remember where I threw them, and shifted into my wolf form. I'd find some animals to hunt. Hunting always helped.

Chapter 23

Blake

It was finally the day of the ceremony. My father was clearly anxious because he was ready to bite the head off anyone in his vicinity. He was barking orders at all of the event staff. My mom tried, unsuccessfully, to calm him. My poor mom, always putting herself in his way to spare others. She looked beautiful in a long navy gown. My mom had always been very pretty, with long brown hair and a tall, slim frame. She was now allowing her hair to gray naturally. It was about half gray now and done up in an elegant chignon for today's event.

I went over to kiss her cheek. She pulled me into a hug and said, "Good luck today, honey. I'm really proud of you, and I know you will do great as alpha of our pack."

Luke and his parents arrived shortly before we were to go on stage for the ceremony. It wouldn't take long, but the whole pack was here, and the event would be projected on big screens so everyone could witness it. The priest of the temple would be leading the ceremony. He was already up on the stage, leading everyone in chants. It was dusk and the changeover would be performed once the full moon was visible.

"Good luck, man," Luke patted me on the back.

"You too, man," I replied.

After we heard the end of the temple choir performance, the pack event planner signaled for us to follow her up to the stage. Luke, his parents, my parents, and I all followed her. I looked up and saw that the moon had come out, a perfect night without a cloud in the sky. Once queued, the six of us walked out onto the stage. We all had meditation pillows set out for us. The priest led us all in meditation. After the meditation, he waved my father over. My father took the microphone.

"Midnight Maple Pack, the night has finally come. After years of watching my son train and grow into the man he is today, it is my pleasure to pass the title of alpha to him. I know he will proudly and magnificently lead this pack like my father before me, my grandfather before him, and my great-grandfather before him. My luna, Sienna, and I have a tremendous amount of pride today. The Moon Goddess has blessed us with a healthy and strong heir who has worked hard his entire life for this moment."

The crowd erupted in a round of applause and cheers. The priest handed my father a knife. He cut down the center of his palm and handed the knife to me. I did the same. My father spoke to the crowd. "I, James Wulfric, pass the title of alpha to my son, Blake Wulfric."

Following my father, I spoke into the microphone. "I, Blake Wulfric, accept the title of alpha from my father James Wulfric." We placed our palms together and a warm sensation spread from my father's palm to mine. We stood that way for about a minute until the sensation passed. I could feel myself becoming tethered to the pack, with a bit of everyone's energy settling inside me.

After we moved our palms from each other, the crowd erupted into cheers again. My father and I moved back to be by my mom as Luke and his father came forward. The same knife we had just used was then handed to them, and Beta Alfred sliced his hand, then handed the knife to his son. He did the same. Beta Alfred moved to the microphone and stated, "I, Alfred Hemming, pass the title of beta to my son, Lucas Hemming."

Luke moved forward toward the mic. "I, Lucas Hemming, accept the title of beta from my father, Alfred Hemming." They pressed their palms together in the same way that my father and I had. Once they separated, the crowd, once again, cheered. Luke's father went back to stand by Luke's mom while Luke stayed forward, and I went to join him.

The priest, once again, handed me the knife. I cut a slit down my other hand and handed the knife to Luke who did the same. I spoke into the microphone. "I, Blake Wulfric, elect Lucas Hemming as my beta, to be loyal to and lead the Midnight Maple Pack alongside me."

Luke followed my lead. "I, Lucas Hemming, accept Blake Wulfric's election to be loyal to and lead the Midnight Maple Pack alongside him as his beta." We touched our newly sliced palms to each other, and I could feel a physical bond being formed between us. Once the feeling passed, we separated, and the crowd cheered even more loudly than previously. I looked down to see that my palms were already healing due to the enhanced werewolf healing abilities. We went to join hands with our families, with the priest in the middle who led everyone in a chant. I could hear the crowd below chanting along with us.

After the chant, we all moved off the stage, and they brought the temple choir back out to celebrate the occasion. As I was heading to exit the stage, I noticed Jasmine pass by, and she gave me a quick smile. After we were all back off the stage, I looked at my father, and the permanent scowl he had held my whole life seemed relaxed, as if he had been relieved of a huge burden that had been weighing heavily on his shoulders. He then did something I hadn't seen him do in years—he smiled. He hugged my mom and tenderly kissed her cheek. I had to do a double take to make sure it was actually my father.

"Come, Sienna, let's go celebrate our retirement," he said, taking her arm. I stared after the two of them walking away, my mouth hanging open.

Alfred came over to pat both Luke's and my shoulders, also looking as if he'd reversed ten years in age over a matter of minutes. "I'd say good luck, but neither of you need it. You guys will both do great, I know it!" He turned to his mate. "Come on, Robin, we should go celebrate too, baby. Although, the real celebration will happen after the pack run." He winked at her.

"You guys aren't even moved out yet! At least keep it quiet!" Luke shouted at them.

Luke's sisters suddenly appeared with their mates and pups. Peyton wobbled over, her hands on her very swollen belly. "Congrats, guys!" they both said at the same time, coming over to give us each a hug. Their mates shook our hands, and all of the pups wrapped their arms around us in a group hug, bringing Luke and me closer together.

"How are you feeling, Peyton," Luke asked his sister, looking concerned.

"The baby should be here any day now. This one's definitely a lively one. I don't think there's an organ or bone within the vicinity of my stomach he hasn't kicked yet. I'm ready to push him out and put him straight into warrior training. Also, Lauren has news to share." She smiled at her younger sister.

We all looked over at her as she glowed. "I'm pregnant too! I've been dying to tell everyone, but I wanted to wait until we were sure everything was okay. But now that it's been two months, we're in the clear." I looked down where I saw just the beginnings of a round belly beginning to show.

"Wow, congrats, Lauren," Luke said, engulfing her in a big hug.

"Yeah, congrats," I said hugging her as well, feeling a wound opening within me. I wanted to shift into my wolf and run but knew I couldn't at that moment. I'd have to hold on until the pack run later that night.

We then all went out to join the crowd that was celebrating. As soon as we emerged, Luke and I found that everyone wanted to come over to congratulate us and shake our hands. We had become overnight celebrities. We must have spent an hour making small talk with just about every pack member. After a while, they all dispersed to go enjoy the fair that was set up for them. Lucy came over and ran into Luke's arms, wrapping her legs around him, forcing him into a deep kiss. Luke took her hand and led her away. I noticed Jasmine looking over at them, an intense glare on her face, her eyebrows set in a deep frown and her jaw tense.

"You know, not everyone's saving themselves for their mates," I said to her, assuming she was irritated due to her prudishness.

"Oh, I'm not bothered by that," she replied, the look instantly wiped from her face.

"You definitely looked bothered. You looked like you were about to kill someone."

"Oh, that's weird," she said, blushing. "I didn't realize I looked that way."

"Hey, come on, let's give them some privacy and check out the fair," I said reaching for her hand.

She moved her hand away, "Not in public, my parents are here. And everyone's looking at you right now!"

"Let's go somewhere private then." I smiled at the thought.

"No, I don't think it's a good idea. My parents will come looking for me. I should go back over to them," she said, turning away from me. I instantly regretted having stayed away from her all these weeks. I desperately missed her and wanted to be close to her again.

At midnight, Luke and I shifted into our wolf forms and led the pack on a pack run through the forest. Most people just stripped in a large group, nudity not being a taboo in packs. Others were more modest and shifted deeper within the woods where they wouldn't be seen. Luke and I stayed at the front of the group, in sync with each other. Everyone else followed as a large group of wolves all ran through the forest, as if on our way to battle. We led them in a loop and back to the packhouse where everyone howled, the sound echoing into the night, and shifted back into their human forms. After the group dispersed to head home, Luke and I shifted back as well.

"Well, let's get to business," Luke said to me, patting me on the back, and leading me into the packhouse.

Let's get to business, I echoed his thought in my head.

Chapter 24

Jasmine

My twentieth birthday was three days after the alpha ceremony. It was the perfect fall day—the trees in northern Vermont had turned into a palette of red, orange, and yellow, and the weather had now cooled. I had the day off from work and spent it on schoolwork. It wasn't a very exciting birthday, but I wanted to be sure I stayed ahead in school.

At four in the afternoon, while my parents were at work, I heard the doorbell chime. I descended the stairs to the first floor and looked out the window to see that Blake was waiting on the doorstep. I took a deep breath and opened the door, wondering why he was here.

"Happy birthday." He smiled, engulfing me in a hug. I patted his back, unsure of his presence and confused by how he was acting as if he hadn't ignored my existence for three weeks before he bumped into me at the gym. Four if we included the past week, especially after having been so intimate and confessing his secrets to me. I felt a pang in my heart, hurt by how he expected me to just drop everything and go along with him.

"How'd you know it was my birthday?" I asked, pulling away from him, crossing my arms, and putting distance between us.

"Lucy," he replied. "Now, come on, get dressed. I'm taking you to celebrate." I turned around to head toward my room, completely baffled by the sudden appearance of Blake. He spoke again. "On second thought, maybe you should just stay in those leggings." I looked over my shoulder to see that he had a lustful look on his face, his eyes half-closed, staring at me.

"I'll be right back," I replied, not responding to his comment. I was unsure about what to do, irritated by the situation. Maybe I should just pull out my inner Lucy and tell him I already had plans and to fuck off. As much as I was annoyed and wanted to do just that, something kept me from following through. Maybe, I thought, I should talk to him and figure out what his intentions were, and why he was sending such mixed signals. At least then I'd know where I stood with him. Were we friends? Was he only interested in spending time with me if I was putting out? Or was it something else entirely? I ran upstairs and quickly threw on a casual dress and some boots, not sure exactly where he was planning to take me, but deciding the outfit was versatile enough for most occasions. I quickly ran a brush through my hair and threw on mascara and lipstick. I went back downstairs to see him sitting on the entryway bench.

"Nice home," he said.

"Thanks," I replied. We exited the house, and I locked the door. He opened the car door for me, putting out his arm to help me in. I ignored his arm and got in without his help.

After he was settled in his seat, he turned to me with a big smile on his face and said, "I got you a little present." He handed me a small jewelry box. I took it, feeling stunned, turning it in my hand. Not only had he shown up on my birthday, but he had brought me a gift too? I glanced over at him, then opened it to find a silver bracelet with a charm that looked like a Jeep with a sapphire set in the middle. "I saw it and thought it would be perfect, especially since your birthstone matches the color of your car."

"Wow, thank you," I replied, as he helped me put it on my wrist. He squeezed my hand after he did. My breath caught and my heart beat vigorously against my chest as I looked into his eyes, again feeling confused by his intentions. There had clearly been a lot of thought put into this gift, and I didn't think it was something that you could go to the store and just find last-minute, so he must have ordered it ahead of time or, at the very least, had it overnighted from somewhere.

"I know it's kind of silly to wear a bracelet of your car. But it's something that connects us, so I wanted to get it for you. Anyway, we have somewhere to be, so let's go." He reversed out of the driveway and sped toward the downtown area. He said it so nonchalantly, but I started to wonder if maybe he was just playing it cool. This was a really thoughtful gift, and his explanation made it seem even sweeter. I turned my wrist, looking at it as the light streamed in through the window reflected off the sapphire, the sparkles within it rainbow-like.

I was puzzled when we parked across the street from the café where I worked. It was an odd choice to bring me to where I worked for my birthday, especially considering they were now long closed. Once I got out of the car, he tried to take my hand and I pulled it away.

"Not in public," I whispered loudly, horrified at the idea of people seeing us walking around holding hands. What was he thinking? He hung his head for a second but then regained his composure and led me around the building to the back where we had outdoor seating that overlooked a brook There was a whole group of people waiting there. "Surprise!" everyone shouted. Ugh, Lucy had thrown me a surprise birthday party!

We entered to greet the group, noticing there was a large spread of food and pastries. The whole back area was decorated. Lucy came over and said, "Happy birthday, best friend," as she hugged me.

After greeting everyone that had come, Blake took me aside. "Unfortunately, I can't stay tonight. But I want to celebrate with you when I have more time. Just text me when you're free again, and I'll clear my schedule for you." He kissed me on my cheek and left. I felt a longing to leave with him, suddenly feeling a deep desire to pick things back up where we had left off. I shook my head, realizing how dumb the idea was, and turned back to the party.

Lucy handed me a drink after Blake left and led me to mingle with the group. "Actually, I'll just have a water," I said, handing the drink back to her.

"Not today, PJ! It's your birthday!" Lucy put it back in my hand and grabbed my arm to bring me over to everyone. I had to admit, the drink helped me loosen up, and I was soon enjoying myself, laughing with everyone who had come.

After about an hour, Lucy yelled, "Luke, you made it!" I turned to see her pulling him in for a deep kiss. After they separated, she brought him over to greet me. For the first time in over two years, our eyes met, and an inexplicable feeling came over me. It was almost as if I had predicted this would happen, but it still shocked me—the definitiveness of it. His eyes widened as I recognized the same realization had come over him. It took everything within me to suppress the desire to say the word that was forcing itself onto my lips: *Mate*. Fuck!

I could see in my peripheral vision that Lucy was looking between us, completely unaware of what we were experiencing: a gravitational force pulling us toward each other. I suddenly wished I could mindlink in my human form, not wanting to create drama at my birthday party.

After a few moments, I was surprised that a mindlink from Luke was able to come through. *"Jasmine, please don't say anything. We need to talk about this."*

I looked at him, surprised that he was able to mindlink me not being in his wolf form.

"I can mindlink in both forms now that I'm beta of the pack."

Drawing me out of my trance, Luke finally spoke out loud. "Nice to see you, Jasmine. Happy birthday." He reached to give me a hug, spreading sparks and calm throughout my whole body. I was amazed at the feeling he caused, and he smelled so good—his divine and sensual scent much stronger now than what I had remembered. I didn't want to leave the comfort of his arms, feeling like I couldn't get close enough to him. We finally compelled ourselves to withdraw from each other.

I forced myself to speak. "Nice to see you too. Thanks for coming."

I felt like the entire world was spinning around us, everyone else at the party a blur. Luke and I stood staring at each other, realizing that Lucy had disappeared. I shook my head, forcing myself to come out of my trance. I was about to say something to Luke when I turned to see that Lucy was coming out of the café with a birthday cake topped with twenty lit candles. Everyone began singing "Happy Birthday" as Lucy placed the cake on the table closest to me.

After the song was over, Lucy said, "Now make a wish and blow out the candles!" The only thing I could think to wish for was for Luke to be mine. I blew on the candles, all of them blew out and relit again. Lucy had put trick candles on the cake. I blew again and realized it would be futile to keep trying other than just for comedic effect. The candles could not be blown out. I wondered if this was an omen. Everyone laughed, in good spirits, unaware of the feelings I was experiencing—the anxiety pulsing through my body.

Suddenly, I felt it. My chest contracted and a dizziness come over me. My canines were lengthening, and fur was sprouting from my arms and legs. I ran as fast as I could until I reached the bathroom at the back of the café. I slammed down the cover to the toilet seat and fell onto it, forcing myself to take deep breaths, bringing my thoughts to anything other than my birthday and Luke. This was not happening.

Luke

A strong desire washed over me as I watched Jasmine blowing out her birthday candles, an illicit thought entering my mind—I hoped she was wishing for me. I observed her whole body. I had always thought she was cute, but now I felt lustful watching her bent over, her lips in the shape of an O. It took everything within me not to imagine my arms around her, my hands under the skirt of her dress while she was pushed up against me. I could feel my pants becoming tight, thankful everyone's eyes were on Jasmine at the moment. I shook my head, trying to rid myself of all my dirty thoughts. I looked up to see Lucy smiling and laughing at the trick candles she had placed on Jasmine's cake. Everyone joined her in laughter, the whole party enjoying themselves.

Suddenly, I noticed that Jasmine wasn't laughing with everyone at the silly party prank. No, she looked like she was struggling. I noted that fur was sprouting along her arms and legs, and I realized what was happening—she was having a panic attack. I started to step toward her to try to comfort her when she sprinted from the party, causing shock to appear on everyone's faces.

"Is she okay?" Kyle asked, looking concerned.

"Oh no!" Lucy threw her hand over her chest, appearing distraught at the situation. "I'll be right back," she yelled to everyone, turning to go.

I stopped Lucy and said, "Hey, stay here and keep everyone entertained. I'll go check on Jasmine." She nodded, appearing thankful. Of course, she couldn't know my desire to be with Jasmine at that moment. If she did, she would never have been so trusting.

I entered the café and inhaled her intoxicating scent. It led me to the bathroom door. I knocked on it. When she didn't respond, I knocked again and said, "It's Luke. Can I please come in?" After a few moments, she finally opened the door to the bathroom and I entered, shutting the door behind me. Her scent filled the small room. I didn't think I'd ever been in a bathroom that smelled so good before. She was sitting down on the toilet, and I squatted down in front of her, taking her hands. "Are you okay?" I asked, looking into her beautiful amber eyes. Sparks darted up my arms from touching her. It was a mesmerizing feeling. I suddenly understood how strong the mate bond was. In that moment, I wanted nothing more than to pull Jasmine against me and claim her as mine.

"Yeah, sorry, that was really embarrassing. I just needed to be alone for a minute." We stayed like that, just looking into each other's eyes. Finally, Jasmine broke the silence. "So, what now?"

I knew exactly what she was asking. She wanted to know if I would break up with Lucy, her best friend and my long-term girlfriend, to be with her. It should have been an obvious answer—the Moon Goddess had fated us to each other. But I found myself paralyzed—unable to answer. While new feelings had emerged for Jasmine, I couldn't push the love and affection I felt for Lucy away.

After considering how to reply, I finally said, "I don't know." She removed her hands from mine. The sparks were replaced with a feeling of immense emptiness without her touch. I spoke again. "Can you please just give me some time? I honestly don't know what to do. I need time to think."

"Time to think?" she asked, her eyes penetrating mine. "Time to think about what?"

"About this," I replied. "About the fact that we're mates."

"What about it?"

"You have to agree that it's a lot to find out that my mate is my girlfriend's best friend."

I could see that tears were threatening to fall from her eyes. I rubbed her knees with my hands, seeing that it was having a calming effect on her as she closed her eyes. She finally opened her eyes and asked, "Are you going to tell Lucy?"

"Not yet," I replied, not knowing how I would explain what happened to her. I knew I couldn't keep this from her forever, but I needed time. This had been sprung on me so suddenly, and I had trouble deciding the right course of action.

"We can't keep this from her."

"We won't. Let's just give it some time before we throw this curveball at her. You know she's not going to take it well." I couldn't help but cringe at the thought. I could already envision the impending car crash, and knowing Lucy, it was going to be bad—five-car pileup bad.

"Okay," she replied, looking unsure, a sadness in her eyes. I felt like I could almost read all of her emotions now, being connected to her. "I need to go home. This is too much for me."

"Okay, I'll let everyone know you didn't feel well."

Frustration played across her face as she sighed. "Damn it, I don't have my car. I got a ride here. It's okay. I can just walk."

"I'll drive you home. I'll mindlink Lucy to let her know." I put my hand out to help her up. She took it and I pulled her to her feet. I put my arm around her, leading her to my car, loving the feeling of having my arm around her shoulders. I quickly mindlinked Lucy to let her know that I was taking Jasmine home because she didn't feel well, adding that she had probably drunk too much, giving an excuse for her ill feelings.

I drove through the pack toward her house, remembering vividly where she lived. When we got closer, she asked, "Do you mind dropping me off down the street? I don't want my parents to see you, and I don't want them to know about this."

"Yeah, it's fine. Look, I'm really sorry about this. If I knew you were my mate, I never would have started the relationship with Lucy."

Jasmine glared at me. "Isn't that the point though? You knew all along that you had a mate somewhere out there. But you still chose to get involved with someone else, not even considering how your mate would feel once they found you."

I felt like I had been punched in the stomach. Jasmine was right. I had been a complete idiot and now I found myself immobilized when forced to make a choice. We drove the rest of the way in silence. She didn't say anything as she exited my car and walked away down the street. I sat there baffled by the situation, unable to drive back to the party and face Lucy. As if reading my thoughts, I saw a text come through. *Hey is everything ok, baby? Everyone's heading home now. I can meet you at the packhouse.*

After reading and rereading her text, I finally replied, *I have some pack business tonight so go home and get some rest. Love you.*

A text came back almost immediately. *Ok love you too.*

Chapter 25

Jasmine

As soon as I entered my house, my parents came over to give me hugs. I told them I wasn't hungry after having eaten at my party. They still forced me to have birthday cake with them. I had to find the strength to act normal as I made strained conversation with them, wanting to be anywhere but there. This had to be the worst birthday I'd ever had.

After I was finally excused from the table, I went up into my room and shut the door, so many emotions flooding me. How did I end up in this situation? I sighed and lay back in my bed, subconsciously playing with the bracelet on my wrist. I needed to talk to someone about this, to organize all of the thoughts floating through my mind. I couldn't talk to my usual confidant, my best friend. I also couldn't talk to my parents or grandparents, not that I ever really went to them about anything. I didn't feel close enough to Emma or Madison, them being more Lucy's friends than mine. Either way, I couldn't trust they wouldn't say anything to Lucy. I knew I had to tell her, but I didn't want to without Luke's agreement to do so first. Either way, I wasn't exactly sure what I would say, imagining the awkward conversation.

Hey, you know your boyfriend? Yeah, the one you're in love with and want to be your mate? Well, funny thing about that—he's actually my mate!

This was a huge mess.

It was so ironic. For two years, I had secretly longed for Luke to be my mate. Now that he was, he didn't even want to be with me. Then, I realized something else. Maybe all that time that I had a crush on him wasn't a coincidence at all. I had felt the connection, my inner wolf pulling me toward him. I just wasn't able to confirm the reason for the feelings until now. That's why no matter what I did, I couldn't push him from my mind for all of that time. That's why his relationship with Lucy upset me. But what about him? Had he ever felt the same way I did?

I put the back of my wrist to my forehead, the charm of my new bracelet landing on me before my hand did. Realization hit me—I could talk to Blake. Okay, maybe he wasn't the best person to speak to in this situation, but I didn't have many options, and I felt I could at least trust him. He'd been a friend to me all summer, and plus he had confided in me about how he had lost his own mate. I turned to my side and picked up my cell phone.

> ***Me**: I know it's short notice but any chance you're free now? I need to talk to someone.*
> ***Blake Sexy AF**: Do you want to come to the packhouse? Happy to give you another birthday gift in my bed ;)*
> ***Me**: No, packhouse is a bad idea. Can we go somewhere more private?*
> ***Blake Sexy AF**: What about the party lake? I can have patrol avoid it tonight and we can be alone*
> ***Me**: How soon can you get there?*
> ***Blake Sexy AF**: I just have to finish up with something*

and I can be there in 20 mins
Me: *Ok see you in 20*

I changed out of my dress into jeans and a sweatshirt and threw my hair into a ponytail. I ran down the stairs, not even bothering to tell my parents that I was leaving, something I'd never dared to do before. I just didn't have the energy to come up with some convoluted story of where I was going. Anyway, I was twenty now and well past the time I should still be asking my parents' permission to do everything.

I jumped into my car and sped toward the lake at the outskirts of the pack territory. I had to park at the edge of the woods and make my way over by foot. Upon exiting the car, my night vision kicked in, allowing me to clearly see the path in the dark forest. I reached the clearing by the lake and sat down on a patch of grass, waiting for Blake to arrive. I saw that my parents were texting me asking where I went. I didn't bother responding, knowing I'd get an earful whenever I finally returned home. Moments later, I felt my dad attempting to mindlink me, and blocked the connection. He was going to be pissed, but it seemed like small guppies compared to the tiger shark I had to fry now.

Before long, Blake appeared and sat down next to me. "I know I asked you to text me when you were ready to celebrate your birthday with me, but I didn't think it would be so soon. Won't lie though, if I knew I could celebrate with me and my body, I wouldn't want to wait either."

"This is serious," I replied.

His eyes searched mine. "Tell me."

"I found my mate."

"You did? Why do you look so upset then? Where is he? And why are you with me instead of him right now?"

"My mate doesn't want me."

"I don't believe that for a second. What kind of idiot wouldn't want you?"

I choked out, "My mate is Luke."

"Luke? Like my beta, Luke?"

"Yes."

"Your mate's my best friend and beta, Luke Hemming?"

"Yes."

"Well, shit. That's a plot twist." He took a seat next to me, his shoulders slumping. "And you never realized he was your mate until today?"

I looked into his eyes, and if I didn't know better, he almost seemed sad, his brows furrowed and the corners of his eyes downturned. "He left before I turned eighteen. Now that I think back, there were signs. I just didn't realize what they meant at the time. Like, months before I turned eighteen, I thought he had gotten a new cologne. He always smelled so good! But I recently found out he doesn't even wear cologne. And the night before he left for Quebec, he touched me—"

"He touched you?"

"Not sexually. In conversation, he would touch my leg or arm, and I felt this calm feeling being emitted from his hand. I thought I was just drunk. But when he touched me today, it was the same thing but so much stronger, like sparks."

"So, what happened today? When did you figure it out?"

"When he came to my party. As soon as I looked in his eyes, I just had this feeling come over me, like we were meant to be together."

"Damn."

"Yeah, and when I asked him what now, he said he didn't know. He didn't say it, but I could tell that he didn't want to leave Lucy for me." Tears fell from my eyes, pained with the rejection from earlier.

Blake wrapped his arms around me, holding me against him, and I put my head against his chest. "Jasmine, don't cry. It will be okay," Blake whispered in my ear while he brushed his hand down the back of my head. After some time, he asked, "So, what did Luke say he was going to do?"

"He said he didn't know and asked for time to decide." I sniffled, my throat tight and lungs heavy, unable to shake the misery and helplessness. I lay against Blake's warm body, feeling safe with his huge, muscular arms wrapped around me.

After a minute or so, Blake spoke again. "I hope he doesn't take too long to decide. Otherwise, I hope you have a really strong vibrator."

"What!" I pushed away from him, seeing a smirk on his face. "Why would I need a vibrator? This is serious, and you're making your sex jokes!"

He simply replied, "Well, you're going to go into heat."

"Heat?" I looked at him, wondering what he could possibly mean.

"Wait, you didn't know that werewolves go into heat?" He looked at me with his eyes wide. "Damn, first order of business is to update the health program at the pack school. Things are so outdated around here. I can't believe your mom never told you about heat, or really anyone else for that matter."

"My mom doesn't tell me anything. We pretend sex doesn't exist in our house. Why would I go into heat?"

"After you meet your mate, you go into heat every month until your mate marks you. That means you get super horny. That's how the Moon Goddess encourages werewolves to mate." He then chuckled to himself, clearly laughing at some inside joke I wasn't privy to.

"What's so funny?"

"I'm just remembering when Ria used to go into heat. One time she was so horny that she begged me for anal sex. We never marked each other, so she used to go into heat all the time. Best sex I ever had."

I looked at him, considering this new information.

Then Blake continued, "You know, if Luke's that big of an idiot that he actually needs to think about being with you, I'm happy to offer my services. I have tons of experience sleeping with a woman in heat." He smiled at me. "Anyway, more seriously, nothing against Lucy, but if he doesn't see how amazing you are, that's really his loss. He was always the smart one but now I'm reconsidering what I thought of him. Someone would have to be a complete moron to reject you."

I considered what Blake said, not sure if I agreed with him. After all, Lucy looked like a supermodel. And while she could be a bit flighty, she was a very loyal friend and great at making someone feel loved. After thinking for a bit, I asked, "When will I go into heat?"

"I'm pretty sure it coincides with when you ovulate. When was your last period?"

"How do you know so much?"

"Well, besides the fact that my mom's a doctor, my mate used to go into heat every month, so now I have very intimate knowledge of it."

"Oh. My last period was about a week ago."

"If I had to make an educated guess, you should be going into heat in about a week."

"Oh."

He put his hands on my shoulders, giving me a stern look as he stared into my eyes, "Make sure you stay away from all unmated males when you're in heat."

"Wait, why?"

"They can sense it and it's really hard to resist the desire they will have for you."

"What about my parents?" I asked, panicked. "Will they sense it? What about my dad?!" I was practically gagging at the thought.

Blake softly chuckled and replied, "Don't worry about that. Parents can't sense their daughter's heat, and they're mated and marked anyway, so they can't sense it in anyone else either. It's only the unmated ones you have to worry about, and really only the males in most cases."

"Thank the Goddess." I gave a relieved sigh, relaxing back against Blake's body as he brushed his fingers through my hair.

"If you really wanted to seduce Luke, that would be the time to do it. I can guarantee you he won't be able to keep it in his pants if he's around you."

"I don't want to seduce him. I want him to *want* to be with me, and not because I took advantage of him!"

"Technically it would be the Moon Goddess that's taking advantage of him since that's how this whole thing works. She gives you a mate and encourages you to be with them. Part of that tactic is putting you into heat so that the two of you mate with each other. But, anyway, if you don't want to encourage any type of mating, definitely stay away from all unmated males."

He tightened his grip on my arm and continued, "If any man as much as touches you without your permission, you let me know." I turned my head so I was facing him, and he had the look of someone I would never want to cross, his eyes taking on a devil-like appearance. "The punishment for mating by force in our pack is death, and I will not hesitate to kill anyone that does." The way he said it made me shiver. It was evident that he didn't mean metaphorically.

I put my hand to my forehead, feeling overwhelmed by all this new information, tears flooding back to my eyes. Noticing my reaction, Blake pulled me tightly against him, holding me against his chest. "Hey, it's going to be okay. It will all work out," he whispered against my ear. "I promise." My tears dropped freely, soaking his shirt.

I lay against him as he rubbed my back, comforted by the feeling of being against his body. And then a thought came to me—why couldn't Blake have been my mate?

Chapter 26

Jasmine

The next day was Saturday, and I was scheduled for the late shift at the café. Checking the schedule and seeing that I was supposed to work with Lucy for several hours, unable to face her, I texted Valerie to tell her I was sick. I knew she'd be very concerned for a couple of reasons. For one, when adult werewolves got sick, they got really sick. There was no such thing as a small cold, since our wolf was capable of healing us. Only young werewolves who had yet to shift were capable of getting colds. In summary, she would likely assume that I had to be hospitalized. Second, I never called out from work, so she would definitely think I was hospitalized. But I couldn't even bring myself to care enough to make a believable excuse.

Of course, next thing I knew, I had a frantic text from Lucy that said, *OMG! ARE YOU OK! YOU'RE SICK????*

Okay, maybe I shouldn't have made such a dramatic excuse. I replied, *Too much birthday drinking haha. Late night.* It was still pretty dumb, but werewolves could get hangovers if we drank enough, so it was a semi-believable excuse. It wasn't really believable that I, personally, would call out due to a hangover, but it wasn't completely outside the realm of possibilities.

She replied with, *Nice! I guess someone had an after party last night. Hope it was with Mr. Hot Alpha!* If only she knew. At least she would relay the information to Valerie so she wouldn't worry too much about me.

I went downstairs to face my parents, who were home from work that day. I found them sitting on the couch, anger on both their faces as soon as they saw me descending the stairs. My mom was the first one to stand. "Do you have any idea how worried we were last night, you leaving and staying out so late without saying anything to us? And you wouldn't even answer your phone."

My dad spoke next. "This is absolutely unacceptable behavior. What has gotten into you?"

My mom chimed in, "Is this Lucy's doing? That girl is no good. I wish you would find some more suitable friends. She's not a good influence on you."

My dad asked, "Where were you?"

I couldn't meet his eyes.

"Answer me!" he yelled.

"I was getting drunk at the party lake." Okay, so my answer was half true. But drinking would be far less bad than what I was actually doing in my parents' eyes. My mom audibly gasped.

"I thought they patrolled that lake these days." My dad narrowed his eyes at me.

"Well, there's a new alpha in town!"

"I don't want you going anywhere near that lake anymore. I'm going to submit an official complaint. That's just asking for a security breach. The whole pack should be being patrolled at night. What else do we pay pack fees for?" My dad looked irritated.

"I am very disappointed in you right now. This is not how we raised you to behave." My mom slapped me across the face. I was completely shocked. My mom had never raised her hand to me before. "Next time, the claws come out," she warned and turned away to leave the room.

In order to get out of the house, I decided to go to the gym. I needed to do something with all of the anxious energy within me. Hitting something would help. And that was exactly what I did. I spent at least fifteen minutes pounding my fists into a punching bag. Suddenly, I saw from the corner of my eye that someone stationed themselves next to me. I turned my head to see that Blake was doing the same thing I had just been doing. When he saw me looking, he turned to face me, a smile on his face.

"I can't lie, seeing you beat the shit out of that bag was really fucking hot. Now you've got me all worked up."

"Don't you have your own gym?"

"This one has hotter women. Do you want to spar with me?"

I agreed and he led me outside to the sparring field. We spent the afternoon working on our fighting techniques. He shifted into his wolf form, and I stayed in my human form as I practiced my kicks while he attacked me.

He mindlinked me, *"Damn you kick like a badass. I need you as one of my warriors."* We switched, and I did the same thing, attacking him in my wolf form while he kicked me. I practiced how I fell as a wolf after being kicked, so I could recover quickly and get back into the fight immediately. Once we'd had enough, I went back behind one of the partitions that were set up to switch back into my human form and put my gym clothes back on.

After we were dressed, I walked back over to him. "I need to ask you for a big favor."

"I'm good at favors, especially the sexual kind." He winked at me. I hesitated, then he spoke again, more seriously. "What is it? I won't judge. Although I'm hoping it is a sexual favor."

"Goddess, it's so embarrassing," I trailed, wondering whether I could ask Blake for this.

"Hey, Jasmine, whatever it is, you can tell me. I won't think any less of you. I promise." He spoke softly, touching my arm in a friendly gesture. The way he said it made me believe he was being sincere and gave me the courage to proceed.

"Can you please order me a vibrator and have it shipped to you?" I said very quietly, practically whispering. I could sense my whole body overheating with embarrassment. What was I thinking asking Blake for this?

"Are you serious?" He studied my face, his piercing blue eyes penetrating me.

Responding frantically, I blurted out, "I have cash. I'll pay you back for it plus extra for the trouble. I don't have my own credit card, and my Amazon Prime account's connected to my parents,' so they will see anything I order. And I definitely can't have it shipped to the house in case my parents get to it before I do. I don't know who else to ask."

"Couldn't you have just gone to a sex shop?"

"I can't go into a sex shop!"

"Goddess, you really are sheltered. Yes, I can do this favor," he replied, suddenly smirking. "But I want a detailed play-by-play of you using it in return. I'd also accept being able to watch." I widened my eyes in shock at what he was asking. "I'm kidding! You should have seen your face. I'll get it for you without anything expected in return."

"And make sure it's quiet."

He shook his head. "Luke's a fucking idiot."

"Thank you for being so understanding and nonjudgmental," I said.

"Hey, it's no problem. Friends?" He wrapped his arms around me. I put my head against his chest, which was currently soaked in sweat. I didn't even care. I just liked the feeling of being close to him, a warmth from him I couldn't explain.

After I went home, I couldn't help but want to press Luke some more, hoping he wouldn't leave me in this awkward limbo I was currently in. Maybe he could at least give me a timeline for how long he would take to make his final decision. As much as this was torture, a part of me hoped he wouldn't decide too soon. I wasn't ready to be rejected outright by him. I knew deep within me that it would tear me apart.

After hesitating for several minutes, I finally texted him.

> ***Me***: Hey, Luke, any chance we can meet and talk today?
> ***Luke***: Yes, we should talk. Come to the packhouse after five. We'll be the only ones here
> ***Me:*** Ok, see you then

Chapter 27

Jasmine

At five that evening, I told my parents that Madison had invited me over for dinner. My mom rolled her eyes but didn't stop me as I left the house. I drove over to the packhouse and noted Luke's silver Toyota 4Runner was the only car parked in the packhouse lot when I arrived. I took a few deep breaths, feeling a tightness in my chest as I approached the front door, not knowing what to expect. My hand was practically shaking as I rang the doorbell, but I did my best to hold myself together.

Moments later Luke let me in, welcoming me with his enchanting scent. I inhaled deeply, having almost forgotten how amazing he smelled. My stomach fluttered, and I couldn't help but smile widely, taking in his handsome face. He smiled back at me, showing off his perfect white teeth. He pulled me into a hug to greet me as sparks danced across my entire body, putting me instantly at ease. When he pulled away, he asked, "Can I give you a tour?"

"It's okay, I already had one," I replied.

"From whom?" He looked surprised, his eyebrows raised.

"Blake."

"Blake brought you here before?"

"I came over a couple months ago, and he showed me around."

"I didn't know you guys hung out."

"We're just friends."

"That's news to me." Although he said this with a poker face, I could sense he seemed irritated. I found myself exceptionally perceptive to his emotions, as if they were being emitted from his body. "Well, how about we go sit down in the living room." I followed him over to the couch, where he gestured for me to sit. "Can I get you a drink? I'm going to make one for myself. I think it will make the conversation easier."

"Okay," I replied, agreeing that alcohol was a good idea in this situation. I could sense his nervousness and it was intensifying my anxiety. Yes, alcohol was a necessity tonight.

"Is red wine okay? I'll open a bottle." He rubbed his neck, shifting a bit on his feet. Yes, he was definitely nervous.

"Sure, red wine would be great." He nodded and walked out of the room. Moments later, he reemerged, balancing a bottle of red wine, a wine opener, and two wine glasses. He pulled out a couple of coasters and placed the wine glasses on top of them. He proceeded to open the bottle of wine and pour a generous glass for each of us.

Once he placed the bottle down on the coffee table, he sat down next to me and took a sip. I followed his lead and did the same. He turned to me and sighed. I stared at him, wondering if I should say something. Finally, he spoke.

"Goddess, you smell amazing. I can barely even concentrate on what I want to say with how good you smell."

"Thanks, you smell good as well," I replied, delighted with the compliment from him. Maybe things between us would work out. I felt myself relax a little, taking another sip.

"It must be the mate bond." He smiled. He then put his hand on my knee, setting off sparks, a gentle pulsing shooting up my leg, rousing me. "Touching you also feels amazing. I bet kissing you would too."

I swallowed, wondering if he would kiss me. Being in such close proximity to him, there was nothing I wanted more. It was like a gravitational pull toward him. It took everything in me not to lift his shirt and rub my hands all over his well-sculpted chest, which I was presently vividly recalling in graphic detail from two years earlier. The image conjured all sorts of feelings within me. If I had believed my thoughts at the time were inappropriate, they were nothing compared to the ones coming to me now. All I knew was, if Luke had been trying to remove my bikini bottoms, there was no way I would have stopped him with how intense the throbbing between my legs was at that moment. It caused me to shift in my seat, the friction at the crotch of my pants practically inducing me to moan with how sensitive that area was. I shook my head, forcing myself to sit still, trying to remove the thoughts from my mind.

I took another sip from my wine glass, now distracted by the fact that I could sense Luke's similar arousal, realizing it was likely the same for him with me. We were so close together, I could hear every breath he took and feel the heat of his body.

The sexual tension between us was so thick that you could cut through it with a knife. I could sense we were both resisting what we wanted, the mate bond pushing us toward each other. As the glasses emptied, Luke refilled both of them with another generous pour.

Shaking my head again and forcing my mind out of the gutter, I spoke, breaking the silence. "How long do you need to decide what you're going to do?"

He closed his eyes and sighed. "I don't know. I know that's not what you want to hear, but I've been with Lucy for four years now. I can't just throw away a four-year relationship so easily. I feel all these amazing things when I'm with you, but I barely know you."

His words broke the spell I was under. Tears built up in my eyes, my emotions heightened by his presence, and his rejection hurt far more than it probably should have. Clearly noticing my devastation, he rubbed my knee to show me he didn't mean to hurt me with his words. His touch calmed me, the sparks emitted from his palms having a soothing effect. "I just don't want to make a hasty decision just because something feels good. That wouldn't be fair to Lucy."

I took a deep breath, trying to understand where he was coming from, struggling to ignore the sting in my chest. Lucy was my best friend, and I knew she loved—nay—was obsessed with Luke, so I knew I should feel more guilt, much how Luke was feeling torn right now. But I couldn't help how heartbroken I was that he didn't return my feelings and didn't want to honor the mate bond.

Luke continued, "I know the Moon Goddess wants us to be together and fated mate bonds are the strongest of all bonds. But they're not always perfect. You probably don't know this, but Alpha James cheated on Luna Sienna for years even though they were fated mates. The bond kept them together all these years, but at what cost?"

"What does their relationship have to do with us?" I asked, trying so hard not to feel wrecked by the conversation we were having, doing my best to speak evenly with the acute scratching at my throat and heaviness in my chest.

He sighed heavily and replied, "I just want you to understand why this is so hard for me. I can't help but wonder if I break up with Lucy for us to be together if it will be enough. Will I be able to just walk away completely and never look back? You deserve someone who's able to give you all of them. I'm just afraid that my feelings for Lucy will always hold me back from being able to do that." He closed his eyes and put his head in his hands.

The back of my throat prickled at his words. I took deep breaths, trying to rid myself of the agonizing feeling that was building within me. Finally, I responded, "But we all only get one fated mate and that's it. If you reject me, there won't be anyone else for me. I'll have to hope that I can find a chosen mate. And that's not even taking into consideration that rejecting your mate's an insult to the Moon Goddess. You know how religious my family is. My parents will disown me." I couldn't hold back my tears anymore as they fell down my cheeks, the reality of the situation hitting me. What was I going to do? Luke was my one mate that I had been planning to save myself for completely, and he didn't even want me.

Luke looked up and at the sight of my tears, he used his thumb to wipe them away. "Please don't cry, Jasmine. We don't have to decide anything tonight. We have plenty of time. But this is what I mean. I don't want to make a rash decision like rejecting you tonight instead of giving us a fair chance. Can you at least give me the opportunity to get to know you better?"

I nodded, grabbing a nearby napkin to wipe away my own tears, feeling so embarrassed by what a slobbering mess I was being. He rubbed my arm, the feeling cheering me up. That's all he had to do—just touch me, and suddenly my tears began to dry. He had clearly figured it out, because that's what he kept doing every time I showed signs of emotion.

Luke then poured the remainder of wine into our glasses and stood up. "I'll be right back. I'm going to get another bottle." He took the empty bottle with him to dispose of it and returned with a fresh one. He topped both of us off and put the bottle down, immediately grabbing for his wine glass. We both took more sips of our wine.

He broke the silence again, "So, let's get to know each other." He gave me a small smile. "What have you been up to for the past two years?"

"Nothing too exciting. I'm taking college classes full-time now, living with my parents still."

"Why didn't you go away for college?"

"I didn't like the idea of living with humans. Plus, there's the whole problem with my—" I couldn't say it, ashamed of my biggest weakness, the thing I used to get teased about when I was younger.

"Panic attacks," he finished for me, being well aware of them, having known me in high school.

"Yeah, it would be too risky." He took my hands in his, rubbing his thumbs against my palms, instantly sending sparks and calm through my body. "What about you? What have you been up to?"

"Well, you know I've been up in Quebec, doing investigative work. Now that I'm back, I enrolled in a couple college courses at the local community college. I figured I could knock out my degree slowly, especially since there's no rush to complete it."

"How was it being away for two years?" I asked.

"It was pretty fun actually," he smiled. "The guys I was with were all my age and unmated, so we'd go out and party a lot. Kind of like a college experience, I guess. When you ignore the fact that you're putting your life in danger every day, of course." He chuckled.

"Was your life really in danger?"

"Sometimes. We definitely had some close calls. But you shouldn't worry too much about that. It's just part of the job."

I nodded.

"So, changing subjects, you're an only child, right? No siblings?"

"Nope, no siblings. You have two sisters, right?"

"Yes, I have two much older sisters. One is thirty-six and the other is thirty-four. They're both mated with pups. My oldest one, Peyton, actually just gave birth to a little baby boy a couple of days ago. And we just found out my other sister, Lauren, is having another baby. So I'm going to have six nieces and nephews all together soon! They're a rowdy bunch! Especially my oldest nephew, Noah. He's a riot."

"Wow, so you must have been a surprise being so much younger."

"Oh yeah! My parents tried for years to make a beta heir and had practically given up until I popped out. My dad was about ready to hand the title over to one of his brother's pups."

"It must be nice having such a big family," I said wistfully. I'd always envied Lucy and her huge family and how fun and chaotic it seemed being a part of it, especially in comparison to my stringent and quiet parents. My dad was also an only child, and I barely knew my cousins who lived in Alaska.

"Maybe one day you can meet them. My sisters are really nice, and my brothers-in-law are actually pretty funny. We usually laugh while they bounce jokes off each other. They definitely keep us entertained."

We took more sips of our wine and Luke topped up our glasses some more. He spoke again. "Look, Jasmine, I know I made a huge mistake four years ago. I should never have started such a serious relationship. To be fair, at the time I didn't think it would ever get this serious. For years we told ourselves that we would just break up with each other if we were mated to others."

"That's not true! At least not for Lucy. All I ever heard from her was how much she loves you and how you're meant to be together and that you're going to be chosen mates."

He shook his head. I could sense a feeling of deep regret. "Lucy's very resolute. When she puts her mind to something, she won't stop until she gets it. Once I found out we weren't mates, I tried to encourage her to consider us ending things, but she wouldn't hear of it. I eventually gave in. I was in too deep to fight it anyway. It's hard to justify ending something tangible for something theoretical."

I sipped my wine in understanding. Lucy could be really pigheaded. Arguing logic with her was useless. She always found justification for what she wanted, oblivious to the harm she caused. I wondered how she would react once she knew her best friend was mated to her boyfriend. While Lucy had always been a very good friend to me, I knew deep inside that she would never give Luke up. That was where she drew the line, even to the detriment of our friendship. Luke poured the remainder of the second bottle and went to grab a third. After opening it, he, once again, gave us both generous pours. We both sipped some more. I felt the buzz from all the wine hit me and put my glass down.

As I sat back on the couch, Luke followed. He then put his arm around my shoulder, pulling me closer to him. I snuggled up against him, feeling comfortable against his warm and muscular body now after so many glasses of wine. I inhaled his scent and enjoyed the feeling that came over me from being so close to him. My whole body was aroused, my thighs tingling, spreading a warmth throughout my entire lower half. A familiar feeling of fluttering in my stomach emerged, and I had an impulse come over me that Luke's body should be against mine, filling me. A graphic thought emerged: an image of his hands grabbing my hips and pulling me against him, pushing himself inside me.

My legs tensed. I could sense that his thoughts were in sync with mine—his chest rose and fell slowly from his deep breathing. We sat there for an indeterminate amount of time, just listening to the other breathe, incapable of separating ourselves from each other. We were so close right now—it wouldn't be much effort to give in to exactly what we both desperately wanted at that moment. But we continued to deny ourselves, acting out the fantasy in our minds rather than in reality, both too nervous to make the first move.

We finally finished the third bottle, and I noticed it was getting late. A text appeared on my phone from my mom asking when I'd be home. I replied, barely able to see straight enough to type. *Soon. Just finishing up dessert. Banana cream pie.* Holy fucking Artemis, I was even turning texts to my parents into sexual innuendos. I turned to Luke and said, "I should go home," getting up and wobbling.

He got up to stop me, grabbing me by the hip. My cheeks reddened as I realized he had just reenacted what I had been imagining moments earlier, but much differently of course. Luke quickly removed his hand, and I noted his cheeks were red too. He blinked and said, "You're too drunk to drive home. To be honest, I'm not in much better shape. Let's wait for Blake to get home and he can drive you."

"I have to go home. My mom slapped me earlier today."

"She slapped you? Why did she do that?" He pulled me back down onto the couch and looked at me inquisitively.

"Because I was out really late last night."

"You were? You went out after I dropped you at home yesterday?"

"Yes, I was upset, and I had to get out. It was the only time I didn't tell my parents where I went, and they were pissed."

"Wow, but you're an adult now."

"I know, but they think I'm still a kid."

"I'll mindlink Blake and see when he'll be home." His eyes turned up toward the ceiling. After a few moments he brought his eyes back to mine and asked, "Can you wait twenty minutes? I'll make you something to eat for now to sober up."

"Okay," I agreed. He took my hand and pulled me toward the kitchen. He sat me down at the table and heated the skillet, putting slices of bacon into it. "You also like peanut butter, banana, and bacon sandwiches, right?"

My eyes lit up at him remembering that fact from so long ago. He made us both sandwiches and sat down with me at the table, giving me a coy smile. I returned the smile, feeling like we shared a special connection through our mutual love of a weird sandwich.

As we were finishing up, Blake walked into the kitchen. "Hey." He waved to both of us. I suddenly felt very awkward with both of my love interests in the same room as me. Luke nodded at Blake and cleared the table, placing our plates into the sink.

Luke helped me up to gather my purse and walked me outside to my car, holding me close with his hand on my lower back. I could sense this was intentional to stake his claim on me in front of Blake. He opened the passenger door to my car and helped me into my seat. Before I could close the door, he took my hands in his. He rubbed his thumbs against my palms and looked into my eyes, the soothing feeling radiating up my arms. It seemed like he was hesitating to let me go, finally saying, "I'd drive you home myself, but I'm in no position to right now. But it was really nice to spend some time with you, Jasmine. I'd like to see you again soon." He kissed me on the cheek but didn't move away.

"I'd like to see you again soon too," I replied, wondering if this meant he really did want to get to know me and consider honoring our mate bond. I felt a hopeful swelling in my chest.

We stared at each other for a few moments, and he finally touched my shoulder and said, "Good night, Jasmine." Then he closed my door gently. I watched as he walked back into the packhouse.

Blake climbed into the driver's seat. I looked over at him, watching his eyes scan my body. "Damn, you smell like a bar. How much booze did Luke give you?" he questioned as he started the car.

"We shared three bottles of wine."

"It's like he was trying to get you as drunk as possible so he could get in your pants."

"I don't think so," I groaned.

"You sound like you were hoping he'd get in your pants."

"Mm," I responded noncommittally.

He pulled out of the packhouse lot and drove down the dark and quiet streets. "Are you sure you want to go home in that state? You're really drunk right now and there's no question that your parents will be able to smell it on you."

"Oh Goddess, my mom is going to claw me," I moaned.

"Claw you?"

"She slapped me this morning because I told her I drank at the party lake last night. And she told me she'd use her claws next time. I am so screwed."

He burst out laughing. "You know, I did get an official complaint today that the lake wasn't being properly patrolled."

I groaned again.

"Maybe we should make a pit stop to check on the patrolling. It will give you a chance to sober up." He turned and drove toward the lake instead. Once parked, he helped me out of my car and walked me to the same place we were last night.

After we sat down, I pulled out my phone. "I should text my mom to tell her I'll be home later than expected." Thinking quickly, I wrote, *Madison's family pulled out a game of Monopoly. Going to join.*

Peering over my shoulder, Blake asked, "Monopoly? Seriously?" He started laughing again.

"It's a nice, wholesome game," I replied. Then added, "And it takes a long time to play."

"It's more wholesome than the games I want to play with you, I'll give you that. So how was your evening with Luke?"

I groaned in frustration again. "This whole thing really sucks. It's not fair."

He put his arm around me. While I did not feel the same sparks and calm from Blake, I did note that I fit much better with him, as if his body were molded for me. I snuggled against him, enjoying how close I felt to him.

He sighed. "Life's rarely fair."

"Thanks for being my friend," I said. He kissed me on my head in response, eliciting a warm and comforting feeling inside me.

"By the way, I stopped by the sex shop today and got you what you asked for."

"Oh Goddess. I can't believe I'm actually going to use it!" I cried out.

"To be honest, I'm surprised you don't already own one. But maybe I shouldn't be." He smirked at me.

"I've never even—" I stopped, not able to say the word, feeling a flush spread across my cheeks.

"Masturbated?" he finished for me. He then pulled me up off him and looked deeply into my eyes. "Are you fucking serious?" I nodded.

"Can you show me how?" I asked, liquid courage pulsing through my veins, the thought of it suddenly seeming like a great idea. I touched his bicep, a la Lucy, trying to look seductive as I did it.

He groaned loudly, in a tone that made it clear he was severely frustrated. "There's nothing I'd like to do more than to show you, but you're not even close to sober right now. This is crossing into really unethical territory. If you still want me to show you tomorrow when you're sober, I will show you several times over."

"Do you think Luke would show me?"

"Why don't you ask him and find out? I can't say I won't be bitter with jealousy if you do, but I have a feeling it would take a massive, ungodly amount of willpower to say no to that proposition."

"Is it true your dad cheated on your mom all the time?"

"Did Luke tell you that?" He narrowed his eyes at me. I nodded. "Yes, it's true."

"Oh."

"My father's not a good person. Why did that subject come up anyway?"

"Luke said that a mate bond doesn't guarantee a good relationship, so he wanted to be sure before he made any decision."

"Luke's right. Not every mate bond's a good one, especially when one or both of the people in the bond is a bad person. Having a mate doesn't change who you are. But that was a dumb comparison because neither you nor Luke is a bad person. In fact, you're both some of the best people I know. Both your hearts are in the right place. I know Luke's being frustrating right now, but I also know it's because he doesn't want to hurt either you or Lucy. At some point, someone's going to have to get hurt, and he's going to have to decide who it will be."

I snuggled against Blake, the position feeling so natural with how well our bodies melded together. He wrapped his muscular arms back around me.

After some time, he took me back to the car and drove me home. "How are you going to get home?" I asked.

"I'll just shift and run home. I brought a bag to put all of my clothes in and carry home in my mouth." He pulled into the driveway. I was relieved to see that all of the lights in the house were out, meaning my parents had already gone to sleep and not waited up for me. He parked the car and slipped out. I looked at his empty seat and noticed that a shopping bag was left behind.

Chapter 28

Jasmine

On Monday, after temple, I was once again working the late shift at the café. Reena had opened, so she left as soon as I walked in at ten o'clock. Just Valerie and I were working together, which was a relief. After everything that happened this past weekend, I was not ready to face Lucy yet.

"So, major hangover on Saturday?" Valerie eyed me suspiciously when I walked in.

"Yeah, major. I was out all night celebrating my birthday on Friday night."

"If you were Lucy, I'd maybe believe you. But even Lucy's never called out hungover before."

"There's a first time for everything!" I shrugged.

"Hmm, ok. I'm going to pretend to believe you since you've never called out before and you're one of my best employees. But don't let it happen again."

After doing some cleaning, I pulled out my textbook to get some reading in before the lunch rush. But I found that I had trouble concentrating, rereading the same words over and over again. After a while, I closed my textbook, giving up.

Valerie walked by. "Hmm, it's not often I see you close your textbook when it's dead in here."

"Mm," I replied, not knowing what else to say.

"A lot on your mind? You seem really spacey today."

"You could say that," I replied.

"Well, come on, spit it out. I'm dying to know what kept you from coming to work on Saturday. Did you finally get a life?"

I looked at her crossly. "Hey, that's not very nice!"

She laughed. "I'm only saying. You've spent too much time living your parents' life, and it's about time you live your own. So, I'm going to use my imagination until you tell me what's really happening. And the alpha's one fine man, so I have some very vivid images of him in my imagination right now—of what you did with him all day Saturday." She grinned.

"Do I even want to know?"

"Oh, trust me, you do. I'm imagining some intense porn in my head right now. Some of it may possibly be illegal in this country." She laughed.

"I definitely don't want to know. Anyway, the alpha and I have decided to just be friends."

"Why would you do something crazy like that?"

I groaned.

She continued, "I'd be groaning too if I were friend-zoned by him."

"It's not that—"

"Well, what is it?"

"If I tell you something, can you please not tell anyone, especially not Lucy?"

"Now I'm really dying to know. And yes, I can keep a secret. My lips are sealed." She made a gesture of zipping her mouth.

I hesitated, not sure if I should confide in Valerie. But she had never given me a reason to distrust her, having been almost a second mother to me during the time I'd worked in the café. She crossed her arms and tapped her foot in a waiting gesture. I finally replied, "I met my mate."

"What! Why would you keep that a secret?"

"My mate is Luke."

"Like Lucy's boyfriend, Luke?" Her eyes were wide open with shock.

"Yes. Lucy's boyfriend, Luke."

"Well, damn, this story's more interesting than I imagined." Just then, a group of customers walked in, forcing us to end the conversation. I went to take their orders. We had a steady stream of customers for the rest of the day, many who sat in the café, so Valerie didn't ask for any more information until I flipped the sign to Closed.

I went to begin the closing checklist when she approached me. "I can't lie, I may have imagined a threesome with the alpha and the beta. Please tell me that's what happened on Saturday."

"That's absolutely not what happened on Saturday," I replied.

"So disappointing." She shook her head then continued, "So what's the deal? I know Luke didn't break up with Lucy because I definitely would have heard about it by now."

"No, he didn't." I looked down at the floor.

"He can't seriously be considering rejecting you and staying with Lucy?" she asked, her face concerned.

"I don't know. I guess that's exactly what he's doing," I replied, feeling defeated.

"What an asshole!"

"I mean, Lucy had him first, right? They've been together for years."

"But Lucy has no right to him. He's your mate. I can't even believe he's able to consider it, to be honest. As soon as I met my mate, it was like every other man I'd ever been with was wiped from my mind. I guess things with him and Lucy must have been much more serious than any of us thought."

"I guess so," I replied.

The next day, I arrived at the temple an hour before choir practice in the afternoon. I figured that since this was Artemis's doing, that maybe someone at her house of worship would have some answers. At this point, I was grasping at straws, hoping someone had something enlightening to offer me and a way out of this mess.

I went to the priest's office and knocked on his door. He waved me in. He was a nice older man named Bernard, and my family all knew him well, being regulars at the temple. He gestured for me to take a seat in front of his desk while he sat back in his office chair.

"It's always nice to see you, Jasmine. What brings you in today?" he asked.

"If I tell you something, is there any chance you would tell my parents?" I questioned him.

"Absolutely not. I take my vows very seriously, and you can tell me anything. I would never repeat anything that's told to me in confidence." I sighed in relief. He continued, "Is everything okay?"

"No, it's not," I replied, fidgeting with my hands, not able to make eye contact.

"Please, let me know what's happening so I can try to help."

"I met my mate."

"That's wonderful news. Why would that possibly be bothering you?" This reaction was becoming irritating. Was meeting one's mate the best thing that happened to everyone except me?

"My mate's with someone else."

"Oh, of course. Now I understand!" He appeared as if he found the answer to a very difficult question he'd been pondering.

"You do?" I asked, leaning forward in my chair.

"Yes, this is very common. Many people have concerns that their mates haven't been chaste when they themselves have. I am not surprised that you would have the same concern. After all, you are such a pure and devout young woman. Unfortunately, not everyone takes their worship of Artemis and their dedication to their mate as seriously as you do. But this is very common, very common indeed."

I looked at him in shock at what he was assuming my problem was.

"Anyway, Jasmine, you shouldn't worry. Artemis does not make mistakes and there is a reason she mated you with whom she did, and the mate bond allows us to overlook someone's past transgressions. In no time, it will all be in the past and you will be happily mated."

I stared at him for some time, in shock at his response. I finally snapped out of it and said, "But that's not why I came here."

"It's not?" He looked surprised.

"No, the problem is my mate doesn't want to be with me. He wants to be with the person he was with before he realized I am his mate."

Bernard looked at me sadly. "Unfortunately, this does happen sometimes, that someone chooses to take a chosen mate in place of a fated one. It's not common, but I've seen it during my many years as a priest. Of course, you know the temple's beliefs on this—that it is forbidden. We will not marry anyone who rejects the mate they are gifted by the Moon Goddess. It is an insult to our deity, and it is believed she curses anyone that does so, so it is also highly discouraged."

"But what if I'm not the one who rejects my mate, but it's my mate who rejects me?"

He shook his head sadly. "It takes two to reject. One must initiate the rejection and the other must accept. Without both steps taking places, the rejection does not take effect. You cannot simply blame a rejection on the other person."

"Does that mean I'll never be able to get married?"

"You can still be married, but not in the temple. You can obtain a legal marriage the same way humans do."

I felt sick at the reality of the situation. After considering what Bernard told me, I asked, "But why does the Moon Goddess choose the mates she does for us?"

"Well, we can't know how her mind works, but there are theories. It has been observed that, through the mate bond, one mate will enhance the other, so one popular theory is that she finds us someone who improves certain aspects of ourselves that are necessary. For example, often alphas are mated to strong women that will consequently strengthen the pack as their luna. Another theory is that our mate is a soulmate—someone that is our other half, someone we are spiritually connected to. This is a popular belief for those who believe in reincarnation."

"I see," I replied, wondering if either of those theories were true.

"If you don't mind me asking, who is your mate?"

I hesitated and then decided to answer his question after some thought. "It's Beta Luke."

He caressed his beard. "Well, isn't that something? Yes, I do recall he had a girlfriend. And, if I'm not mistaken, his girlfriend is your friend?"

"Yes, that's correct." I felt defeated. "It just doesn't make sense. I always did everything right. I listened to my parents, did well in school, came to every temple service. Why did I get stuck with a mate who wants someone else? And why does that person have to be my best friend?" I could feel a pain in my chest at how unfair the situation was, a scratch at the back of my throat. I sniffed back the early stages of tears, trying to stay strong, not sure if I could.

He appeared lost in thought, considering my question. After some time, he finally replied, "The Moon Goddess works in mysterious ways. I've been a priest for almost fifty years now, so I've witnessed many different people's stories. Sometimes things happened that didn't make sense at the time, but would eventually work out better than imagined. I have faith that things will work out for you as well."

I shook my head, not seeing how this was going to work out well. I finally resigned myself to the fact that nothing was going to be answered today, thanked him for his time, and made my way to choir practice, a scratching, awful pain in my throat as I sang that day.

I'd be lying if I said I wasn't completely crushed. I had spent my entire life devoted to Artemis and faithfully awaiting the day she would gift me my mate. Now that it finally happened, I had to accept the painful truth that my mate was contemplating rejecting me, and I might not be allowed to get married in the temple I grew up attending. I knew I couldn't force Luke to be with me. That left me with no choice but to wait for him to finally make his decision, bringing an uncomfortable sickness to my stomach. Normally when I wanted something, I just had to find a way to accomplish my goal. With school, all I had to do was study harder. With strength training, all I had to do was lift heavier. But what do you do when someone doesn't return your feelings?

Chapter 29

Blake

Luke and I were in the packhouse office one morning, meeting with the pack accountant and office manager, when, suddenly, Luke and I received a mindlink from Mike, one of the high-ranking warriors on patrol.

"Alpha, Beta, we found the scents of a stranger pack in the northern border. Could be a sign of casing since it's not the scent of any neighboring packs."

I mindlinked Mike and Luke, *"Thank you, Mike, we'll be by your patrol station in an hour so we can discuss in more detail."* Being able to mindlink in human form was one surprisingly useful perk of being an alpha.

"Ok, Alpha," he replied.

Luke looked at me. "Well, that sucks."

"Yes, yes it does," I replied.

We spent the next hour continuing our conversation about fund allocation. The accountant and office manager were both competent, having survived my father who would never have put up with anything less than, so the conversation didn't take any longer than that. As soon as we were done, Luke and I headed outside and drove over to Mike's patrol station.

When we arrived, Mike bared his neck in submission. "Good morning, Alpha, Beta."

"Good morning, Mike," I replied. "So, what exactly happened?"

"The northern border morning patrol took our positions and we sent two of our juniors to walk fifty yards out from the border, as per patrol guidelines, and they noticed an unfamiliar scent. I, personally, went out to smell for myself and confirmed that the scent was indeed unfamiliar and werewolf, as suspected. We walked the area but weren't able to locate the culprits. That's when I mindlinked you. It's similar to what happened a year ago."

Luke nodded in understanding.

"Since I wasn't here a year ago, do you mind explaining what happened?" I asked.

"Two werewolves from the Bois Sombre Pack were discovered after their scent was detected at the border. They were tortured and killed, per your father's orders. We then mailed their eyes back to the pack and have not seen any evidence of them approaching our territory since. I am familiar with the Bois Sombre Pack scent, so I can confirm it was not the same. However, we cannot rule out that members of an ally pack were sent to do their dirty work."

A shiver ran up my back. It would make sense that they would not continue to send their own pack members as the majority of our pack warriors had fought in the battle five years ago and would be familiar with their scent.

"I can take you over to the area where we found the scent," he offered.

"That would be great," I replied, as Luke and I followed him. He brought us into the forest and the three of us peeled our clothes off and shifted into our wolves to make tracking easier, not having to crawl on our hands and knees in our human form. We followed the scent to a cave but found it empty when we arrived.

"It was the same earlier," Mike mindlinked Luke and me. "I can send some of my patrol group out on a mission to try to track farther if you'd like, Alpha."

"Yes, please do," I replied.

"Consider it done."

"Thank you, Mike. I will double the bodies patrolling that area moving forward and require two additional juniors to walk one hundred yards out from the border at the beginning of each patrol shift. Hopefully it's not the case that other packs are casing the area but we can't be too careful."

"Noted, Alpha."

"I will take care of updating the schedules and send a memo out to everyone," Luke chimed in.

"Thank you, Luke," I responded, then added, "Mike, we'll be on our way. Keep us posted on the mission."

"Will do, Alpha and Beta," Mike replied and turned to go back to his patrol station.

After we returned to the packhouse office, I turned to Luke and said, "I guess we should call the Lune Nordique Pack."

"I'll get them on the phone." Luke was able to get Alpha Antoine on the conference phone who, luckily, was fluent in English. While we were all required to take French in school, I had never quite picked it up.

"Bonjour, Alpha Blake and Beta Lucas. I'm going to assume you have news," Alpha Antoine greeted us in his French Canadian accent.

"Good morning, Alpha Antoine. Alpha Blake speaking. One of my patrol officers has informed me that the scent from an unfamiliar werewolf pack was discovered just outside the borders of our pack. We're concerned that our pack might be being cased. Do you have any information on your end?"

"That is very bad news, Alpha Blake. It could be a sign that Alpha Édouard is preparing for war, as I'm sure you have concluded yourself. I don't have anything new to share from my end, but please keep me informed if the situation becomes dire. We are prepared to travel if necessary."

"Thank you, I appreciate it," I replied. "We will keep you posted, and you do the same."

"Absolutely, Alpha Blake," Alpha Antoine replied. We said our goodbyes and hung up.

I sat back in my chair and sighed. War was looming. Ever the optimist, Luke responded, "We'll figure this out. I'll start drawing up the new patrol plans."

"I also want the new training requirements for the pack put in place. I want all pack members who are over the age of eighteen and under the age of sixty to be required to spar for at least two hours a week with the warriors. I also want more accountability for everyone's training. I've gone down to the pack gym and spoken with some of the trainers. They've agreed to personalize a training schedule for everyone. And I spoke with the school trainers who have agreed to make the curriculum more rigorous. We have reason to believe that the next battle might be fought on our soil, and I want everyone to be prepared."

"Got it. I'll get this all put together and have the office manager get the information out to the entire pack."

"Thanks, man." I smiled at Luke. Then I thought of something, "You know, on the topic of updating school programs, there are a lot of things they don't cover in the health program at the pack school."

"Well, you know how your father was. He was really traditional. I'm pretty sure he'd have blown a gasket if they started covering things like birth control."

"Well, yes there's that. But they also don't cover heat."

"Heat? You mean like what happens to a woman during the mating process?"

"Yes, that's exactly what I mean."

"Hmm, yeah, I don't think the temple would have approved of that getting covered."

"It's probably an important topic to cover, don't you think? It's not exactly something you can just google if you don't know."

"Well, of course. But I think most people know about heat anyway."

"Are you sure about that? How did you learn about heat?"

"Well, you know, probably the same way you did. Guys talk about it, you hear rumors about it. Eventually you talk to someone who knows someone that's been through it, or you catch the scent of someone that's going through it and realize what it is."

"So, I have a question for you. Do *you* know what brings on heat?"

He appeared lost in thought and finally responded, "Actually, I have no clue. I guess I never thought about it too much besides, obviously, what happens during heat." He smirked.

"Well, I can tell you exactly what brings it on. Once you meet your mate and the mate bond's in place, your mate will go through heat every month to encourage the mating process until you finally mate and mark them."

"Is that what happened with Ria?"

"Yes, that's exactly what happened with Ria. I never marked her, so she used to go through heat every month. It would be the same for your mate as well." I watched as his eyes glossed over, deep in thought. I couldn't help wondering what he was thinking. Working and living with Luke now, we had rekindled some of our old friendship, but it still wasn't the same as it had been before I left.

I eventually dismissed myself and decided to do a run to check on patrols, feeling irritated—a bubbling feeling under my skin. I exited the packhouse, throwing off my clothes, and shifted to begin my daily run of all the patrol sites.

I couldn't lie, the situation was killing me. It almost seemed like a cruel joke at first, when Jasmine told me she was mated to my best friend—someone that was practically a brother to me! Someone I lived and worked with! I mean, what are the odds? The girl I was now falling head over heels for had found her mate, and it was none other than the one person who could, unknowingly, rub my face into it the most. *Fucking Artemis!* I tried to laugh and joke it off—one of the ways I used to cope with my pain before, well, Ria, and I could no longer laugh and joke anymore. That was, until Jasmine came along, and I finally got my sense of humor back. Yep, this had to be a joke. That Goddess had a really dark sense of humor.

To make matters worse, I couldn't help but feel downright irritated with how uninterested Luke seemed to be in Jasmine. He hadn't even mentioned her once since he'd invited her to the packhouse a week earlier. Granted, our friendship wasn't what it had once been, but I couldn't help but compare his reaction to my own years earlier. When I found out who my mate was, I wanted to sing, shout it from the rooftops. There wasn't a single person I didn't want to tell. My obsession with Ria was all-encompassing.

Hell, I couldn't help but compare Luke's behavior to how I felt about Jasmine now, not able to stop thinking about her, trying so hard not to let it kill me. Luke's reaction just seemed so wrong, unnatural. I knew it was important to her to be with her fated mate, but Jasmine deserved better.

I shook my head, knowing I shouldn't meddle. But, Goddess be damned, Jasmine deserved better.

Chapter 30

Jasmine

On Friday, I woke up feeling very hot and aroused. I knew that I had been having an erotic dream, but I couldn't recall what it was about. I kicked the blankets off me, feeling the cool air on the sweat that was covering my body. I rubbed my thighs together, discovering an unbearable swelling between my legs and a strong desire to have something inside me. I looked at the time and saw it was ten o'clock. I had slept longer than usual, and my parents had already left for work. I opened my bedside drawer where the unopened shopping bag Blake had left for me lay.

As I was about to reach for it, I saw a text come through. I reached for my phone instead. I was surprised to see it was from Luke. It read, *I need to talk to you. Can I come see you now?*

A warm shiver traveled up the entirety of my body at the thought. I couldn't help imagining him in my bed, completely naked, his hands exploring every untouched part of me, his skin brushing against mine, gliding against me, relieving me of the pressure I currently felt between my legs. But I was also unsure about it. My whole body longed for him, so much it was practically unbearable, but I recalled my conversation with Blake. My feelings hadn't changed. I didn't want him to be with me because I had seduced him. I wanted him to be with me because that's what he genuinely wanted. I replied to him, *It's not a good time. I think I'm in heat.*

I saw the three dots pop up on my screen instantly and then a text returned.

> **Luke**: Are you alone? You're not out, right?
> **Me**: No, I'm home alone
> **Luke**: Good, don't leave your house today
> **Luke**: I'm coming over right now

I looked at my phone, shocked, blinking. He was coming over *right now*? I ran to freshen myself up. I changed out of my pajamas and put deodorant on. I quickly brushed my hair and teeth and swiftly made my bed. Just as I was fluffing the pillows, I heard my doorbell ring. I ran downstairs to answer it.

"Can I come in?" he asked. I held the door open for him so he could walk through and closed it behind him. "Goddess, you are in heat," he said, seeming surprised even though I had just told him the same minutes earlier. I noticed he was clenching his fists. "This is what I wanted to talk to you about, but I didn't know it would be this damn hard. Your scent's so irresistible."

"What's it like for you?" I asked, being able to imagine, wanting so badly to run my fingers over his entire body.

"I want you so badly right now. It's taking everything in me not to just jump you." He moved closer to me. Before I could stop myself, I grabbed him into a kiss, desperate to feel his lips against mine. He instantly returned the kiss, grabbing my ass, pulling me tight against his body. I could feel his erection throbbing against me. It was like fireworks were exploding as our tongues intertwined, our bodies engulfed in sparks. It was intoxicating.

After some time, we pulled apart, gasping for air. "Do you want to come to my room?" I asked, feeling bold, eager to continue what we'd started.

"Goddess, yes," he replied. I led him upstairs to my bedroom. We both sat down on my twin-size bed. Before either of us could stop ourselves, our lips and tongues crashed together, our hands feeling for every part of the other's body. I pushed my hands under his shirt, feeling his abs, stroking his sculpted body, moving my hands up to his chest as he removed his shirt. He then did the same to me, pulling my shirt over my head and unclipping my bra. His mouth instantly fell to my bare skin, and he kissed up my stomach, massaging my breasts, then brought his lips back to mine. He pulled both my pants and underwear off at the same time, switching from his hands to his foot to kick them off my legs. I reached for his belt, desperate to be completely naked with him. He finished unbuckling it for me, unzipping his pants, and pulling them down with his boxer briefs, his erection springing free. I was like a wild animal, completely consumed by my heat, not able to get enough of Luke. I wouldn't be satiated until he was inside me.

Luke pulled me against him, his touch only making me more crazed with desire. We feverously kissed each other, our bodies pressed together, lying side by side. Suddenly, Luke pulled away slightly and asked, "Have you done this before?"

"Done what?" I asked.

"Had sex with someone," he replied, matter-of-factly.

I felt myself blush. "No, I haven't."

"We shouldn't then. It wouldn't be right."

"Does that mean you don't want to?" I asked, practically crying from how desperate I was to feel Luke inside me, filling me, rubbing against my inner walls.

"No, I absolutely do. I want you so badly right now, and it's going to take everything in me not to, but we should wait. Your first time should be special, and not something you might regret later because you were influenced by your heat."

"But I want it so badly right now," I whimpered, not able to imagine ever regretting this. I was throbbing between my legs, overtaken with lust for Luke.

"Here, it's okay, we can do something else." Before I could ask what he meant, I felt his finger slip inside me, followed by a second. "Goddess, you're so wet and tight," he whispered in my ear, moving his mouth back against mine. He moved his fingers in and out of me, then curled them, feeling around my inside walls. Suddenly, he hit a spot that released sparks of pleasure throughout my body, causing me to moan against his mouth. "You like that?" he asked, and kept rubbing against the same spot, provoking me to moan more loudly in confirmation, throwing my leg over his hip.

He flipped me on my back, moved down my body, spread my legs, and put his head between them. His tongue slid from bottom to top, licking the whole length between my legs. Once he got to the top, he began sucking the most swollen part of me, causing my whole body to tense, overwhelmed by the pleasure his mouth was causing. His tongue found my most sensitive spot, and he ran it back and forth, the pleasure from his tongue mixing with sparks being emitted by his body touching mine. My whole body began to tremble as he put additional pressure and flicked his tongue back and forth more quickly. My moans were now so loud that I wasn't sure the neighbors couldn't hear. Before long, firecrackers exploded within my body, followed by bliss flowing to all of my limbs. Luke lay down beside me as I turned to him and said, "Wow."

He snuggled me against him. I could feel that his erection was still very prominent. I looked up at him, touching it, and asked, "Should I?"

He groaned against me, and I could sense that he absolutely wanted me to return the favor.

"What should I do? I've never done this before." I looked at him, feeling myself go red at the confession.

His eyes softened, looking at me. "It's okay. If you haven't done it before, I can take care of it when I go home. I can feel your heat dying down now, so it's not as difficult to resist. But it will probably start up again at some point, so please just stay home today. I'm not the only person that can sense it."

"Yeah, Blake told me already," I responded.

"Blake? You talked to him about this?"

"He was the one who told me about heat. I didn't know about it before."

I could sense he was irritated. After some time, he asked, "How close of friends, exactly, are you with Blake?"

Something within me told me that I couldn't be completely forthcoming with Luke about this topic. I replied, "We hang out sometimes. He's nice to me."

"Nice in what way?"

"He listens to me when I have no one else to talk to."

"I see." His jaw was tense.

"Anyway, what did you want to talk about when you came over?"

"It doesn't matter now. Mostly I just wanted to make sure you knew about heat and not to leave the house and stay away from all unmated males. Your heat affects me more than anyone else, but it still affects others as well. And we've all heard stories of men who didn't resist. While most men will, some are scumbags." He kissed me on my forehead. "Anyway, I should go. Not because I want to, but I have a lot of work to do today." He got up and began dressing. I followed his lead and did the same.

I walked him to the door. He grabbed me into a kiss, dipping me as he did, and then he walked out the door. He turned to look at me and said, "Goodbye, Jasmine. Have a good day." He hesitated to turn around and then finally did. I closed the door and slid down the back of it, sitting myself on the tiled floor, trying to process what just happened.

Luke

I hopped in my car, desperate to get home and rub one out. The visit with Jasmine did not go as planned at all. I hadn't intended to do any of the things we did. All I'd wanted was to explain how heat works to her, assuming she didn't know, so she'd be prepared. After my talk with Blake, I became worried, knowing Jasmine had been raised so conservatively. I had assumed that everyone knew about heat, but something told me that Jasmine might not, at least not how it affected unmated men. And while I knew how it affected men, having sensed it before unwittingly, I, myself, hadn't known what actually brought it on.

Fuck, why did I allow things to escalate so much?

After she grabbed me into a kiss, I surrendered, all my senses overwhelmed. I reprimanded myself—what was I thinking anyway, going to her house when she was in heat? Why had I thought it would go any other way? But I couldn't lie to myself. She tasted absolutely delicious. Kissing her was even better than I imagined. I couldn't stop the image of her completely naked and aroused from entering my mind, now recalling the beautiful curves of her body, her pert breasts, and her toned legs. And she was so wet and so tight. There had been nothing I wanted more than to bury my cock inside her. I had the worst blue balls of my life.

I parked in the packhouse lot, relieved that Blake's car was absent. He wouldn't stand in my way as I ran up to my room to take care of myself and how horny I was at that moment.

I sprinted into the packhouse and up the stairs, only to find Lucy waiting for me in my room, seated on my bed. "How did you get in here?" I asked, knowing we kept all the doors locked at all times.

"The housekeepers let me in."

"Why are you here?" I questioned.

"I missed you, Luke. You've been so busy, and I feel like we're long-distance all over again." She came to me, wrapping her arms around me. Then she started sniffing and I knew I'd been caught. "Why do you smell like Jasmine?"

"There's something we need to talk about," I said, taking her hands and bringing her to sit on the bed with me. I hesitated, feeling sick at having to reveal this information to her.

She looked at me, her eyes burning into mine. "Well?" she asked. "What is it?"

"Lucy, I don't know how to say this. So, I'll just come out and say it. I've met my mate."

She pulled her hands out of mine, and I watched as she closed her eyes. After some time, she asked, "And who's your mate? Although, I think I know the answer."

"Jasmine."

"And you just figured it out today or what?" She opened her eyes and looked at me.

"No, I figured it out a week ago at her birthday party," I confessed, realizing how much I'd screwed up.

She had a death glare in her eyes. "And you didn't think to tell me before today? Is that why you've been avoiding me? Is that it? You're going to leave me for Jasmine now and forget about me? You didn't even have the decency to tell me?"

I pulled her hands into mine again, feeling sick at my actions toward her. "No, that's not it at all. I just wanted to give myself some space to think about it. This was all sprung on me so suddenly, and I just needed time to figure out what to do. My feelings for you haven't changed. I still love you very much. But what am I supposed to do? The Moon Goddess gives us all one mate, and mine happens to be Jasmine. I can't help the way I feel toward her now. I wish this never happened, but I can't change it."

"So, reject her then! You won't have these feelings anymore if you just reject her. Then we can just go back to how things were." I was a bit shocked at Lucy's demand that I just reject her best friend. How could it be so simple in her mind?

"Lucy, please, be reasonable. I don't want to hurt you. I just need some space right now so I can make the right decision."

"It doesn't seem like you needed any space from Jasmine. I smell her all over you." She took my hand, smelling it, catching me red-handed. Tears filled her eyes. I watched as they spilled over, running down her cheeks. I felt a deep affection for her, her pain affecting me in my chest. I reached for her, bringing her against my body, holding her tightly, and inhaling her scent. As much as Jasmine affected me, I still felt very deeply about Lucy, and hated myself for hurting her.

She pulled away and stood up, unzipping her dress, revealing that she was completely naked underneath it. I instantly felt myself go rock-hard. I didn't think I'd ever been so hard in my life, my cock throbbing with desire. I was already horny when she arrived, and now she was putting me over the edge. I was surprised I hadn't prematurely ejaculated with how worked up I was.

She walked over, and lifted my shirt over my head, kissing me down my chest and abs. She then undid my belt, pulling it clean out of the loops. Her hands unbuttoned and unzipped my pants, pulling them down, urging me to lift myself off the bed so she could remove them completely. She kneeled down on the floor in front of me, easing my legs apart, and instantly put her hands and mouth on my cock. I was putty in her hands as she used her years of practice and knowledge of exactly what I liked to get me off. She cupped my balls in one hand, while she used the other hand to rub up and down my shaft in sync with her mouth, coating and lubricating me with her saliva. She pushed my cock so deep into her throat that I was surprised she wasn't gagging. I groaned in pleasure at the feeling of her mouth on me. I knew it wouldn't take me long to come. Then she suddenly stopped.

"You like that, huh?" she asked.

I nodded in confirmation, not being able to speak.

"You like when I fuck you with my mouth? You like feeling your cock jammed down my throat?" She pushed me back forcefully so I was lying on the bed. Knowing I'd let her do anything she wanted to me, I watched as she climbed on top of me and lowered herself onto my cock. I moaned in the pleasure of feeling myself inside her. She was so warm and wet and I didn't think I'd ever loved the feeling of being inside her so much. She began riding me fervently, her breasts bouncing, her ass hitting against me as she landed, her moans loud as if she was performing in a porno. Less than a minute after my cock had entered her, the strongest orgasm I'd ever felt exploded within me as I felt myself forcefully spray the inside of her with my come.

She withdrew herself from me as I watched semen drip down the insides of her legs. She got up and pulled her dress back over her body then looked at me and said, "There's no fucking way Jasmine fucks you as good as I do." She grabbed her purse and walked out of my room. I sighed as I lay back in my bed, wondering what just happened, feeling as if the day so far had all just been a dream.

Chapter 31

Jasmine

The day after Luke came over, I could tell that my heat had eased. I no longer felt the same intense swelling between my legs. I still desired Luke, but it was not the same desperation I had felt the morning prior. It was dark outside when I woke. After I shut off my alarm, I lay in my bed with my eyes closed, reliving everything that had happened the day before, recalling Luke's naked body and how he made me orgasm for the first time in my life.

After imagining what it would be like to be with someone for so long, the actual encounter turned out better than my imagination. I reminisced about the feeling of Luke pressed against my body, his hands on my bare skin, and the sensation of sparks between my legs. My thighs were tingling in memory of the encounter—I could still feel his fingers inside me. He knew what he was doing. And then another thought came to my mind. After hearing Lucy talk about how good Luke was in bed, I could now confirm that she had not just been talking—he was good. And, I realized with horror, he was good because he was experienced, with years of practice hooking up with Lucy.

Shit, we still hadn't told her! My arousal shifted to guilt. I was a horrible friend. I had gone behind Lucy's back, practically slept with her boyfriend, and she still had no clue he was my mate. I knew it wasn't exactly an excuse but, to be fair, I hadn't exactly been lucid. The person I was the day prior wasn't me—I had turned into a rabid animal, ready to mount the first victim that turned up. I hadn't even invited Luke over! He just came—and in only one sense of the word.

I wondered what it all meant. Why had Luke come over while I was in heat? Had he decided he wanted to be with me? And what did it mean that he had just rushed out right after? Was he unhappy with something I did, or, well, didn't do? I grumbled as I forced myself to get up, confused by the mixed signals Luke was sending.

I quickly got ready for my early shift at the café and jumped in my car to drive over. I knew Lucy was working that day and groaned to myself at the thought. I had managed to avoid her for the entire week, but I'd finally have to face her. It would be even worse knowing what I had done with her boyfriend yesterday.

I entered the café at five, performing all the opening tasks. Valerie had hired a new girl named Liz to bake all the pastries early in the morning. She stocked the glass case while I worked. Her shift was normally short, ending soon after we opened. She never talked much. I was relieved that we wouldn't have to make strained conversation, and I could be left to my own thoughts.

At six, I flipped the sign to Open. As customers began slowly filing in, Liz slipped out. Valerie came in at seven thirty and took my place at the register while I prepared the drinks. Lucy was late, as usual, running in at eight.

"Half hour late today!" Valerie yelled, shaking her head. After Lucy dropped her things off and put her apron on, she replaced Valerie at the register. But something was off. Lucy wasn't her usual flirty self. She barely even spoke as she took customers' orders. I felt dread in the pit of my stomach.

"Good morning, sweety." I saw one of the regular customers address Lucy.

"Hi, Americano and chocolate chip muffin?" Lucy replied, pulling a muffin out of the glass case to put into a to-go bag. This was not like her at all. He looked disappointed at her response. She kept her back to me the entire morning rush. There was no question that Luke had told her and didn't even inform me that he had done so, leaving me completely unprepared for the tension that penetrated the air between Lucy and me.

After the rush ended and the restaurant was practically empty, Valerie came out from the back. Lucy stayed with her back turned, leaving me paralyzed, unsure what I should say or do.

Valerie broke the silence. "Well, don't just stand there, go clean some tables! This place is a mess. I'm surprised we don't have rats yet."

Lucy grabbed for the spray bottle and a clean rag. Without even turning to look at her, she said, "You must be blind, Valerie. There's a huge rat standing right next to you."

"That's not fair, Lucy!" I retorted.

Lucy turned to look at me, murder in her eyes. "What part isn't fair? The part where you didn't tell me that my boyfriend is your mate or the part where you fucked him behind my back yesterday?"

I stepped back, clasping my chest in shock. I couldn't believe that Luke had confessed everything to her, leaving me completely blindsided. How could he do that and not even let me know? I became light-headed, wondering what exactly he had told her, not knowing where I stood. And that's when I felt it again—the contractions in my chest, my breathing becoming shallow and the whole world crumbling under my feet. I knew I wouldn't be able to control it this time. I ran out of the café, just as I shifted into my wolf form, shredding my clothes, and sprinted away into the woods.

I ran through the forest, allowing myself to succumb to my wolf, delighting in the smells of wet tree bark, moss, and decomposing leaves.

My paws pounced off the dirt as the wind blew through my fur. I had to have run for at least two hours before I stopped and rested, not far from the border of our pack, not ready to reenter. I wondered if I could just stay in my wolf form and live as an animal in the forest. I'd never spent more than a few hours as a wolf, but I was now tempted to just remain in this form. Everything was simpler as an animal. Only my instincts mattered. I found a brook and drank deeply from it, savoring the taste of the cool water on my tongue.

I finally allowed myself to come back to reality, knowing I'd have to face what happened at some point. I tried to force a link to Luke, hoping that I wasn't too far from him. I was relieved to see that it was able to go through, the link clicking into place.

"What exactly did you tell Lucy?" I asked him.

"Shit, I was going to tell you."

"When were you planning to do that? It would have been nice if I could have at least prepared before I had to work with her."

"Shit. I'm really sorry, Jasmine."

"At least tell me what you told her so I know what's going on."

"To be honest, I didn't tell her much. I just told her we were mates."

"And that we fucked yesterday?"

"I didn't tell her that."

"So why did she accuse me of that?"

"She probably assumed the worst. I wasn't even planning on saying anything to her yet, but she came to the packhouse yesterday while I was out and smelled you all over me when I got home."

"Great, just great."

"I'm really sorry, Jasmine. You don't deserve any of this."

"Can you at least please help me with something? I had a panic attack and shifted while I was still dressed, and now I'm stuck in this form while my house keys are at the café. My parents are probably home, anyway, and I don't want to go home naked."

"Don't worry, I'll get your keys. Who else is working at the café?"

"Valerie."

"Okay, I'll mindlink her so she can meet me and Lucy doesn't see me taking your stuff. I'll also get you some clothes from my sister's house. Meet me in the woods behind the packhouse in a half hour."

I lay down and sighed. I wasn't sure if things could get worse.

Luke

I was in the pack office with Blake, deep in discussion about training, when the mindlink from Jasmine came through. I knew I'd fucked up. But maybe I could fix things. I wasn't sure how, but I would try.

"Who were you mindlinking with?" Blake asked.

"Jasmine," I replied. "Sorry, man, I really have to go."

"What happened?" he asked.

"She's stuck in her wolf form. I have to find her a change of clothes so she can shift back."

"Why doesn't she have her clothes?" he looked concerned.

"She had a panic attack."

"Is she okay? Do you need my help?"

"No, let me handle it," I replied. I was becoming annoyed with his concern for my mate. I didn't trust at all that he had good intentions with her either, especially after his comment at the temple service. Moreover, what was he doing discussing heat with her?

I jumped into my car and drove to my sister Lauren's house. Peyton had had her baby a couple days after the alpha ceremony, so I didn't want to bother her, knowing she was preoccupied with a newborn at the moment. I told Lauren I needed the clothes for a rogue werewolf who had wandered into our territory, deciding it was best to share as little information as possible. This was not a completely uncommon situation, so she didn't question it. She handed me a pair of shorts, a T-shirt, and some flip-flops.

I then mindlinked Valerie and asked her to meet me down the street from the café so I could collect Jasmine's things. Not long after I arrived at our agreed-upon meeting spot, she sauntered up to me, her hips swaying. She was very curvy, reminding me of Jessica Rabbit with her red hair. I'd heard rumors about her younger days, and I could believe them. Even well into her forties, she was a very sexy woman.

"Well, if it isn't Casanova in the flesh." She grinned at me.

"What do you mean by that?" I asked.

"Well, you have all my employees fighting over you. I can't blame them. You are one fine-looking man. If I were mateless, I'd probably be fighting over you too."

I crossed my arms, deciding to ignore her comment. "Thank you for bringing Jasmine's stuff."

"You're welcome. Not that it's my business, but Jasmine's a good girl and she doesn't deserve the shit that you're putting her through. I know you've been dating Lucy a long time, blah blah blah. And I like Lucy too. But she's not your fucking mate. So, grow a fucking pair and do the right thing."

I nodded at her in acknowledgment as she handed Jasmine's purse to me. I then got back into my car and drove to the packhouse.

I walked into the woods and sat on a tree stump, waiting for Jasmine to arrive. A stunning wolf with brown and black fur with white on her paws and on the tip of her tail sprinted out from behind some pine trees, stopping in front of me. Jasmine's intoxicating scent wafted through the air. Her wolf was beautiful, with thick fur, brilliant amber eyes, and perfect pointed ears. She almost reminded me of a fox. For a moment I considered running my hands through her fur, wanting to know how it felt. But I resisted, knowing this was not the time or place. I stood up and put the clothes I brought onto the stump and turned around, giving her privacy as she shifted back. Not that I didn't want to look, recalling how amazing her body was, feeling my blood rushing south at my indecent thoughts. I shook my head, forcing myself to act appropriately.

"I'm decent," she said. I turned around to see her standing in front of me. As soon as I saw her, I had a desire to hold her in my arms—to feel her body against mine. When I was away from her, I could sort of control how I felt. But when she was standing in front of me like this, I couldn't help but want to be close to her, the mate bond like a magnet.

"Are you okay?" I asked, sensing her anxiety, feeling terrible about my actions. Jasmine didn't deserve what had happened. She had always been so sweet and kind.

"Well, not really," she said, sitting down on the stump. An overwhelming guilt came over me. I'd really fucked up. I knew I had to do something about it but felt so ill-equipped.

"Do you want to come into the packhouse for a little bit before you go home?" I asked, hating the idea of her just leaving—wanting to spend more time with her and try to cheer her up.

"It's probably best that I go home now. The day has already been kind of a disaster."

"Why don't you come in and eat something? We can talk." I took her hand, pulling her inside of the packhouse. I took her into the kitchen and sat her down at the table. The cook had left us some lunch on top of the stove that I hadn't had a chance to eat yet. I looked to see what it was. "Do you like macaroni and cheese and hot dogs?"

"Sure," she replied.

I spooned some of the food onto two plates and put them in the microwave. "What can I get you to drink?"

"Just water is fine."

I dispensed water out of the fridge into two glasses, placing them on the table, squeezing her shoulder in a friendly gesture as I did. I sighed deeply as sparks traveled up my arm, the feeling magical. I grabbed the food out of the microwave and took a seat beside her. "I know it's childish, but mac and cheese and hot dogs always cheers me up. There's nothing else like it. It brings me right back to my childhood." I tried to make conversation with her.

She gave a small smile, and I felt a swelling in my chest that maybe she was cheering up, hopeful that things would be okay. We sat in silence eating our food. Finally, I spoke again.

"Jasmine, I know I've fucked things up and I'm really sorry. I'm going to try to make things right. I'll talk to Lucy and ask her for some space. I know it's a lot to ask from both of you, but I really need some time to digest everything. Deciding the one person to spend the rest of your life with is a huge decision and none of us should make it lightly. I don't think what I'm asking is unreasonable. We have plenty of time to mate and get married. All of us are really young. There's no reason we can't take a few weeks or months to figure it out. And, who knows, maybe Lucy will meet her own mate during that time, and then we'll all really understand our options."

"I spoke with the priest earlier this week," Jasmine replied.

"What did he say?"

"He said that the temple forbids taking a chosen mate over a fated one, and that by doing so, I wouldn't be allowed to be married in the temple. He also said it's believed that the Moon Goddess curses those who take a chosen mate."

I sighed, considering what she was telling me, not knowing how to respond, certain that a temple wedding would be important to Jasmine and her parents. After all, her whole family attended every week. I also reflected on what my own parents would think if I wasn't allowed to be married in the temple. They had always been adamant about following temple traditions, especially as leaders in the community. I knew my mom would be pretty upset, but I was sure she'd eventually get over it. Although religious, my parents had always been understanding. Either way, I couldn't choose my mate based on what my parents thought—they weren't the ones marrying them!

We continued eating our food silently. Finally, Jasmine spoke again. "I've thought about it, and I don't think what you're asking for is unreasonable. It just hurts. We're supposed to be together. Artemis wants us to be together. I won't get another mate if you reject me. It would be one thing if we were human and we had no idea who we're supposed to be with, but in this case, we do. The Moon Goddess tells us. And I feel like there must be something severely wrong with me for you to consider rejecting me given that information." Her voice cracked as she completed the sentence and tears spilled from her eyes.

I moved my chair closer and wrapped my arms around her, allowing her to cry into my chest, her pain sinking into my bones. I didn't want to hurt Jasmine, but I also didn't want to lead her on either, going along with the mate bond even if my heart wasn't into it. I did feel a lot for her, especially now with my arms wrapped around her, her head against my chest. Whenever we were close to each other like this, it was like a magnet pulling me toward her, making it impossible to imagine myself away from her. That's why I needed space. I needed to clear my head and figure out what I should do—do what was expected of me and be with Jasmine or follow my heart and be with Lucy.

Finally, I replied, "No, that's not true, Jasmine. There's absolutely nothing wrong with you. You're perfect. If I had never met Lucy, there would be no question and I would have been over the moon to have you as my mate. But I can't change the past. I made mistakes and I have baggage now. You don't deserve any of this, but I also can't change how I feel about Lucy now that I feel it. I'm going to do my best to do the right thing. Please, just give me some time."

She nodded into my chest and lifted her head up. "I'm going to go home. Thanks for getting me some clothes and my stuff."

I stared into her amber eyes, the whites red, her face blotchy. My chest ached seeing her like this. But I wasn't sure how to fix the situation without being disingenuous. I just hoped that time would fix everything that had gone wrong in the past week.

"Do you need a ride?" I asked, getting up and putting my hand out to help her up.

"No, it's okay, I'll just walk over to the café to get my car. It's not far from here. Plus, it's best if Lucy doesn't see me with you." She ignored my hand and walked toward the front of the packhouse.

I followed her to the door and watched her walk down the street. I closed the door to find Blake looking at me with his arms crossed. He shook his head at me and said, "You're a fucking idiot." And then he walked away.

Chapter 32

Blake

It was mid-October, and Luke had put the new training requirements in place. I checked the sparring rosters to see who was signed up. I noted that Jasmine had enrolled in a two-hour stint that day and got an idea. I mindlinked the trainer that was leading that session and asked to switch with him. It had been a while since I'd heard from her, and I missed her. This was a harmless way I could spend some time with her. Plus, I couldn't lie. Watching her fight was really fucking hot. I still vividly recalled that day when we had sparred together.

    I walked out on the field, my heart skipping a beat when I saw Jasmine. She was wearing a tight-fitting gym outfit that showed off her entire body. She looked so sexy I almost forgot what I was there to do. Coming back to reality, I began leading everyone in the warm-up. I had everyone do push-ups, planks, and burpees. I couldn't help watching how good Jasmine looked performing all the exercises as I barked orders at everyone.

    To begin the session, I decided to have everyone practice the wolfman's carry. This was essentially the wolf version of a fireman's carry and was important for warriors to be proficient in during battle. When wolves became too weak, they were forced back into their human form, and we had to be able to carry them off the battlefield to safety. I had all the civilians that came that day stay in their human forms while the warriors all shifted into wolves and practiced flipping them onto their backs.

I watched in delight as Jasmine giggled while one of the female warriors practiced the exercise with her, thinking she looked so cute. Jasmine would lay on the ground, and the warrior used her snout to flip Jasmine onto her and secure her by holding Jasmine's arms in her mouth, giving a little shake to make sure she was safely in place. Jasmine was clearly enjoying herself, and I could already picture her as part of the warrior team.

After I was satisfied that the warriors had done a solid job, I began assigning everyone partners for sparring. I decided to pair Jasmine with Logan. He was a big man and one of my best warriors. While he could easily overpower Jasmine in a fight, I knew she was a fair match for him in technique. I was looking forward to watching her take him on.

We started with practicing the ground and pound, a move meant to bring one's opponent to the ground and pound them with one's fist. Everyone's opponents were supposed to avoid being taken. I walked around, observing and correcting anything I saw. Logan went first with trying to ground Jasmine. I was excited to see that Jasmine did a great job outsmarting him, not getting grounded most times that he tried. I had everyone switch and was amazed to see that Jasmine was a quick thinker. She outmaneuvered all of his blocks and was able to ground him most of the time. Hot damn!

I began shouting out other sparring moves, and it was the same. If Logan had been allowed to use all of his strength, he would have likely knocked her out in at least one of the blows he made. But because this was more of an exercise in technique, Jasmine was outperforming him. I could see that he was becoming frustrated. I, on the other hand, was getting extremely turned on.

After running through additional moves, I decided to end the sparring session with the spinning backfist. Everyone was supposed to spin and try to hit their opponent with the back of their fist, the spin allowing one to generate more force from the punch. Jasmine went first, and it was amazing. Most of her punches landed. This was not an easy move to master, and most people missed most of the time. But she was quick on her feet. We then switched and Logan struggled. Most of his punches missed. I could see that he was growing very frustrated.

Suddenly, I noticed something in his eyes. I knew he sometimes had trouble controlling his anger, but I didn't think that would happen during a sparring exercise. Before I could stop the exercise, he spun and threw a punch with full force, throwing Jasmine back. Everyone gasped, noticing what happened. I shifted into my wolf in anger, tearing my clothes, and attacked him. I grabbed him by the center of his body with my mouth, swinging him violently and throwing him into the grass. I had to stop myself from killing him I was so pissed.

I went over to Jasmine and whimpered, seeing that he had left her with a huge black eye. I mindlinked Logan, *"Get the fuck out of here before I actually fucking kill you."* He got up and ran off the field, bleeding from his middle. I knew he'd be fine and heal quickly. Jasmine would too.

One of the warriors handed me a fresh pair of shorts. Because Jasmine was present, I went behind the partition to shift back into my human form, thinking I should stay modest in front of her, even though I normally wouldn't have bothered. I came out and yelled at everyone, "If anyone else ever fucking pulls that again, I will personally escort you to the cells and torture you. We have non-warriors sparring with us now, and it's unacceptable to use full force during these sessions. Dismissed!" Everyone walked away as Jasmine slowly got up. I went over to help.

"Are you okay?" I asked.

"Yeah, I'm fine. Just wasn't expecting that."

"Let's get some ice for that." I took her hand and brought her into the warrior gym. I sat her down on a bench while I went to grab an ice pack from the men's locker room fridge.

I saw Logan wrapping himself with a bandage when I entered. Upon noticing me, he said, "I'm really sorry, Alpha. Is she okay?"

"Yeah, she's fine. Don't ever fucking do that again. I will fucking kill you if you do. You're one of my best warriors, but you can't be punching women. Pick on someone your own size."

"I know, you're right. She was just so good." He shook his head, looking wounded.

"She was, wasn't she?" I smiled with pride.

I took an ice pack out of the freezer and brought it out for Jasmine. She put it on her eye, and I sat down next to her. "I guess you got a taste of your future today."

"My future?" she asked.

"Yeah, once I finally convince your parents to let me recruit you as a full-time warrior. I saw you out there today, and you were really good. Logan wouldn't have lost his cool like that if you didn't bruise his ego with your skills. Those big tough guys hate when they get beat by a girl." I smiled at her.

"I feel like you're not really selling it by saying my future consists of getting the living daylights punched out of me."

I laughed and hugged her. "Let me see your eye." She moved the ice pack. I could see it was already starting to heal, the deep purple becoming more of a brown shade. "You know what will help make it better?" I asked.

"What?"

"If I kiss it."

"Is that so?"

"One hundred percent. My mom's a doctor and that's how she used to heal all my wounds. Worked perfectly every time."

"Well, if your mom's a doctor, she must know about healing wounds." She closed her eyes and lifted her head up to me.

I put my lips to her closed black eye, planting a soft kiss on it. Not being able to help myself, I softly kissed around it. "So, what do you think? Is it feeling better yet?"

"You know what, I think it is."

"Good, if it doesn't heal fully in the next few hours, let me know, and I will kiss it some more. In fact, any time anything hurts, just let me know, and I'll be happy to provide my healing services."

She chuckled. "Thanks, I appreciate the offer."

"So, where are you off to now? I'll walk you over."

"I was just going to go home and do some schoolwork. I've been falling behind and I need to catch up."

"In that case, I'll walk you to your car." I helped her up and walked with her, wishing I could spend the whole day with her. Before she got in her car, I said, "Don't forget, you still owe me a ride in your car and lunch." I was elated at the idea of spending more time with her.

As I watched her drive away, I sighed to myself, feeling a dull ache in my chest. I knew I should stop thinking about her and try to move on. But I just couldn't bring myself to stay away. She had this warmth about her. When I was around her, I could slowly feel my old pain melting away, my affection for her growing each time I saw her. Anyway, we were friends, and there was nothing wrong with being friends, right?

Chapter 33

Jasmine

After the whole situation with Lucy, Valerie redid the work schedule so that we wouldn't be working shifts together. It wasn't too difficult because I had dropped down to two days a week after school started. It was weird not having my best friend in my life anymore. To be honest, I missed her. She was my only real friend in the pack, and now I didn't even have her. But I could understand why she was upset with me, even if it hadn't really been my fault. I knew it would be best to just give her space. I didn't think there was anything I could say that would change how she felt.

I had also agreed to give Luke space, so I hadn't seen him since the day of above situation. Yep, I was now best friendless and mateless. To make matters worse, I was almost positive I wouldn't have all As this semester. I was having trouble concentrating in school and putting in the effort required. I was tempted to see if I could take a leave of absence and resume next semester, but I wasn't sure how my parents would react to something like that. My mom was really on edge lately. I felt like she could snap at any moment.

At dinner one night, my mom spoke. "You know, Jasmine, I've been hearing rumors around the pack. People have been asking about you.

I've been telling them it's nonsense, but I'm getting very concerned. You've been acting out a lot lately and I feel like I don't even know you anymore."

"What rumors?" I asked.

"People are saying they've seen you with the alpha. They said they've seen your car parked at the packhouse, and that he was kissing you at the warrior gym the other day."

I felt a knot in the pit of my stomach. This could not be happening.

My mom continued, "Where are these rumors coming from?"

"I don't know," I mumbled.

"It's a small pack, Jasmine. I really hope you're not acting inappropriately. What will your mate think?" Goddess, if she only knew. Luckily, that rumor hadn't gotten around yet. I was secretly thankful that Lucy hadn't started telling everyone, and partially surprised. She wasn't usually quiet when she had a vendetta against someone.

"Sometimes people just make things up because they're bored." My dad winked at me, surprising me. It wasn't often he took my side.

"Goddess, I hope so." My mom sighed.

After dinner, I received a text from Blake.

> ***Blake Sexy AF***: *I hope you didn't forget you owe me a ride and lunch*
> ***Me***: *Take your pick of almost any day. I have no life anymore.*
> ***Blake Sexy AF***: *Tomorrow*
> ***Blake Sexy AF***: *Come to the packhouse at 10?*
> ***Me***: *Can we meet somewhere else please? My car can no longer be seen at the packhouse*
> ***Blake Sexy AF***: *Sounds like you're in trouble*
> ***Blake Sexy AF***: *Wild guess…your car isn't banned from the library yet? Meet there?*

Me: *Haha no it's not. I'll meet you there tomorrow at 10*

The next morning, I waited until my parents left at eight fifteen and then began preparing us lunch for the day. I checked through the fridge to see what we had and ended up making Italian sandwich roll-ups and pasta salad. I also packed some Oreo cookies. I placed everything into a small tote bag and got in my car to meet Blake.

I pulled up next to his car at the library. He moved from his car into the passenger seat of mine, and we sped away from the pack. He gave me directions to our secret spot where I parked at the side of the road. We hiked up the mountain and sat down to eat once we got to the summit.

"This is really good." Blake smiled. "You're on lunch duty from now on."

"Thanks," I replied.

"So, why can your car no longer be seen at the packhouse?"

I groaned. "I guess there are rumors around the pack now. People have seen my car at the packhouse, and they saw you kissing my eye the other day. So now everyone thinks we're involved."

"So, let's get involved and make them true. They're already talking, so why not?" He smirked.

I lay back and groaned again. "My life's a disaster right now."

He lay down next to me. "How so?"

"Neither my best friend nor my mate is talking to me anymore. There are rumors about me around the pack. I'll be lucky if I get Bs in my classes this semester, I'm doing so bad at school right now."

"So, I take it Lucy knows about Luke now?"

"Yep, she called me a rat."

"Why'd she do that?"

"Because Luke came over when I was in heat and things got really, well, heated. Of course, that same day Lucy happened to show up at the packhouse and smell me all over him. She assumed the worst, not that I really blame her. That's probably not the best way to find out your best friend and boyfriend are mates."

"Luke went over your house when you were in heat?"

I felt myself blush. "Yeah, he did."

"Holy fuck. Well, what happened? Did he pop your cherry?"

"No, he didn't. He just went down on me."

"Damn, I am dying of jealousy right now. What else?"

"That's it. He left after that."

"He just left? You didn't finish him off?"

"I offered to, but when I asked him what to do, he said he'd do it himself." I could feel that my whole body was crimson.

"That's fucking crazy. He declined? What the hell is wrong with that man?"

I groaned.

He smiled and said, "Well, if you're desperate to finish someone off, I'll volunteer myself. His loss."

As Blake said it, I couldn't help but imagine it, a warm feeling on my skin and my stomach fluttering as my imagination ran wild, tempted to take him up on his offer. I quickly pushed the dirty thoughts from my mind.

He then sat back up again and continued eating. I lay back, realizing that it was nice just spending the day with Blake. It was comfortable being around him. There was no pressure to be anyone but myself. After he finished eating, he moved my head onto his lap. We stayed like that for some time, staring into the fall foliage that was dying down, many of the leaves now fallen.

We eventually hiked down the mountain and made it back to my car. I drove us to the library. Before he exited my car, he said, "Honestly, Jasmine, don't worry too much about the Luke and Lucy situation. It will eventually work itself out. Put your mind on studying for now. And, hey, if studying's no longer your thing, I know a certain alpha who would love to recruit you as one of his warriors. Just saying."

I looked at him. I had been wondering something and asked, "When you say that, do you really want to recruit me, or is that just a joke? I sometimes can't tell when you're serious and when you're joking."

"First of all, I'm pretty sure everything I've said that's sounded like a joke has been serious. Yes, I want to get in your pants. And yes, I want you as a warrior."

"But wouldn't you be worried after what happened to Ria? I mean, I know I'm not your mate. But we are friends. So, I was just thinking it's strange that you'd want to recruit me."

He looked at me sadly. "Yes, I'd worry. But there are other ways to die than being a warrior. It's impossible to avoid all of them. As alpha, it comes with the territory anyway. Normally, the luna's expected to lead alongside the alpha, including in battle. The only reason my mother doesn't is because she's a doctor. If I ever take a luna, I'd be honored for her to help protect the pack by my side."

"I hope you find a luna one day," I said, touching his arm. I hated the idea of him being alone for the rest of his life. I imagined what it would be like to be his luna—the idea of it somehow comforting and familiar. I almost felt a little sad that I couldn't be.

He sighed and continued, "The thing is, you're really damn good at fighting. As alpha, it's my job to recruit the best team, and I've seen you in action. Plus, you'd learn how to fight and defend yourself, so you'd be less likely to die if there was an attack on our pack. Obviously, it's up to you if it's something you're interested in, so think about it. If it is, I will personally speak to your parents for you. So just let me know. And no pressure if you're not interested."

"Okay, I'll think about it."

"Good. Either way, I'd like to watch you work out again. It's really damn hot." He leaned over and kissed me on my cheek and exited the car. I watched as he climbed into the driver's seat of his own car. Then I backed out of the parking space and drove home, the sadness lingering. I couldn't help but think about how Blake's and my friendship had developed over the past few months and what a good team we would make. Yes, it was unfortunate that things hadn't worked out differently for us.

Chapter 34

Luke

The same day that I spoke with Jasmine after bringing her clothes, I went to the café and waited for Lucy to end work for the day. After she got out, I had essentially the same conversation with her and asked for space. It had now been three weeks since I'd seen her. I couldn't lie and say I didn't miss her. Over the years, she had become my best friend, and I felt lonely without having my best friend in my life anymore. When we were long-distance, we at least texted and spoke by phone regularly, but now it was just silence between us. It felt unnatural. Every time something happened, the first thing I wanted to do was tell Lucy, but I'd have to remind myself that I had asked for space.

But, just like that, after three weeks, the silence came to an end. Much like three weeks earlier, I walked into my room one day to see that Lucy was already waiting for me, sitting on my bed. I sighed, torn about what to say or do. Finally, I asked, "What are you doing here, Lucy?"

She got up and wrapped her arms around me. "Please, Luke, this time apart's killing me. I miss you so much, and I'm so horny."

Being so close to her, against her body, I could smell that she was aroused, instantly making me go hard. Before either of us could stop ourselves, we had our mouths on each other, the time apart making us more desperate to be together. It wasn't long until we were completely naked, pressed up against each other in my bed. I opened the drawer to my bedside table, pulling out a condom, knowing this wasn't going to end in any other way.

The next day, the same thing happened again. This time Lucy had donned lacy lingerie for the occasion, making me powerless against her. She was so beautiful, and I couldn't deny my desire for her. The day after that, the same thing.

Lying naked with her, she moaned, "I am so horny lately. All I want to do is fuck you all the time." Before I knew it, this had been going on for a week. I began to look forward to her waiting for me in my bedroom, ready for me to defile her as soon as I walked in.

On the seventh day, I entered my room to see her in my bed, on her hands and knees, completely naked, her legs spread, giving me a perfect view of her ass and pussy. I instantly stripped the clothes from my body and began kissing her ass, shoving my fingers inside of her pussy, feeling how wet she was.

She moaned, "I'm so horny, and I want you so badly, Luke." I rubbed my thumb against her clit, her moans echoing throughout my room. "Please, just fuck me. I want to feel your cock inside me," she pleaded.

I instantly pulled out a condom and did exactly as asked. She grabbed my headboard as I pounded against her.

"Harder, Luke, fuck me as hard as you can." I started pounding harder against her, her arousal transferring to me. I found myself slipping a finger into her ass, causing her to moan even louder with her approval. I moved my finger in and out of her ass as I pounded her, enthralled. Before long, her whole body trembled with orgasm, setting off my own release. We both collapsed onto the bed, panting heavily.

I quickly ran into the en suite bathroom to clean myself and returned, snuggling up against her naked body. I felt intoxicated by her. I brushed my fingers through her hair, and kissed her gently, enjoying being close to her. After some time, we finally dressed, and I walked her downstairs to see her out of the packhouse.

Blake

I was home at the packhouse one evening, going through some emails on my laptop, when I heard moans from up above. I felt myself go hard at the noise, aroused by the thought of sex. It had been a long time, I thought to myself. Because the moans were barely audible from where I was sitting, it was hard to determine exactly who was making them, or if Luke was maybe just watching porn very loudly in his room. After some time, they stopped, and I forced myself to concentrate on my work again.

Before long, I could hear footsteps coming down the stairs. I snuck over to an area where I'd be unseen but able to see who was coming down, wondering if Luke had had Jasmine up in his room, feeling envious of his luck. But then I spotted the long legs and the blond hair. No, it wasn't Jasmine at all.

I waited until Luke walked Lucy to the door, kissing her deeply, and shutting it behind her. He smiled to himself and was about to head back upstairs. Before he could move too far, I jumped out and punched him in the face, breaking his nose. He fell backwards, a faucet of blood drenching his T-shirt.

He looked up, shock on his face. "What the fuck, man!" he yelled at me.

"I should be asking you, what the fuck, myself!"

"Why did you just punch me?" he shouted, adjusting his nose and standing up.

"Don't you have a fucking mate?"

I was enraged on Jasmine's behalf. He shook his head, his eyes closed, not answering me. I stood there, waiting. Finally, he spoke. "You're one to talk. You're the one who wants to make my mate your next pump and dump."

My fists clenched at his words, ready to deal another blow. "That's not fucking true! Why would you say that?" I bellowed.

"What, all of a sudden you're some saint? You act like I didn't witness what went on before you met your mate, and after. Let's see, there was Ashley, Tiffany, Andrea, Tina. Should I continue the list?"

"Look, man, I know I wasn't an angel in high school, or the year before I left for college. Hell, I wasn't an angel in Siberia either. But I like Jasmine. I care about her. And what you're doing to her is not cool. It's not right to string her along if you have no intention of dumping Lucy. If you want to be with Lucy, then at least reject Jasmine so she can move on. But don't pretend you need fucking space while you're in here fucking Lucy. That's really not cool, man. And what's even less cool is that you're showing up at her house while she's in heat, taking advantage of her."

"She told you about that?" I stared at him, not responding to his question. He continued, "My intention was not to take advantage of her."

"Then why would you go to her house when you knew she was in heat? What did you think would happen? You knew she wouldn't be able to make rational decisions in that state."

"I don't know. I just wanted to talk to her to make sure she knew not to go out and, you know, what happens during heat."

I rolled my eyes. "A phone call could have sufficed." I watched as he looked pained. His mouth and chin were covered in drying blood.

He shook his head. "Goddess, it's so fucking hard. I love Lucy, but the mate bond's just so strong with Jasmine. I can't even wrap my head around the idea of rejecting her. I don't know if I want to."

"Well, she's pretty fucking amazing. If she were my mate, I'd know to never reject her." I walked away, leaving Luke in his bloody state.

Chapter 35

Jasmine

Taking advantage of my willingness to run errands, my mom sent me to the grocery store with a list on a Saturday morning at the end of October, before work. I was placing zucchinis into a plastic bag when Lucy's mom pulled up next to me with her grocery cart.

"Ah, Jasmine! I'm so glad to see you!"

I was pleasantly surprised to hear that she was glad. There was hope that Lucy hadn't swayed her to believe that I had sprouted whiskers and a wormy tail. I replied, "Good morning, Ivy."

"It's been forever since we've seen you! I've been waiting for you to come by so I could tell you something."

I was wondering if Lucy had told her anything. I decided it would be best to just act like everything was normal. "Oh, what's that?"

"Well, I'm not sure if you remember, but a while back I told you a story about my old friend Katie."

"Yes, I remember that story. Did you ever get in touch with her?"

"As a matter of fact, yes, I did! We've been chatting through Facebook, and I was happy to learn she found a chosen mate at her new pack. What I've been dying to tell you is that she'll be coming here with her son to visit our pack over Thanksgiving weekend. She was able to book a room at the casino, and I really want you to meet her and her son. I think you'll really like both of them."

"I'd love to meet them," I replied, interested.

"She went to school with both your dad and me, so she'll probably have tons of stories about our old high school days to share with you." Ivy had a glint in her eyes as she said this.

"I'm looking forward to hearing all the stories."

"Perfect, I'll be in touch once she's in town so we can all plan to meet." She hugged me and strolled away.

Luke

After resolving to make things right, I fucked them up all over again. It was like taking one step forward and three steps back. The next day, my nose was fully healed, and Lucy was waiting in my room again. Thank the Goddess because she had clothes on this time. Otherwise, I wasn't sure my little head would have cooperated with my big one. Lately, it seemed to have a mind of its own.

"I'm wet and ready for you." Lucy ran over, reaching for my belt.

"No, wait, stop, Lucy." I used whatever little willpower I had to move her hand from my groin area. "Let's sit down. We need to talk."

"Talk after, fuck now." She tried again to reach for my belt.

"No, Lucy, I'm serious."

"Your cock definitely isn't." She looked down at my crotch where I was clearly sporting a boner.

"Okay, but he's not in charge right now. Let's sit down." I tried to pull her down to sit on the bed next to me.

"That's too bad, I like when he's in charge." She sat down and instantly grabbed for my crotch, causing me to groan. She wasn't going to make this easy.

I removed her hand and said, "Come on, Luce, please don't make this more difficult than it has to be."

"Well, you have no problem making this difficult for me. I've been horny all day and I want to fuck."

I sighed, putting my head in my hands. "Lucy, we can't do this anymore." I lifted my head and looked into her wide eyes, taking her hands in mine, and continued, "I have a mate. We've talked about this. I love you but we're not meant to be together. You have a mate somewhere out there too, and you'll meet him someday. Artemis wants us to be with our mates. I don't know why she chooses who she does for us, but I owe it to my mate to at least try to make things work. This isn't just about you and me. If I reject Jasmine, she doesn't get another mate. At least have some empathy for the person you've been friends with since grade school."

Lucy was silent. I searched her eyes, wondering if she would accept what I told her. It wasn't like her to just quietly accept anything. Finally, she exploded.

"I fucking hate Artemis. I fucking hate being a werewolf. And I fucking hate this pack. This whole place is so backward! But you know what I hate the most right now? Most of all, I hate you! I've loved you for four years. I've been loyal to you even while being apart from you for two years. You know my deepest, darkest secrets and I know yours. Your family's friends with my family. We've always been good together. When we have sex, our bodies fit, like we're two puzzle pieces coming together. And you're willing to just throw all of that away for someone you barely ever even spoke to before you found out she was your mate? I know both of you, and I just don't see it. You're not right for each other. And you know what you are? You're a fucking coward!"

She then grabbed her purse, ran out of my room slamming the door. Not long after, I heard the front door being slammed. I put my head in my hands, groaned, then got up and slammed my fist into the wall.

Jasmine

That evening, after taking a shower and returning to my bedroom, I was surprised to find a text from Luke. I hadn't heard from him in a month and had finally started to take Blake's advice to stop thinking about him. Out of sight, out of mind.

> *Luke*: Hey, sorry I've been out of touch for so long. I'd like to make it up to you. Can I take you out to dinner one night?
> *Luke*: I have pack duty tomorrow night, but maybe Monday evening if you're free?
> *Luke*: There's a nice Italian restaurant in the casino

I blinked at his texts. It seemed so out of the blue after not hearing from him for so long. But I had nothing to lose at this point, so I replied.

> *Me*: Sure, I will be free Monday evening
> *Luke*: Great, I will pick you up at 6?
> *Me*: Can we meet somewhere?
> *Luke*: Why?
> *Me*: My parents...
> *Luke*: We're mates right? I think it's time we tell them.

> *They can't be against your mate taking you out to dinner. I want to do the right thing now. I hope you'll give me a chance.*

I was baffled. I wondered what had caused his change of heart. Either way, I could feel my heart beating in my chest, a warm feeling in my body. Luke had come around. I was no longer mateless.

Not long after Luke's texts, I received one from Blake as well.

> **Blake Sexy AF**: *Have the day off tomorrow. Hiking?*
> **Blake Sexy AF**: *If your life's still a disaster, seeing my sexy body climbing a mountain will cheer you right up :)*
> **Blake Sexy AF**: *And don't forget, you have lunch duty from now on :)*

I stared at my phone. Two guys asking me out in one night. And not just any guys—the beta and the alpha. Never did I ever think something like this would ever happen to me.

Chapter 36

Jasmine

Since my parents were home on Sunday, Blake and I met at the library again. This time we took his car. I packed turkey sandwiches and cut-up vegetables to go with a ranch dip. I told my parents I had a lot of schoolwork and would spend the day at the library.

After driving to our secret spot and parking, Blake reached for his cell phone to remove it from the mount when a string of texts came in.

"Just a second, Jasmine. These look important," he said as he began reading through them.

Suddenly, I started to feel very warm. I pulled off the sweatshirt I had worn in preparation for the cool weather that day. I looked over at Blake, my eyes scanning his whole body, and felt a strong desire to touch him. I put my hand on his thigh and began rubbing it, distracting him from his phone.

He looked over at me and dropped his phone. "Fuck!"

"What?" I asked, inching my hand toward his crotch. I watched as a bulge formed.

He abruptly grabbed my hand and moved it back into my lap, then reaching to the floor of the car where his phone had fallen. He came back up with his phone and looked at me.

"Fuckin' A, you're in heat!" He closed his eyes, gripping the steering wheel, breathing heavily. After rolling down the windows he continued, "I have to drive back. There's been a security breach at our border. And holy fuck, I can barely concentrate right now." He shifted his car into drive and banged a U-turn to head back to where we'd come from.

After driving for some time, I leaned over, shoving my hand inside the bottom of his shirt, and rubbed my hands on his well-sculpted abs. I could feel him flex against my hands as I touched him, my panties becoming soaked with arousal, my breathing now heavy.

"Dear Goddess, Jasmine, please don't do that. It's taking everything in me not to pull over and throw you in my back seat so I can fuck you in every position that's physically possible in a car. You touching me is not helping at all."

"I want that so badly right now," I moaned, imagining Blake's chiseled body naked with me in the back of the car, the swelling between my legs practically becoming unbearable. I moved my hand down to his crotch to feel his bulge.

"Please, Jasmine, I'm begging you. I am going to do something I regret if you don't stop touching me." His jaw was clenched, and his knuckles were white from gripping the steering wheel so tightly. I shook my head and took my hands off him, realizing what I was doing.

In a moment of clarity, I had a thought. "I'm supposed to go to temple service tonight."

Blake replied, "You are not going to temple service tonight."

"But what will I tell my parents?"

"We'll think of something."

It wasn't long before I was possessed with desire again, wanting to feel every last inch of him, my whole body shivering with yearning. He stopped at a stop sign, and I boldly unbuckled my seatbelt and jumped across his lap, grabbing his face and bringing his lips to mine, my fingers against the rough stubble, his tongue instantly finding mine. We kissed fervently as he grabbed my breast with one of his hands, provoking me to moan against his mouth. My body backed against his steering wheel, resulting in a loud honk, which woke us from what we were doing, and I was able to gain enough awareness to move back into my seat.

Blake immediately hit the gas. I sat on my hands, finding it difficult to overcome the overwhelming longing I felt for Blake at that moment. After some more time driving, Blake said, "We're getting closer now and I can mindlink the pack again." After about a minute, he said, "It's not safe for you to be alone outside right now. I'm having Jack meet us at the border and he'll drive you to the packhouse in my car."

"Jack? Lucy's brother, Jack?"

"Yes, my friend Jack who's Lucy's brother."

"But he doesn't have a mate."

"You're safe with him."

"How am I safe with him?"

"Because he's gay."

"What!" I screamed.

"I'm surprised you didn't know considering he's your best friend's brother."

"No, I had no clue," I said. Blake stopped at another stop sign. I couldn't help myself as I, once again, grabbed for the bulge in his pants, completely abandoning our conversation. Blake had the steering wheel in a death grip as I reached for his belt buckle.

"Please, Jasmine, for the love of Artemis, don't do it. I will not be able to control myself. I am so fucking horny right now, and I don't think I have enough willpower to resist whatever you're planning to do." I looked up at his face. He appeared to be in pain looking down at me, his breath quick and shallow. "It's not much farther until we reach Jack."

"Why are you resisting? I thought this is what you wanted. This is all you ever talk about, and now you're rejecting me when I want it so badly," I cried out. Tears brimmed in my eyes, pained that he'd have spent so much time dangling a (huge) carrot in front of me and then pull it away just as I wanted it the most.

A car honked behind us and we both looked up. Blake then pulled over to the side of the road to let the car pass. He put the car in park and turned to me. "Jasmine, please look at me."

I turned my head so I was looking into his piercing blue eyes.

"I am not rejecting you. Even when you're not in heat, I want you so fucking much. But it's like how you said you didn't want to seduce Luke—you want him to come to you because he wants you. I also want to do things the right way. I want you to make this decision with a clear head. I don't want to take advantage of you right now just because I caught you while you were most vulnerable. So please, for the love of Artemis, just hold on a little longer until we get to Jack!"

I forced myself to sit back down on my hands. Blake then turned away from me and maneuvered the car back onto the road. I felt a pulsing between my legs that was becoming painful from the need to be relieved. I groaned.

"What's wrong?" he asked.

"I'm so horny that it hurts right now," I replied.

"Holy fuck."

After driving a few more minutes, Blake pulled over. Jack came to his window, looked down at Blake, and said, "Damn, never thought I'd see the day you'd be so hard for me. Must be my lucky day!" He grinned.

Blake laughed. He threw Jack his keys, patted him on the back, and said, "Thanks, buddy, I appreciate your help." He then sprinted toward the woods.

Jack sat in the driver's seat, looked over at me, and said, "Hey, Jaz, how's it going? Haven't seen you in a while."

"Hi, Jack," I replied.

"Blake told me a bit about your situation. I'm going to take you to the packhouse and set you up in one of the guest bedrooms for now.

Some warriors on patrol caught stranger werewolves just outside the pack border, so Blake has to deal with them." I nodded, having a hard time speaking from the pressure I was feeling between my legs. Jack continued the conversation. "So, what's this I hear about Luke being your mate? I take it that's why we haven't seen much of you lately?"

I groaned. "Has Lucy said anything?"

"Not to me, she hasn't. She must be devastated, though. To be honest, I think she was closer with Luke than even Kyle is with Emma."

I nodded, barely able to concentrate. The only thing I could think of was relieving the pressure between my legs, the swelling overwhelming. An image of Blake's naked body on top of me, gliding between my thighs, wouldn't leave my mind. I squirmed in my seat, trying my best not to act obvious in front of Jack. Once we got to the packhouse, Jack unlocked the front door and walked me in. He brought me upstairs to what was now Blake's old bedroom turned into a guest room. His old furniture was still there, but it was emptied of all the other contents. I sat on the bed, inhaling. Blake's scent, while faint, still permeated the room, clinging to the curtains and mattress.

"Just stay here for now. I'll be back in a bit. You can walk around the packhouse if you need anything while I'm out. No one's here right now."

I didn't want to do anything but lay down and take care of myself. I closed the door after Jack left and fell into the bed, my head falling against the pillow. I realized it must have been Blake's old pillow with how strongly it smelled of him. I breathed it into my lungs—and with it all my memories of Blake's amazing body, warming all my limbs. I unbuttoned my jeans, my hand finding its way south as I imagined what it could have been like had I not stopped Blake that day when he tried to remove my bikini bottoms. At that very moment, there was nothing I wanted more than to feel Blake's hips between my thighs, his chest brushing up against my erect nipples, the scratching of his stubble against my lips as I kissed him, and his deep breathing in my ear.

About an hour later, I heard a knock on the door. "It's Jack. Blake asked me to get something for you." I made sure I was presentable and opened the door. "Sorry, this is really awkward, Jasmine. I'll pretend it never happened." He handed me a bag that looked just like the one Blake had left in my car a month earlier.

My whole body burned with embarrassment. "Thanks, Jack," I said, and closed the door. I couldn't lie, though—I was appreciative for the gift, my right hand was now cramped.

After some time, a mindlink came through from Blake. *"I'm going to talk to my mom and have her call your parents to tell them you're in the clinic recovering after accidentally ingesting wild wolfsbane. Luke and I won't be home tonight so you can just go home whenever the heat passes."*

A shiver traveled the entirety of my body at the sound of his voice, and a disappointment followed that he wouldn't be returning home that night. Goddess, what I wouldn't do for a taste of Blake at that moment.

Chapter 37

Luke

I fell into bed around eleven the next morning. After the scent of a stranger pack was discovered by one of the junior warriors during his rounds, Mike and some of the other senior warriors tracked it. They discovered a den where two stranger werewolves were staying. They asked the wolves to shift into their human forms so that they could talk. But the wolves refused, attacking instead. Luckily, our warriors were able to take them down and force them into their human forms. They were then dragged into the cells and jailed.

After Blake arrived, they were brought out for interrogation and, up until that point, I hadn't realized how fucked up Blake was. I'd heard stories over the years of his father's interrogation techniques, but it was a whole different story to personally witness them. Blake had clearly picked up every trick in his father's book.

After chaining the strangers to the wall, he shoved a knife into each one of their thighs, only to pull it back out and allow their legs to partially heal and do the same thing again, continuously reopening the wound. He took a sword and cut their hands and feet off, one by one. Then he cut their ears off. At one point, he cut the balls off one of the strangers and forced the other one to eat them. I'd stayed strong until that point, but that pushed me over the edge. I doubled over and emptied the contents of my entire dinner onto the floor. But Blake seemed like he enjoyed it—got a sick pleasure from it. He smiled while they screamed and thrashed in agony, a glint in his eyes.

Blake didn't give up and continued the torture for hours while the few warriors that joined us kept running out to bring coffee and food. If torture were an art, Blake was an exceptionally creative artist. Once the strangers were completely mutilated beyond recognition, they were finally begging for death, and confessed that they were from the Silver Moon Pack in Maine. They had formed an alliance as a promise for reinforcement in their own ongoing disputes. Luckily, Silver Moon Pack was a smaller pack and not a true threat to us. However, it wasn't clear how many other packs may be forming alliances with the Bois Sombre Pack—it was likely they were not the only one.

Blake had the present warriors put together two packages—the left hands in one to mail to Silver Moon Pack, and the right hands in the other to mail to the Bois Sombre Pack. He then wiped his hands clean and, with a sick smile on his face, exclaimed, "Can't wait until another pack tries to case this place. I'm ready for round two."

It was already light out by the time we exited the cells, forcing me to squint after being in the dark for so long. I drove home with Blake. While we were driving, I decided to try to make amends with him after Friday's blowout. I glanced over at him quickly and said, "I want you to know that I'm going to do the right thing. I thought about what you said, and I ended things with Lucy. I've asked Jasmine out on a date tonight. Artemis chose us for each other, so I am going to make a sincere effort and try not to screw things up again."

When I glanced at him again, Blake nodded, not replying. I wondered what he was thinking. We used to be like brothers, practically able to read each other's minds. But ever since Ria died, he wasn't the same. He had closed himself off. There were times when it seemed like the old

Blake was still there, especially when he'd lighten up and joke around. But it was always short-lived. Most of the time he had only two personalities—serious or angry.

After I parked the car, we got out and headed to the house. Before we separated to go to our own floors, he said, "If I don't see you before you leave, good luck with your date." At least that was something.

I set my phone alarm for four thirty and fell into my pillow, completely exhausted.

Jasmine

I woke around eight the next morning, feeling that the heat had finally passed. I typed a quick text to Blake to let him know I'd gone home, in case he came looking for me whenever he came back. Then I cringed at my behavior the previous day. I couldn't believe how much I'd lost control in front of him, when I had a mate no less.

I turned completely red as I thought about how he had asked me to stop several times and I still persisted to try again and again to seduce him. Ugh! How embarrassing! Then I thought, with horror, if the tables were turned and I had been the man in that situation that, well, I had definitely not acted appropriately. I couldn't stop thinking about what a fool I'd made of myself. I walked over to the library, where my car was still parked, and drove it home to an empty house.

I logged in to my online classes and cringed as I checked my grades. It was not good news. I had completely slipped in every class. I knew if I didn't do something, my GPA would nosedive. It was now November and more than halfway through the semester. I'd have to request a leave of absence. I knew these grades didn't reflect who I was.

I decided to write the dean an email and tell him I'd been having mental health issues, trying to stay as vague as possible. I wasn't sure what options he'd offer me. My first year of college, I'd gotten an A in every class, no problem. I'd never been in this position before.

I then decided to get some different tasks done to take my mind off Blake and school. I did my laundry, cleaned my room, and organized my closet. Once it got closer to time for the date, I showered, did my hair and makeup, and picked out a nice dress to wear. I finished the look off by applying red lipstick. Then I cooked dinner and set the table for two. At least things with Luke seemed to be improving. So, it wasn't all a complete disaster anymore.

My parents walked through the door at around five thirty and I went over to greet them.

"Are you okay, Jasmine? What happened?" My mom ran over to me, her arms encircling me in a hug.

"I didn't even know wild wolfsbane grew in this area," my dad added. "How did you ingest it?"

"I was stressed out so I went for a run in my wolf form, and there must have been wolfsbane in the brook when I drank from it, because I suddenly felt really sick and ran to the clinic," I replied, recalling a story I'd heard of someone in the past who had done something similar.

"We were so worried when Dr. Luna called. I'm so glad you're okay," my mom said, releasing me from the hug and holding me at arm's length, looking me up and down. "Wow, you look nice. Are you going somewhere tonight?"

"I have a date," I replied.

"A date?" My mom raised an eyebrow at me.

"Yes, I met my mate," I replied.

"Well, that's wonderful news," my dad said, throwing his arms around me.

"Yes, very good news, honey!" my mom agreed.

"So, who's the lucky man?" my dad asked.

"Beta Luke." Both of them went silent.

"I think I need to sit down," my mom finally said, going to sit on the entryway bench.

"Well, that's certainly surprising," my dad said. "When did you find out he's your mate?"

"Just recently. He's obviously been gone a long time and just came back. The last time I saw him I was seventeen so I didn't realize until now when I saw him again."

"Well, being a beta's mate is very honorable," my dad said, but he didn't sound convincing.

"I'm sure the Moon Goddess knew what she was doing." My mom pressed her lips together in a thin line. The conversation definitely went a lot more awkwardly than I was expecting.

At six, the doorbell rang, and my father went to answer it, with me right behind him.

"Good evening, Mr. Dale," Luke said, putting his right hand out for a handshake. He had on a fall jacket that was unzipped to reveal a button-down shirt and tie underneath. In his left hand, he had a bouquet of colorful flowers.

"Good evening, Beta," my dad replied, shaking his hand. "So, Jasmine tells us you're her mate?"

"Yes, sir," Luke replied.

"Well, come on in."

"Hi, Jasmine." He came over to me and kissed me on the cheek. "You look beautiful." He handed me the flowers.

"Thank you," I replied, inhaling his intoxicating scent, feeling nervous.

"Can I get you something to drink? We have water, Coke, juice," my dad offered.

"Sure, water would be great, thank you."

"Jasmine, I'm going to take Beta Luke into the living room. Why don't you prepare those waters for us?"

"Okay," I replied, heading into the kitchen. He led Luke into the living room. I listened to hear what they were saying while I put the flowers into a vase and prepared two glasses of water.

"Well, it was certainly a surprise when we found out you were Jasmine's mate, Beta. How do you feel about it?" my dad asked him.

"Jasmine was the smartest and sweetest girl when we were in school together, and she's also beautiful. I am lucky that the Moon Goddess picked someone so perfect for me. I look forward to getting to know her more now that I know she's my mate."

"Okay, I'm glad to hear that. Now, it's no secret that you were, until recently, as far as I know, dating her friend. My assumption is that relationship is no longer?"

"Your assumption is correct. Lucy and I broke up now that I found the woman I am meant to be with. I'd like to, with your permission of course, take Jasmine out to a nice dinner tonight so we can begin our new relationship."

"Well, of course, Beta. Who am I to stand in the way of the Moon Goddess? I hope the two of you have a nice night and that we'll be seeing more of you around here."

"Thank you, sir. I'm sure you will."

I then went in to hand them their waters. Luke's responses were very polite, and I hoped they satisfied my dad. My dad took a couple sips of his water and said, "Well, I have to go eat my dinner now. But have fun tonight. And bring my daughter back in one piece, Beta."

"I certainly will, sir," Luke replied.

Once my dad left the living room, I led Luke outside after throwing on a jacket and grabbing a shopping bag. After I closed the door behind us, he stopped me at the doorstep and brushed his fingers through my hair. "You look so beautiful tonight, Jasmine. And you smell amazing too."

"Thank you," I replied. He took my hand and brought me to the car, opening the passenger door for me.

After we were both seated, I handed the shopping bag to Luke. "Thank you for letting me borrow your sister's clothes. Can you please return them to her?" Luke took the bag and thanked me, throwing it into the back seat. He then shifted into reverse to back out of the driveway.

As we were driving, Luke began conversing with me. "I'm glad you agreed to go out with me tonight. I want to take you somewhere nice as an apology for how I've acted since realizing I'm your mate. I'm hoping we can start over tonight." He glanced over at me, smiling.

A warmth spread through my chest. Being in the car with him, his whole scent surrounded me, making me feel relaxed and lustful. I couldn't help but want to forgive him.

I finally replied, "Thank you for inviting me out. Is it true what you told my dad—that you broke up with Lucy?"

He knit his eyebrows together and blinked his eyes a few times, then replied, "Yes, it's true."

"Why the sudden change of heart?"

"Because it was inevitable anyway. Ultimately, I'm meant to be with you and not Lucy. And Lucy's also meant to be with someone else. I've done a lot of thinking. I've screwed up and I want to make things right. Plus, to be honest, I've always kind of had a crush on you."

He quickly smiled at me, turning back to the road and continuing. "It's kind of funny, I used to dream about your scent sometimes." He laughed. "I'd go into department stores to try to figure out what it was, but I never could. Now it all makes sense." He took my hand, which sent sparks and calmness throughout my body. He kept my hand in his for the remainder of the drive.

Luke pulled into valet parking, where the valet helped me out of the car. I walked toward the entrance when I felt Luke's hand brush against mine, clasping his strong hand around mine, leading me into the casino.

I smiled to myself at how comforting the gesture felt. We walked through the halls, the loud sound of slot machines echoing, creating an exciting and vivacious ambience. We cut through the gaming floor, and I looked around, observing the bright lights of the slot machine screens reflecting off patrons, and people having lively conversations at card tables. The excitement of the casino penetrated me, and I found myself smiling brightly, feeling optimistic about the evening.

When we reached the restaurant, Luke went up to the host stand. "Good evening, Mr. Hemming. It's nice to see you tonight," the man behind the stand said. "We reserved the best seat in the house for you." He led us to a round booth at the back of the restaurant where we had a view of everything. The host handed us both menus after we sat down.

After a few minutes, a waiter came over to ask if we'd like anything to drink. I replied, "Just water for me, thank you."

"What wine do you recommend?" Luke asked.

"Ah, we have the perfect bottle for you, Mr. Hemming. It's on the house, of course. We'll bring it right out," the waiter replied.

Once he walked away, Luke turned to me and said, "They know me here since the pack owns the casino, so don't worry about being carded. But that's not why I brought you here. There's just not many other restaurants in the area, and I know this one's really good."

After some time, the waiter poured us both wine from a bottle after he presented it and opened it for us. After he walked away, Luke said, "Cheers," and touched my glass with his. We sipped from our glasses, and I was pleased to find the wine was actually really good. I normally found wine a bit too bitter or harsh, but this one had a nice sweetness to it.

After the waiter took our orders and menus, Luke moved closer to me until we were almost touching. Then he turned to me and said, "I know we never talked about what happened when I went over your house, and you were in heat. I really hope you don't regret anything that happened. It's been bothering me."

I flushed and replied, "I made a huge fool of myself, didn't I? How embarrassing. I won't do that again."

He looked at me, his eyes wide. "What? No, you didn't make a fool of yourself at all. Why do you think that?"

"Well, I obviously had no idea what I was doing. But I'll learn. I'm a quick learner." I looked in his eyes eagerly. I was sure my whole body was red.

He put his hand on my knee. "I can't believe you're even worried about that. That's not what I meant at all. I meant, I hope you don't regret that we, you know, got really intimate with each other."

I looked down at my lap, fidgeting with my hands. "Oh. No, I don't regret that. I actually really enjoyed it." My chest tightened, and my face, neck, and ears burned from the candid admission.

"Okay, good. I just really want you to know that it wasn't my intention to take advantage of you. So, I'm glad you don't regret anything that happened. I enjoyed it a lot too. Kissing you and being with you is so amazing. I've never felt anything like it." He put his arm around my body, pulling me against him, setting off calm and sparks throughout my body.

The waiter brought out bread for us. Then a different waiter came out with a charcuterie board. He placed it in front of us and said, "Compliments of the chef. Here we have some parmesan flown in from Italy this morning, aged twenty-four months, our most popular imported salami, prosciutto di San Daniele, and our house-made mozzarella." He pointed out each item as he spoke.

After our main course was served, a tall man dressed in a suit came over to our table. As soon as I inhaled his scent, I instantly recognized that he was a werewolf from our neighboring pack that owned the pharmaceutical company my parents worked for.

"Good evening, Beta Luke. It's nice to see you joining us tonight. And may I ask who this beautiful lady is?"

Luke stood up, pulling me up with him. "Of course, Nate. Let me introduce you to my mate, Jasmine." Luke then looked at me and said, "Jasmine, this is Nate. He manages this restaurant. He's from the Autumn Moon Pack."

Nate held out his hand for me to shake. Once I took his hand, he said, "It's such a pleasure to meet you, Jasmine." I noticed his eyes glanced at my collarbone. After letting go of my hand, Nate looked at Luke and said, "No mark on her yet, I see. Must still be early days."

"That's correct," Luke replied. "We just very recently realized that we're mates, and it's our first date."

"Well, I hope she's marked next time I see you," he winked at Luke. "Anyway, I wanted to come by and say hello to our VIP guests. Anything you need, just let our staff know and we'll take care of you."

We sat back down to eat our meal. Luke turned to me and said, "I hope you don't mind taking things slowly, Jasmine. I'm still processing everything. But I'm guessing you'd want to wait until after marriage for marking anyway?"

"Yes, I think my parents would have a fit if we marked each other before marriage, and I like that we're taking things slowly," I replied. I could sense that he felt relieved by my response. I began to consider if I actually was ready to bind myself to him for the rest of our lives. Usually, werewolves marked each other almost immediately after meeting their mates, the desire to do so was overpowering. I felt it too, but I also felt a resistance to it, as if it didn't feel quite right. It was probably due to starting things off on the wrong foot.

After we had coffee and dessert, Luke led me outside the back of the building where there was a golf course. We threw our jackets on, feeling the chill of the beginning of November. He took my hand to bring me over to a line of golf carts. "Stay here, I'll be right back," he said, unlocking a door next to the golf carts.

He came back out with a key and waved me over. He helped me into the driver seat of one of the golf carts and then got into the passenger side. "Let's go for a ride!" he said and showed me how to start up the cart. I drove it out onto the green. We drove around aimlessly, just talking and laughing.

He finally told me to stop. We found ourselves in the middle of the golf course, far from the casino. He came around to draw me out of the golf cart and dropped to the ground, pulling me down with him into the grass. We lay together on our backs, staring at the stars up above. "Do you know anything about constellations?" he asked.

"Nope," I replied.

"Well, let me educate you." He smirked. "See those stars over there? The ones that are all clustered?" He pointed toward the sky.

"I think so," I replied, thinking that his description was not specific enough to know which stars he was talking about.

"Well, that's Princess Wolf Enim-saj."

"Princess Wolf Enim-saj, really?" I turned to look at him, raising one of my eyebrows.

"Yes, Princess Wolf Enim-saj." He had a silly grin on his face. "She was a beautiful, beautiful wolf with amber-colored eyes. So beautiful that Zeus wanted her all to himself. But Enim-saj was not interested in Zeus and preferred a more handsome and stronger gentleman wolf name Ekul." I laughed and Luke continued. "Artemis saw how perfect the two wolves were for each other, so she blessed them as mates."

"What about Zeus?" I asked.

"He challenged Ekul to a duel to the death."

I played along, gasping dramatically. "So what happened?"

"Well, Princess Wolf Emin-saj was afraid they would kill each other. And she was such a selfless wolf that she sacrificed herself, turning herself into stars. And it's now said that when someone wishes to meet their own beautiful wolf, they should make a wish on her constellation." He then turned to face me smiling. "But, for the record, if the duel went on, Ekul would have won."

I laughed, punching him playfully and asked, "So, did you make a wish?"

"Of course I did. That's how I met the beautiful Princess Wolf Jasmine." He beamed, his whole face lighting up. "Princess Foxy Jasmine actually."

"Foxy?"

"You remind me of a fox in your wolf form. So beautiful. And foxy."

"Foxes are orange."

"Some are brown. The quick brown fox jumps over the lazy wolf." He snickered.

"You're missing a *d*." I laughed.

He looked at me, confusion on his face. Staring at me intently, he replied, "I can guarantee you I'm not. Missing a *d*."

A flush burned across my cheeks as I realized what I had accidentally implied. "I meant, *d* for *dog*. When you're typing. The *dog*'s the *d* on the keyboard. You said wolf so the sentence didn't have a *d*," I frantically tried to explain.

"Relax, I know." He smiled. "You're so cute. But, for the record, Ekul does have a *d*. Of course, you know that already."

I couldn't help but now recall what I knew in graphic detail, feeling my whole body overheating even with how chilly it was outside. He kissed me on the cheek, the ensuing spark practically zapping me with how sensitive I felt at that moment, breathing in Luke's scent, being so close to him, buzzed off the wine.

"So do you actually know anything about constellations?" I asked out of nervousness, thinking I should change the subject.

"Nope." He laughed. "But I wanted to impress you, like in the movies," he said, pulling me toward him and kissing me. Fireworks erupted as his lips touched mine. He deepened the kiss, pulling me closer to him, his hands all over my back. I completely lost myself in the kiss as our bodies moved against each other, rolling all over the grass. I felt abandoned and didn't even care that I was rolling on the ground in a nice dress and jacket. I wrapped my legs around him, my dress hiked up so high my underwear was exposed. And yes, I felt his *d*, which was very much not missing, throbbing against the thin fabric of my panties.

Once we were gasping for air, we finally separated. Luke lay on his back as I put my head on his shoulder. He pulled me close to him and said, "Kissing someone you have a mate bond with has to be the most magical thing I've ever felt. I've had a lot of good kisses in my life, but nothing like this," he said.

"Mmm," I replied in agreement. He was right. I enjoyed kissing Blake, but kisses with Blake didn't emit literal sparks like they did with Luke.

"Even just lying here with you is magical. It feels like we're supposed to be together. I can't even bring myself to stop touching you."

I snuggled closer to him, and we began kissing again, the mate bond pulling us forcefully back toward each other.

Cold droplets falling from the sky interrupted us. Luke pulled me up and helped me back into the golf cart. We drove back to where we had come from and parked the cart in the same spot we originally got it. Luke put the key back and then we walked toward the casino entrance as a drizzle fell on us. Luke looked at me once we entered the building and brushed down my hair with his hands. His hair was tousled, which was actually kind of sexy, and he had traces of my lipstick all over his face. We both started laughing looking at each other. "We should probably clean ourselves up," Luke said as he led us to the bathrooms.

I entered to some girl looking me up and down. I then looked in the mirror to see my hair was in complete disarray and my lipstick had spread widely from where it had been applied. I also had grass stains on my jacket and the skirt of my dress. I laughed at my reflection.

So much for Perfect Jasmine.

I brushed my fingers through my hair, trying to put it back in order, and wet a paper towel to clean my face. I had worn a rich, red lipstick, which I had reapplied after dinner, and it had stained the skin surrounding my lips. I eventually gave up on trying to remove it, knowing I'd need to use makeup remover.

I exited the bathroom to find that Luke had had the same problem that I had. He took my hand and led me to the valet area. The valet person smirked and asked, "Good night?" Luke and I looked at each other laughing. He then went to retrieve the car after Luke handed him the ticket.

Luke drove me home. I sighed in relief when I saw that the lights were all off, so my parents wouldn't bear witness to my disheveled appearance. Luke got out and opened my door for me. He then walked me to the front door.

"I had an incredible night with you tonight, Jasmine. I'm looking forward to our next date." He pulled me against him until our entire bodies were touching. He looked down at me and brought his lips to mine. We must have kissed for at least ten minutes before finally pulling apart. "Have a good night, Jasmine," Luke said and turned to go. Before I entered the house, he turned to look at me, smiling and waving goodbye.

I ran up into my bathroom to clean myself before my parents could possibly have a chance to take in my appearance. I sighed as I washed my face, thinking that this had to have been one of the best nights I'd ever had in my life. That night I dreamed about Luke's scent overtaking all of my senses and woke up aroused, tangled in my bedsheets.

Chapter 38

Luke

The day after my date with Jasmine, I ran the border of the pack grounds in my wolf form to do a patrol check. When I got to Mike's location at the northern border, I stopped and mindlinked him to see how things were going.

"*All good, Mike?*"

"*All good today, Beta. Sent the juniors out one hundred yards at the start of the shift.*"

"*Good.*"

"*That was the first time you witnessed an interrogation on Sunday, wasn't it?*"

"*Yes.*"

"*You'll get used to it.*"

"*Yeah, that was definitely an interesting experience.*"

"*Alpha Blake's so much like his dad it's uncanny. The sick shit he comes up with, like feeding one guy's balls to another.*"

My stomach churned recalling the incident.

"*His dad used to do the same shit. One time he cut a dick off and shoved it in the guy's ass. I think his son may have actually been there for that one too. That was many years ago.*"

I recalled that Blake used to be forced to attend tortures with his father. I couldn't imagine having to witness what I did at only ten years old. Even at twenty-one I felt like I had endured some form of psychological damage watching Blake mutilate live people.

When he was a kid, Blake would often come into my room, woken from nightmares, and ask if he could stay the night. He'd be shaking, with tears in his eyes, so I'd let him sleep in my bed with me to try to comfort and help him. Even back then I noticed that he'd begun to change. He had always been such a happy-go-lucky kid, but it was as if his dad had stolen his innocence, forcing him to grow up too soon as he became more serious and withdrawn.

After he met Ria, it seemed like he'd begun to heal. A lot of the happy-go-lucky parts of him, from when he was a kid, began to come back. He joked and laughed more easily. We were all really happy for him, and everyone loved Ria. She had a biting sense of humor—very sarcastic. She teased Blake relentlessly, which he took in good humor. Their bantering was always hilarious to listen to. She was a perfect match for him. We all cried when we found out she'd been killed in battle. That was the final straw that completely crushed Blake. He was never the same again after that. The old Blake had been completely wiped from existence. Now Ria was a topic we all did our best to avoid.

*** *Four and a half years ago* ***

It was early January—the time of year that's dark, cold, and snow is a permanent part of the landscape. The roads were so terrible out where we live that it was almost impossible to leave the pack territory, especially if you didn't have a vehicle made for off-roading.

I had a fully loaded schedule. I was in my junior year of high school and was now training with the warriors after school three times a week and all day Saturday. It didn't leave me much time for a social life, but I still found time to hang out with my buddies when I could—anything to get out of the packhouse. Ever since the battle in late August, it was like a cloud had descended over our residence and never left. Blake, who I'd always been close to, no longer talked to me. Instead, it was a constant show of arguing and throwing of objects between him and his father. At this point, we may as well have hired a permanent, live-in handyman with how often someone had to come over to make repairs. Of course, that was when Blake was home, which most of the time he simply wasn't. No one knew where he went. He disappeared sometimes for days at a time.

At first, I tried to talk to him. We all did. But it was fruitless. Blake, as we knew him, was gone, and all that was left was an empty shell of who he had been. His father had been cracking away at him for years. And then Ria finished him—breaking him for good.

I had been sitting at the dining room table one afternoon, working on homework, when the doorbell rang. Being the closest to the entrance, I got up to answer it. I opened the door to a very attractive girl, who I instantly recognized as the older sister of one of the guys in my class. Her name was something with a *K*—Kayla, Karla, Kara? Her eyes were bloodshot, and she looked disturbed as she looked at me.

"Is Blake home?" she asked.

"Wait here, I'll go check." I sighed, closing the door on her. The polite thing was to let her in, but I knew that could be a recipe for disaster.

I walked up the stairs to the alpha floor and knocked on Blake's door.

"Yes?" Blake's voice sounded.

"There's someone here to see you. A girl."

"Not interested," he replied curtly.

"She looks upset." I tried to encourage him to speak with her.

"Just tell her I'm not here."

I walked back downstairs and opened the door again. "He's not home," I said.

"Please, I need to see him. I can see his car in the lot." She was quickly becoming hysterical. "He won't answer any of my texts or calls. I need to talk to him."

"I'm sorry, he's not home." I reached out to touch her arm, seeing how desperate she was.

"Please, help me. I know there was something between us. I can't believe he would just ignore me after everything." She started sobbing, her entire face turning red, fat tears rolling down her cheeks. I was dumbfounded, not knowing what to do. I soon sensed the scent of my mom and Blake's mom as they entered the room. I stepped outside, shutting the door behind me so they wouldn't witness what was happening.

"I'm sorry, I can't help you. I'm sure Blake didn't mean to hurt you. He's just not in a good place right now."

"So he thinks it's okay to just play with people's feelings? He thinks it's okay to just sleep with someone and then pretend nothing ever happened?"

I shook my head. Blake had always been a player, but he had become even more callous in the past few months. I was surprised that women still flocked to him even with his reputation. It was always the same story—they thought they were going to be the one to change him and change his ways. But Blake was Blake, and now he was an even more fucked-up version of Blake.

"You should go. I'm sorry," I said, not knowing what else I could say. I didn't think explaining that she wasn't the only one would help the situation. She sniffed, likely resigning to the fact that it was over, and walked away feebly.

"Who was that?" my mom asked as soon as I reentered the house, her, Blake's mom, and my dad all staring at me.

"Just some girl," I said.

"One of Blake's girls?" Luna Sienna asked. I nodded. They turned away and walked toward the living room. I went back to the dining room to return to my homework.

"I don't know what to do," Luna Sienna cried. "I can't stand seeing Blake like this." I continued to pretend to do my homework, but I instead turned my attention to the conversation, which I could easily overhear with the open floor plan of the packhouse. She continued, "He was always such a sweet boy growing up. This isn't my Blake."

"He is James's son. I'm really sorry, Sienna. I pray to Artemis it isn't the case, but this is how it started with James. After his father died, he acted out in exactly the same way. It's almost like watching history repeat itself."

"I just want to help Blake so much. But he's shut me out." I could tell Sienna was speaking through tears.

"He's shut all of us out," my mom responded.

Luna Sienna spoke again. "He's grieving. And James isn't helping the situation. He's fixated on Blake becoming alpha. No matter what I say or do, he won't listen to me. Blake needs to heal. He can't become alpha now. I know James is worried after so many people died during the battle, but can't he see that Blake isn't in a position to take on so much responsibility right now?"

"Sienna, I'll speak with him," my dad said. "I can understand where James is coming from. We can't deny that the pack is growing weak, but we also can't have a leader that's so unstable right now. Maybe we can find a compromise."

"Ria was so good for him." Luna Sienna sniffed. "After everything James put him through, it seemed like Blake would finally be okay. Why did she have to die? Why did Artemis take her life? Why does my Blake have to suffer so much? I just wish I could take it all away from him. I just want my son back. All I do is pray all the time, but I'm starting to lose hope." She was sobbing now.

"Don't lose hope, Sienna," my mom consoled her. "You can't. Blake will heal. He just needs time. Al and I will talk to James. We'll figure something out. And we'll pray for him too. Artemis never gives anyone more than they can handle. Blake's a strong boy. He'll find his way through this."

"His grandmother didn't," Sienna cried.

"They never marked each other, don't forget." My dad was speaking now. "There's hope. The pain would be much worse if they had marked each other. Blake still has a chance to get past this."

After they left the living room, I made my way back upstairs and knocked on Blake's door.

"Yes?" his voice sounded.

"Can I come in?" I asked. I knew this was a stupid idea, but we had been close before all this happened. Maybe there was still hope that some semblance of our friendship was still there.

"Fine," he said. I opened the door. Blake sat up in his bed. I looked at him to see that he had practically grown a beard—it had clearly been a long time since he'd last shaved.

"We're all worried about you, man," I said. He looked at me, not saying anything. After a pause, I spoke again. "What happened with that girl that came by today?"

"Which one was she?" he asked.

"I think her name starts with a *K*. Kayla? Karla? Kara?"

"Christa," he said.

"She was really upset."

"I don't know why. She came onto me. What did she expect was going to happen?"

"Maybe she really liked you?" I offered.

He scoffed.

"Don't you think it's a little fucked up that you're sleeping around with the same people that you're going to be leading?"

"It's just sex," he replied.

"Maybe to you, but clearly it means more to these girls."

"Did you come in here just to lecture me, Luke? Because if so, then I'm done with this conversation."

I nodded and walked out of the room.

I continued my run after saying goodbye to Mike. Kyle and his dad, Haydon, were at the next stop. I felt awkward approaching them, but I had no choice. Since Haydon was the senior in charge, I mindlinked with him. *"All good today, Haydon?"*

"All good, Beta." He sounded sad.

Feeling like I couldn't avoid the topic, I broached it. *"How's Lucy doing?"*

"She's okay. She'll eventually get over it and meet her mate. I just hate seeing her like this. I know why you broke up with her, and I don't blame you, but it's just hard seeing your daughter in so much pain."

"I'm sorry, sir. I wish things had gone differently. I love Lucy and I hate that I had to hurt her like this. I should have never allowed the relationship to get as serious as it did. We were kidding ourselves thinking things wouldn't end like this."

"Hey, it's ok, Luke. Lucy's a strong girl. She comes from generations of warriors. So don't worry too much about her. That's my job. Go enjoy your mate. There's nothing like the mate bond. I'm pretty sure Ivy and I lasted only two days before we marked each other. One day it will happen for Lucy too."

"Thanks, sir, I appreciate it." I felt an ache in my chest.

Chapter 39

Luke

I had the evening off on Wednesday night, so I decided to surprise Jasmine once she ended her shift at work. While on my way, I stopped at the grocery store and picked up a bouquet of roses. I removed a single rose and told the cashier that I'd like her to have the rest. I waited until Jasmine got out of work and met her at the front door as she and Valerie were closing up.

"Well, hello there, Casanova. Have you come to seduce me too?" Valerie laughed. She then lightly punched me in the arm and walked away.

After Valerie disappeared down the street, I turned to Jasmine and said, "I'd like to exchange a single rose for a single Jasmine." I internally cringed at myself, thinking how corny that sounded. Jasmine giggled, likely out of politeness because that was lame even for me.

She took the rose and smiled, saying, "Thank you."

"I couldn't wait to see you again. I hope you didn't make any other plans tonight."

"No, I didn't."

"Ok, perfect. How do you feel about ice-skating?"

"That sounds great." She smiled. She was so cute looking up at me with her amber eyes. I couldn't help but pull her in for a deep kiss, enjoying the feeling of sparks as I kissed her. I kissed her down her neck and wished we were alone so I could keep kissing her farther down.

I walked her to my car and opened the door for her, helping her get in and getting a glance at her ass as she climbed into her seat. She did have a nice ass. After closing her door, I hopped into the driver's seat and sped toward the closest ice-skating rink, which was about a half hour away.

During the car ride, we fell into easy conversation. Being with Jasmine was easy. We had so much in common and laughed at the same things. It was almost like she was the female version of me in some ways. I held her hand during the drive, enjoying the feeling of sparks and calm that fell over me.

Once we got to the rink, I rented two pairs of figure skates for us. After putting them on, we went onto the ice and held hands as we skated around in a large circle. I could tell Jasmine would be easy to fall in love with.

After skating for some time, we exited the rink, and I bought us some hot dogs and hot chocolate from the concession stand. We sat on the bleachers surrounding the rink, far from others, and I snuggled her close to me as we ate and drank.

Suddenly, she turned to me and said, "I've been wondering something."

"What is it?" I looked into her eyes. I could sense she felt nervous. I instinctively put down my hot chocolate and took her hands in mine to calm her.

She looked down. "That day you came over my house when I was in heat—you didn't want me to return the favor. Why was that? Was it because you thought I'd be bad at it?"

"No, that's not it at all! Is that what you thought?" She looked up at me and I searched her eyes.

She looked down again and continued, "I don't know. I thought that might have been the reason, since I'm not experienced. I know that you're probably used to being with someone who knows what they're doing."

I shook my head, wondering how I kept getting everything wrong, and replied, "That's not the reason at all. Trust me, I wanted it so badly. But when you said you'd never done it before, I felt like it would have been wrong to ask you. I knew if you hadn't been in heat, then we would never have gone that far, especially since I still hadn't told Lucy anything about us yet. Mostly, I didn't want you to end up doing something that you'd regret later."

"Oh," she said, looking down.

"I was trying to do the right thing. And I feel terrible if I insulted you. It doesn't bother me at all that you're inexperienced. I'm just trying not to rush things. But if you wanted to take things faster, I definitely wouldn't complain."

She laughed nervously, continuing to look down. "I think I do want to take things faster. When I'm around you, I just have all these feelings. But I've never acted on them before, so I don't really know what to do."

"What kind of feelings?" I asked, knowing because I felt them too. Plus, the mate bond allowed me to sense what my mate was feeling. I could feel myself going hard, forcing me to adjust how I was sitting so it wouldn't be obvious. I was dying for Jasmine to tell me using her words.

She laughed nervously again. "Well, you know—I know you feel it too. I get really warm and turned on, especially when I smell your scent."

"Yes, I know exactly how you feel because I feel it too." She looked in my eyes as I smiled at her, wishing we were somewhere more private. "How late can you stay out tonight? Instead of taking you home, I could always bring you back to the packhouse. But I won't be hurt if you say no. I don't want to rush you into anything you don't want to do."

"Yes, I'd like to go to the packhouse tonight," she said. I brushed her hair back with my fingers, kissed her, and we smiled at each other as we separated. I wished we were already there. I could only imagine how good a blow job would feel with the added bonus of the mate bond. After we finished our hot chocolates, we returned our figure skates, and I drove back. The anticipation was killing me during the drive home.

I opened her passenger door and helped her out of the car. I had asked the office manager to get someone in right away to fix the hole in my bedroom, and it had been fixed yesterday, thankfully. That definitely would have been an awkward story to explain.

When we entered, Blake was home. He greeted us and smirked at something when he looked at Jasmine. I gave him a hard stare, wondering what he could be smirking about. Then I noticed his eyes glossed over, turned skyward, clearly in a mindlink, and her face turning red. He walked away from us to go do something else. My body tensed in rage that they were sharing secrets, and right in front of me no less!

Once we were in my room, I asked, "What did Blake mindlink you?"

"Oh, Goddess, it's so embarrassing. I can't tell you." Jasmine covered her face with her hands, covering a flush that crept across her cheeks.

"What is it? Please tell me." She shook her head. "Please," I asked again, more softly, taking her hands so I could look into her eyes. "I'm your mate. You can tell me anything."

I let go of her hands and looked on as she stared at the floor, clearly deliberating on whether to tell me or not. She finally sighed and said, "While you and Blake were out on Sunday all night, I slept in the guest bedroom here. I don't know if Blake told you the whole story, but I went into heat and Jack bought me a vibrator. I completely forgot about it and the housekeeper discovered it."

"Blake definitely failed to mention this story to me, and I have so many questions now." I tried to keep my voice even as I spoke, clenching my fists into balls as my muscles quivered and my body heated.

"It was a weird situation. I couldn't go back home because my parents would expect me to go to temple service, which was obviously out of the question. So, Blake had his mom call my parents and tell them I'd ingested wolfsbane so they wouldn't know I was in heat."

"But why was Jack involved in all this?"

"Did you know he's gay?"

"Jack's gay?" I was shocked. I couldn't believe that I had been friends with Lucy's entire family for so many years and had never known.

"Yeah, I didn't know either until Sunday. I didn't even know werewolves could be gay, to be honest."

"Yes, they can, but you probably don't know of any because Alpha James would banish them from the pack. That's probably why Jack was never open about it."

"But when they get mates, are they male or female?"

"Male."

"If the Moon Goddess is willing to grant male mates to males, why would the temple and pack be against it? The Moon Goddess doesn't make mistakes."

"Alpha James was very traditional. But Blake's definitely not. I think you'll see a lot of changes to the pack in the coming years. Jack's one of Blake's closest friends, and I very much doubt he'd ever banish him."

She nodded.

"Anyway, next time you go into heat, can you please not involve Blake? I'd rather be the one that's there for you as your *mate*." I emphasized the word, something deep within me compelling me to make it clear to her. "I know we were on bad footing this time around, but I'm going to be a good mate to you moving forward, so you can come to me for anything."

She nodded again.

Not wanting to waste more time with this conversation that was just causing me to become irritated, I moved in to kiss her, starting out gentle, nibbling on her bottom lip. She returned the kiss, parting her lips, drawing my tongue into her mouth. Before long, we fell into bed together. I eased her shirt off, kissing down her chest, and unhooked her bra, pulling it off her. I kissed down to her right nipple, sucking on it as a moan escaped her lips. I then kissed across her chest to the other one and did the same thing, savoring the feeling of her erect nipple against my tongue. Before long, I removed my own shirt, and her hands flew to my abs, gliding up my body to my pecs. I loved the feeling as she ran her hands up and down my torso, emitting calm and sparks. The sparks flowed right to my cock, which I could feel throbbing within my pants, begging to be freed.

I kissed down Jasmine's belly very slowly, as she flexed her core, revealing that she had her own set of abs. My tongue brushed against the ridges. When my lips reached her jeans, I undid them and pulled them off her. I slid mine off too. I lay down next to her and kissed her again. After pulling away, I asked her, "How far do you want to go?"

"I want to learn how to give you a blow job," she replied, a deep blush spreading across her cheeks. I could feel my cock was rock-hard at this point. I couldn't help but picture her lips sliding up and down the length of it.

"Okay," I replied. "If you feel uncomfortable at any point, just let me know. It's okay." I removed my boxer briefs, my erection springing free. She moved down, putting her hand on it, provoking me to groan from how good it felt. "Just put your mouth and hand on it, suck very gently, and move your mouth up and down. And make sure you avoid using your teeth."

As I'd imagined, it felt amazing. The sparks emitted by the bond and the feel of her mouth on me were like nothing I'd ever experienced before. She worked intently, following my instructions. I guided her gently as needed, but found she was a natural. I watched her as she bobbed her head up and down, glancing at me for reassurance, her enchanting amber eyes locking with mine.

The mix of seeing Jasmine's beautiful naked body with her mouth on my cock and how good it felt with the bonus addition of the sparks, well, I didn't last long. My lower body was trembling as I was brought to the edge of climax and said, "I'm going to come." Before I could pull out of her mouth, I came inside it. She looked a bit shocked but swallowed. "Sorry about that. We probably should have discussed that beforehand. You didn't have to swallow it, but it was really hot watching you do that." I smirked.

"I didn't know what else to do with it." She turned red and looked down, saying very quietly, "Lucy told me before that you like when she swallows." Then she looked up and said, "Sorry, I don't know why I just brought that up."

I looked at her, dumbstruck, the reality of the situation hitting me. I didn't even know how to respond to that comment. I pulled her down to lie next to me and said, "You don't have to do what Lucy does. If you don't want to swallow, I would enjoy the blow job either way." I put my fingers through her hair and said, "You did a great job for your first time. I was really impressed. Now let me return the favor."

I got up and slid her panties off, then kissed inside her thighs, using my hands to massage the sides of her ass. I inhaled her delicious scent, which compelled me forward. I began using my tongue to lick her from bottom to top until I found her clit. I sucked it, which caused her to produce a loud moan, encouraging me to continue. I licked her clit, brushing my tongue back and forth, gently at first but adding pressure, enjoying the sound of her moans from above. I glanced up to where she was lying with her eyes closed, lost in the pleasure. I took my pointer and middle finger and pushed them inside her, searching for her G-spot, something that was much easier to do when I could practically sense what she was feeling. Goddess, she was so tight. I continued to lick her while stimulating her inside at the same time. Before long, I could feel her body contracting and her legs shaking, then she gave off one final, long moan, indicating she had come. I kissed the inside of her thighs before I went back to lie down next to her.

I held her naked body against mine, inhaling her beautiful scent. Yes, Jasmine would definitely be easy to fall in love with.

Chapter 40

Luke

The following Friday, my whole family came over to the packhouse for dinner. My parents had come home for the weekend after spending the past month in Quebec, my father having taken over my old job. My sister Peyton brought her newborn, whom my mom was desperate to finally meet. Blake and his parents were also in attendance. They'd become an extended part of the family over the years.

I invited Jasmine to introduce her as my mate to everyone. I brought her around to all the guests so she could meet my family.

My mom pulled her in for a huge hug. "Oh my goodness, Jasmine. I am so happy that Lukey found his mate! And what a wonderful mate the Moon Goddess gave him. I couldn't have picked a better one myself." She started dabbing a tissue at her eyes, being melodramatic as usual.

All of my nieces and nephews came over to hug Jasmine, welcoming her to the family. Noah, who was ten, asked her, "Have you guys done it yet?"

I lightly whacked him on the top of his head. "That's not how you speak to a lady, Noah. Now go learn some manners."

He rubbed his head and gave me a pointed look. "I don't think you guys did it anyway because you're not marked."

"Where did you learn about that?" I asked him.

"My friend Bobby told me. He said that mates mark each other after they do it. His older brother told him that."

I shook my head at him.

While sleeping with your mate was not guaranteed to end in marking each other, the feeling to do so was usually so overwhelming that it frequently occurred after the first time. Religious people normally waited until they were married to mark each other, to not make their sinful behavior obvious. No one actually believed that anyone waited until after marriage—not even sure how a female going into heat would make that possible—but people liked to keep up the image. That was the reason Blake and Ria had waited—his parents thought it would be disrespectful to the temple if an alpha didn't wait, being the leader of the pack and representative of the pack's beliefs.

"Ugh, I am not looking forward to having a teenager in the house!" Peyton sighed, overhearing the conversation. She walked over and asked Jasmine if she wanted to hold her new baby. Jasmine took my new nephew in her arms. I felt a warm feeling in my body as I watched her hold him. After a minute, she handed him back to Peyton and said, "Congratulations, he's incredible."

My dad came over and hugged Jasmine saying, "Welcome to the family, Jasmine. We're so happy that Luke met his mate. Now, get busy producing a beta heir for us, will you? It took us forever to make Luke, so I suggest you get started as soon as possible." He laughed.

"Dad!" I gave him a warning look. Jasmine blushed.

Blake's mom jumped in. "There's no rush. I didn't have Blake until I was thirty and everything worked out just fine." She smiled. "I'm sure Jasmine wants to finish school first anyway. I've heard she's a great student."

"Just don't wait too long," Blake's dad chimed in. He looked over at Blake and said, "You either, Blake. Let's make sure the pack stays nice and strong for the next generation."

Blake rolled his eyes at his dad. My dad pulled me aside and said, "Hey, Luke, while I'm here, do you mind fixing something on my iPad for me? I can't get into my emails anymore." I told Jasmine I'd be right back and walked over to the living room, where my dad's iPad was lying on one of the end tables, to see what was wrong with it. Last time he had accidentally put it in airplane mode.

As I played around with his iPad, I glanced back over at Jasmine who was laughing at something Blake whispered in her ear. She pushed him on his arm, and he snickered at her, smiling much wider than I had seen him smile in years. She returned the smile, her eyes shining as she looked at him. In reaction, my hands gripped the iPad very tightly, practically breaking it. They were clearly much closer than they had both led me to believe, their chemistry evident. Jealousy at the pit of my stomach, I observed as they were lost in their own world, apparently oblivious to everyone around them.

Blake's mom finally tapped Blake to ask him something, and I could see that he was surprised, as if he'd forgotten where he was. He followed his mom to the kitchen while Peyton and Lauren went over to talk to Jasmine.

I finally figured out that my dad had simply moved the icon for his email on accident, so it was no longer in its usual place in the bottom menu, but on a different screen instead. I moved the icon back to where it was previously and handed it back to him. Blake, his mom, and my mom helped Connie bring all the food out to the dining room table and then they called us to be seated.

I sat next to Jasmine, Lauren on one side of me and my mom next to Jasmine. I looked down to where the former alpha was sitting at the head of the table. Blake was sitting next to him, smile replaced by his usual scowl. I wrapped my arm around Jasmine's shoulder, feeling the need to show that she was mine.

The dinner went smoothly, Blake's dad abstaining from his normal running commentary. I wasn't sure that Jasmine was ready to be exposed to his brute personality quite yet—better to ease her in.

During dessert, my nieces and nephews all made plates and went over to the living room to play Xbox while the adults stayed at the dining room table. "How are you feeling, Lauren?" Blake's mom asked my sister.

"Not too bad actually. Not too many symptoms, thank Goddess! Last time I feel like I lived in the toilet bowl I was throwing up so much. But no nausea this time around."

"But she definitely has some of the better symptoms." Lauren's mate, Isaac, winked and smirked at the table.

"I know exactly what symptoms you're talking about," Ryan chimed in. "That's definitely the best part of pregnancy. It was like heat all over again. Peyton was so horny all the time. That's how we figured out she was pregnant this time around actually." He laughed.

Peyton hit his arm and said, "My parents are sitting right in front of us, Goddess!" Everyone began laughing, including my parents.

"I'm definitely going to miss these days once the baby's born," Isaac added, bringing Lauren closer to him. He turned to me and said, "Don't worry, Luke, you're next. My advice, though? Don't mark her until after marriage. Enjoy heat sex for now—it's the best."

"Oh my Goddess, Isaac! You guys are the worst!" Lauren yelled. "How did my sister and I end up with such pigs for mates!"

Ryan and Isaac started snorting, setting off laughter again.

Something about this conversation made me feel uneasy though. And then I thought to myself, *No, Lucy and I had always been careful, hadn't we?* It was impossible. I kissed Jasmine on the cheek, pushing the thought from my mind.

Chapter 41

Jasmine

On Saturday morning, I headed to the gym early, before work. I was surprised to see Blake again once I got there, especially with it being so early in the morning. "Why do I keep bumping into you at this gym?"

"I told you, the women are hotter at this one than mine." He smirked. "Actually, I got here early because I have to meet with some of the trainers in an hour to discuss training plans for all of the pack members. Most members come in on Saturdays for their training appointments, since they work during the week, so we thought it would be a good idea to meet ahead of their day. I figured I might as well get my own workout in beforehand. And, since you're here, you can be my benching partner now." He winked at me.

"I feel like I don't have a choice."

"Come on, you know you want to watch me work these guns. I'll even take my shirt off and give you a whole show."

I smiled and playfully pushed him on his arm, shaking my head at how arrogant he was. He led me to the benches and strolled over to the racked weights, ready to pull some off to place on a barbell.

Glancing over at me, he asked, "So, how much do you press?"

"About 180."

"Nice," he said approvingly, and placed the plates onto the barbell for me. He went behind the bench and waited for me to lie down so he could spot me. I began lifting as he kept his hand under the barbell, ready to catch it. "Damn, watching you bench all that weight's so fucking hot. I think we need to become official gym partners."

I got up after eight reps. He added weights to each side for himself. Then he removed his shirt, and—dear Goddess!—I couldn't help myself as I stared at his broad shoulders and perfectly formed pecs. My eyes traced the flawless ridges that outlined his statuesque abs, to his stomach with a dusting of hair that trailed from his belly button and disappeared underneath the waistband of his sweatpants. Damn, was it hot in here, or was it just me?

He lay down and I spotted him as he benched, not able to pull my eyes off his body as all his muscles flexed while he lifted the barbell and breathed heavily. I felt a tingle between my legs as I watched him, completely turned on. I couldn't deny how hot he looked.

"Don't get too distracted watching my ripped body. You still need to spot me." He laughed. A flush burned across my cheeks at getting caught.

After we both finished four sets, we moved to the free weights and began doing different upper body exercises together. We started with bent-over rows. I looked at Blake, my shame coming back to me, and said, "Sorry again about how I acted when, you know, I went into heat."

"Once again, I'm not sure what you're sorry about." He looked at me. "I mean, if I were horny and I was sitting next to me, I'd be all over myself too."

"I acted completely inappropriately. I wasn't any better than those men you told me about who can't control themselves when they sense a woman in heat."

"It's different for men, though." He looked at me.

"What do you mean?"

He smirked and said, "Well, unmated straight men will literally want to screw any woman in heat, no matter who she is or what she looks like. They don't discriminate. Frankly, not much different than men in general, but I digress. Women, on the other hand. . ." He paused looking at me.

"Yes?" I waited for him to continue.

"They're much more selective. Most of the time, they only want to mate with men they're otherwise interested in."

"Oh," I replied, feeling myself go completely red.

"Of course, you clearly have excellent taste." He winked at me.

"Great, all I did was feed your already overinflated ego," I grumbled.

We switched to curls and lateral raises. Blake looked at me in the mirror and asked, "So, how's the mate thing going? Seems things worked out as I thought they would."

"It's good," I replied, not knowing what else to say.

"Good. Luke's a good guy. I knew he'd do the right thing in the end. I'm happy for you."

"What about you?" I asked.

"What about me?"

"Is there anyone you're seeing? Or anyone you're interested in?"

"That's not really my thing. I just like to play the field. Anyway, right now there's a lot going on with the Bois Sombre Pack. I don't really have time for a social life."

"What's going on with the Bois Sombre Pack?"

"Nothing you need to worry about. We've got it under control for now."

"I'd like to learn more about your job." I looked over at him.

"It's not that interesting." Blake seemed a bit distant suddenly, giving curt answers, as if he wanted the conversation to end. I wasn't sure what to make of it. We kept lifting our dumbbells, switching to an Arnold press.

I tried again. "By the way, thanks for everything you did on Sunday. I appreciate it."

"Don't mention it," he replied.

"I'm really grateful. My parents believed your mom when she called."

"Don't worry about it."

Blake seemed off and I couldn't figure out how to get things back to how they were between us. After we finished with free weights, we went to stretch together.

As I got up to head to the locker room to shower before work he said, "Good workout today. Glad I bumped into you."

I smiled at him, taking in his entire appearance. He was still shirtless, and I couldn't help but look him up and down. Luke was also very muscular—he'd filled out significantly since high school. But it was hard to explain, I didn't get the same primal feeling that I did when in Blake's presence. I stepped toward him and hugged him goodbye. He wrapped his arms around me instantly and held me tightly against his body for a few moments. I enjoyed the feeling of being pressed against him, wishing I could stay like that all day. We finally separated and I walked toward the locker room.

I walked into work at seven thirty, Valerie right behind me. When we entered, Reena was already there after having opened that morning. As soon as I got there, I took my place at the coffee machines, ready for the morning rush.

During downtime, Valerie came out from the back and asked me, "So how are things going? Things are good with Mr. Hot Beta now?"

"Yeah." I thought for a moment and asked, "How's Lucy doing? I haven't seen her since that day we fought."

"She's not great, but don't worry too much about her. The beta's your mate and she has no right to him. She'll eventually get over it."

I sighed, wondering if we'd ever be friends again, wondering if I should try to reach out to her, but also fearful of her reaction. On the surface, it seemed like everything turned out the way it was supposed to, but I couldn't help but feel like everything was still wrong.

Luke surprised me by coming in at lunchtime. He ordered a couple coffees and said hi to everyone. I made the coffees and came around from the counter to hand them to him.

He placed them on a table behind him and put his arms around me, pulling me in for a hug. "I was grabbing some sandwiches for lunch from the sub shop next door and wanted to stop by and say hello to my mate." He smiled at me.

I inhaled his scent, instantly wishing I didn't have to continue working for the rest of the day.

"I have to work tonight, but I will text you so we can get together again soon. I hope my family wasn't too crazy for you yesterday."

"No, I enjoyed it. I have a really small family, so it was nice being around so many people. I like how your family's so much more open with each other. We can't talk about anything in mine."

"Okay, good. My parents and sisters loved you." He took my hands in his and kissed me on the head. "I'll see you again soon." He picked up his coffees and we walked to the door together so I could see him out.

I walked back around to the other side of the counter. "That beta's one fine man. You're a lucky girl," Valerie said to me. I nodded my head, a smile on my face.

Chapter 42

Lucy

I was still in shock. I couldn't believe that I had lost both my boyfriend and best friend in a matter of weeks. Even more shocking was that the Moon Goddess had both shoved a dagger into my heart and then turned it until she could draw every last bit of pain out of me. It's one thing to lose the man you want to spend the rest of your life with, taking with him your whole future, but the fact that he's now with your best friend? I wanted to vomit every time I thought about it. It was so heartbreaking that I didn't think I could ever be friends with Jasmine again.

When I told my mom, she held me while I cried. But everyone knew there was nothing I could do except move on, if such a thing was even possible. Both my parents kept reassuring me that I'd eventually find my mate, and then I'd forget this ever happened. But I didn't believe that either. Luke had been my life—he was the reason I got out of bed in the morning. The fact that he didn't fight for the two of us still hurt me. I always felt like we were closely connected—like we could tell each other anything without judgment. He got me better than anyone else. And we just fit together, as if our bodies were molded for each other. But perhaps I'd just always felt our bond more strongly than he did, which was even more painful to think about.

On Saturday, my mom forced me out of bed. I had Saturdays off from work since Jasmine normally took that shift. Valerie had separated our shifts so we wouldn't have to work together, something I was very thankful to her for. I didn't think I could ever look at Jasmine's face again. She was my best friend, and she didn't even hesitate to take my boyfriend from me after knowing, for so many years, how much I loved him. It felt like the ultimate betrayal.

That afternoon, Kyle and Emma came over to spend some time with the family. After lunch, the men all went outside to play football while my mom cleaned up. Emma and I were seated in the living room together.

"How are you doing, Lucy?" Emma looked at me, pity on her face.

"Horrible," I replied. "I still can't believe what happened."

She pulled me in for a hug, "It'll be okay. You'll meet your mate soon and you'll forget about him. Having a mate's the most incredible thing, better than just a boyfriend."

"How do you know? You never had a boyfriend."

"I guess that's true. But mates come from the Moon Goddess so no one else can take them from you. They're meant to be yours. You won't have to worry."

"Can we please talk about something else?" I asked, feeling sickness in my stomach all over again, especially at the thought of Luke finding his new mate to be better than his long-term girlfriend.

"Okay, I have some news for you. I wasn't sure if I should tell you because of what you're going through right now. But you're my sister now, so I want to tell you."

"What is it?" I asked.

"I'm pregnant." She smiled. "We've only told family so far since it hasn't been two months yet." I looked at her glowing, making me feel more despair at my situation.

I forced myself to say, "Congratulations. When did you find out?"

"About a week ago. My boobs were hurting so badly. I kept telling Kyle not to touch them during sex. And I just felt really weird and realized I'd missed my period. So, I took a test and got the two lines! I took another one because I couldn't believe it."

An even sicker feeling came over me after what Emma said. My breasts had been extremely sore for the past few weeks. I thought it was just my period coming, but it never actually came. And my breasts just got more and more sore. Now, with Emma sitting in front of me, I realized I had been feeling off and not like myself. I thought it was the depression, but it could have been more than that.

"So how do you feel?" I asked, keeping the conversation going.

"It's amazing. Kyle and I are so happy. I know it will happen for you soon too. I can't wait until our pups are cousins and can play together while we sit around and gossip."

The next day, I made my way over to the pack clinic after my shift at the café ended at one thirty. I was relieved to see it was empty of other patients. I sat down in the waiting area until a nurse called my name and brought me to an examination room. She took my vitals and then asked me to sit and wait for the doctor.

A few minutes later, the former luna entered. My stomach dropped. Luke had grown up with Luna Sienna in the same packhouse, and she certainly knew by now that Luke was mated to Jasmine. Unaware of the gravity of the situation, she sat down in front of the computer and pulled up my file, turning toward me after she did. "So, Lucy what brings you in here?"

"I'm sorry, Dr. Luna. It's very personal. Is there any other doctor I can see today?"

"Unfortunately, since it's Sunday, only one of us is working today. But please be assured that anything you tell me will be kept completely confidential. There's no reason to worry."

I sighed, hesitating, wondering if I should come back another day. But then I finally decided to just come out with it, not wanting to wait any longer. "I think I'm pregnant."

She blinked a few times, clearly taken aback by the news. "Oh, I see. Have you taken a pregnancy test yet?"

"No, I haven't."

"Okay, well, let's just start there. I'll be right back." She walked out of the room and came back moments later with a cup, then led me to the bathroom so I could pee in it. Several minutes later, she came back and took me into another room.

After closing the door and gesturing to a chair to sit down, she looked at me and said, "We ran the test on your urine, and it came back as positive. I'd like to do an ultrasound on you to confirm. I'm going to exit the room. Please remove your pants and underwear, and here's a blanket to cover yourself for modesty." She handed me a sheet. "Just lie down on this table and put your feet into the stirrups."

I did as she said and she reentered.

I lay back, and she said, "Now relax, this might be a little uncomfortable. I am going to insert a wand into your vagina. You might just feel a little pressure." She did exactly as she warned and looked at a screen. I waited until she finally spoke. "Well, Miss Lucy, you're measuring around ten weeks along for a human pregnancy. That means you're about seven weeks along as a werewolf. Let me go ahead and print you a picture. I'll want you to come back for a longer appointment when the full staff is here so we can run all the tests necessary. You're already quite far along and will be in the second trimester next week since werewolf pregnancies develop much more quickly than human ones."

I couldn't speak, trying to digest all the information I was being given. The former luna continued. "I'm going to step out so you can get dressed and then let's talk."

I dressed, feeling like I was in a trance. I couldn't believe what was just confirmed. I sat down in the same chair from earlier and the former luna knocked and came in.

She sat down and asked, "So, Lucy, can I answer any questions?"

"What are my options?"

"If I understand what you're asking, your only option, if you continue to seek treatment at this clinic, is to carry this pregnancy to full term. You can certainly place the resulting baby for adoption if you so desire. We have programs through the temple that will assist you with this option. But abortions are banned in our pack. Either way, the Moon Goddess wanted you to have this pup. There's a reason you were blessed with this pregnancy. May I ask, is Luke the father?"

"Yes," I replied, feeling like the entire world was spinning around me, making me dizzy.

The former luna sighed, and continued, "I know the situation isn't ideal, but Luke's a good person. I have known him since he was born. I know he will do the right thing and support both you and your pup. Additionally, you have all the services of the pack. Pups are highly valued by our pack, and you will never need to worry. Werewolf pregnancies are considered sacred as they're granted by Artemis herself."

I nodded, trying to digest all the information I was being given. After a minute, the former luna asked, "Are there any other questions I can answer?"

I shook my head, in too much shock to ask anything else.

"If that's the case, I am going to make an appointment for Tuesday when the full staff is in so that we can run all of the necessary tests. Please let Luke know. I know he will do the right thing and he's welcome at the appointment, of course."

She wrote out a card with an appointment time for Tuesday and handed me the ultrasound picture. As much as I had always imagined Luke being the father of my future pups, I had never imagined it to be like this. After the former luna stepped out, I began crying, unable to hold back the tears. But then I had an illicit thought. Maybe, if he knew I was pregnant, just maybe he'd come back to me, and we could be a family like I'd always imagined. If I explained the situation to Jasmine, even she'd certainly agree that Luke should be with the mother of his baby.

I pulled out my phone and wrote a text to Luke. *Can we please talk? I have something important to tell you.*

Chapter 43

Luke

After Lucy texted me, I agreed to meet with her during her lunch break from work the next day. She asked me to meet her at the central park. When I arrived, I was surprised to see her already sitting on a bench. Punctuality was not something I often saw from Lucy. I felt uneasy about this, like something must be really serious.

My heart skipped a beat as I approached. As much as I tried to push Lucy from my mind, I still felt a fondness for her. Seeing her made all my feelings for her rush back to me. I quietly sat down next to her and smiled. "Hi, Lucy."

"Hi, Luke." She frowned back at me.

"What did you want to talk about?" I asked, looking into her blue eyes. I could see how sad they were. Lucy was someone who wore her heart on her sleeve.

"I'm pregnant." I stared at her, wondering if I had heard what she said correctly. I could feel my heart sinking and a sick feeling coming over me.

"You're pregnant?" I asked, trying to confirm if what I had heard was correct.

"Yes."

"When did you find out?"

"Yesterday. I went to the clinic and Dr. Luna did an ultrasound on me. Here, I have the picture." She dug into her purse and pulled out a black photo. I stared at it in disbelief.

"And it's mine." I sighed as I stated the fact, knowing in my heart it had to be.

"Yes, who the fuck else's would it be? I'm not the person that was screwing around with two different people. I was always faithful to you." She had delivered a punch to my stomach.

"And Luna Sienna knows?"

"Yes, she was the only doctor that was in the clinic. It's really a messed-up situation—you almost want to laugh." She shook her head. I just stared at the photo, trying to process everything.

When I didn't say anything, Lucy continued, "Dr. Luna scheduled me for an appointment for tomorrow morning to run tests. And she invited you to come, seeing as you're the father."

Two feelings came over me simultaneously. I was both in awe that I had created a life with Lucy but also sickened by the situation and what it meant for Jasmine and me. I didn't know how I would tell her. Our relationship had already started so rocky, and this was only going to make things worse. I looked back up at Lucy who was staring at me, waiting for a response. "Yes, I'd like to come," I replied.

"Oh, Luke, I miss you so much." She sighed, throwing her arms around me. I hugged her back, enjoying the feeling of being with Lucy again.

After some time, I spoke again. "Lucy, I just want you to know that I will always support you and our baby. I don't want you to worry. No matter what happens." I pulled her close to me, smelling the shampoo in her hair. She began sobbing into my shoulder, making my heart sink. I hated how much I had hurt her. I didn't want to hurt her anymore.

Blake

Luke and I were seated in the office at our individual desks, catching up on work, when I looked over at him. He was staring aimlessly into space, his eyes wide.

"Yo, is everything all right, man?" I asked him. He blinked a few times, bringing himself back to reality, then stared at me for a few moments. I looked back at him, wondering what he was thinking. I decided to try to make more of an effort to be a friend to him. "I'm happy to listen if there's anything on your mind."

"Goddess, I've really fucked up this time, Blake."

"What did you do now?"

"I'm still processing it. I just found out that I'm going to be a father."

A sick feeling came over me, making me regret ever starting this conversation. "Jasmine's pregnant? How's that even possible?"

"No, not Jasmine! Lucy!"

"Holy shit, man. Well, that's. . ." I didn't even know how to finish my sentence.

"I know. I don't even know how to tell Jasmine."

"So, what are you going to do?"

"What can I do? I'm going to be a father. I'm going to help Lucy raise our pup."

"What about your mate?"

"I don't know, man. I mean, she's my mate, so I am going to commit to her. I am trying so hard to do the right thing and I just keep fucking up."

"Well, what do you *want* to do?"

"Does it matter? The Moon Goddess chose this fate for me and, at the end of the day, we're all at her mercy."

I shook my head, wondering if I should press Luke harder for a real answer. Eventually I decided against it and said, "Well, congrats, man, on the pup. You'll be a great father. And I'm sure all of this will work out. Just look at Tom Brady. He knocked up his first supermodel girlfriend right before he got with Gisele, and now they're all some happy, blended, supermodel, Super Bowl–champion family."

Luke chuckled, and then went back to spacing out. Just then a mindlink came in from Mike to Luke and me.

"There's a new scent on the northern border. We tried tracking it, but nothing was found."

"We'll be right there," I mindlinked back, including Luke. I looked at Luke who was coming back out of his trance again.

"Shit. Let me text Jasmine and cancel our date," he said. He almost looked relieved as he did it. While I was initially irritated by his blasé reaction, another stronger feeling came forth—maybe it wouldn't work out between them. But I pushed it away, not wanting to get my hopes up only to be crushed later.

It was best if I prepared for the worst. I already cared too much, had gotten too close to Jasmine. And I knew that being with her mate was important to her. Once again, I pledged to myself that I wouldn't meddle, tried my best to ignore everything within me that desired things to be different.

We stepped outside of the packhouse and threw our clothes off, shifting into our wolf forms. We ran over to Mike's patrol station, where he met us in his wolf form. We followed him as we tracked the scent that was found. It smelled faintly familiar—I had met someone from this pack before, but I couldn't put my nose on exactly who. We followed the scent deep into the woods, but it disappeared once we hit a brook. Whoever it was must have swum away, taking their scent with them.

We were a week into November now, so the temperature had dropped significantly. I couldn't imagine that the culprit had gone far in the freezing water. We tried walking down the side of the brook for a mile with no luck. We backtracked and tried going a mile the other way. Nothing. Whoever it was, was able to swim more than a mile in freezing water.

After we returned to Mike's patrol station, Luke and I ran the pack border, checking on all the other patrol stations. We confirmed with the senior warriors that the juniors were walking one hundred yards out at the beginning of each new shift, and that we were alerted any time anything suspicious was found. Luke and I finally returned to the packhouse, and Luke wrote up a report to send to all the warriors, informing them of the security breach and reminding them of patrol duty directions.

"I can't wait to fuck these next assholes up" I grimaced. "These motherfuckers think they can come here and fuck with my pack? They're going to regret the day they cooperated with the Bois Sombre Pack."

Luke looked up at me from where he was working on his laptop and shook his head. "Please remind me to never get on your bad side. I think I'd like to keep my balls."

Chapter 44

Lucy

On Tuesday morning, Luke met me in front of the clinic. We walked in together, and Luke sat with me while we waited for my name to be called. He went into the examination room with me while the nurse took my vitals and had me produce another urine sample. Luke held my hand while the nurse took several vials of my blood.

The former luna came in after and asked me a bunch of questions about my health and eating habits. She then had me sit down on the examination table and gave me a full physical exam. After she was done, she asked Luke if he wanted to see the baby. He nodded and came over. She pulled out the ultrasound machine. After she was able to get the image up on the monitor, she turned it so it was facing Luke and me. Luke held my hand and said, "Wow, that's amazing." I watched as his eyes sparkled, engrossed in the image he was seeing on the monitor.

"I calculated the due date for March 24," the former luna said. Luke squeezed my hand.

After the ultrasound was done, the former luna came and sat down with us to talk. "Luke, thank you for coming in and supporting Lucy. I know this must have been a bit unexpected and unplanned, but having a pup is a wonderful thing and I know you will be a great father. Congratulations." She leaned forward to give him a hug.

After separating, Luke rubbed the back of his head and said, "Thank you, Luna. It was definitely a shock and I'm still wrapping my head around it, but I told Lucy that she'll never have to worry."

"Of course, I wouldn't expect anything less. Do you have any questions?"

"To be honest, I'm still processing all of this. But I'm sure you won't mind if I call you another time."

"Of course not. You're practically a second son to me, Luke. I know this will be quite a shock to everyone at first, but everyone will eventually get used to it. I know your mother will be very happy—she loves all of her grandchildren, and I am sure she will dote over this pup as much as all your future ones."

"Thank you, Luna. I appreciate it."

After we spoke a little while longer, the former luna left and gave Luke and me some time alone. He took both my hands in his and said, "I'm so amazed, Lucy. Seeing our pup on that screen was incredible. I can't believe that you and I created a life together." He smiled at me, and my heart melted. I had missed seeing him smile at me like that. "I meant what I said yesterday. I don't want you to worry about anything. I'm going to make sure you and our pup are always taken care of."

I took my hands from his and leaned in to hug him. He held me against him like he used to. Then he asked, "Do you mind if I touch your belly?"

I lifted my shirt, and he rubbed my belly very gently. I had been feeling a little bloated lately, but my belly still didn't appear pregnant. Feeling some courage, I said, "You know, Luke, we don't have to raise this baby separately. We can be a family just like we always wanted."

He pulled his hand from my belly and sighed. "Lucy—"

"Why not, Luke? We love each other, and the Moon Goddess wants us to have a baby together. Maybe this is her way of showing us we should be together."

"Lucy, if she wanted us to be together, she would have made us mates." He looked at me sadly. Looking into his eyes, I knew that he knew I was right. Maybe I didn't win the battle today, but that didn't mean I hadn't won the war. I still had until March 24 to convince him. And if not him, I could always accomplish my goal through Jasmine.

We finally left, and he held the door open for me as we exited the clinic. He then walked me to my house. I didn't live too far. Before I went inside, he stopped me and said, "Lucy, I want to be there for you. If you ever need anything, please let me know. I know we're no longer together, but I still want to do the right thing and support you through everything." He leaned over and kissed me on the cheek. "Take care of yourself."

Jasmine

After not hearing from her in over a month, I received a text message from Lucy on Tuesday morning while I was working. I was shocked when I checked my text notifications after the morning rush was over.

Lucy: *We need to talk.*

I could feel my lungs contracting as I read the text message, but I took deep breaths, staving off a panic attack. Her message was so cryptic. It could mean a million things. How could she send such a vague text message and not expect my anxiety to go into overdrive?

After reading and rereading the message, wiping down the tables, and sweeping the floors, I finally replied.

Me: *Do you want me to call you tonight?*

I waited for a response to come back, checking my messages every few minutes. Eventually I gave up and got back to work. During another lull, I still hadn't received a message back, so I decided to reread the email I'd received from the dean at my school. He had sent me a form to complete in order to request the leave of absence. It additionally required a written recommendation from a health provider. I hadn't gone to see a therapist in a few years, so I wasn't sure whom I could ask to complete the recommendation letter. I started to wonder if it was easier to just accept the bad grades for this semester.

At four, I left work and drove home. My doorbell rang a few minutes later. I looked out the window to see Lucy standing there, just as beautiful as ever, holding her head up high, intimidating me. I took a few deep breaths and then finally opened the door.

"Are you home alone?" Lucy asked.

"Yes," I replied.

"Can I come in?"

I gestured for her to come in and closed the door behind her. She walked into the living room, not even bothering to remove her shoes or jacket. She sat down on the couch, so I sat down on the adjacent love seat. I took in her appearance. I had almost forgotten how poised and confident she presented herself, sitting up tall, extending her long body, making me feel short and hopeless in her presence.

I finally asked, "What did you want to talk about?"

"I'm pregnant," she replied, not even bothering to ease into the topic of conversation.

I felt my heart pounding, a sick feeling coming over me. The room was beginning to spin around me. I lay back into the couch, closing my eyes, forcing myself to breathe. When I felt like I had the panic attack under control I spoke. "Are you sure?"

"Yes, I went to the clinic and Dr. Luna did an ultrasound. I'm seven weeks along."

I'd recalled learning in my college Biology 101 class that pregnancy was measured from the last period rather than conception. Doing the math rapidly in my head, if one could assume her period had been about two weeks prior, it would put her at five weeks since conception. I quickly thought back and realized, with horror, that she had conceived after my birthday—after Luke already knew I was his mate. I continued to force myself to breathe.

Finally, I asked, "Are you keeping it?"

"Are you serious, PJ? Miss super religious, never do wrong, would actually insinuate that I should get an abortion?" She gave me a hard stare and then continued. "Anyway, I told Luke and he wants me to keep it. He said he will always support me and our baby."

"Luke knows?" I was shocked that he knew and hadn't said anything to me. I wondered if that was why he had canceled our date the prior night. Was he planning to reject me and be with Lucy now?

"Of course he knows. He's the father."

I nodded, trying to wrap my head around everything.

Lucy sighed and continued. "Come on, Jasmine. You know how much I love Luke. This is a sign from the Moon Goddess that we should be together. You always get everything—good grades in school, top marks in training, a nice car, a perfect family, and a nice house. But that's not enough for you. You want my perfect boyfriend too! Can't you just, for once, let me have something?"

"He's my mate, Lucy. We're meant to be together. And if I reject him, that will mean I can't get married in the temple."

"Who cares about getting married in the temple? You can still get married."

"I care! My family cares! Anyway, if I reject him, I also won't get another mate. I'd have to find someone else who no longer has a mate and hope that he wants to be with me too. I'm not like you who goes around stealing other people's mates!"

"You speak like you're superior to me, stealing my boyfriend without a second thought."

"He's my mate, Lucy! You knew he'd find his mate one day! You just deluded yourself into believing that things would work out differently than they did."

Lucy huffed and said, "I'm done with this conversation." She stood up and walked herself out. I heard the front door slam as I lay back on the love seat, clutching my stomach, feeling a sickness come over me. When I couldn't hold it in anymore, I ran to the toilet and vomited.

I went outside and shifted into my wolf form, disregarding completely my dinner duties. I was so stressed that I ran all the way to the secret place that Blake had brought me to in the past, remembering the road there now. I ran in the woods, parallel to the street that led me there, as the sun set in the distance. When I arrived at the base of the mountain, I stopped at the pond to drink some water, and then climbed the mountain in my wolf form, finding it much easier than as a human.

I reached the top to find Blake was there, also in his wolf form, staring out into the woods which, by now, had descended into darkness. He looked up at me, and I walked over to lie down beside him, his eyes glowing in the darkness. He used his tongue to lick my face affectionately.

"Are you okay?" he mindlinked me, looking into my eyes.

"Not really," I mindlinked him back. *"But I don't really feel like talking about it."*

He nodded and laid his head back down.

Chapter 45

Jasmine

I got home around ten that night after Blake ran home with me. I found where I had tossed my clothes in the backyard and threw them on. My parents stood up from the living room couch as soon as I walked in.

"Jasmine, where in Artemis's name were you?" my dad shouted. "Do you have any idea how worried we were? Your car and phone were at home, and you were missing for several hours without a note or text about where you went."

I looked at him, not wanting to answer. Finally, I said, "I'm an adult."

"You may be an adult, but you still live under our roof! We called your mate, and he also had no idea where you were. He inquired with the patrol on duty and thank Goddess they were doing their job and knew you had crossed the border in your wolf form."

My mom chimed in, "Jasmine, it's like we don't even know you anymore. Ever since your birthday you've not been acting normal. What has gotten into you?"

I shook my head, not wanting to respond.

"Well, where were you?" My dad pressed. "Why did you run off?"

"I was stressed, okay?" I replied, becoming irritated.

"I don't like that you're taking runs outside of the pack territory, especially at night. It's not safe. Last time you ingested wolfsbane. Who knows what might happen next! I've heard there have been security breaches at the border. That's the last thing we need is for a rival pack to kidnap you. I'm going to speak with the beta about this. As your mate, he should be more concerned with your safety."

"You're going to tell on me to my mate?"

"Maybe he'll do a better job controlling you." My dad sighed.

"Controlling me?!" I yelled.

"Yes, you're completely out of control right now!" my mom shouted.

"Don't you think you're overreacting? I just went for a run. That's all."

My mom shook her head. "Just go to your room, Jasmine."

I turned to walk upstairs, not able to believe that my parents were sending me to my room at twenty years old. I grabbed my cell phone on the way up and plopped down on my bed once I got there. I found that I had several texts from Luke waiting for me.

> *Luke*: Hey Jasmine, are you ok?
> *Luke*: Your parents just called worried about you
> *Luke*: I hope you're ok
> *Luke*: When you get this message please text me and let me know you're ok
> *Luke*: Also I'd like to see you tomorrow. Sorry I had to cancel our date yesterday...

I sighed, looking through the texts, no indication that he had something to tell me. I began to wonder if Lucy had made the whole thing up. I didn't think she was that crazy to fake an entire pregnancy, but she had been known to do some outlandish things in the past.

I finally replied to him.

> *Jasmine*: I'm ok. Just got home and parents are pissed
> *Jasmine*: Lucy came by today...

I waited for his response to come through. A minute later, three dots appeared, indicating he was typing back. After what seemed like over five minutes, I finally received a reply.

> *Luke*: Please can I see you tomorrow so we can talk in person?
> *Jasmine*: I'm free all day.
> *Luke*: I'll come by in the morning. Text me when your parents leave for work
> *Luke*: Please get some sleep tonight. I don't want you to worry. You're my mate and I want to be with you no matter what

I stared at my phone, feeling another wave of nausea come over me. I couldn't help myself as I ran to the bathroom and threw up in the toilet again, sickened that Luke had more or less confirmed everything I'd been told earlier. I couldn't believe that my mate had gotten my best friend pregnant. It was like I was living in a bad dream. Because it had been several hours since I'd eaten, mostly just stomach acid that burned my throat came up. Once the nausea passed, I stepped into the shower and tried to wash the day away.

I tossed and turned all night, falling in and out of sleep, feeling my anxiety choking me. My stomach rumbled with hunger, but I found I couldn't bring myself to even want to eat, the idea of food making me feel ill. I woke up early the next morning and waited for the sound of the garage opening and closing before I finally got out of bed and got ready. I texted Luke as I brushed my teeth to let him know I was home alone.

About twenty minutes after I sent the text, I heard the doorbell ring. I walked to the front door and opened it to his tall, brawny frame standing before me. He walked in with his hands in his pockets. I could sense he was nervous.

I led him into the living room where he sat down on the couch, pulling me down to sit next to him. He rubbed the top of my thighs, making me feel calmed and aroused by the feeling emitted from his hands. I was almost ready to forgive him.

Finally, he spoke. "I'm sure Lucy must have told you most of what I came here to say. I'm sorry you had to hear about it from her first. I didn't know she'd tell you before I had the chance to."

I moved away from his touch and anger bubbled within me. I began to see a pattern. Luke was putting off every important decision and conversation, just burying his head in the sand. I nodded, deeply frustrated. This was not the first time it had slipped his mind to tell me something that affected my life!

"Jasmine, I'm so sorry." He closed his eyes. I could sense that he was remorseful. Then he opened his eyes again, looking at me for a response. I couldn't find the words to say anything, seething within.

After some time, he finally spoke again. "I'm sure the reason you ran off was that you were stressed, and I don't blame you. I asked the warriors on patrol to mindlink me once you returned, and they did. But I was surprised to find out you weren't alone when you came back."

I could sense there was some anger behind his words even though he said them calmly.

"Why were you with Blake?"

At his question, I became triggered, finally finding my voice and confronting him. "How dare you ask me about Blake when you knocked Lucy up after you already knew I was your mate? You told me to give you time and space, and meanwhile, you just continued your relationship with Lucy as if nothing ever happened. Is that why you didn't want to tell her? Because you wanted to continue being with her?"

He shook his head, a pained look on his face, his eyes clenched shut and nose scrunched. He put his thumb and pointer finger to the bridge of his nose. I stared and waited until he finally said, "I know I messed up, Jasmine, and there's nothing in the world I can do to make up for it. I know you probably won't believe me but what happened wasn't my intention. It just happened."

"What do you mean 'it just happened'? You just tripped and fell on top of her?"

He tried to take my hands and I pulled them away from him, moving farther away from him on the couch.

"Please, Jasmine," he pleaded. "I will spend the rest of my life trying to make this up to you if I have to. I know I messed up and there's no excuse. But you're my mate. When I asked you for the opportunity to start over, I meant it. I want to be with you, my mate. I broke up with Lucy and have committed myself completely to you since then. I wanted to put everything in the past behind us and give our relationship the chance it deserves—I still want that."

"Don't you think that will be a bit difficult when you're going to have a pup with someone else?"

"I will, of course, take responsibility and support Lucy and our pup, but that will not take away from what you and I have. I know it's a lot to digest right now, but I know one day we'll move past this and be happy together."

I shook my head, not knowing if that was true. Would we be happy together one day? Would we move past this? Or would I spend the rest of my life bitter that my mate, instead of immediately coming to me, took a detour and knocked up my best friend? Why was that something I should put up with and accept?

He moved in closer to me, his scent overwhelming me. He began rubbing my shoulders and arms, the sparks and calm spreading throughout my body. Before I could stop myself, I lay back on the couch as he pulled me against him in a cuddle.

I could feel the remorse seeping from his body as he rubbed my back. I closed my eyes, enjoying the feeling of being against him, his scent, and the sparks that traveled up and down my body, making it impossible to continue seething, the mate bond taking control of my emotions. We stayed like that for several minutes.

Finally, Luke pulled away and said, "I'm so sorry, Jasmine. I want to be a good mate to you. I really do. I don't expect you to forgive me today or any time soon. But I am hoping that, with time, you will see that I am committed to our relationship and want to be with you."

He snuggled me close to him, kissing my head, making me powerless to object. No matter how much I wanted to hate him, the mate bond wouldn't allow me to. Being so close to him made me forget that anyone even existed outside just the two of us. It was like Blake said, I was willing and ready to forgive any of his worst transgressions.

We continued lying against each other on the couch, intertwined. After some time, a thought from earlier came to me and I asked, "Are you sure Lucy's pregnant?"

He looked at me sadly. "Yes, I'm sure. I went to an ultrasound with her, and it couldn't have been any clearer."

"How did this happen?" I demanded.

He sighed and said, "We were always careful and just one time I slipped up. Just one time. And that's when I'm sure it must have happened."

"Why did you slip up?" I asked, feeling sickened by the conversation, part of me not even wanting to know.

He looked into the distance. "You're not going to like this story, but I don't want to hide anything from you anymore. I want us to be straightforward and honest with each other from now on."

He looked in my eyes sadly. "It happened after I came to see you when you were in heat. I left with the intention to, you know, take care of things myself, but Lucy showed up. I wasn't planning to do anything with her, but she just took control. I was so horny that I let her. Because I wasn't thinking straight, I forgot to put a condom on and that was that."

I rolled off the couch and began crouching on the ground, dry heaving. I was dizzy, as if the whole world was spinning around me. Fur was sprouting up my arms and legs, and my claws were beginning to extend out from my fingers.

Luke jumped off the couch next to me and held me against him. "Breathe, Jasmine, breathe." I followed his instructions, taking deep breaths as the feeling of his body touching mine calmed me. "Just breathe," he repeated, brushing my hair out my face.

After the feeling passed, I asked, "How could you?"

"I know, I really fucked up, Jasmine."

I looked into his eyes which were now red and pooled with tears. I put my head against his chest, sighing. He petted the back of my head, holding me against his chest. I could feel the regret radiating from his body.

"I hate how much I've hurt you. You don't deserve any of this."

"What will I tell my parents?"

"I will help you tell your parents if you want me to. It's my fault and I need to own up to it. I will let them know that I will still honor our mate bond and intend to take care of you for the rest of my life."

I pulled away from Luke and sat back on the floor, my back against the couch, letting out a heavy sigh. "Let's not tell them yet. They're not happy with me right now, so let's wait for them to cool off a bit."

"Whatever you want, Jasmine. I'm here for you." Luke crouched in front of me and took my hands. "I'd like to invite you over to the packhouse for dinner tonight, just to hang out, nothing more. I just want to start making up for how badly I've acted."

I nodded, unable to bring myself to decline.

"Good, I'm so happy you're still willing to give me a chance. I'll see you at six tonight." He kissed me on the head. "I have to go now but I'll see you later."

He got up and I followed his lead. I walked him to the door. Before I closed the door behind him, he turned around and said, "See you tonight, Jasmine. I'm looking forward to it." He then turned and walked to his car.

Chapter 46

Jasmine

A few minutes before six, I pulled up next to Luke's 4Runner in the pack parking lot. I made my way to the front door and rang the doorbell. Luke opened the door, stepping aside so I could walk in. As soon as he shut the door, he wrapped his arms around me in a hug.

"Thank you for coming, Jasmine. You look and smell so good." He helped me slip out of my jacket, hanging it in the entryway closet. He took my hand and led me into the dining room where he had laid out dinner with two place settings. "I wish I could take the credit, but Connie's a much better cook than I am." He smiled, pulling out my chair for me. I sat down and he pushed me in to the table.

I looked at the food in front of us to see there was crisp salad, warm dinner rolls, and a savory beef roast surrounded by fingerling potatoes. When Luke carved into the roast, the juices dripped from the perfectly cooked beef.

"This all looks and smells delicious!" I commented.

"Connie does a good job. Now help yourself," he said, waiting for me to take some food. I served myself a little bit of everything and put it on my plate. Meanwhile, he grabbed a bottle of wine from the table and poured some for both of us. He put some food on his own plate. We both began eating. Luke looked at me and said, "How do you like it?"

"It's really good," I replied, smiling.

"Good, something to look forward to."

"What do you mean?" I asked

"Once you move into the packhouse. Connie's our cook, so you'll get to enjoy this every day."

"Oh," I replied, digesting the information. It was strange to think that I would one day be living in the packhouse with Luke. And Blake. I took a drink from my glass of wine. I was unsure about spending my entire future with Luke. Something about it didn't seem right.

And then I recalled the news I had recently been given and started to feel nauseous again. I tried to push it from my mind, trying to enjoy the night. I took another drink from my glass of wine. Would Luke and Lucy's pup also live with us? Probably not full-time, but likely sometimes. I took another drink.

"Slow down there, Jazzy," Luke said, standing to refill my wine glass.

"Sorry, just a lot on my mind," I said, taking another sip. He flinched and sat back down. We continued eating our food. "Let Connie know this is really good," I added.

"I will, absolutely." He looked at me for a second then continued. "Look, Jasmine, I don't mean to keep repeating myself but I'm really sorry about everything. I know we'll get past this with time. And I will never ever be unfaithful to you. I want you to know that. I made some mistakes recently, but that will be the last time."

I nodded, sensing he was being sincere.

After we finished eating, Luke took our dishes to the kitchen. I followed him with the leftover food. He placed it into containers and left the platters in the kitchen sink.

After we finished clearing the table and putting everything away, Luke took my hands in his and said, "I have a surprise for you for dessert. Go sit down in the living room and I'll be right over."

I went to sit on the couch and waited for him. He came out with a tray with two mugs and a bottle of Baileys. He put the tray down and then went over to the fireplace. I watched as he threw a couple logs into it and started a fire, lighting a fire starter.

He came back over to me and asked, "Would you like some Baileys in your hot chocolate?"

"Sure," I replied. He poured some of the bottle into both the mugs. He then went over to a stereo and turned some music on, playing it fairly loudly.

"Now sit back and relax. I'll be back again." I sipped from my mug as he headed back toward the kitchen. He came back with a shopping bag, which he unpacked in front of me to reveal a couple of skewers, graham crackers, Hershey's chocolate bars, and marshmallows. "I thought it would be fun to make s'mores."

He opened all the ingredients and slipped a marshmallow onto each skewer, handing one to me. Then he gestured for me to follow him to the fireplace. We knelt next to each other as we sipped from our mugs and roasted our marshmallows. I noted that we both slow roasted our marshmallows rather than allowing them to just burn, like most people I knew.

"I like your roasting technique." Luke smiled at me, as if reading my mind. "Blake and my sisters just burn theirs."

"Is this something you do often?" I asked.

"Growing up, we used to make s'mores during the winter all the time." He smiled widely, clearly recalling the memories.

Once both our marshmallows were golden brown, we put them between the graham crackers with chocolate and sat back down where we had been previously kneeling, next to the warm, crackling fire.

After we finished our s'mores, Luke leaned over, putting his hand on the side of my head, and gently kissed me. As soon as his lips touched mine, desire came over me and I kissed him back, shoving my tongue into his mouth.

We fell back onto the floor, narrowly avoiding my mug. I was feeling buzzed and loved the feeling of Luke's lips on mine, sparks and calm flowing through my body. No matter how much I fought against it, I couldn't stay mad at him, succumbing to my desire for him, a prisoner to the mate bond. Our bodies rubbed together as we hungrily kissed each other.

He inched his hand under my shirt, cupping my breast. I brought my hand to the arm he was using to support himself, loving the feel of his muscles as my hand slid down it. He kissed down my chin and neck, trailing kisses down to my chest, stopping once his lips hit the fabric.

He removed his hand from my breast and pulled my shirt off me, pulling his own off right after. He lowered his lips to my chest, continuing to kiss down to my breasts, using his lips to trace the fabric of my bra from breast to breast. He unhooked my bra, pulling it off me, and looked down at me. "You're so beautiful, Jasmine."

He brought his hands to my shoulders, tracing them down the side of my body, and bringing them to my breasts, gently caressing them, brushing his thumb against my nipples. I looked up at his face, seeing that he was looking at me lustfully, his eyes half-closed.

Suddenly Blake's scent entered my nostrils and we both looked up to see that he had just walked into the dining room, the loud music clearly having drowned out the sound of him entering. The open floor plan of the house gave him a full view of us. Upon seeing him, Luke yelled, "Fuck!"

"Sorry," Blake quickly apologized and turned to walk upstairs.

I got up and went to put my bra back on.

"Sorry, I didn't know Blake would be home so early. Although, it's probably getting late," Luke said as he went to grab for his phone. As the screen lit up, I noticed he had a string of texts from Lucy on his lock screen.

He unlocked his phone and began focusing on his phone, presumably reading the texts that had come in. I threw my shirt back on as Luke stayed absorbed in his phone.

I grabbed my mug and went to sit back down on the couch, unnoticed by Luke. He began energetically typing. I sipped my mug observing Luke shirtless, completely immersed in his phone. He stayed like that for several minutes.

I pulled out my own phone to see that it was now nine thirty. I had a text from my dad asking when I would be coming home. I quickly wrote, *Soon*. Finally, Luke turned around to look at me and said, "Sorry about that."

"Was it Lucy?" I asked.

He winced and said, "Yeah. She was just telling me about her pregnancy symptoms. I want to make sure I'm there for her through this."

"I see," I replied, feeling sickness come over me again. I stood up and said, "I should probably go home. It's getting late."

He nodded and also stood. "I'll see you out." He followed me and pulled my jacket from the closet. He helped me put it on and then walked me to my car. Before I got into my car, he pulled me in for a hug. "Thank you for coming, Jasmine. Sorry we got interrupted but I'd like to see you again soon." He then leaned in for a kiss and I moved my head, so he kissed my cheek. After I got into my car, he stood outside and watched as I drove away.

Chapter 47

Luke

During my lunch break on Thursday, after I had spent the morning leading training classes at the pack elementary school, I made my weekly FaceTime call to my parents. Both of them were seated in front of my dad's iPad staring back at me.

"How are you doing, Luke?" my mom asked, leaning forward.

"I'm good," I replied, knowing I'd have to break the big news to them during this call, but I couldn't help but stall, knowing it would be a huge shock.

"How's the situation with the security breaches? Did you catch the latest offenders yet?" my dad asked.

"Not yet."

"How's Jasmine? Any discussion of a wedding yet?" My mom winked and smiled at me.

I cringed internally, knowing I'd have to tell them. "Jasmine's fine. Actually, I have some news."

"Already?" My mom's eyes widened. "It sounds like the two of you didn't waste any time. How long have you been mates now again?"

"Erm, well, actually, the news isn't about Jasmine."

"Oh, what is it then, honey?"

"It's actually about Lucy."

"Lucy?"

"Yes, actually, I found out earlier this week that Lucy's pregnant." My mom gasped and fell back in her chair and my dad looked over at her. She had her hand to her chest, breathing heavily.

My dad turned back toward the screen and looked at me sternly. "Dear Goddess. Please tell me it's not yours, Luke."

I felt my cheeks redden as I rubbed the back of my neck from nervousness. "Actually, it is."

"Fucking Artemis!" my dad shouted, surprising me as my dad didn't often swear. My mom began crying, pulling a tissue from beyond where I could see on the screen. We stared at each other, no one saying a word.

Finally, my mom spoke. "I knew we shouldn't have encouraged the relationship. This was only bound to happen. I tried to be open-minded to this whole girlfriend thing—I liked Lucy. But this is too much. What will the pack say?"

"I hope you're not planning on dumping your mate for Lucy," my dad chimed in.

"I wasn't planning to," I replied, seeing this conversation was not going at all the way I imagined. After Luna Sienna had seemed so open-minded to the situation, I thought my parents might be too.

"Good, because I will not allow it," his jaw was tense, eyebrows scrunched together. "The last thing we need is for another pack to have a vendetta against us."

"What are you talking about?" I asked.

"Jasmine comes from an alpha family. They're notorious on the West Coast, and that pack is much larger than ours. We're already not on the best terms with them and this wouldn't be the first time that they've threaten us to ensure a mate bond is consummated."

"Jasmine comes from an alpha family?" I asked, shocked by the information. I had known Jasmine for years and was surprised that I didn't already know this tidbit about her. My mom started sobbing, and my dad put his arm around her.

"Yes, and what has happened is exactly why dating is discouraged in werewolf society. But what's done is done. Just, for the love of Artemis, do not even think about rejecting Jasmine under any circumstance."

I blinked at my parents, taken aback.

My dad continued. "I won't be so callous as to tell you to banish Lucy from the pack like James has with all of his mistresses with illegitimate children. But, dear Goddess, you better make sure that you keep Jasmine happy. Her family in Alaska is no joke. If you think James is bad, just wait until you meet the alpha family of the Jade Moon Pack."

I stared at my dad, speechless. I was not expecting the conversation to take this turn at all. I had always assumed that my parents would support any decision I made, even if it was taking a chosen mate. I now realized how naive I had been in my thinking.

"Listen to your father, Luke. You need to take responsibility for what you've done and put the pack first. As beta, you can't make decisions without it affecting everyone. Now, I need to lie down. Honey, I love you," my mom said and walked away.

"Bye, Luke," my dad said, hanging up the call. I sat at the kitchen table, staring at the cell phone in my hand.

After some time, Blake walked in, checking the stove to see what had been made for lunch. He then turned to look at me and said, "What, did you knock someone else up now?"

"Fucking A, Blake. Did you know that Jasmine comes from a family of alphas?"

"What? No." Blake raised his eyebrows, staring out into the distance. He then turned back to me and continued. "But it does make sense. That girl lifts and fights like a badass."

I stood up, put my empty dish in the sink, and walked out of the packhouse. I got into my car to drive to my college classes. I was dazed as I drove, lost in thought. The community college was in the town near the casino, which was a bit of a drive from the pack territory. I couldn't lie and say that I never once considered rejecting Jasmine. It's not that there was anything wrong with her—no, she was perfect. It was just that I had already been in love with someone else when we realized we were mates.

When Jasmine and I were together, it felt like we were the only two people in the world, lost in each other. But when we were apart, I couldn't help but long for Lucy. And now that she was pregnant with my pup—I would be lying if I said I hadn't considered Lucy's proposal to be a family. But I tried to brush my feelings aside and would now have to try harder. As I drove, my car alerted me to texts coming in from Lucy. I kept hitting *Ignore* on my screen. She had been texting me incessantly since I told her I wanted to be there for her.

Once I parked at the community college campus, I pulled up my text thread with Jasmine and wrote, *Have class and training today, but would love to see you tomorrow night :)*.

Immediately after, I pulled up Lucy's frantic texts and began responding, assuring her everything would be okay.

Chapter 48

Jasmine

I had signed up for my weekly two hours of sparring on Friday morning. I arrived early, sitting down on the bleachers while I waited for the group on the field to end their session. I sensed someone sit down next to me. Blake's scent alerted me to whom it was. I turned to look at him to see him smiling at me.

"Well, hello there, Miss Alpha."

"What's that supposed to mean?" I asked.

"You didn't tell me you come from a family of alphas. You're just full of surprises."

"Oh yeah, I always forget about that. We don't really keep in touch with my mom's side of the family. How'd you find out?"

"Luke told me."

"Oh, I don't remember telling him that, but maybe Lucy told him."

"Seems like a pretty big flex for you to keep this hidden from everyone."

"It's not really a big deal. It's not like my dad's an alpha."

"Still, it's pretty fucking hot. Now I know where you get it from." The bell rang, signaling the end of the current sparring session. Blake got up and put his hands out to help me up. "I can tell you that this alpha," Blake pointed to himself, "can't wait to see what Miss Alpha does today."

"I didn't see your name on the schedule when I signed up for this session."

"There's been some logistical changes." He smiled, leading the way to the field and taking his place at the head of the group. Had Blake been trading places with trainers to spend time with me? My stomach fluttered at the thought.

My grandparents came over for dinner that night. They had, of course, met Luke in the past, him being beta of the pack, but they were excited to finally meet him as my mate. I had let my family know that he would be picking me up for our date. My mom still wasn't completely happy about the situation, but she did her best to hide her feelings.

I wasn't looking forward to telling her about Lucy. People at temple had always gossiped about Lucy and Luke's relationship, especially since they had always been so open about it, something that wasn't common in our pack. Now that I was mated to Luke, I'm sure people had something to say about it and would have even more to say once Lucy was showing and everything was out in the open.

At six the doorbell rang, and my dad went to answer. He brought Luke into the living room where we were all sitting, waiting for him. My grandfather got up first and put out his hand. Luke extended his own hand to shake it.

"Congratulations, Beta. You have a good girl here. Jasmine was the top of her class in school and learned how to cook from the best—her grandmother. Of course, you've already met my mate, Mary." My grandma got up and shook his hand next.

"Thank you both. I'm very lucky to have Jasmine as a mate."

My dad nudged my mom to stand up and brought her over to Luke. "Miriam wasn't available last time you came over, but she was very happy to learn that our Jasmine has met her mate."

"Yes, very happy, Beta." My mom put her hand out limply, a scowl on her face. Luke shook it.

"I'm so fortunate that the Moon Goddess thought I was deserving of Jasmine. I'm a lucky man." Luke smiled at everyone.

"Now, we don't want to keep both of you. Have a good night, kids," my dad said, gesturing for us to leave.

We walked out and Luke helped me into the car. After he jumped into the driver's seat, he turned to me and said, "Your mom didn't seem very happy."

"My mom has been in a bad mood for a while now."

"Is it because I'm your mate?"

I shrugged, not wanting to answer his question.

"Well, is it?" he pressed.

"It's not the only reason."

He nodded and began backing out of the driveway. He put the car into drive and asked, "Can you please elaborate on why your mom wasn't happy?"

"Does it matter?"

"Yes, it does matter. I want to know. I didn't know that your mom comes from an alpha family."

I sighed. "It doesn't matter. We barely even keep in touch with that side of the family. How did you find out anyway?"

"My dad told me. Please, Jasmine. It's really important to me to know why your mom isn't happy. I want to fix anything that's a problem," he pleaded with me.

I considered how much to tell him and finally settled on being honest. "She's mostly not happy with me. I've been leaving the house without saying anything and there were rumors about Blake and me at one point, which didn't help. But yeah, she's not happy that I am mated to someone that she and her friends used to gossip about all the time. I mean, you don't exactly have the best reputation in the pack, openly dating Lucy. It's only going to get worse once everyone finds out she's pregnant."

Luke let out a deep breath. "Goddess, I really fucked up, didn't I?"

I didn't know how to answer. Just then, text messages began coming in, the alert popping up on the console of Luke's car showing they were from Lucy. He kept hitting *Ignore* as the message alerting him popped up. I felt the familiar sick feeling come over me again, wondering why I kept torturing myself trying to make things work with Luke. I started to wonder if I should just let him go be with Lucy. I was starting to forget why I ever even wanted him in the first place. It didn't seem worth the torture and losing my best friend.

As soon as I started considering giving up on our relationship, Luke reached over and took my hand, emitting sparks and calmness through my arm. I sat back in my seat, enjoying the feeling coming over me.

"Don't worry, Jasmine. We'll figure it out. I'm going to step it up and prove to everyone that I'm a good man and worthy of being your mate. Let's just enjoy the time we have together tonight and not worry about it right now."

Luke pulled into the parking lot of a bowling alley. He came around to open my door and help me out of the car. He then took my hand and led me inside. We went up to the desk to rent bowling shoes and claim a lane. Once we were seated at our bowling lane, Luke got onto his knees and helped me put my shoes on. He looked up at me and smiled. "See? If you stick with me, you'll get waited on hand and foot. Now let me go order us some food."

I quickly looked at my phone to see a text from Blake.

Blake Sexy AF: *You looked good out there today, Miss Alpha*

A smile spread across my face. I quickly put my phone away before Luke returned. He had two cups in his hand, which he set down on the table. "Sorry, I forgot to ask what you wanted to drink so I got us both Cokes. I hope that's okay."

I gave him a thumbs-up. "Coke's good."

"So, how much do you know about bowling?" he asked.

"To be honest, not much."

"Okay, good. That means it'll be a fair match because I know close to nothing." He laughed. He let me go first. I picked up a purple-colored bowling bowl, observed what others were doing, and did the same thing, flinging the ball straight into the gutter. I tried again and was able to hit a couple of the side pins. On my third shot, I was able to knock one more pin down.

"Hmm, well, it's good to know you're not perfect at everything." Luke snickered. He went next and didn't do much better. "Damn, this is much harder than it looks."

We slowly started to improve as we continued bowling, giving each other high fives as we'd knock over bowling pins. Eventually, a waitress brought over a pepperoni pizza and cheesy fries. I dug into the food while Luke bowled.

"Hey, save some for me!" he yelled from the lane.

"Well, you better hurry up, because this pizza's really good. I can't guarantee I'll be able to stop eating it."

He ran over and sat next to me, flinging his arms around me, "Sounds almost like how I feel about you." He began nibbling on my ear. "Mmm you taste so good. I haven't tried the pizza yet, but I'm pretty sure you taste better."

He kissed me from my ear to my chin, making my body come alive, desperate for more. I inhaled his scent and melted into his touch, enjoying the feeling of having him close to me. Suddenly, I couldn't remember why I ever doubted our relationship.

He put his mouth to my ear. "I've been thinking about you ever since we got interrupted the other night, imagining how the evening should have ended."

"And how's that?" I looked into his eyes.

"I'd tell you, but I'd rather show you later." I snuggled into him, feeling lust overtake my entire body. He then grabbed a slice of pizza and bit a piece off. "Mmm, this pizza's good. But I stand by my word that you taste better."

We finished eating and went back to bowling. We stopped paying attention to the score and just bowled, taking turns, finding excuses to constantly touch each other. After some time, I excused myself to go to the bathroom. When I returned, I saw Luke engrossed in his phone, frantically typing. My stomach dropped, instantly knowing who he must be texting.

I sat down, and he didn't even lift his head, continuing to concentrate on his phone. I eventually cleared my throat and he looked up, surprise on his face. "Oh, sorry," he said as he slipped his phone back into his pocket.

"Lucy?" I asked. He wouldn't make eye contact with me as he nodded. I let out a deep breath and sat down.

"I'm sorry, Jasmine. But I have to be there for Lucy. I have to take responsibility. I can't just abandon her."

"Yeah, I understand." As much as it hurt, I agreed with him that he should take responsibility. But I couldn't bring myself to look at him, the pain still raw. I wondered if I would ever get used to the whole situation.

He wrapped his arms around me, which began to calm me, and asked, "Hey, do you want to get out of here?" I nodded. Luke paid for the food, then we returned our bowling shoes and went back to the car.

As we were driving home, Luke said, "I just can't help but wish I could go back in time and tell seventeen-year-old me to do things differently. I feel like I've really made a mess of everything. I'm really sorry, Jasmine.

I'm really trying to do the right thing—and while I know it's mostly all my fault, I can't help but feel like I just can't catch a break."

I looked over to him. I could sense regret as I listened to him. After reflecting on what he said, I asked, "Why did you start dating Lucy anyway? And did your parents really not care?"

He stared straight ahead silently. After some time, he finally responded, "To be honest, Blake's and my parents never really cared much about what we did during our personal time. Don't get me wrong, they were tough on us with our training—especially Alpha James with Blake. You can't even call what Blake went through 'training'—it was abuse, plain and simple. But I think because we were sort of the golden children, they just let us get away with everything. Blake used to have girls in the packhouse all the time, and his parents never batted an eye. But, then again, it's not like his dad wasn't doing the same thing, so maybe it was just par for the course for his family."

Luke paused and I looked at him, waiting for him to continue. He shook his head and said, "Sorry, I don't mean to talk badly about Blake and his family. That was wrong of me to tell you that. I guess I just wanted to be open with you so that you understand more of the environment I grew up in."

"Did you have girls over the packhouse like Blake did?" I asked.

"There was one girl before Lucy, but it didn't last very long. She wanted to keep things secret, and we eventually decided to just break up."

Luke glanced at me, and I nodded.

He continued, "Anyway, I wasn't even that interested in Lucy when I first saw her. I honestly thought she was just a blonde bimbo. To be honest, she's not the type I normally went for. Before Lucy, I liked girls more like you—quiet and intelligent. But as I started speaking to her, I just became completely charmed by her. She has this confidence about her—she knows what she wants and she's not afraid to go for it. But underneath all the layers, she has this vulnerability that's so sweet. I couldn't help but fall for her. Plus, I couldn't believe my luck that such a hot girl was pursuing me. I mean, Blake's gotten some really hot girls, but, man, Lucy was something else."

I wrapped my arms around my stomach, an unpleasant feeling coming over me listening to Luke's story, but I wanted to hear it because I was curious and wanted to learn more about him and his past.

He must have sensed how I felt because he paused and said, "I don't have to keep going if you don't want me to."

"No, I do. It's just hard to hear, that's all. But I want to know more about you, so please continue."

"Ok," he replied. "Well, things just moved really fast. Her parents, as you know, are really liberal and didn't mind that Lucy had a boyfriend. And my parents never really paid attention past my training. Anyway, they were mostly preoccupied with my sisters because they had pups, and my mom was busy helping with raising them. Plus, Lucy's dad and her brothers are warriors, so both our families instantly became friends. They would say things like, 'Don't get too attached. You may not be mates,' and stuff like that. But they never really pushed on any of those points and sort of just let us be. It just felt natural. I imagine it's like a human relationship where you just meet someone, and you have no idea if it will go anywhere, but it's exciting and fun. And you like getting to know the person, so you just keep seeing them over and over again. One day you wake up, and you realize you're in love and you want to spend the rest of your life with that person. But because we're werewolves, it gets complicated because we have mates. But what can I do now that I'm in way too deep? It's like you go so far down a path and it almost seems pointless to backtrack. I hope that makes sense."

I looked over at him, feeling a stabbing pain in my chest. I'd already sensed everything he told me, but it was even worse to hear it spoken out loud—to have him confirm all my worst insecurities. Up until they were verbalized, I could deny everything, tell myself it was all in my head.

Now it was out in the open, and I'd be forced to acknowledge it. He was staring ahead as he drove.

"Yeah, it makes sense. It just sucks," I replied, not knowing what else I could say, feeling a scraping in my throat and chest. "I just never thought that meeting my mate would be like this. Do you even feel anything for me? Or do your feelings for Lucy just override the mate bond?" I looked up to see that we were in my neighborhood and Luke was pulling up to park his car in front of my house.

After he put his car in park, Luke took my hand and said, "I do feel a lot for you, Jasmine. And I can feel that it could lead somewhere. When we're together, there's no one else I'd rather be with. And I don't mean to hurt you by being honest, but I want us to have an honest relationship, especially knowing that we're meant to be bonded for life. That's why I'm telling you all these things. The main problem is that my past with Lucy has created this sort of block for me. And I'm trying so hard to move past it. I really want this to work, and I promise I will try as long as you still want to be with me. How do you feel? And please be honest with me too." He looked over at me, his eyes searching mine.

"I feel the same things you do. I know I don't have a past, but I know exactly the block you're referring to. I think because you have it, I have it too. And Lucy's my best friend. It hurts me that things have turned out this way."

He used his thumb to rub my palm. "I'm glad we could have this conversation tonight. Let's just take things slow. We're both still young, so there's no reason to rush into anything. Let's just get to know each other more."

The sparks from his touch rushed up my arm, calming my whole body, practically forcing me to forget how nauseous the conversation had made me earlier. I shook my head and asked, "Do you honestly think us getting to know each other more will change how you feel?"

He looked at me for a few moments and said, "Yes, I do. The more I get to know you, the more I like you. I think this could lead somewhere good."

Chapter 49

Jasmine

The next day, Saturday, I worked the early shift and got out of work at one thirty. It had dipped below freezing, and snow flurries were falling from the sky. As I walked past the sub shop toward where I was parked, I noticed two familiar faces inside. Luke and Lucy were seated across from each other, Luke's hands on top of Lucy's on the table between them. I stared, the two of them lost in their own world and completely oblivious to the fact that I was gawking at them through a huge window.

    A person sitting directly in front of the window looked up at me, clearly wondering why I was staring creepily into the restaurant. I turned away and continued walking. Once again, I wondered what it would be like to have this as the rest of my life—forever competing for Luke's attention with my former best friend and mother of his first born.

    I drove home to an empty house. My parents had gone out. I went upstairs and turned on my laptop to check the grades on my latest assignments. I cringed. Ugh, I was completely disgusted with myself. I had completely slipped in school, being so affected by my mate situation. Every time I opened my textbooks, I could barely concentrate. When I did my assignments, I rushed through them. I couldn't even be bothered to study for any of my exams. I'd be lucky if I got away with Bs this semester. For a normal person, this would be perfectly okay, but I had never even received an A minus in my life.

I fell into my bed, feeling completely defeated. I tried to nap, throwing on some headphones to listen to music, but found it was no use. I was too anxious. I knew I'd have to do something physical to get it all out.

After spending around an hour trying to relax, I finally ran downstairs and stepped outside. The air was crisp and perfect for going for a run in my wolf form. I stepped into the woods and found a place to leave all my clothes, sheltered from the snow flurries. I stripped naked and quickly shifted. It was therapeutic allowing my brain to succumb to my animal side, and the frozen leaves crunched under my paws. I sprinted north, eager to explore the forested area beyond our pack territory.

As I ran, I dodged different trees, taking in my surroundings. The skies were gray, and the branches of the trees were bare. Around three miles outside the border, I sprinted around a huge rock, and that was when I realized that this was a bad idea. I found myself face-to-face with two huge wolves. I was close enough that their scents filled my nostrils—the scent of an unfamiliar pack. I knew it wasn't from any neighboring pack because I had never smelled it before. I was about to run away in another direction when one of them pounced toward me. My reflexes were fast, and I was able to dodge the attack. I could probably fight off one wolf if I had to, but in this case, I was outnumbered. They both growled and bared their teeth at me. Fear overtaking me, I mindlinked the first person that came to mind.

"Blake, help!"

Blake

I was in the middle of eating soup that Connie had made that day for lunch when I heard the mindlink come through. Jasmine. I felt all the hairs on my body stand up. The way she mindlinked me, it was pure, primal fear. I tried to force a link back to her, to try to get more information, but it was blocked. She must have been too busy concentrating on whatever scared her to accept the mindlink back. The fact she could mindlink me made it clear she was in her wolf form, a hint to her whereabouts.

I instantly shot up and ran outside, mindlinking the seniors that were normally on duty at this hour, having almost memorized the schedule by now. *"Did anyone see a young pack female wolf pass through the border recently?"*

I didn't know how much time I'd have, so I ran outside and ripped the clothes off my body, heading toward the northern border, that being my best bet based on recent events. As I ran, I mindlinked Luke, *"Northern border, now. Jasmine's in trouble."*

As I ran, Mike mindlinked me back, *"Yes, one of the juniors saw a wolf pass through our patrol area not too long ago."* Perfect.

I replied, *"Stand by."* I sprinted as fast as my paws would take me, stomping hard against the frozen soil. I ran to the northern border, where one of the juniors on patrol pointed me toward where he had seen Jasmine run.

I ran straight past him and instantly picked up her scent, following it to a large rock. I continued to follow it around the rock when I spotted her. Bloody, but, goddamn, she was a fucking fighter. The two wolves would have easily overpowered her in brute force, but I knew her technique was what kept her alive. I knew how good she was at dodging and landing attacks.

And she was tough. They'd clearly gotten a good many bites and scratches in, the white parts of her fur now stained red, but she was still fucking going.

I immediately pounced, bringing the bigger of the two wolves down, taking him by surprise and getting in a huge gash down the entirety of his back. He got up and pushed me off him, spraying blood as he shook. He lunged back at me, and I caught one of his legs between my teeth, tearing into it and savoring the taste of blood as it filled my mouth. Before my teeth hit bone, he finally kicked me off.

Just then, Luke arrived and went after the other wolf that was left battling Jasmine. I looked over to see that she had been knocked over, distracting me, a protective feeling taking over seeing her like that. In that split second, the wolf I was fighting grabbed hold of my neck with his mouth, ready to kill me. I used my front paws to stop him before he could behead me.

Fuck, I should have had the patrol team follow me. That was reckless to try to play hero. I couldn't even mindlink now, needing all of my concentration to fight off these wolves.

With my paws in the wolf's mouth, I used my strength to pry it open far enough so that it snapped, breaking his jaw. I heard bones crack—music to my ears. The sadistic part of me woke up. I quickly looked over to where Luke had the other wolf pinned down, currently attempting to injure him—so he'd be forced to shift back to his human form—and then I turned back to my target.

I began shoving my claws deep into his body, dragging them, enjoying the vision of blood as it spilled out of the ripped seams of his body. He fought back, scratching me across the face. And then he lunged for my throat with his claws. I dodged the attack and bit down on his neck. I did not intend to kill him, but I couldn't stop myself as I felt my teeth break through his skin and snap his neck in half, pulling his throat out with my mouth. I spit it out onto him as I saw his lifeless body on the ground, shifted back into his human form. Damn it. We still had one left that we could interrogate, at least.

I pulled my attention from the lifeless man to where Luke was fighting the other werewolf. Jasmine was standing by as backup. She was so injured that I was surprised she hadn't shifted back into her human form yet—her fur matted with blood and deep cuts along her face.

I was running over to help Luke when that wolf dodged Luke's attack, throwing him back, and went straight for Jasmine, pushing her over and snapping one of her back legs against a rock, a clean break. We watched in horror as her howl turned into a shriek as she finally shifted into her human form. Anguish ignited within me at the sound. All I could see was red as both Luke and I leaped on him. Luke went for his head, and I went for his spine as we completely annihilated him, Luke beheading him and me pulling his vertebrae out of his body with my claws, feeling gratified as his limp body fell to the ground.

And now he was dead too. Fuck! The pack they were from would remain a mystery, although the scent was still familiar. Why couldn't I place it?

Luke and I both shifted into our human forms as we ran over to Jasmine lying naked on the ground, completely bruised and covered in blood. Luke put his head to her chest. "She's still breathing." Then he looked at me pointedly and said, "Would you mind at least pretending to avert your eyes?" I turned my head away as he picked her up and said, "I'll run her to the clinic."

"Ok, I'll get these bodies burned," I replied. We ran back toward Mike's post. They had clothing waiting for us once we arrived, clearly having been mindlinked by Luke. He quickly threw some shorts on himself and a large T-shirt on top of Jasmine. Mike drove them to the clinic.

I also pulled on a pair of shorts and had a few of juniors follow me into the woods. We dragged the dead bodies back to the patrol station where we threw them into a large firepit, throwing wood and pouring gasoline over the bodies. I lit a match, tossing it into the firepit, and watched them burn, the smell of burning flesh and gasoline filling our noses. I was used to it by now, having burned dozens of dead bodies over the years.

As the flames blazed, I walked away, removing the shorts I was wearing and shifting to run back to the packhouse. Once I entered, I ran upstairs to take a shower. The injuries I had sustained were fairly minor for a werewolf. After I got out of the shower, I looked in the mirror to see that the scratch across my face and the bite marks on my neck were healing. I dressed myself and went downstairs where I saw Luke had planted himself on the couch.

"Your mom was working. She's taking care of her," he said. I nodded. Luke got up and went into the kitchen.

That gave me the opportunity to sneak out. The clinic was not far from the packhouse. I was desperate to see her for myself, and I would easily have a way since my mom was working.

I walked down the street until I reached the clinic. I waved to the woman who was working the front desk and walked directly to the back. I found my mom seated in her office. She got up as soon as I entered. I hugged her and said, "Mom, please, I need to see Jasmine."

She nodded and led me to the room where she was. "I set her leg and gave her medication for the pain. She just needs to heal, but she'll be fine."

I entered quietly and knelt by her bed. I brushed her hair out of her face, smoothing it down, and listened to her labored breathing. She stirred; her eyes snapped open. "Blake," she whispered, her eyes glossy as she looked at me.

"Shhhh," I said. "It's okay, just rest for now."

She closed her eyes again. I laid my head next to her, enjoying being near her. I must have dozed off because the next thing I felt was someone's hand on my shoulder gently shaking me awake. I lifted my head to see my mom was standing over me.

"Go into my office. Jasmine's family is here with Luke to see her. I'll get rid of your scent before they come in."

I did as my mom said and snuck over to her office where I sat down in her office chair.

After some time, she walked in and closed the door with her arms crossed. "Blake, I've noticed you seem very close with Jasmine. Is there something going on between the two of you?"

"We're just friends."

"Blake, I know you. I'm your mother. This seems to be more than friendship. This is now the second time I've had to be deceptive to cover for you when it involved Jasmine."

"There's nothing more to it than friendship. I just care for her as a friend."

She closed her eyes and pinched the bridge of her nose. "Blake, please, just be careful. That's your beta's mate. He's practically a brother to you, and I would hate to see the leadership of the pack torn apart over this. Your father may come off too harsh most of the time, but he's right when he says the pack needs their leaders to have their heads in the game. Especially after what happened today. I'm worried, Blake. This could be the difference between life or death. You're my only son, and I can't lose you." She came over and hugged me, kissing me on the forehead. "Now, go home and let Luke take care of his mate."

Chapter 50

Jasmine

I awoke on Sunday morning feeling much better than I had when I initially arrived at the clinic. I could tell that the deep gashes that the wolves had put into my body were now just scratches. My leg was still sore when I moved it, but not to the extent it was the night before when the pain was excruciating. I still probably couldn't walk today, but maybe tomorrow.

A nurse came in and exclaimed, "Ah, you're awake now! Good! Let me bring your breakfast and medication in then." She disappeared and returned a few minutes later carrying a tray. She adjusted my bed so I was sitting up and set the tray on the bed so I could easily eat from it. Before she left, she said, "Your mate asked me to call when you wake, so I'll go do that now."

I felt my stomach grumble, I hadn't eaten since my lunch break at work the previous day. I quickly ate the bagel and fruit she brought me and drank from the mug of coffee. Not long after I finished, the nurse came back and took the empty tray from me. "Your mate will be here soon. Let me help you use the bathroom before he comes."

She helped me use some crutches so that I could maneuver myself into the bathroom. I was able to freshen up, combing out my hair and brushing my teeth. I could see in the mirror that the scratches that had covered my face yesterday were almost fully healed now. Once I was done, she helped me lie back down in the bed.

Luke came in not long after and ran over to my bedside. As soon as the nurse walked out, he laid his body next to mine on the bed, using his hand to brush back my hair. I enjoyed the feeling his hand emitted, calming and relaxing my whole body. "You look much better today," he said, smiling at me. "How are you feeling?"

"Better," I replied.

He grabbed my hand and held it. "Please don't do that again, Jasmine. I spoke with your father and we both agree that it's best that you don't leave the territory anymore when you're alone in the forest. It's too dangerous right now."

I nodded.

"Why were you out there anyway?"

I felt the nausea returning, the walls closing in. "I was just really stressed. I needed to run."

He used his thumb to rub my palm, calming me. "Please don't stress, Jasmine. We'll figure everything out. Everything will work out, I promise."

"How can you promise that?" I demanded. "How do you see this working out?"

He looked away, letting out a deep breath. I could sense anxiety, a feeling I was very familiar with. He shook his head and then looked back at me. "I know it's bad now. I know a lot's happening, but I'm going to take responsibility. I'm going to be a good mate to you. Please believe me, Jasmine." He searched my face, looking for confirmation.

I sighed, not able to give him any, wondering if everything really would work out—not sure that it could. But as his body touched mine, the sparks and calm flowing through me, I began to believe it might, against my better judgment.

He continued, "I'm so glad we were able to get to you in time. I can't stop thinking about what would have happened if we didn't. When Blake mindlinked me, I dropped everything and just ran." He snuggled closer to me, kissing me on the cheek. "Although, how did Blake know you were in trouble?"

"I mindlinked him," I replied, realizing I probably shouldn't admit to this as I said it.

"You mindlinked Blake but you didn't mindlink me?" I looked at him, not answering his question. "But why him?"

"He was the first person I thought of," I admitted.

"Do you have feelings for Blake?" he asked, staring straight into my eyes.

"What, no!" I exclaimed.

"It just seems like there's something going on between the two of you."

"We're just friends."

He let out another deep breath and said, "I know I haven't been the best mate to you. But I'm trying, Jasmine, I really am. Please, I want you to come to me when you need help and you're in trouble. Please don't go to Blake anymore."

Blake

I was alone in my office, seated at my desk, when my father barged in. Before he even spoke, I could tell he was in a bad mood. His face was red, eyebrows furrowed, and hands clenched in tight fists. I had come to recognize when my dad was going to blow up over the years, and I knew he wasn't just coming in for a friendly chat. He stormed in, stopping in front of my desk, and banging his fists down on it.

"What's this I hear about trespassers being killed on the spot?" he bellowed.

I sighed. "They technically weren't trespassing."

"I don't fucking care about technicalities. They were clearly the same assholes who have been casing this place for at least a week. And now we have no fucking clue what pack they're from or what their motivation was. What was the first fucking thing I taught you about trespassers?"

I shook my head. I knew I fucked up, and it was not surprising that my father was pissed. Everyone knew to interrogate first, kill later. I'd made a rookie mistake. It was just, at that moment, I couldn't think straight, especially after seeing how the asshole had hurt Jasmine, even though I knew better.

My father continued on his tirade. "What the hell is wrong with you, Blake. All those years of training and you still don't fucking know what you're doing. You clearly didn't get your mom's brains, that's for sure! Goddess knows why she sent you to me as my only son. I only hope she lets me die before I have to witness this whole place go to shit under your leadership."

I was becoming enraged by my father's outburst. I had my hands balled into fists, restraining myself from swinging one right into his face. I was completely sick of how he always talked to me and others, as if there was nothing wrong with verbally abusing anyone in his path.

He continued, "What fucking good are two dead and burned bodies? They can't fucking tell us anything. We don't know if we should be expecting a fucking war tomorrow. Because you didn't do your fucking job. What kind of alpha are you? You're a fucking embarrassment, that's what! All those years of trying to knock some sense into you and nothing to show for it!"

I was really pissed now and shouted, "Get the fuck out of the packhouse before I beat the shit out of you!" I used my alpha aura and he couldn't help himself as he bowed his neck to me, scrunching his face in pain.

Before he could say another word, he walked himself out.

"That's right! I'm the alpha now so fuck off!" I yelled to him as I heard his footsteps disappearing toward the front door.

That night, I went to the temple service. I sat in a different location than I normally did, not wanting to be anywhere near my father. I saw him enter with my mom and take their usual seat up front. Not long after, I spotted Jasmine's parents enter sans Jasmine. She must still be recovering. A bone completely snapped in half could take a long time to heal. Luke entered and was about to sit with my parents when he noticed where I was sitting and sat down next to me instead.

"Hey," I said to him as he sat down.

"Hey."

"How is she?"

"Still recovering," he replied.

I wanted to push for more information but didn't want to seem too interested. I'd ask my mom, but after her speech I knew that would be a bad idea as well.

Suddenly, Luke turned back toward me and asked, "What's the deal with you two?"

"What do you mean?" I asked, taken aback.

"I just feel like there's something going on between the two of you."

"We're just friends. She's your mate."

"You've never really had female friends before unless you were trying to get into their pants."

"Let's not talk about this right now. She's just my friend, okay?"

He shook his head, but he clearly agreed this wasn't the best place for this conversation and turned his head forward as the priest walked on stage to begin the service.

After the service, the two of us walked home together. Luke turned to me again, "Blake, please be honest with me. Do you like Jasmine?"

"I like her as a friend," I replied, trying to put emphasis on the word *friend*.

"I don't know. It just seems like you might like her as more than that."

I sighed, knowing I'd have to be more convincing. "Look, Luke, you're practically a brother to me. I'm not going to go after your mate. Jasmine's incredible and you're really lucky to have her. I just care about her well-being, that's all. Just be good to her, okay?"

He nodded, and his eyes glossed over. I could see he was lost in thought. I found myself once again wondering what he was thinking. Once we got back to the packhouse, he split from me and continued walking toward the clinic.

I walked inside, only to hear the doorbell ring minutes later. I answered it and came face-to-face with Lucy.

"Is Luke in?" she asked.

"No," I replied, looking her up and down. She was very beautiful and had this confidence about her in the way she held herself, as if she were too big for this place. I could understand the attraction Luke had for her. He wasn't always so sure of himself, and I could see how he'd be mesmerized by someone so poised and assertive.

"Can I come in?" she asked.

"What are you doing here?"

"I haven't been feeling well, and I need to see Luke. I can wait for him."

"Shouldn't you be seeing a doctor in that case?"

"It's nothing serious. I just need the support from the father of my baby."

I stepped aside and she walked in, shoving past me. I watched as she went to climb the stairs to his room.

"Where are you going?" I shouted at her.

"Where do you think?" she replied.

I followed her up the stairs, annoyed. "Is Luke okay with you just going into his bedroom when he's not home?"

"Why wouldn't he be? I've been in there hundreds of times. I mean, we had to make this baby somehow."

I couldn't believe her audacity. "Luke has a mate."

She suddenly narrowed her eyes at me, a sour expression on her face. "I had him first. The mate thing's just a bump in the road between us. Believe me, Luke wants to be with me. He's just too much of a coward to think for himself. He feels obligated to Jasmine because of this whole mate bond thing, but they're not going to last long. She's not right for him. Anyway, I'm carrying his baby."

"Isn't Jasmine your friend?"

"She *was* my friend, past tense. Until she went behind my back and stole my boyfriend from me."

"Are you serious? Jasmine and Luke are mated to each other."

"I'm sick of hearing mate, mate, mate. What about what Luke and I want? Why does some invisible person get to decide our fate for us? Why does it mean that she's better for him than I am?"

"Because that's how it works, Lucy. If you take Luke away from Jasmine, she won't have anyone. Why don't you see that?"

"Is that really the end of the world? I mean, she could find someone else. Not too long ago, you were all over her yourself."

I stared at her openmouthed, shocked at her selfishness.

After gathering my thoughts, I said, "But Jasmine doesn't want someone else. She wants to be with the person she's supposed to be with. It may not make sense to you, but she's been raised very religiously, and her family has certain expectations of her. In fact, even leaving religion out of it, most people want to be with their mates. I have yet to meet someone that doesn't. I've experienced the mate bond myself and I'm still in pain from losing it."

I felt a prickle at the back of my throat. I was surprised at my admission to Lucy. I didn't often confess my feelings about my own mate bond, especially to people I wasn't close with.

If I didn't know better, I'd think she suddenly seemed to soften, her facial features taking on a downturned appearance, a sadness playing across her face. Maybe Lucy wasn't as awful as she was acting. But before I could consider it more, she turned and walked into Luke's room.

I sighed and decided to mindlink Luke. *"Lucy's here."* Then I went back downstairs to find leftovers to eat for dinner.

I was seated in the kitchen when he popped his head in. "Where is she?" he asked, looking tired.

"Upstairs," I replied. He shook his head and was about to close the door and walk upstairs when I stopped him. "Luke." He looked at me. I continued, "Do you wish you were mated to Lucy instead of Jasmine?"

He stepped into the kitchen and closed the door behind him, looking at me for a few seconds before he replied, "It doesn't matter what I want. I spoke with my dad, and I have no choice. Apparently, Jasmine's related to the alphas of the Jade Moon Pack, and they've threatened our pack before. I don't know when or why, but my dad was adamant that I need to see this relationship through, or they could be a threat to us. This is bigger than me. I have to think about the pack now."

I looked at him wondering if I should say more. Finally, I just nodded my head in understanding, resigned to both the fact that he was partially right—we did have to consider the pack above all else in our positions—and that I shouldn't interfere. Ultimately, Jasmine was Luke's mate, not mine. He turned around and walked out the door. But I couldn't help but feel that it wasn't right.

Chapter 51

Jasmine

When I woke on Monday, I could feel that my leg was finally fully healed. Luke picked me up and drove me home. My parents were already gone by the time we got there. After he parked in the driveway, he followed me as I went out back to where I had left my clothes and keys before I had shifted days earlier. I walked to the back door to unlock it.

"Would you like to come in?" I asked.

"Yes," he replied, following me into the kitchen. Once I shut the door, he wrapped his arms around me. His body was warm against mine, the sparks it emitted provoking my muscles to tense and my heart to beat rapidly, my whole body becoming aroused. As soon as his mouth touched mine, I pressed my pelvis against him in desperation.

After pulling apart, I dropped everything in my hands onto a kitchen chair. He grabbed me again, pulling me tightly against him. I used my free hands to touch every bit of him as he kissed me—his abs, chest, and broad shoulders.

"I want you so badly," he moaned between kisses. "It's been too long. No interruptions today. I'm turning my phone off." He pulled out his phone and demonstrated as he turned it off and put it down on the kitchen table.

I took his hand and led him upstairs, his scent and the feeling of him touching my body setting off the same desire. Halfway up the stairs, he picked me up and carried me into my bedroom, throwing me on the bed. Crawling on top of me, he pushed my hair behind my ears and put his mouth back on mine. He settled between my legs, pressing his erection exactly where I could feel myself tingling, sparks being emitted and dulled by our clothing. He kissed me hungrily, stopping to pull the shirt off his body. I watched as he revealed his muscular torso to me, heightening my desire for him. He then peeled my shirt off and kissed down my chest, quickly unsnapping my bra and throwing it.

He placed his hands on my breasts, gently massaging them, and brought his mouth down on one of them. My breathing deepened—his soft, warm tongue against my aroused nipple was intoxicating. He kissed down my breast and moved his mouth to my torso, quickly kissing his way down, stopping once he reached the top of my jeans. He impatiently unbuttoned and unzipped them before pulling them off me. Once my legs were completely bare, he took his jeans off as well.

"Goddess, I just love touching you. Everything about being with you feels so good," he exclaimed, staring down at me.

He brought his hands down to my panties and pulled them off, sliding them down my legs slowly. Once they were completely off, he kissed me up my legs, prompting my muscles to contract from the feeling of his mouth against them. When he started kissing the inside of my thighs, a moan escaped my lips, the pleasure and anticipation almost unbearable.

He looked up, locking eyes with me, and said, "You smell so fucking delicious. I want to taste every bit of you."

He teased me, kissing the inside of my thighs, not moving any closer to where I wished he would kiss me. He slowly circled his mouth closer and closer to the target and finally shoved his fingers inside me. I yelped in surprise at the feeling as he pushed them in and out of me, eventually curling his fingers to find that spot that spread bliss throughout the lower half of my body, provoking me to moan loudly.

"Goddess, it's amazing. I can almost feel your pleasure through the mate bond," he exclaimed just as he lowered his mouth between my legs, first kissing me, and then sucking gently, a shiver traveling up my body in response. He eventually began using his tongue, flicking it against me, emitting sparks and pleasure. I completely lost myself in the feeling, my toes curling, grabbing at the bedsheets, wishing it would never end.

I tried to hold on to the feeling as long as I could but eventually found myself at the place of no return, my body shaking against his mouth, feeling euphoria pulse through my body. I gasped in a loud moan, and he pulled away, laying himself next to me. I turned to look into his eyes as he pushed my hair back.

"How was it?" he asked.

"Amazing."

"Good." He smiled.

"Let me." I got up, wanting to return the favor. He rolled onto his back, and I pulled his boxer briefs down. He kicked them off his legs. I was unsure of myself as I tried to do the same thing I did last time. I put my hand on his erection, lowering my mouth to it, feeling it pulse in my hands. As soon as he was inside my mouth he groaned.

"Goddess, it feels so good. You could probably just keep your mouth on it and not do anything and I would still come from how good it feels."

I knew that probably wasn't what he wanted, so I moved my mouth up and down as he let out another groan. I allowed my hand to glide up and down his shaft in sync with my mouth. Before long, I found myself in a groove, my tongue pressing against him as I moved.

Soon I could feel the lower half of his body pulsating. "I'm going to come," he exclaimed, and I kept going. I could feel as he throbbed a final few times before hot, salty liquid entered my mouth. I licked it up off him and swallowed it.

He had told me I didn't have to, but I still wasn't sure what the alternative was. Certainly, he didn't want me to spit it out on either him or the bed.

"Damn, that's so fucking hot when you swallow my come," he sighed. I lay down next to him and he kissed my forehead. He pulled me closer to him, cuddling my naked body against his. "This is nice, just lying here with you," he said against my ear. "Are you comfortable?"

"Yeah, it feels nice," I agreed.

"How's your leg feeling?"

"Much better. Good as new."

"I know I keep saying it, but I'm so glad you're okay." He looked into my eyes. "You're my mate and I will always protect you. That's exactly what I told your family. I think after what happened, your mom's finally starting to warm up to me."

I nodded, knowing it would be short-lived. I was terrified of revealing to my parents that Luke had impregnated my friend. I knew it would not go over well. As the thought came to my mind, I started to feel sick again, dry heaving, rolling away so I was no longer touching his body.

"Are you okay, Jasmine? What's wrong?" he asked.

"My parents don't know."

"Your parents don't know what?"

"Lucy's pregnant." I could sense a dread come over him as soon as I said it.

"Jasmine, please, don't get stressed again. I'll talk to them. I'll explain everything and let them know that it won't get in the way of our mate bond."

"But how can you promise that? It already has." I looked into his eyes. "Every time I turn around, she's texting you. She's relentless. I know she won't give up until she has you back. I just wonder if it's even worth fighting it anymore. Maybe Lucy's right, and the pregnancy's a sign that you're meant to be with her. That the Moon Goddess made a mistake fating me to you."

"Don't say that, Jasmine. Please. I know it will all work out. If I were meant to be with Lucy, I would have been mated to her. But I'm not. I'm mated to you."

"You didn't even care before. You thought we should all think about it before committing to each other. Why are you so adamant that we should go along with the mate bond all of a sudden?"

"Because I realized I was being selfish and immature. I arrogantly thought my personal will was superior to that of the Moon Goddess. But that's not the case, is it? At the end of the day, she decides our fates for us, and we can't circumvent them without creating bigger problems than we anticipated. Anyway, I know that being with your fated mate's important to you, as is getting married in the temple. And I don't want to be the person to take that away from you."

"But those things aren't important to you," I responded, a bit taken aback that he was only doing this for me.

He sighed and said, "They're important to me too. I also went to temple every week with my parents. I guess I just ended up on the wrong path for a little while. Anyway, part of being in a relationship is doing things that make the person you're with happy. I've done a lot of thinking, and I want to make you happy, Jasmine. I don't ever want to be the reason you're sad." He pulled me against him, and the sparks emitted from his body possessed me once again, forcing me to forget what I was ever even upset about, the bond taking charge.

I sighed, snuggling into his chest. It did feel really nice being so close to him. I became calm just by touching him. It was like my entire body craved him, and he was the cure to all my ailments. I could tell that he felt the same way as he held me closer to him, rubbing his hand against my back. We lay like that for a long time, just enjoying the feeling of being with each other.

Eventually, we got up and went downstairs. I was starving. "Would you like me to make you something for lunch?" I asked Luke as we entered the kitchen and he picked up his phone, switching it on.

"Actually, I better get back to the packhouse. I've been avoiding work while I've been here with you. Not that I regret it, of course." He smiled and pulled me in for a hug. "But I obviously can't avoid work forever."

Suddenly, his phone started dinging. I glanced over to see that text message alerts were coming in from Lucy. I sighed, stepping away from him. He threw his phone into his pocket and looked back up at me. "I have to go, but I will see you again soon." Then he turned to go to the front door to leave. I followed him, seeing him out. He kissed me one last time at the doorway before he descended the front stairs and got into his car.

As I watched his car drive away, I felt deep within me that things weren't going right at all.

Chapter 52

Jasmine

On Wednesday I was supposed to return to work, but Valerie canceled my shift, saying I needed more time to recover, and she'd see me on Saturday. I tried to argue but she wouldn't hear of it. Not wanting to sit around, especially with my leg now fully healed, I went to the gym.

I decided to avoid leg exercises just in case. I began with several minutes of stretching followed by different floor exercises. First, I worked on my core by doing crunches, Russian twists, and planks. Then I transitioned to push-ups, seeing how many I could do in three minutes. When I was on the second minute, I sensed a familiar scent and couldn't help but smile. I completed the last minute of push-ups and finally fell to my knees and looked up.

"I see Miss Alpha's already back in action." Blake smirked at me.

"I'm starting to think you're stalking me."

"Okay, this time it wasn't a coincidence. I saw your car parked out front as I was passing by." He put his hands up. "But I'm due for a workout anyway."

"Stalker."

"Oh please, you love it. I know you're secretly happy that you'll get to stare at my ripped body with no shame again."

"Sounds like something a stalker would say."

He smiled and put his hands out to help me up. "Come on, let's go do some pull-ups and TRX exercises." He led me over to a large power rack in the center of the gym, pulled off his shirt, and hopped up, grabbing hold of the pull-up bar. He gripped the bar as he pulled his body up, all the muscles in his upper body revealing themselves.

Oh Goddess, I felt a strong tingle between my legs. I couldn't deny my attraction to Blake.

I went after he did, using a bench to reach the bar. As I was pulling up, Blake started speaking. "You know, you were really tough on Saturday. I don't think most women would have made it that long and still stayed in their wolf form, especially without formal warrior training. I was impressed."

"Thanks," I replied, finishing up my set. I got down, and he hopped back up. "Probably best I don't leave the territory for now though. I didn't realize how dangerous it is."

"That's probably Luke's and my fault. We should have been pursuing those assholes more, but I think we've both been distracted. That was a huge wake-up call for both of us. People leave the territory all the time, and they shouldn't have to worry that they're going to get attacked."

"Where did they come from anyway?"

Blake hopped down and looked at me. "We don't know, unfortunately. I accidentally killed both of them before I got a chance to interrogate them." I hopped back up and he spoke again. "How's your leg doing?"

"Much better."

"Good, I knew it would heal in no time. Fucking badass Miss Alpha, future warrior. Did I mention how hot it was watching you do all those push-ups?"

After we finished with the pull-ups, we switched to the TRX exercises. We each took a set of straps and Blake called out different exercises as we did them together. As we were doing TRX rows, Blake looked over at me and asked, "So how are things with Luke going?"

I groaned, unable to answer.

"That doesn't sound good."

"Can I be honest with you and not worry that you'll say anything?"

"Of course. We're friends, right?"

"I just know you're close friends with Luke, so it makes it a little weird. But I have no one else to talk to. I sometimes wish I had an older sister or something. At least then she could help me with my parents, but I don't have anyone anymore. I used to have Lucy, but you know how that is."

He nodded. "I'm happy to listen anytime, Jasmine. And I won't say anything. I honestly don't talk much to anyone either. I think I've had more conversations with you than I have with anyone in the past five years. Let's switch to TRX chest press."

I flipped my body over, following his lead. I was surprised at his confession. I sighed and decided he could be trusted.

"I just don't know if it's worth fighting for the mate bond anymore. I'm so torn. When I'm with him, it's like it's just the two of us and no one else matters. As soon as he touches me, I'm willing to forgive anything and everything as long as I can be close to him. But then, when I step away, I realize how much of a disaster the whole relationship is. I've broken my closest friendship to be with him. He knocked up my best friend after he already knew I was his mate! And now, every time I turn around, he's texting with her. And I understand that he has to take responsibility since he's the father of the baby, but it just hurts." My voice cracked and a tear fell down my cheek. "At first, he didn't even want to commit to me and now, all of a sudden, he won't hear of us breaking things off."

"Maybe he realized you're worth fighting for." I looked at Blake whose piercing blue eyes stared into me as if they were seeing into my soul.

"You're definitely worth fighting for. He might have just been a little slow to figure it out for himself."

"I don't know." I turned back to look at the floor as I pressed.

"Well, what do you want? If you didn't have to worry about making your parents happy or getting married in the temple, what would you do? Would you still want to be with Luke?"

I pondered Blake's question and finally came back with my own. "We only get one mate, and the Moon Goddess wants me to be with him. What if I reject Luke and don't find anyone else?"

"I don't think that's even possible. If Luke can't see how fucking lucky he is to have just been handed you on a silver platter, then, quite frankly, he doesn't deserve you. And someone else will definitely realize it. There are plenty of men out there who have lost their mates, and I'm sure there are loads that would be more than happy to scoop you up. TRX biceps curl."

I flipped my body so I was facing the ceiling and began curling. We were mostly silent for the remainder of the workout as I considered what he said. I couldn't help but wonder if Blake was one of the men that would be willing to scoop me up. I wasn't sure.

From everything he'd said to me, it seemed that he was no longer interested in relationships and only wanted something casual. It seemed like Ria was the one time he ever swayed from his usual ways, and that was only because she was his mate. Either way, I knew that I definitely couldn't count on Blake if I broke things off with Luke and that should not even be a consideration. A deep sadness came over me at the thought. I should just assume I'd be alone for a while until I found someone, if I ever found someone, and that suddenly felt very lonely.

After we finished with the TRX exercises, we went back onto the mats to stretch out. It was nice just being with Blake. I felt calm in his presence, I realized, not needing the touch of the mate bond to give me that effect.

After we finished our stretches and got up to leave, he pulled me in for a hug, holding me against his sweaty body.

He put his mouth against my ear. "You're a tough girl, Miss Alpha. You'll be okay." He separated from me and walked away. As I watched him go, I wondered what he thought of me. Were we just friends, or was there maybe something more?

Chapter 53

Jasmine

On Thursday afternoon, I ran to the grocery store, a list in hand that my mom had left me that morning. I was in the produce section when I spotted them. Lucy and her mom were together, walking the store. But that wasn't what bothered me. She was wearing a dress. And not just any dress, but one that was tight on her body, revealing every imperfection. Since Lucy had no imperfections, she'd normally have no problem pulling it off. Except for, of course, that her belly had popped.

On any normal person, one could easily assume that maybe she had eaten too much. But Lucy was not a normal person. No, she barely had an ounce of fat on her body, and it was obvious that her normally flat stomach was no longer so. No, she was very clearly pregnant.

I watched as she rubbed her belly, wandering the store with her mom, sociably greeting other pack members as they shopped. I quickly turned my carriage, and flung myself down a different aisle, trying my best to avoid them. It was not a large store, so it would not be easy. As a severe sickness come over me, I made the decision to abandon my grocery cart and sprint out of the store. Maybe I could come back later.

I jumped into my car and sped home. All this time, I'd been dealing with a ticking time bomb, and it wouldn't be long before it exploded.

My mom was closely connected to all the busybodies in the pack, and if Lucy had become open at all about her pregnancy, it wouldn't be long before it got back to her.

I decided to text Luke, especially after he'd asked me to go to him for help whenever I needed it.

Me: *Hey, are you around?*

I waited and didn't see a reply after a few minutes. Then I remembered he had class on Thursdays. I decided to busy myself with cleaning. I did my laundry, vacuumed the house, scrubbed my bathroom. I thought about doing my homework, but I couldn't stomach it.

At four forty-five, I started dinner. I then remembered that I had never returned to the grocery store, but I made do with whatever ingredients I could find in the fridge and pantry. I dug some frozen meatballs out of the freezer and put together a large batch of spaghetti and meatballs. We still had some salad ingredients left, so I was able to put together a pretty good salad. I added hardboiled eggs and crumbled bacon to spruce it up.

My parents walked in just as I was putting the final touches on the meal. I quickly looked over at my phone where I finally had a response from Luke.

Luke: *Sorry, I was in class. Heading home now.*

As soon as I saw my parents' faces, I knew they were in a bad mood. It was like I could see the future, and I had already predicted what was going to happen once they got home. My dad went to reach for the liquor cabinet. They never drank—ever! The liquor cabinet was literally only there for when other people came over. He pulled out a bottle of whiskey followed by a glass. I watched as he poured a drink. My mom just walked over to the kitchen table and slumped down in her chair.

My dad stood, staring at me, sipping from the glass. He finally spoke. "Your mom got some interesting text messages at work today from her friends."

"Oh, what about?" I played dumb. Inside, I was crumbling.

He took a sip of his whiskey, then looked at me. "Is Lucy pregnant?"

I stared at him, knowing the answer would have to come out. Finally, I whispered, "Yes."

"Fucking Artemis!" my dad yelled. I'd never heard him swear in my life. I cringed. He then seemed to compose himself and asked, "So, what are Luke's thoughts on all this? Is he still committed to his relationship with you?"

"I think so," I replied.

"But you're not sure?" He narrowed his eyes at me.

"Maybe it's just not meant to be," I replied, the first thing that came to my mind after contemplating everything I'd discussed with Blake the prior day.

"Fucking Artemis," he said more softly this time and shook his head, taking a gulp of his whiskey.

My mom got up and ran to my father. "Don't worry, honey. I'll call my brother and nephew. They'll take care of this. There's no reason to worry." She put her arms around him, rubbing his arm.

"No!" my dad yelled, shocking both my mom and me. "That's insane. And threaten our beta? It's one thing to threaten someone with no rank or title, but the beta of our pack?"

"They'll just talk to him, honey. Just a conversation. Pack to pack."

"No, I won't allow it. I'm not taking his choice away. He has a right to choose for himself."

"Why? Do you regret this?" My mom swung her arms, gesturing around her.

"No, I don't regret it at all." He took another sip of his whiskey.

"Then what's wrong?" My mom glared at him. He glared back, locked in a staring contest.

"What's going on? What are you talking about?" I asked, looking between the two of them.

My mom turned to me and said, "Don't worry about it, honey. These are things that happened long ago and don't concern you." Then she turned to my dad. "I'm calling my brother right now."

"No! I won't allow it!" he shouted. "If he doesn't want to be with my daughter then she deserves better than that. Moon Goddess be damned! I had my choice taken away. And while I don't regret it, I will not allow someone else's to." He poured more whiskey into his glass, sat down at the kitchen table, and started putting food on his plate.

My mom hesitated and sat down next to him at the table. She put some salad on her plate and then looked over at him. "Honey, think about what you're saying. We can't be allowing our daughter to disrespect the Moon Goddess. He has obligations, especially as the beta of this pack. Just think about it, okay?"

"My word is final," he shot back at my mom. When I looked at her, I saw she looked devastated, eyes brimming with tears. Both my parents began eating in silence. I sat down at the table and took some food, having completely lost my appetite. I spooned small portions of both the salad and spaghetti and forced myself to shove some in my mouth.

After we were done eating, I silently helped my mom put everything into the dishwasher. Silence. Just silence. No one spoke. Feeling brave for a moment, I considered asking my mom for the whole story, knowing they were hiding something from me. But when I looked at the emotion in her eyes, I couldn't do it. After years of being conditioned to never question them, it was terrifying and unnatural.

Finally, I went up to my room and texted Luke. *My parents know.*

A few minutes later, I received a text back.

Luke: Should I come over? I'll talk to them
Me: It's not a good time. They're not talking right now...
Luke: Are you ok? I'd like to see you. Can you come to the packhouse?
Me: It's better I don't leave right now
Luke: I'm coming over
Me: Just park down the street and I'll meet you. Don't come near the house!

I threw on a jacket and went down the stairs, spotting my mom sitting on the couch.

"Where are you going?" she asked.

"I'm just going for a walk."

"Don't leave the territory," she warned.

"I won't," I replied and slid out the front door. I made my way down to where Luke would need to turn to come onto my street. I waved as I saw his headlights. He pulled over and I jumped into the passenger side of his car.

"What's going on?" He looked at me.

"Can we just park somewhere and talk?" I asked.

"Okay, let me just drive farther down where there aren't any houses around." He put his car into drive and drove ahead until he reached a forested area and pulled over. Then he turned to look at me, taking my hand. "Jasmine, what happened?"

"My parents know."

"You told them?"

"No."

"How did they find out?"

"Because Lucy has made it completely obvious. My mom's basically president of the pack rumor mill. She got texts from all her busybody friends at work today. So, I basically got ambushed as soon as my parents got home."

"How did they take it?" He took my other hand in his so he was holding both my hands now, looking intently into my eyes.

"How do you think they took it? Not well at all."

"What did they say?"

"I don't know. It was weird. My mom told my dad she would call her brother and nephew, and my dad wouldn't let her. They started arguing about something that happened a long time ago, but when I asked what they were talking about they wouldn't tell me."

"Fuck."

"What?"

I looked over at Luke who covered his face with his hands and then removed them to look at me. "My dad mentioned something about this to me."

"What did he say?"

"Your mom's brother or nephew—is one of them the alpha of your mom's pack?"

"Yes, her nephew's currently the alpha. Her brother used to be."

"She clearly wants them to come and make sure that I honor the mate bond, Jasmine. My dad told me about this. Look, Jasmine, I'm *not* planning to *not* honor it. There's nothing to worry about. I will go to your house right now, and I will speak with your parents just like I planned to. We'll fix all this." He rubbed his thumbs against my palms, spreading a calm through my body.

"That ship has sailed," I replied bitterly. I knew I had told him to hold off on speaking with my parents, but I didn't mean for so long. Why hadn't he taken more initiative? Why did he keep promising to take responsibility and then avoiding it until it was too late?

"Jasmine, it hasn't sailed." He straightened up. "I can still speak with them. Yes, they heard through the pack gossip, but they still haven't heard from me what I intend to do. I will assure them that they have nothing to worry about."

"I don't think it's a good idea."

"Why?" I could sense his concern as he looked at me.

I looked at Luke and felt anxious at what I was about to say, knots twisting in my stomach. But I pushed through it and said, "Because I'm not sure we should do this anymore. My whole life's falling apart over this mate bond. This is not how it's supposed to be. Everyone else is happy when they meet their mate, and I've just got tons of anxiety. I don't know if it's worth fighting for anymore. Plus, you're having a baby with my best friend—my best friend whom I lost because of all of this. The whole situation's a huge mess."

He reached over and pulled me against him as much as he could with the center console in the way. "Please, Jasmine. Don't say that. It will work out."

"Maybe the best way for it to work out is for it to not work out at all."

He held me tighter and said, "Please just sleep on it. I'm not ready for us to reject each other, Jasmine." I nodded into his chest, the sparks and calm being emitted from him forcing me to forgive him. "This is really uncomfortable, by the way, maybe we should get into the back seat." He chuckled. I chuckled too, and we got out to move into the back.

"Much better." He pulled me against him. "It feels nice cuddling with you. I will definitely miss this if you choose not to be with me anymore."

It did feel nice. Being so close to him, once again, made me forget how frustrated I was with his behavior, the bond flexing its power over us. We stayed like that for a while and, the next thing I knew, I was waking from sleep.

"Did I fall asleep?" I looked up at Luke.

"Yes, you did. And you looked so cute. I didn't want to wake you." He smiled. "You were like a sweet little fox."

"Oh Goddess, I hope I didn't drool on you." I wiped my hand against my mouth.

"It's okay," he said, leaning forward to kiss me. Before I knew it, we were making out at the back of his car, parked in a forested area, like a couple of teenagers. He pulled away and said, "I'll miss this too. Kissing you is really magical." He put his mouth back on mine.

Eventually we stopped, falling back into a cuddle, and I said, "I should probably get home."

He nodded and got out of the back seat. I followed. He came around and opened the front door before I could get to it and helped me in. Then he got back into the driver seat and stopped at the end of the street. "Are you sure you don't want me to drive you all the way home?"

"No, it's better that my parents don't see your car. Things are really weird right now."

"Okay, can you at least text me when you get in, so I know you made it back safely?"

"Sure," I replied.

He then got out of the car and came around. I had already opened the door, so he just helped me down once he got there. He then pulled me in for a tight hug and kissed me. "Please think about staying with me, Jasmine. I promise I will always be good to you. I know things are complicated with Lucy now, but I know they will eventually work themselves out."

He gave me one final kiss and let me go. I began to walk away and turned around to see that he was standing there watching me go. I waved to him, and he waved back, and then I continued walking. As irresponsible and frustrating as Luke was being, he was very sweet.

Chapter 54

Blake

On Friday morning, I was alone in my office going through different financial reports that the accountant had left me to review. A knock at the door broke my concentration. When I looked up, I was surprised to see my mom in the doorway.

"Can I come in?" she asked.

"Of course." I waved her in.

She softly closed the door behind her and walked over to give me a hug and kiss me on the forehead. Then she sat down at a chair in front of my desk. "Blake, I need to speak to you about your father."

I groaned. "What about him?"

"I know your father's very difficult sometimes, but I would like for you to make an effort to work with him. He has a lot of experience with running the pack and going to war, and, quite frankly, you need his help. It's not that I don't have faith in your leadership skills. It's just that you are still new at this position, and everyone needs a mentor when they're first starting out. I couldn't have succeeded as a doctor if I didn't have more experienced doctors to help and guide me."

"My father owes me an apology," I replied, annoyed by the conversation.

My mom let out a sigh and continued, "Your father's not good at apologizing, and you know that. But that doesn't mean he's not sorry. I spoke with him, and he's going to make more of an effort to tone down his speech when he speaks to you. Unfortunately, I don't think it's something he has much control over. He's too old now for me to force him into therapy." She snickered a little.

"Why have you stayed with him all these years?" I asked, surprising myself with the question. It was not something I ever asked my mom in the past, although it was something I wondered about my whole life. While divorce with werewolves was very rare, and the mate bond couldn't be severed, it still seemed like it would have been an improvement to split up rather than continue to put up with his philandering and verbal abuse.

She let out a deep breath and sat in silence considering the question. I waited until she finally spoke. "Your father's a very complicated man. Once you're marked by your mate, you're able to feel what your mate feels when they're nearby, running alongside your own feelings, even more acutely than before marking. And your father has a lot of pain. I don't know where the pain comes from since your father isn't one to open up about his feelings. But I feel the pain, constantly, all the time, like a heart that broke and never healed, maybe several times over. He carries it around with him every day. While I don't agree with the way he directs his pain most of the time, I am able to understand it. But I also know that beyond the pain, your father feels other things too. I can feel that he has both love and pride when he looks at you. He may never say it, but it's there. I stay with him because the mate bond allows me to both understand and forgive him. But I also stay for the good parts of your father. He's not all bad. I do know that he cares very much about you and this pack, and he's afraid now, especially with the loss of his control."

I nodded and said, "I'll think about it."

She didn't get up. She stayed sitting, looking at me. Finally, she said, "Please, Blake. Can you please be the bigger person and put aside your grudges toward your father? I know he's difficult to work with and be around. If you don't do it for yourself, at least do it for me." When I didn't reply she got up, kissed me on the head, and walked out of the room.

I returned my attention to the financial reports and thought, *We all have pain. It's not an excuse.* But I also loved my mom, and she knew I'd do anything for her. I let out a deep breath, knowing I'd have to find a way to continue working with my father.

I walked to the kitchen to make myself more coffee. I stepped toward the machine to see the pot was already full.

"One step ahead of you," Connie chimed from where she was preparing food for the day. I gave her a nod and grabbed a mug. After I filled my mug, I returned to my office and sighed, forcing myself to write my dad a text message.

> **Me:** *We have a Zoom call today with Alpha Antoine and Beta Alfred at 12. I'll send you an invite.*

The call only brought more bad news. Beta Alfred had gotten word through some of his sources that an attack on our pack was likely to happen within the first two weeks of December. It quickly changed to a logistics call where we'd need to set up housing for the Lune Nordique Pack warriors in preparation. Fortunately, barracks had been built years ago for situations such as this, so I assigned the office manager the task of finding cleaners and maintenance people to prepare the building for the incoming guests. I also asked our housekeeper to prepare one of the bedrooms on the alpha floor of the packhouse for Alpha Antoine and his mate, who would be arriving in a little over a week.

As Luke and I were in discussion, my father walked in. I sat back in my chair and stared at him, wondering what he would say.

Luke, always polite, stood up and put out his hand to greet him. "Good afternoon, Alpha James."

"Luke," my dad replied as he briefly shook his hand. Then he looked at me and said, "Have you spoken with the Autumn Moon Pack yet?"

"About a month ago, I briefly mentioned the situation," I replied.

"I will speak with Alpha Marc. Their pack's one of our very closest allies, and we've always supported them over the years with their disputes. It would be bad politics to turn their back on us now. I have a good relationship with their alpha, so I will take care of it. When it comes to war, you can never have enough friends."

I nodded at him in acknowledgment. He looked at me for a moment, as if he wanted to say something else. But he clearly abandoned the idea and walked out of the room, pulling his cell phone out. Luke and I listened as his footsteps faded down the hallway.

Luke sat back in the chair he'd pulled over to my desk. I looked over at him and said, "I know you have a lot going on in your personal life right now, but we both need to have our heads in the game. Shit's getting real."

As if on cue, Luke's cell phone, which was sitting on top of my desk, lit up with a string of text messages. I looked over at his screen to see Lucy's name repeated down the screen. Luke let out a deep breath and yelled, "Fucking Artemis!" He shook his head and shoved his phone in his pocket. I raised my eyebrows at Luke in a questioning gesture. He sighed and said, "I'm fucking trying, Blake. I really fucking am!"

"What's going on with Lucy?" I asked, although I more or less had guessed at the situation, especially after my confrontation with her.

"It's a fucking disaster. Every hour she has some new pregnancy symptom that she needs to tell me about. She sends me regular updates on how big the baby is. Apparently right now it's the size of a lime. And I want to be there for her, but it's constantly, all the time, and it's clear that she's only doing this for attention. Of course, I can't say that because I'm the bad guy in this situation. I'm the asshole that knocked her up and now wants to marry her best friend. And that's a whole other debacle. Jasmine has some crazy alpha family in Alaska that will apparently be out for blood if I don't honor the mate bond. I have no idea how they feel about the whole situation with Lucy. But that's something we're going to have to deal with, no question!" He put his head down on my desk.

"Damn," I replied.

"This is where you can feel free to shower me with your words of wisdom. Because I can't figure this shit out anymore," Luke said, his voice muffled from within his arms.

Just then, my father walked back in, clearly having finished up his phone call. Luke got up and sat up straight in his chair. My dad looked between us and said, "I spoke with Alpha Marc, and he said they will honor the alliance."

I gave my father a thumbs up. He smiled and walked out again. I turned to Luke and said, "Man, you have to get yourself together. You need to tell Lucy that she can't be doing this shit. We have a war on our hands."

"Have you ever tried telling Lucy what to do before?"

I shook my head and said, "Good point. But come on, man. You need to do something about her. She can't be distracting you like this all the time. I know you always want to be the good guy, but sometimes you have to put your foot down."

He closed his eyes and nodded.

I continued, "And what about Jasmine? Is the only reason you're honoring the mate bond because of her crazy family?"

He opened his eyes and said, "It's not the only reason."

But he didn't seem confident when he said it. When I didn't say anything, he continued, "At some point you have to grow up and do your duty. You realize playtime is over."

"Is Jasmine a fucking duty to you?" I raised my voice at him.

"No!" His eyes were wide. "I mean, not completely. But there's a part that is."

I shook my head and said, "I can't have this conversation anymore, Luke. Just figure it out. And Jasmine deserves better than to be someone's fucking duty. I'm sure both she and her family would feel the same way." My blood boiled as I walked out of the office, completely frustrated with Luke and how he was behaving toward Jasmine, knowing that I would never take my mate for granted like he was—especially if my mate were Jasmine.

Chapter 55

Jasmine

On Saturday morning, I arrived at work at seven thirty, right on time for the late shift. Valerie was inside working the register when I walked in. I quickly dropped all my things in the back and came out front to help her make drinks. After the rush was over, I grabbed the spray bottle and rag to wipe down all the tables and chairs.

When I made it back behind the counter, Valerie came out. She looked me up and down and asked, "How's your leg? Are you okay?"

"It's better, good as new," I replied.

She then put both her hands on my shoulders, stared into my eyes, and said, "How are you?"

"I'm fine," I replied, confused by the question. But she didn't remove her hands.

"How are you taking the whole thing with Lucy? I know it can't be easy to know your friend's pregnant with your mate's baby."

I almost choked, feeling uncomfortable. "What have people been saying? What has Lucy been saying?"

She removed her hands from my shoulders and replied, "Well, people talk, but who cares what they say? And, Lucy, well, she obviously has her own spin on the situation that she's happy to share with anyone who will listen. But that's Lucy for you, and people know how Lucy is."

I started to feel uneasy, considering what Lucy might be telling people. Did I want to know? Before I could think about the question more, I asked, "What's Lucy saying? What's her spin?"

"It doesn't matter," Valerie replied, clearly not wanting to tell me.

"Please, Valerie, tell me. I want to know," I pleaded with her.

She looked at me and said, "It's nothing that bad. It's just nonsense that I think she tells herself to make herself feel better about the situation."

"What kind of nonsense?"

She sighed and said, "Just stuff like how Luke truly loves her and wants a family with her, and that's why the Moon Goddess blessed the two of them with a baby. So he would realize who he's really supposed to be with."

"Maybe she's right." I looked down at my feet, knowing deep within me that Lucy probably wasn't wrong.

"Why would you say that?" Valerie raised her voice. I looked up at her. "You're Luke's mate. If the Moon Goddess truly wanted Luke to be with Lucy, don't you think she would have mated him to her? Why are you doubting the bond the two of you have? He seemed very interested in you that day he came by to visit."

"I think he's interested"—I sighed—"But he doesn't love me. He's even admitted to me that he still loves Lucy several times."

"Goddess! I mean, I love Lucy. She's a bit exasperating and stubborn, but she also has a part of her that's strong and loyal when it really comes down to it. She's also beautiful. But seriously?" She shook her head.

"What, you can't believe that Luke loves Lucy?" I asked.

"It's not that I can't believe it. She has a lot of good qualities. But between you and her, I would have put a hundred bucks on you. And

I don't want to trash Lucy because, like I said, I love her too. But you're just more what I would expect a beta to want."

"Lucy's really beautiful though. You even said that half the reason we have all the customers we do is because of Lucy."

"She's beautiful, but that's not why. It's because she flirts with all of them, and they love all the attention. Either way, beauty doesn't make someone love you. And you're beautiful too. Just in a different way than Lucy."

"Not like Lucy at all. Men cross rooms for her."

She shook her head. She was about to say something when a customer walked in. I took my place at the register to take the order and Valerie walked out back. As I worked, I started to wonder if I could reject Luke. Something deep within me was struck with pain as the thought crossed my mind. It would not be easy. It was unnatural. We were mated to each other, and we would be fighting against our fate to reject each other.

I didn't personally know anyone who had rejected their mate. I'd heard about it throughout the years. People would tell stories that you had no way to know if they were true or not. I suddenly wished I knew their stories. What had gone so wrong in their mate bond that they chose to reject their mate? Did they have a story similar to mine? It gave me comfort that I wouldn't be the only one.

Valerie left at one thirty and then I was alone. I pondered my relationship with Luke until it was time to close. Any time it crossed my mind to reject him, I could feel my inner wolf howling with pain. I may as well have been considering suicide—with eternal darkness as the only result. I didn't know if I'd be able to go through with it. But either option seemed daunting.

When I locked up at four, I was shocked to see Luke waiting for me outside. "Let's go for a walk," he said, taking my hand and walking me toward the central park. Once we'd fallen into a stride, he said, "How was work?"

"It was okay," I replied. "How was your day?"

"To be honest, not great. We have an impending war on our hands, and I'm trying to fix things with both Lucy and you."

"Impending war? Does it have to do with the wolves you rescued me from?"

"Kind of. They were definitely casing our pack territory. But the war isn't because of them. The alpha of the Bois Sombre Pack wants revenge after all the males in his family were killed by our pack in the battle that happened five years ago. Plus, he hasn't given up on getting his mate back—I'm sure because being away from her has made him and his pack weak. He'd probably take another mate if possible, but since he can't until she dies, he's probably becoming desperate now. And, even if she did die, the pain from losing her would never go away. It doesn't help that he was unhinged to begin with." Luke let out a deep breath.

"Wow."

"Anyway, this is along the lines of why I wanted all of us to take some time to really consider the permanence of the situation. There's no divorce from a mate bond. Once we mark each other, that's it—we're bonded for life. I know I am only repeating everything you already know. But it's something that's weighed heavily on my mind. I don't want to make a mistake and force either you or Lucy to suffer with it for the rest of your lives."

"I get it," I replied, feeling my stomach churning and my chest tightening, a deep unease coming over me.

"I know you do, and I appreciate you being so understanding." Luke pulled me against him for a hug. "But Lucy isn't understanding at all. I'm really trying, Jasmine. I want you to know that."

"Are you though?" I asked.

He let out a deep breath and said, "I'm being pulled in so many directions between leading the pack into war, becoming a father, and trying to be a good mate. I didn't know this would all be so hard. I wasn't prepared to take on so much responsibility all at once." He slumped his shoulders and his voice was heavy with emotion. "I keep screwing everything up. Maybe if it was just one of those things I could have handled it, but everything's coming down on me at once."

He paused, shook his head, and continued, "I know it's not fair to you. But, Goddess, Jasmine, I want you to know at least that I do care. I'm not trying to hurt anyone. I wish there was a handbook or something I could read so I knew what to do. But I feel like I'm just grasping at straws, and I keep pulling the wrong one."

I reflected on what he said, and I felt some empathy for him, understanding his struggle. But did he understand mine? I wasn't sure. He let me go and took my hand again so we could walk into the park. He led me over to a bench so we could sit down, and then turned toward me, putting his hand on my leg, rubbing my knee.

We sat there, looking at each other. I wrapped my arms around myself to warm myself as the cold breeze blew. Upon seeing my reaction to the cold, Luke pulled me against him. I snuggled into his warmth and into the dulled sparks his body emitted as it touched mine through our jackets. The familiar feeling of calm and arousal came over me, and suddenly I couldn't be close enough to him. Luke rubbed his hands up and down my back and I inhaled his delicious scent. I couldn't imagine being anywhere else in the world.

After some time of just snuggling against each other, Luke spoke again. "I've thought about it, and I want to make this work, Jasmine. I'm going to speak with Lucy and ask her to give me some more space. I have no idea if she'll comply"—he chuckled—"but I'll at least try for the sake of our mate bond."

"Is that what you really want to do?" I asked, and further clarified, "If we weren't mates, would that be what you want?"

He looked into my eyes and took my hands in his. "But we are mates, Jasmine. You can't separate that from the issue now. We're supposed to be together. And, either way, you have a family that wants us to be together and has the power to ensure the bond's honored. As beta, I have a duty to the pack to avert any threats. It will be the same for you once you become a beta mate."

I realized then and there that his heart wasn't in the relationship, even with the power of the mate bond. Maybe over time he would come to love me. But wasn't that a huge risk knowing how permanent the bond was? Like he said, there was no divorce. We'd be bonded until one of us passed away, and even then, the bond would affect us, driving us possibly to insanity at the loss of our mate. After juggling all my thoughts in my mind, I finally spoke.

"There's something I didn't tell you the other night, Luke."

"What is it?" He searched my eyes.

"My family won't threaten the pack. My mom wanted to call her brother, I assume for exactly the reason you guessed at. But my dad didn't let her. He wants you to have a choice. He said he had his choice taken away, but he won't take yours away. I don't know what he was talking about. As far as I know, my parents have only ever been with each other, and they've always been happy with the mate bond since they met in college. With the way they are, I can't imagine that not being the case. But, either way, he wants you to have a choice. So, if you'd rather be with Lucy, you can be with Lucy. I want you to know that."

"But what about the temple wedding?"

I looked at him, feeling my throat tingle with the threat of tears. "If that's the only reason you want to be with me, then I don't care about the temple wedding anymore."

"Oh, Jasmine," he said, holding me tightly against him. "But what will you do if we reject each other? You won't have a mate anymore. It hurts me to think of you being mateless. You deserve to have a mate."

My eyes brimmed with tears, and I sniffled to keep them from falling. "I'm not the only one. Blake also deserves a mate, and he doesn't have one either. There are others. I'll just have to find someone the old-fashioned way, or new-fashioned way I guess." I chuckled sadly.

"Is that what this is about? Are you hoping to be with Blake?" He pulled away from me and looked at me. I could sense a pained feeling.

"No, it's not. It doesn't matter anyway. Blake's made it clear that he doesn't want a mate anymore."

"Jasmine, I'm not saying this to convince you either way, but please believe Blake when he says that to you. I've never known him to be the type to care about any of the girls he's been with. The only exception was Ria, and she was mated to him. So please don't reject me if you're hoping to be with Blake. I say this to you as a friend and someone that has come to care about you. I worry about Blake. He isn't quite a brute like his dad, but there are a lot of similarities between the two of them. I just don't know if he's capable of loving anyone anymore. Losing Ria really fucked him up."

I nodded as Luke held my gaze. After some time, I said, "Blake's irrelevant anyway. I just don't want you to be with me out of pity. And if that's the reason you're convincing me to stay with you, please stop. It makes it harder to fathom the rejection. I already feel a lot of pain when I consider it. And you fighting against it makes it harder. Just please be honest with me and tell me the truth. If you could choose between Lucy and me, who would you choose?"

He shook his head. "I feel a lot of pain when I think of rejection. It's the same for me, Jasmine. And I've enjoyed this time that I've spent with you. I think we have a lot in common and, under normal circumstances, would have been perfect mates. I've regretted my life choices every single day since your birthday. I really screwed up something that should've been perfect and easy."

"You're avoiding the question I asked."

"I know, it's because I can't answer it. I need more time to think about it."

"Don't you think that just the fact you have to think about it means something? Shouldn't you be sure about the person you will be bonded to for the rest of your life?"

"Please, Jasmine," he pleaded with me.

"Okay, take the weekend. But please let me know your answer by Monday. I don't think we should drag this out anymore if your heart's really with Lucy. As much as I am angry with her, I still care about her as a friend. Besides this, she has always been a good friend to me, and I'd rather not fight against her any longer. I don't even know if it's possible anymore, but I would like to have my friend back. And she deserves to be with the father of her baby if that's what the father wants."

Luke kissed me on the head and said, "You are too good for me, Jasmine, honest. I don't deserve you. I will tell you my answer on Monday." He gave me one last hug and walked away. I watched as he left the park and walked toward the packhouse. After he was out of my sight, I walked toward my car, a pain deep in my heart.

When I finally got behind the steering wheel, I cried. He didn't tell me his answer, but I already knew what it was. I recalled one of our earliest conversations, when he had first invited me into the packhouse and said, *"I just want you to understand why this is so hard for me. I can't help but wonder if I break up with Lucy for us to be together if it will be enough. Will I be able to just walk away completely and never look back? You deserve someone who's able to give you all of them. I'm just afraid that my feelings for Lucy will always hold me back from being able to do that."* I knew that I needed to gather enough strength to properly reject him on Monday.

Chapter 56

Jasmine

On Sunday morning, I awoke to my phone vibrating next to me. I rolled over to find that Lucy's mother was texting me. I quickly unlocked my phone to see the text messages.

> *Ivy*: Good morning Jasmine
> *Ivy*: I hope you are well. We miss seeing you. Haydon and I do not have any hard feelings toward you and we both hope that you and Lucy will one day be able to be friends again.
> *Ivy*: I am messaging you as I hope you are still willing to meet my friend Katie and her son. They will be here for Thanksgiving and we made reservations at a restaurant on Wednesday for dinner. I can pick you up at 5. Lucy won't be there so no need to worry.

I stared at my phone wondering why Ivy was so adamant about me meeting her old friend and son, especially If she wasn't even bringing Lucy. I had almost forgotten that I had bumped into her in the grocery store almost a month ago. It seemed like a lifetime ago after everything that had happened since then. While I had been so curious to meet Katie previously, and learn more stories about Ivy's and my dad's high school days, it now felt like a last priority. It was especially unappealing considering I'd be forced to spend time with Lucy's family, a bitter reminder of everything that had gone wrong.

But I had previously agreed, and a part of me was still curious. I finally replied confirming I would attend and see Ivy on Wednesday at five. Then I rolled over and sighed. I'd tossed and turned all night, falling in and out of sleep, stressed from Luke's impending decision.

I got out of bed, feeling unrested. I went downstairs to the kitchen where my dad was having breakfast.

"Good morning," he said as soon as he spotted me.

"Good morning," I replied groggily. My parents had been acting weird since the other night. They had always seemed so aligned and in sync, as if they were two halves of a whole. But something about the news of Lucy's pregnancy had caused them to detach from each other.

"How are things with Luke?" my dad asked, looking at me curiously.

I went to grab for cereal and a bowl. I wondered how much I should share. I had never shared anything more than the most superficial with my parents. I wasn't sure if I was ready to open up to them now. It felt unnatural. Finally, I said, "Fine."

My dad stared at me. I was uncomfortable as I pulled milk out of the fridge and a spoon out of the drawer. When I sat down, he spoke again. "When you say 'fine,' what does that mean?"

"It means things are fine," I replied, feeling trapped by the fact that I'd now have to sit at the kitchen table with my dad while I ate. I couldn't get up and go somewhere else without it being completely awkward.

"Jasmine," he said softly. "I'm your father and I will support you no matter what happens between you and Luke. I understand both your and his predicament, more than you know. Don't worry about your mom. She will come around to whatever you decide."

I was now certain there was something that my father wasn't telling me. I began to wonder how well I knew my parents. My whole life I'd taken for granted that they were just how they were. But maybe there was a point in time when they were different. Maybe Valerie was right—there were skeletons in their closet that would ultimately fall out. Was I ready to accept this new knowledge of my parents? Knowing them only one way was comforting and safe. Similarly, I'm sure knowing me in just one way was the same for them. We spent my whole life having only a superficial relationship to avoid confronting difficult emotions within each other, pretending everything was perfect to the point where we came to believe it.

Feeling courageous, I finally decided to confront my dad. "What does that mean that you understand our predicament?" I asked.

He shook his head and said, "I was young once too, and I had to make some hard choices."

"What kind of choices?" I pressed him.

"It doesn't matter. They're all in the past now. It's nothing for you to worry about."

"But...," I started to say, wondering if it was worth continuing to press my father.

Before I could continue, he spoke again. "Just don't make your decision based on how you think your mom and I will feel about it, okay? Be with Luke because you want to, not because you feel obligated to. I am your dad, and I will be on your side no matter what happens. I've denied it for a long time, but I have to finally accept that you're an adult now, a very intelligent and capable one at that. It's time we start trusting you to make your own decisions."

Before I could respond, he turned and walked out of the kitchen. I couldn't believe the exchange we'd just had. My dad had never been so understanding before. I let out a sigh of relief, feeling like I could breathe easier now that I no longer had the weight of my parents' approval on my shoulders.

After I finished my breakfast, I put my bowl into the dishwasher. I knew I couldn't remain in my human form for the rest of the day, still feeling anxious about what Luke would decide on Monday. I knew that running outside of the territory borders was unsafe, but maybe I could run within the confines of it, not that there was much forested area to do that in. But I would have to make do.

I walked outside to find that a dusting of snow had fallen overnight, coating the ground in a thin layer of white. I stepped into the woods behind our house, my breath turning into a cloud in front of me as I walked. I quickly stripped, feeling the frozen air on my skin, my bare feet touching the frozen ground. As soon as I removed the last layer of clothing, I shifted. I ran within the forested area of our territory, skimming the border. I felt trapped, desiring to run free without confinement.

Eventually, I stopped at the lake on the outskirts of the border. I looked toward the lake which was beginning to freeze over. The ice was thin and crispy with a big hole in the center of the lake that appeared to extend to the other end, which was outside of our territory. I walked over to the lake, gently putting my paw onto the ice. And that's when I smelled the scent. It was a similar scent to the two wolves who had attacked me. It was on the ice. I put my nose closer, and it was clear that it was there. Someone must have been entering the territory through the lake, and their scent had clung to the solid ice.

I quickly mindlinked Blake, *"I can smell the stranger wolves' pack. It's on the party lake ice."*

"I'll be right there," Blake instantly replied.

I walked back toward the beach area and lay down. After some time, Blake appeared in his human form. As soon as I saw him, I got up and walked over to the lake, gesturing with my nose where to sniff. He went over and got down on his hands and knees, smelling where I had pointed.

"Holy shit," he said. "I've been having my warriors check this area every day, and yet it's Miss Alpha that discovers the scent. Clearly my team needs more training, and we need you to join us." He smiled. He got up, and I saw he was mindlinking someone, his eyes glazed over in concentration. He looked back at me. "I'm having some of the warriors on duty help me track the scent. Maybe I can get some action today." He smiled mischievously. "Nothing like a little torture on a Sunday afternoon."

"*Torture?*" I asked.

He looked like the Cheshire cat as he smiled, his eyes appearing evil. "Yes, torture. How do you think we find out what pack these motherfuckers are from? Nothing like the sweet taste of death to force a man to open his mouth."

I continued looking at him, not knowing what to say.

"You're welcome to come help us track, of course. It could be your first warrior experience. Although, probably best you don't come to the torture portion."

"*What happens during a torture?*" I asked him. I heard a noise behind me and turned to see that some warriors were approaching.

He looked at them and then turned back to me, mindlinking me, "*I get to practice my butchering skills on live mammals, with very sharp knives.*"

I shivered. I'd never seen him look so evil before, it was almost frightening. One thing was clear—Blake Wulfric was not someone you'd ever want to cross.

"*I think I'm good with the tracking,*" I mindlinked him back, the other warriors now standing next to me.

"Men?" Blake said out loud. They instantly all stripped and shifted into their wolf forms, following the border of the lake, leaving me behind.

I'd be lying if I said I didn't look as Blake stripped completely naked in front of me, not even remotely interested in the others. There was something dangerous about him, and I'd never felt so turned on. He both terrified me and wakened something deep within me simultaneously. I never thought I was the type, but I knew I'd let him do anything he wanted to me, consequences be damned.

He was the type of man you went crazy for and, next thing you knew, you found a knife in your hand, tearing through the rubber of his tires. If I didn't pull myself together, I knew I'd end up as one of his deranged exes.

Chapter 57

Jasmine

I woke to my alarm on Monday. I readied myself for the day and joined my parents downstairs to go to temple service. I felt a sickness inside me. Not only would I see Luke at the service, but today was the day he was to verbalize his decision. I knew deep within me what it would be, but it didn't make it easier to face his rejection so head on and fearlessly.

My parents were silent in the car on the way to temple. The tension was so thick you could cut a knife through it. I'd never seen my parents like this in my life. Their bond normally seemed ideal—they agreed on almost everything, their minds an extension of each other's. I had barely ever even heard the two of them bicker. It was the type of bond I wished for myself, though now that dream had departed.

We took our normal place in the pews. Not long after we arrived, I saw Blake and Luke take their seats next to Blake's parents. Blake looked over at me and gave me a quick smile. I smiled back, and he turned back to the front.

After the service, Blake, once again, found me outside of the bathroom when I exited.

"It's convenient that you always have to pee at this time, predictably." He smiled.

"You're such a stalker."

"Yesterday you were the one that called me over to you. You're sending mixed messages to your stalker. I can't help it if I think you enjoy it." He smirked.

"What happened yesterday? Did you catch the culprit?"

He shook his head. "No, this wolf can swim miles in freezing cold water. Makes it really inconvenient for tracking. We just got lucky that some of his scent attached itself to the ice. Good job, though. Let me know if you smell any other strange scents anywhere."

"Were you really going to torture him?"

"Of course. I still regret not torturing the assholes that attacked you. I would have loved to watch them squirm and cry like babies while I carved them into little pieces. After what they tried to do to you, it would have been one of my favorite tortures." His eyes looked evil again. Maybe Luke was right—Blake was fucked up.

He seemed to snap out of it and said, "So what's on the agenda today? Gym? I think we're both due for some squatting."

"Actually, I have to meet with Luke today."

"Hmm," he said, his whole demeanor changing. I was compelled to reach my hand out in a comforting gesture. Not sure why that was my reaction, but it seemed Blake may have been hurt by my response. "Well, don't let me stand in the way of your mate." He then walked away. I felt like I should go after him and say something, but I wasn't sure what, eventually deciding to leave it be.

I walked back to where everyone was to find my parents so they could take me home before heading to work. I saw them deep in conversation with some of my mom's friends and their mates. Luke stepped in front of me before I could get closer to them. He grabbed my hands, holding them between us.

"Jasmine." He looked deeply into my eyes. I saw a sadness behind his as he spoke, sensing sorrow. "I'll be in the packhouse all day. Just come by whenever you have time, and we can talk."

I nodded, then turned back to get to my parents.

They dropped me at home, and my chest ached as I watched them drive away through the front window. I paced the house, trying to calm myself down. I didn't want to delay it anymore, but I also wasn't in any rush to be handed my fate. The anxiety and aching within me were becoming unbearable. After around an hour of pacing, I finally jumped into my car and sped toward the packhouse.

I rang the doorbell and waited outside until Luke opened it. He encompassed me in a hug and then led me inside, into the living room, gesturing for me to sit on the couch.

"Would you like something to drink? It might make this easier."

I nodded, knowing I would need more courage than I naturally had.

"Any preference or drink of choice? I was planning to make some gin and tonics. I think this occasion calls for something stronger than wine."

"Gin and tonic sounds good to me," I replied. He nodded and walked away toward the kitchen. I sat down on the couch, and he returned with a spoon and two glasses filled with ice. He put them down on a couple of coasters on the coffee table, reminding me of the first time I'd met him at the packhouse, bringing back a feeling of nostalgia.

He grabbed two bottles off the bar cart and brought them over to the table. He sat down next to me, poured a mixture of gin and tonic into our glasses, and used the spoon to stir them. He placed the spoon onto an empty coaster and lifted his glass in a toasting gesture. I clinked my glass to his and we both said, "Cheers." We both downed a good amount of our drinks and placed them back onto the coasters.

I looked at him and asked, "So what did you decide?"

"Right to the point, I see," he responded, sighing. "Let's enjoy our drinks first and then we'll talk. Are you hungry? I can also bring out some snacks."

"I'm good," I replied, knowing I wouldn't be able to eat even if I were hungry.

"Let me know if you change your mind. It's not good to drink on an empty stomach."

"Mm," I replied.

"So how was your weekend?"

"It was okay. How was yours?"

"Miserable." He took another drink and refilled his cup. I did the same and he topped me off.

"What was so miserable about it?"

"Come on, Jasmine, you know this is not an easy decision for me. I've been given an ultimatum and a limited amount of time to decide on the path for the rest of my life. That's a lot of pressure. I can't see the future, so there's no way to know if I'm making the right decision."

"But you know in your heart what you really want, right?"

"Following my heart got me into this mess in the first place. I wanted to rely on my brain for once."

We sat there, sipping our drinks and looking at each other. When we emptied our glasses for the second time, Luke topped us off again. The buzz came over me, confusing my senses. Luke was not pouring light.

I felt a desire to move closer to him to calm myself. But I fought against the feeling, knowing it would make this harder. It was hard enough with his scent wafting through the air, making me feel both tender and aroused toward him.

Finally, Luke put his hand on me, and the buzz and sparks mixed, flowing through my body. I couldn't imagine ever rejecting him.

He quickly retracted his hand and said, "Damn, definitely shouldn't do that. Fuck, this is so hard." He shook his head, then looked back at me. "Jasmine, I just want you to know that you're amazing. You're smart, beautiful, kind, mature, understanding, and I am not worthy of you. If you tell me that you love me and want to be with me against all odds, I will not reject you. You're my mate, and I will spend the rest of my life honoring our bond."

I looked at him, not speaking. How predictable that he was trying to put the choice back on me. Irritating. That in itself should have made me reject him then and there.

But I no longer wanted to let him get away with his indecisiveness and dragging out anything that was difficult. He needed to finally be a man. And that's when I finally realized what I should have known all along. Luke wasn't the right person for me.

"Luke," I said, glaring at him. "Just answer the question I asked. Do you want to be with me or Lucy."

He looked down at his feet, shuffling them. After a while of silence, he finally looked up and replied, "I'm sorry, Jasmine, but I love Lucy. I can't help it." He looked back down at his lap, appearing defeated.

It was as if a knife had pierced my stomach. I clutched my chest, feeling tears fall down my cheeks. As much as I had expected it, it still shocked and wounded my whole body. Luke leaned forward and brushed the tears from my eyes.

"I'm sorry, Jasmine." I could sense his remorse.

"We should reject each other," I said, feeling an even sharper pain from my words, causing more tears to fall from my eyes more rapidly. Before I knew it, I couldn't stop them as they tumbled down my face. I could see that Luke's eyes were also red and brimming with tears. This was paining him as much as it was me.

We looked at each other, waiting for the other to proceed. After some time, Luke softly said, "If this is what you really want, you reject me, and I'll accept."

I nodded. We sat there longer, staring at each other. I tried to force the words out, but they were caught in my throat. My whole body ached, fighting me from saying them. "I can't," I choked out.

"If you don't want to, you don't have to. My word still stands. If you want to stay mates, I will honor your desire."

"No, we need to do this," I replied, feeling more confident. We sat there longer, and the words wouldn't come out no matter how hard I tried to force them out. Why was this so difficult?

Just then, the glass door that led to the back garden opened, and Blake stepped in, wearing a T-shirt, shorts, and flip-flops. He looked at me and said, "What's going on? Jasmine, are you okay?" He rushed over and then looked at Luke with anger. "What did you do?"

"It's okay," I said through my tears. "We're just trying to reject each other."

He looked between the two of us. "Oh, shit. Sorry, I'll be in the office."

Before he walked away, I exclaimed, "I can't do it!" He turned back toward me and squatted down in front of me, taking my hands. I continued, "It hurts too much."

"Yes, you can, Jasmine. If you don't want to be with him, you can do it. Just say the words." We both looked at Luke, who was clutching his chest, not faring much better.

"You can do it, Jasmine," Luke chimed in. Then he said more softly, "If that's what you really want."

"Just shut up, Luke!" Blake snapped at his friend, then turned back to me, letting go of my hands, continuing to kneel in front of me. "Just say the words, Jasmine."

I shook my head, tears drenching my face and neck.

"I know you can do it, Jasmine. You're a strong woman."

"I can't!" I choked out in desperation.

"If you need me to, I will use my alpha aura and help you." He stared into my eyes. "Nod your head if that's what you want." Knowing I didn't have it in me, I nodded my head.

Blake stood up and roared, "Reject each other!"

His aura came over me, paining me as my neck bowed to him and then turned to Luke saying, "I, Jasmine Dale, reject you, Lucas Hemming, as my mate." It felt like a sword had sliced right through my chest, shredding my heart and lungs, the pain practically unbearable.

Luke weakly replied, "I, Lucas Hemming, accept your rejection, Jasmine Dale." As soon as he ended his sentence, the pain became overwhelming, and I fell off the couch screaming.

Blake

I watched in horror as Jasmine doubled over and fell off the couch, just narrowly missing the coffee table. I shuddered as she screamed in agony at the rejection. Before I could think about what I was doing, I picked her up by her waist, her whole body convulsing. I quickly glanced back at Luke who was also doubled over on the couch, clearly also in pain, hesitating and wondering if I should try to help him too.

His eyes locked with mine, red and brimming with tears. "It's okay, Blake. Help Jasmine. I'll be okay," he wheezed out, grasping at his chest. I'd come back for him later and make sure he really was okay. At that moment, all I could think about was taking care of Jasmine.

I swiftly grabbed my car keys from the entryway table and ran to my car, carrying Jasmine over my shoulder. I threw her into the passenger seat, sprinted to the driver's seat, and was soon speeding toward the clinic. It was a quick drive. I parked haphazardly, pulled Jasmine out of the car, and ran in, past the front desk and into the back, practically crashing into my mom.

"Blake? What's going on?" She looked shocked.

"Please, Mom, help Jasmine. Please help her."

She led me into a room with a bed and I gently placed her on it. She had stopped screaming, but we could both see that she was still in agony. "What happened to her?" my mom asked.

"She rejected Luke," I replied.

"Oh my Goddess." She looked at me. "I hope this wasn't your doing, Blake!"

"It wasn't, I swear. It was her choice."

She shook her head and said, "Just go wait out in the waiting room and I'll get you when she has calmed down." I walked out to the front and took a seat, grabbing for a magazine. I wasn't even able to comprehend the words as I read them and eventually gave up. The room was empty, so I began pacing, the woman at the front desk looking up at me occasionally.

After what seemed like forever, my mom finally came out and brought me back into her office. She gestured for me to sit down and then she did the same. "I gave her a sedative. She seems to have calmed down."

"When will she be better?" I asked my mom.

She shook her head and said, "She'll eventually feel better than she does now, but all of the pain won't go away until she finds someone else to mark her. The Moon Goddess does not take well to being insulted. Jasmine has rejected her gift and now she will have to suffer for it."

"Fuck," I replied.

"Why did she reject Luke?" My mom narrowed her eyes at me.

"I don't know. I can speculate, but only she or Luke can answer that. I just happened to walk in while they were trying to reject each other. When Jasmine couldn't do it, I offered to help with my aura, and she accepted. That's all, Mom. I didn't tell either of them to reject the other before that moment."

"You're one hundred percent sure you didn't meddle at all?"

I looked down at my feet and replied, "They both confided in me, and I only gave them each individual advice as a friend. But the decision to reject each other was theirs alone." I looked back up at my mom.

She shook her head. "I really hope you're being honest, Blake. Rejecting your mate is no joke. It's very painful and should only be reserved for the most extreme cases. If you convinced Jasmine to reject Luke for selfish reasons, I will be very disappointed in you."

"Can I see her?" I asked, desperate to make sure she was okay.

"You know where she is," my mom replied, sighing.

I got up and walked quickly to the room where Jasmine was. She was lying on her back, her eyes staring at the ceiling. I pulled a chair next to her bed and sat down next to her. I brushed her hair back and looked at her. "Jasmine, how are you feeling?"

She turned to look at me and said, "I'd rather be dead than feel this anymore. Is this what it feels like to beg for death when you're being tortured?"

I got off the chair and lay down on the bed next to her. "No, Jasmine. You don't want to die. I won't let you die. It hurts now but it will get better."

"Please just kill me. I think whatever you do when you torture people would be better than what I feel right now. Maybe you can use me for butcher practice."

"No, Jasmine."

"It's so painful," she cried. I wrapped my arms around her, holding her close to me, wishing I could take the pain away.

"I know. I don't know exactly how you feel, but I can imagine. I've felt it before too, possibly worse, not that it's a competition."

She looked at me, her face blotchy, her cheeks wet.

I continued. "It does eventually get easier. You still feel it, but you're able to live in spite of it. And you have hope. One day you'll be marked by someone else, and it will all go away. You just have to tough it out for a bit until then."

"Is this how you felt when Ria died?"

A sharp pain stung me as she said her name. I flinched, but instantly softened looking at Jasmine. I pulled her closer to me and said, "Yes, but I didn't only lose Ria."

"What do you mean?" She looked at me, her amber eyes searching mine, the whites now red. "Who else did you lose?"

I almost abandoned what I was going to tell her, but I decided to push through it and replied, "I never told this to anyone, but Ria was pregnant." Jasmine's eyes widened at the revelation, and I continued, "We'd only found out the night before. The only person who knows is my mom. Losing Ria, just her, was the worst pain I'd ever felt. But to know that she was carrying my unborn pup was even worse. I'm not telling you this to say that my pain was worse than yours, so I hope you don't take it that way. I just want you to know that I understand how you feel and it will eventually get better, especially for you. You have a way out one day when you meet the right person. So please don't think about death. If I can live through this pain, so can you."

She cuddled into me and sobbed. After some time, she said, "I'm sorry, Blake. That's horrible."

"I never told anyone before now. I couldn't even talk or think about it. But being around you is comfortable and makes it easier to open up. You're a good person, Jasmine, and Luke's a fucking idiot."

Chapter 58

Jasmine

My parents brought me home on Monday night, picking me up on their way home from work. Dr. Luna told them what happened, so I didn't have to. My mom didn't say anything. She just sat in the front seat of the car as my dad walked me to the back seat. He then helped me up to my bedroom and into my bed. He looked at me, not speaking. I turned away from him, feeling shame at how pathetic I was being. I'd always read books and seen TV shows with female characters who withered away from heartbreak, and I hated that I was doing the same thing. But I couldn't help it. The pain was debilitating. Not that I had personal experience with it, but I imagined it was similar to a bullet being shot through my chest.

   I stayed in bed for the remainder of the night, only rising to use the bathroom. It was the same all day Tuesday. My parents kept bringing me food that I ignored, not able to stomach it. On Wednesday morning, I received a text from Ivy reminding me of the dinner. I decided to ignore it. I couldn't fathom the idea of being in a social situation. I heard my doorbell ring that afternoon. I ignored it. I looked at my phone to see it was four. When I didn't answer, the bell rang again.

Then I heard banging on the front door and a muffled shouting. It was Ivy's voice. "Open up, Jasmine! I know you're in there and you're not getting out of this!"

My phone vibrated and I looked at it. It was a text from Ivy.

Ivy: *If you don't come down, I will have Jack get Blake so he can use his alpha aura on you and force you down.*

I wondered if she'd actually involve our alpha in this. Knowing that Lucy got her persistent nature from somewhere, I decided it was probably not a bluff. I forced myself out of bed and walked down the stairs. I realized the pain was less debilitating now, and I was able to walk. I opened the door and Ivy walked in, followed by Jack.

She took one look at me and said, "You look and smell terrible. I knew we had to come early. Come on, let's get you into the shower." She pulled me by the arm and had me follow her upstairs where she pushed me into my bathroom. After she closed the door, she said, "Now get ready. Jack and I will be waiting downstairs."

The water on my body felt good, therapeutic. I then snuck into my room to throw my clothes on. I couldn't be bothered to do my hair or makeup, and so I went downstairs wearing a sweater and jeans with my hair wet. Ivy and Jack got up from the entryway bench and Ivy said, "Good, much more presentable. Grab your jacket and let's go."

Once we were all in Jack's car, I asked, "Why did you only bring Jack?"

She looked back at me from where she was sitting in the passenger seat. "I didn't only bring Jack. I'm bringing you too. But the reason Jack's here is that he used to play with Katie's son, Tyler. They were only six months apart and used to be the best of friends. I wanted the two of them to reunite now."

"Why are you bringing me?"

"Because Katie has some things to tell you. It's about time you finally hear them from her. But I don't want to give anything away myself."

I stared ahead at Ivy's seat, wondering what was going on. Clearly there was some big secret I wasn't privy to. Even with how much pain I was feeling within me, I found myself becoming curious again, anxious to know what it was.

After driving for some time, Jack asked, "How are you feeling, Jasmine? We heard what happened."

"I'm okay," I replied.

"If it helps, Luke's not doing any better. I'd heard it was painful, but I didn't realize how bad," Jack responded.

"Katie was also rejected," Ivy said. "It took her a long time to recover. I'm sure she can tell you more about it today, so you know you're not alone."

When we arrived at the casino, Ivy led the way to the Italian restaurant where Luke and I had gone on our first date. My chest ached, recalling the date. At the time, it was the best night of my life. Now it just brought back painful memories.

The host brought us over to our table where a middle-aged blonde woman was sitting with a young, sinewy man with brown hair, whom I noted was quite handsome and was familiar somehow, like I'd seen him before. The woman got up and ran to Ivy, engulfing her in a hug. "Oh my goodness, Ivy, you haven't aged a day!"

"You either, Katie. You look just as gorgeous as ever," she replied. Ivy separated from the hug, pulling me over. "This is Drew's daughter, Jasmine. Isn't she so big now?"

Katie studied me. "She looks so much like him. But her eyes are definitely her mother's."

Ivy then went to grab for her son but stopped. Jack and Tyler were both standing, eyes locked on each other. The three of us looked between them.

Finally, Jack said, "Mate."

Tyler spoke next and said the same thing.

It was silent as we all stared and then Ivy burst into tears. "My son found his mate!" she shouted. She brought Jack in for a hug and moved to Tyler, pulling him in too. "Welcome to the family, Tyler."

"I can't believe this." Katie's eyes welled up as she put her hands to her mouth. "Tyler, reunited with two long-lost connections today."

"Come on, let's sit, everyone!" Ivy corralled everyone and got us into our seats. "This calls for a bottle of champagne." But then she looked between the two of them for a moment and frowned, wrinkling her brows.

"Don't worry, Jack. Our pack's very open-minded, and you'll be welcome." Katie smiled at him.

Ivy suddenly looked stricken. "No, Katie! Jack can stay at our pack. He's good friends with our alpha and he won't banish him."

"Yes, but mindsets take longer to change than laws. You should know that!" Katie argued back. "Jack will feel right at home in our pack."

"Stop! Mom, we just found each other! We can decide where we'll live later," Tyler said, ending the argument.

"Yes, yes, let's have a nice meal," Katie agreed.

A waiter came over to take our drink orders. Ivy ordered champagne for the table. The waiter carded everyone, so I didn't get a glass. He brought me apple juice in a champagne flute instead.

It's too bad Luke isn't here, I thought to myself. *I could use the alcohol.* A sharp pain pierced through me. I did my best not to wince.

After all our orders were taken, Ivy spoke. "I'm very excited to be reunited with my good friend Katie today." She smiled at Katie and clinked her glass against hers, then continued, "We were best friends when we were in high school, much like Jasmine and my daughter Lucy, who is not here today. Katie and Tyler, you'll meet her tomorrow at Thanksgiving dinner."

"Great, I'm looking forward to meeting all your children tomorrow." Katie smiled.

"There's quite a lot of them." Ivy chuckled. "Anyway, when we were in high school, my good friend Katie here had a boyfriend, much like my Lucy. And Tyler here resulted from that relationship. So, something good came out of it. But I'd like you, Katie, to tell Jasmine more about your former high school boyfriend."

Katie cleared her throat and said, "Well, Jasmine, this may be a bit of a shock, but Tyler's actually your half brother."

I practically choked on my apple juice. Both Jack and I stared at Katie.

"What!" Jack exclaimed. "Jasmine's uptight father knocked someone up in high school?"

Katie laughed. "Drew, uptight? I mean, his parents, yes."

Ivy joined in laughter. "He's changed quite a lot since you knew him. I think it's his mate."

"To be honest, he had already changed significantly before I left. I shouldn't be too surprised."

I felt a pain in my chest, and my lungs contracting, not able to speak. Suddenly everyone was looking at me.

"Are you okay, Jasmine?" Ivy and Jack spoke at the same time.

"Sorry, this is quite a lot, isn't it?" Katie asked.

"Will you be okay, Jasmine? Do you need to get some fresh air?" Ivy looked at me, concern on her face.

"Here, I'll take her outside." Tyler got up, putting his arm out to me. "I'm sure it's a lot to learn you have a secret half brother and you probably have a lot of questions."

Jack helped Tyler pull me up, and Tyler walked me to a door that led outside where a bunch of smokers were stationed. We walked away from them and found a brick wall to sit down on. Tyler looked at me and asked, "Are you okay? Do you have any questions for me?"

The fresh air helped, and I finally found myself able to speak. "Why didn't I know you existed until today?"

He let out a deep breath. "Well, I don't know the whole story, but I know some. I know that after my mom got pregnant, Drew—er—our father went off to college with the promise he'd always support her. They even considered becoming chosen mates but decided to wait until they met their true mates to decide."

"But how could my dad just deny your existence?" I asked, shocked.

"Sadly, I don't think it's rare with werewolves, especially with alpha families. You hear stories all the time about mistresses of alphas being banished from their packs after they become pregnant, especially in religious packs that forbid birth control and abortions. I think that was probably the expectation with your mom's family."

"It's not right though. And I can't believe he just hid you from me all these years. I had a brother all this time and I didn't even know." I put my head in my hands, feeling overwhelmed by all the information I was being given to process. I couldn't help but feel anger at my parents for hiding this from me all these years.

"No, it's not, but, on the bright side, Drew did keep his word. He's sent regular payments to my mom all these years to help support me and helped pay for me to go to college. He also sent me birthday cards every year. So, he's not completely heartless."

I shook my head, mystified, thinking how surreal this situation was. All this time I had wished for an older sibling, I had one all along. I finally asked, "How long have you know about me?"

"I've always known about you. I just didn't know how you looked. I tried searching for you on Facebook a few times, but I could never find you."

"I use a fake last name on Facebook." I chuckled. "I didn't know I'd have long-lost brothers searching for me."

He laughed and got up, putting his arm out for me. "You seem like you're doing better. Ready to rejoin the group?"

I took his arm and he led me back inside to the restaurant. We sat back down at our seats to see that the food had arrived.

"Are you okay, Jasmine?" Ivy asked as soon as I sat down. I nodded in response, still feeling overwhelmed by the surprise that had been thrust upon me.

"Jasmine, I know it's a lot, and this information probably should have come from your father," Katie started, "but you're an adult now and I thought it was time you should learn the truth."

"But why was this kept from me all these years?" I asked. "Why did my dad think it was okay to just never tell me I had a brother?"

Katie cleared her throat and replied, "It was a bad situation all around. Your mom comes from a very conservative alpha family, and when she found out that your dad already had a pup, she was furious. She got her family involved. Her older brother came with their father and threatened your pack, saying that they would declare war if your father didn't honor the mate bond with your mother. They demanded that no one in the pack speak of the relation between Tyler and any of your mother's future children. Which was a bit of an odd request considering, originally, we were all going to live in the same pack as you. But, after your mom had you, I realized it was not a sustainable arrangement and left with Tyler and my parents for another pack, leaving my old life behind."

I stared at her, trying to digest everything. Just then, the manager of the restaurant came by to greet our table. He looked over at me and said, "Ah! Beta Luke's mate! It's so nice to see you again! Is this your family here?"

I winced at the sharp pain in my stomach and hunched over. Ivy rubbed my back and said to the manager, "You've got the wrong person."

"My apologies. She looks and smells just like her." He blinked at me.

"Well, maybe you should get your memory checked," Ivy shot back. He looked at her in confusion and walked away from our table. Ivy turned to me and said, "Sorry about that, Jasmine. I didn't realize the manager here knew you. Are you okay?"

I nodded, not able to speak, the pain still like an open wound.

She gave me a hug and said, "It'll get better."

After we began eating, Ivy spoke again. "Jasmine, I told Katie about your mate situation while you were outside. I hope you don't mind. I wanted her to tell you about hers. I thought it might help."

I nodded and Katie spoke. "After things didn't work out with your father, I met my mate, Carl Miller. He was very strange, but I couldn't deny the mate bond. At first, it seemed we got along quite well. But after he found out I already had a pup, he became disgusted. I don't even know how it was possible with how strong the mate bond was. But he eventually rejected me. There was nothing I could do but to accept the rejection. And just like you feel right now, I was in agony for months. I did everything I could to continue with my life, raising my pup and going to work. Eventually the pain went down, little by little, until it was manageable. Although it was always there, it became easier to do the things I needed to do and appear normal to the outside world. Eventually, I met my current, chosen mate, and the pain started to disappear even more, day by day. After we marked each other, I felt like a new person. It had completely vanished. So don't worry, Jasmine. It hurts now, but it's not forever. You will climb out of it one day."

I nodded. I wondered how long it would take to meet a chosen mate, and if I ever would. If I didn't, I would just need to find a way to live with it like Katie did and Blake does. I forced myself to eat some of the food. As soon as I swallowed a bite, I realized how hungry I was. I hadn't eaten since breakfast on Monday, except for a few bites of toast here or there. I heartily ate my food.

After I finished my plate, curiosity getting the best of me, I asked, "What was my dad like in high school?"

Katie looked at me and replied, "He was intelligent—one of those guys that liked to talk about philosophy and history, play guitar, and smoke pot." She laughed and continued, "He was also really outdoorsy. We used to go hiking all the time, get high, and just talk about everything. He was really easy to talk to and a great listener."

Ivy chimed in, "He's changed a lot, Jasmine. He grew up and matured. He had to take on a lot of responsibility at a young age—Katie got pregnant our senior year of high school. I know he also loves your mom and wants to do right by her. She was raised by an alpha family, so I'm sure she had to shoulder a lot of expectations growing up. And your grandparents were always very religious and strict, so my guess is he wanted to prove to them he was a good man and make them proud. I'm only speculating, of course, but it's just things I've observed over the years."

"I also wouldn't be surprised if he was trying to prevent the same things from happening to you that happened to me," Katie added.

I nodded at both of them, surprised at the revelation. I couldn't imagine my dad to be the type to smoke pot. It was as if I was learning about a complete stranger. We stayed for several hours, chatting. Ivy ordered another bottle of champagne and we all ordered dessert. After dinner was over, Jack stayed behind to get to know Tyler more, now that they knew they were mates. Ivy drove us home in Jack's car.

"Thank you for coming tonight, Jasmine." Ivy glanced at me.

"Thanks for inviting me," I replied.

"I also want to say, I'm very sorry about what happened with you, Luke, and Lucy. I never thought that Lucy's high school boyfriend would have turned into her chosen mate. I feel terrible about it. You've always been a good friend to Lucy, and it makes me sad that all of this has torn the two of you apart. I just hope one day the two of you will be able to move past this, but I also understand if you can't."

I nodded and said, "Mm," noncommittally.

"Also, please know that I still love you like a second daughter, even if you and Lucy are no longer going to be friends. Please feel free to come to me if you ever need anything. Don't be a stranger, Jasmine."

Ivy dropped me at home, and I thanked her again. I went into the house to find my parents sitting on the couch.

"Where have you been?" my mom questioned. "You left your cell phone at home. We tried mindlinking you and couldn't get through. I hope you weren't going outside the territory alone."

"I know about Katie and Tyler," I replied, narrowing my eyes at both of them. My mom gasped and I turned to the stairs, walking up to my room where I was looking forward to changing back into comfortable clothes and curling up in bed. Before I could grab for my sweats, I heard a knock on my door. I turned around to my dad entering.

"Can I please sit down?" he asked.

"Go ahead."

He pulled out my desk chair and took a seat on it. "Please take a seat as well." He gestured at my bed. I did as he asked, crossing my arms and sitting down. He waited until I was seated and asked, "How did you find out about Katie and Tyler?"

"I met them today."

"I see," he replied. "I didn't know they were in town."

"Ivy invited them here."

"I suppose it was only a matter of time before Katie returned to visit her old pack." He sighed.

"Why did you hide them from me? I had a half brother all this time, and I had no idea."

"This goes back over two decades, Jasmine. All I can say is I'm sorry. At the time, I was doing what I thought was the right thing. Looking back now, I probably would have done things differently. While I'm glad I ended up with my true mate and we have you, I probably should have fought more to keep Katie and Tyler in your life. But, at the time, it seemed impossible to make it work. Since your mom's father was the alpha of her pack growing up, that came with a lot of expectations and responsibility. Her father and brother came here and made a lot of demands that I was too young and dumb to fight at the time. Additionally, Alpha James and Beta Alfred encouraged me to go along with the demands so that your mother's pack wouldn't be a threat to us, and I wasn't going to fight our alpha and beta."

I nodded.

My father continued and chuckled. "It's a bit ironic, isn't it? It's like history repeats itself. With Luke, I mean."

A pain pulsed through me at the mention of his name and I lay down in my bed.

My dad looked at me with concern and said, "I'm sorry, honey. It's really not funny. I know that your mom and I were really tough on you growing up, and it was mostly because we didn't want the same thing to happen to you that happened to me. But I guess you can't escape your destiny. If you'd like to tell me more about why you and Luke decided to reject each other, I'd love to listen."

"It's too hard, Dad," I replied.

"I understand, honey. I want you to know that I love you and am not angry about what happened. I'm concerned, but I know that you will find someone else. You were always too good for Luke. I don't care if he's beta of the pack. You deserve someone that's crazy about you. When he came over that day and spoke with me, I could tell that he wasn't right for you. I didn't want to say anything since you were mates, and I assumed the mate bond would take care of everything. But I guess it's just not enough sometimes. But don't worry, Jasmine. There's someone else out there for you." He bent over to kiss me on my head. "Have a good night, honey. I'll be downstairs if you need anything." He exited my bedroom, softly closing the door behind him.

I forced myself to get up so I could change into more comfortable clothes. After I was in my sweats, I unlocked my phone to look through the text messages that had come in while I was away. There were some from my parents and one from Blake.

Blake Sexy AF: *How are you feeling?*

I looked at it and found I didn't have the energy to reply. I put my phone back onto my bedside table and turned off my bedroom light.

Chapter 59

Jasmine

Thanksgiving was at my grandparents' house. I skipped out and stayed in bed, knowing I couldn't possibly handle another social situation. My dad brought leftovers into my room. I picked at them, barely touching them. I called in sick for both my shifts that week, skipping out on work Saturday. After being the type of person who never called out, I realized I was becoming one flaky employee now. I could add that to my list of things I went from perfect at to bad at. I couldn't even be bothered to do any schoolwork. I realized I didn't even care what grades I got anymore.

I was completely pathetic. I had no more motivation for anything in life. Maybe I could just decay in my bed slowly over several months until I was dead and didn't have to suffer anymore.

Early in the morning, on Sunday, when it was still dark outside, my dad came into my room and sat down on my bed. He put his hand on my back, gently shaking me awake, and said, "There's someone here to see you. But I think you should shower first before I let them up."

I groaned.

When I didn't move, he said, "I'll let them up anyway, but I'm pretty sure you'd rather be showered when I do. You're not smelling so great these days." He helped me out of bed. I grudgingly walked over to the bathroom and took a shower. Once again, I realized it felt really nice, and I wondered why I didn't do it more often.

I returned to my room, throwing on leggings and a sweatshirt. After some time, my dad knocked on the door. "Are you decent? Can I let your guest in?"

"Yes," I replied, sitting on my bed

He opened the door and Blake walked in. My heart nearly leaped out of my chest at the sight of him. I did a double take, not believing that not only was he in my house while my parents were home, but my father had also willingly brought him to my room.

He looked at me and said, "Glad to see you're still alive." I smiled. He came over and pulled me up. "Come on, I'm taking you on a trip."

"What are you talking about?" I asked.

"It's my birthday, so you have to do whatever I want." He smirked. "Well, okay, I won't make you do what I really want, as tempting as it is. I'll give you some time to heal before I really start pushing that agenda again. But, anyway, pack your bags. We're going skiing."

"It's your birthday?" I frowned. "Now I feel bad, I didn't get you a gift after you gave me such a thoughtful one on mine."

"You have until midnight to get me a gift, so you still have time. For the record, I prefer the kind where you're naked and on your knees." He winked at me. "Now, come on, time is of the essence. Pack whatever you need for two days of skiing. And a bathing suit."

"My parents are okay with me going on an overnight trip with you?" I asked. "How did you get them to approve of that?"

"Your father and I had a nice chat, and I let him know it will be a whole group of us. I do have other friends as well, in case you didn't know. Also, I promised him you'd have your own bedroom."

I was still shocked. It wasn't like my parents to agree to something like this. I pulled a duffel bag out of my closet and began throwing different clothing into it while Blake sat on my bed, looking at his phone. When I was done, Blake took my bag and we went downstairs where my dad had already pulled out my skis and ski boots. Blake took the ski boots and my dad took the skis and ski poles, and they loaded everything into the trunk of Blake's SUV. I threw on a winter coat and some snow boots and went outside where Blake had already opened the passenger door for me.

We drove about an hour to get to a house he had rented in Stowe, a ski resort town in Vermont. Blake grabbed both of our bags from the trunk and brought them inside. He took me up to a bedroom and dropped my bag inside it.

"Now get dressed to go skiing and I'll introduce you to everyone that's here." He closed the door behind me, and I heard his steps disappear down the hall.

I quickly threw on some snow pants over my leggings and changed my sweatshirt for something lighter. I exited the bedroom looking around. It was a very cozy house, decorated in a wood and nature theme, with several bedrooms. I walked down the stairs where I found a bunch of people congregated.

Blake walked down right behind me and took my hand to bring me over to everyone. "You know Jack, and apparently you have a brother named Tyler?" He raised his eyebrow at me. "Every time I turn around, I learn something new about you."

"To be fair, I didn't know I had a brother either until a few days ago," I replied.

He brought me over to a couple that I had seen around the pack before, but I didn't know their names. "This is my friend Zach from school and his mate Kim." They both waved at me. Zach was tall with curly brown hair and Kim was petite with dirty blonde hair. He then turned me to another couple that also looked familiar. "This is my friend Brooke from school, and her mate, Tim."

I noted that Brooke was very beautiful, with olive skin, dark hair that fell over her back in ringlets, and green eyes. I suddenly wondered how close of friends they'd been. Her mate Tim was also very handsome, but not quite in the same league as Blake. They both put their hands out to shake mine. He then led me over to two other guys. "This is Charlie, and this is Pat." He pointed them each out. "Both unmated."

"Pleasure to meet you, Jasmine." Charlie smiled at me, shaking my hand. He was a tall redhead. "Blake does it again. When's he finally going to share his tempting conquests with us?"

"Pleasure, Jasmine," Pat took my hand next. He was average height with sandy blond hair. "Don't mind Charlie. He's just jealous. He doesn't have Blake's game." He laughed.

I looked between the two of them, feeling nervous.

"Be nice." Blake looked at them and then pulled me away. We all piled into our cars to drive over to the mountain. Once we arrived, we put on our ski boots, bought tickets, and took a gondola to get over to the base of the mountain.

I spent the morning skiing with Blake and his friends. Blake stayed with me the whole time, staying close by me as we went down the mountain and sharing the chairlift with me. As we were sitting together, being lifted up one of the mountains, Blake leaned over and asked, "How are you feeling, Jasmine? I've been worried. You never responded to any of my texts."

I looked down. "Sorry, I just didn't have the energy to reply."

"Well, you're doing great skiing today." He smiled. "Although not a big fan of those snow pants. The leggings were much better, definitely."

We broke for lunch. Blake deposited me at a table with the other girls while he and the guys went up to buy lunch. Brooke moved closer to me and said, "You're definitely quieter than the others."

"The others?" I asked.

"You know, the other girls he dated in the past. They're usually much more obnoxious. You seem much nicer. Nice change of pace."

"Have you known Blake long?" I asked.

"I've known him since kindergarten. He's a good guy. Just be careful."

"I've heard he's not really the faithful type," Kim chimed in. "Although, I don't know him that well. Zach and I became mates while he was away at school so I only recently really met him, but I've heard stories from the other guys."

The guys all came back with trays of food. Blake slid in next to me, putting his tray between us. "Take anything you want." He smiled at me. "I got plenty of food for both of us." I grabbed a container of chili and a spoon.

After lunch, we all went back onto the slopes. At one point, while Blake was laughing with his other friends, Jack pulled me aside and said, "Hey, Jasmine. It looks like you and Blake have gotten really close." I nodded, not sure how I should respond. He continued, "I say this as someone that's practically a brother. Just be careful with him, okay? He's a good guy, but he's not someone that normally takes relationships seriously. I just don't want you to get hurt, especially after everything that happened."

I nodded and asked, "How's Tyler?"

He smiled widely and said, "Tyler's great. You should get to know him. I think I've almost convinced him to join our pack. He's mostly interested because, I think, he wants a relationship with you now that he was finally able to meet you."

"Tell him sorry for not responding to any of his texts, please. I just haven't had the energy."

"Don't worry, he understands. When you're feeling up to it, maybe we can all hang out." I nodded. Blake came over and took my hand to take me over to the next chairlift.

After we were done skiing for the day, we all returned to the house and made a large order for pizza delivery. While we waited, Zach and Pat poured drinks for everyone. I took a vodka cranberry and Blake grabbed a beer. Brooke and Kim pulled me over to them while Blake went to go hang out with his friends.

"So, Jasmine, tell us more about you." Brooke smiled at me.

"What do you want to know?" I asked.

"You can start with what do you do for work?"

"I'm a college student but I also work part time at the café in town."

"Ah! That's right! I thought you looked familiar. That's where I've seen you before. Jack's sister, Beta Luke's girlfriend, works there too, right?"

"Right," I replied, not liking where this conversation was going. Steering the conversation away from the topic, I asked, "What do you two do?"

"I teach first grade at the pack school," Brooke replied.

"I'm not currently working. Zach and I are hoping to start a family soon, after we get married in the spring," Kim responded. I noted that Kim was already marked.

"Are you married?" I looked at Brooke.

She nodded. "Yes, we got married not long after we realized we were mates."

"So how did you meet Blake?" Kim asked.

"Through friends," I replied, deciding it was best to keep it simple.

"So, what do you think of him?" Brooke asked.

"He's nice," I replied.

"Hmm. Most people don't normally describe him as nice." Brooke looked at me as if she was trying to figure me out.

There was an awkward pause and Kim asked, "Have either of you watched any good shows recently? Zach and I are looking for a new one to start."

I was thankful for the change of subject. As the three of us sat talking with each other, Charlie kept coming over to hand me a new drink. I subconsciously kept accepting them, not keeping track of how much

I was drinking. Before long, I was starting to feel buzzed and realized I really had to pee. I excused myself and walked to the bathroom.

On my way back, Charlie cornered me in the hall, away from the group. "You're really cute, Jasmine. Very shy and quiet though. Not normally Blake's type."

I could smell that he had also been drinking heavily, likely more than me. I was really nervous as he stared into me. I tried to walk away and he put his arm on the wall, stopping me from leaving.

"It's always the quiet ones. I bet you're crazy in bed—that's why Blake keeps you around, right?"

"Please let me go," I said, trying to walk the other way, but he put his other arm against the wall, caging me in. His breath smelled terrible, and I thought I was going to gag.

"Blake's only playing with you though. Why not play with me too?" He grabbed my ass with one of his hands, pulling me close to him. I tried to push him away as I felt a panic attack come on. I started to feel dizzy, the whole world swirling around me. I was losing the strength to push him off me as he grabbed me with his other hand. I started taking deep breaths, trying to gain control of the situation, when he was pulled off me. I looked up to see Jack had thrown him to the ground in the room where everyone was. They all looked up to see what was happening.

"What the fuck are you doing?" Jack growled at him.

Charlie got up and pushed Jack. "I always knew you were a fucking faggot." He then spit in his face.

Jack was about to punch Charlie when Blake yelled, "Stop!" Everyone looked at him and he said, "He's mine." He walked over and grabbed Charlie by the shirt, pulling him up toward him. "If you ever use that word again, I will fucking banish you from this pack." He looked around at everyone and yelled, "If anyone has a problem with either Jack or Tyler, you fucking come to me. I am the alpha now, and I decide who stays and who goes from this pack."

He looked back at Charlie and continued, "And if you ever, ever even fucking look at Jasmine the wrong way again, I will end you. And I can promise you it will not be quick and painless. Now I suggest you get the fuck out of here." After he put Charlie down, he fled. Blake looked back at the group, smiled, and said, "Isn't there supposed to be some birthday cake?"

"Coming right up!" Brooke stood up from where she was sitting and walked toward the kitchen.

Blake came over to me and put his arm around me. "Are you okay?"

"Yeah," I replied.

"Good. He's gone now. Let's go have some cake." He led me over to the kitchen table where Brooke was lighting candles. After they were all lit, everyone started singing "Happy Birthday." When the song ended, Blake blew them all out in one huff, then he winked at me and said, "I hope my wish comes true."

After we ate cake, everyone changed into their bathing suits and we made our way outside to the hot tub. Blake pulled me close to him and whispered, "I wish we were alone in here."

Zach and Pat brought out tequila shots for everyone. We all took one and then they brought out more drinks. I was fully drunk by the end of the night, having trouble balancing.

Once everyone started going to bed, Blake led me to my room. He opened my door and said, "Have a good night, Jasmine. Thank you for coming here for my birthday." He kissed me on my forehead and turned to walk up a set of stairs.

I decided to follow him, wobbling as I did, and dropping the towel that was wrapped around me. He turned around and looked at me. "Be careful." He came down to help me.

"I want to see your room," I said.

"Well, okay then," he said, picking up my towel and helping me up the stairs. He opened the door to a spacious, rustic bedroom with large windows, an angled ceiling lined with wooden beams, soft carpet, and an en suite bathroom. "What do you think? Nice, right?" he asked, smiling at me.

"I should probably rinse myself before I get into bed," I slurred while untying the strings to my bikini top, allowing it to fall to the ground. His eyes didn't leave me as I then slid my bathing suit bottoms off until I was standing completely naked in front of Blake.

"Goddess, you really know how to torture me," he practically groaned.

"Are you going to join me?" I asked, heading into the bathroom to step into the shower.

"Well, this is certainly a new version of you that I didn't know." His eyes were wide as he followed me, dropping his swim shorts as he entered the bathroom. I turned on the water, waiting for it to warm up. I then stepped into the shower and he followed me. He pulled me close to him, kissing me. The two of us lost ourselves in the kiss as the water fell over us.

I begged him for more with my tongue, grabbing his ass and pulling myself against his very substantial erection. He groaned and bit my bottom lip, grabbing me by my ass and lifting me against his body, pressing me against the cold tile wall. I didn't even care how cold it was as I felt Blake's warm body against mine, kissing me as if my lips were the only things keeping him alive.

"We should go to bed," he whispered, his warm breath tickling my ear, my whole body tingling with desire as he turned the water off. He stepped out and handed me a towel to dry off as he did the same.

I followed him out of the bathroom and flung myself onto the bed, trying to position myself seductively. His lustful blue eyes pierced me as I asked, "So how does this work? You just fuck me until you get sick of me and find someone else?"

"What?" he asked, blinking a few times.

"Well, I don't have a mate to save myself for anymore, so I might as well find out what the big deal is. And you seem willing to show me."

"Why are you saying this, Jasmine?"

"It's what you want, right? All your friends told me. You just hit it and quit it."

"They actually used that phrase?"

"No, but it's accurate, isn't it?"

He sighed and lay down next to me. "Please, stop, Jasmine. You're drunk. Let's just go to sleep."

"Why? It's what you want, right? I'm offering you what you want."

"Please, Jasmine. Not now."

"Why are you rejecting me? Does everyone want to reject me?" Tears slid down my cheeks.

"No, I don't want to reject you. Not even close." He pulled me against him. "And I definitely don't want to 'hit it and quit it,' as you so eloquently put it."

"Then what do you want?" I asked, staring into his eyes.

"I just want to be close to you," he said, pulling the blanket over us. "Let's not make any bad decisions after we were just heavily drinking. Although, it's nice having someone in my bed again. I missed having someone to snuggle with while I sleep. Bonus that she's also naked. I can't complain about this birthday gift at all."

Chapter 60

Jasmine

I awoke the next morning to the sound of an alarm, my throat and mouth dry. I heard a male groan next to me and felt movement on the mattress. I could smell Blake all around me. The memory of last night started to come back to me as I opened my eyes. I lifted the blanket I was under to realize that I was completely naked and so was Blake. My whole body turned red as he rolled over, pulling me against him.

"Well, good morning, Miss Alpha," he said, bringing his mouth to mine, kissing me. "How'd you sleep?"

"I'm pretty sure I remember the whole night. Can werewolves black out?"

"It's rarer than it is for humans, but it's possible."

"We didn't—" I started.

"Have sex?"

"Did we?"

"No. But you definitely tried to seduce me." He smirked at me.

"Oh, Goddess!" I put my hands on my face, recalling what I had done.

"You're quite the seductress when you've been drinking. I mean, I can't blame you. I'd want to jump my bones too. Now that you're fully sober, I wouldn't mind a round of morning sex. Get a nice head start to the day."

"Let's just pretend that I didn't do what I did last night."

"Why? I enjoyed it."

I groaned. "And I don't even have any clothes up here."

"I like it." He smiled. "Don't worry, I'll go grab your bag and bring it up here." He got out of the bed, completely naked. He went to throw on some clothes, and I couldn't help but admire his ass while his back was turned to me. It was really nice. He stepped out of the room and I groaned again.

Moments later, he returned with my duffel bag and dropped it on the floor next to his. Then he stood at the foot of the bed watching me with his arms crossed. "Can I get some privacy please?" I asked.

"It's not like I didn't see everything last night—I enjoyed the show by the way." He smirked, then rolled his eyes. "But, sure, I'll go use the bathroom while you get dressed." He entered the bathroom and closed the door behind him.

I quickly rushed over to my duffel bag to throw on clothing for the day. I waited for Blake to come out and I went in after him to pee, wash my face, and brush my teeth. When I stepped out, he was sitting on the bed on his phone.

He got up and asked, "Ready for another day of skiing? We're leaving this evening since the pack needs me back home, so make sure your bag's packed so we can load it into my car."

I nodded. I made sure everything was gathered and checked the room that was supposed to be my bedroom. Once everyone was ready, we drove back to the mountain where we went to a crepe restaurant for breakfast.

We then hit the slopes. Blake, again, stayed with me while we skied, sharing the chairlift with me. When we were on one of the longer chairlifts, Blake spoke. "So, Tyler. How does it feel to meet your long-lost brother?"

"It's weird. He's such a stranger to me. I mean, the timing obviously isn't great since I've been sort of avoiding social situations recently, and I should probably try to get to know him now."

"Thanks again for coming, Jasmine. I know it probably took a lot of effort and I appreciate you making it out for my birthday." He squeezed my hand. "But, anyway, I'm sure you've probably heard the rumors. I supposedly have half-siblings out there somewhere. No idea where they are. But it's weird to think that they may show up one day seeking either me or my father out."

"Do you think the rumors are true?"

"I'm sure they are. My father's an asshole. He's completely incapable of keeping his dick in his pants."

"Are you different?" I asked, realizing how mean that sounded as soon as I said it.

His jaw was tense, and his eyes looked evil as he glared at me. "I am not like my father."

"I'm sorry. I didn't mean to say it like that," I choked out, feeling fearful of his expression. I covered my face with my mittens, realizing I had just completely insulted him. "I was just curious about what all of your friends told me."

"That I just want to 'hit it and quit it'?"

"Well, is it true?"

He sighed. "I'll admit that I haven't always been the most upstanding citizen. But I would never just toss a woman carrying my child away like she was trash. I would also never cheat on my mate. My father disgusts me."

"I didn't mean...," I began to say, but didn't finish, hoping he understood what I had actually meant to ask, but he didn't respond and I chastised myself for my blunder.

We got to the top of the trail and got out of the chairlift. We waited for the whole group to arrive and skied down the mountain, but Blake was distant now. I realized that I had ruined whatever there had been between us.

He continued to take the chairlift up with me, but he was cold now, only giving short answers when I asked him questions. When we skied, he no longer stayed close to me like he had previously, and instead preferred to join his friends. I wasn't looking forward to the one-hour ride home, distraught by how I had screwed things up between us.

Blake had been a nice distraction from Luke, but now that he was no longer paying attention to me, the feelings came back, the excruciating pain returning to my chest. I was slow going down the trails, the whole group having to wait for me at the bottom before we could ascend the mountain again. By lunchtime, tears were threatening to fall from my eyes.

I was relieved when Jack and Tyler approached me. Tyler asked, "Why don't you sit with us for lunch today? I've been here with you for two days and barely spoken with you." I agreed and the two of them went up to buy lunch while I saved a table and waited for them to return. They came back and sat across from me. Blake followed right after them and sat down next to me.

Jack and Tyler both looked at him. Finally, Tyler asked, "Is Blake your boyfriend, Jasmine?"

"No," I replied, feeling insecure and weird having to answer in front of Blake. "He's just a friend."

"Good-looking friend." Jack winked. "I used to have the biggest crush on him growing up."

"I don't blame you." Tyler chuckled. "I'm almost jealous of Jasmine for being the sister."

I looked at Blake and he kept a straight face, not saying anything.

"He's grumpy sometimes." Jack snickered. "Actually, most of the time."

"I can see that. I could work with that. Sulky yet sexy." Tyler laughed. "Lots of passionate, angry sex."

"Mmm." Jack nodded. "He loves to torture too."

"Oooh, he's got some *Fifty Shades* in him. Very nice." They both laughed, sharing an amused look with each other.

"Are you two done?" Blake asked.

"I don't think he likes being part of our foreplay." Jack smirked.

"He doesn't have to be. He could be part of the main event. I don't mind sharing," Tyler responded.

"I don't know, your sister might mind." Jack looked over my way.

"Well, he's not her boyfriend. So he's fair game as far as I'm concerned."

Blake shook his head, the corners of his mouth lifting.

"He's smiling. I think he might be agreeing to the arrangement." Tyler looked at Jack.

"Seems positive at least. All hope is not lost," Jack replied.

"Ok, that's enough," Blake said, a smile now on his face.

"I agree. I was hoping to get to know my sister before this hot man crashed our party and distracted me." Tyler grinned. "So, Jasmine, besides Blake, what else do you like to do for fun?"

I almost spit my water out at the question. "I'm pretty boring," I replied. "I mostly just go to school and work."

"She's also really good in the gym," Blake added. "She can squat 320 and bench 180."

"Wow, that's impressive!" Tyler exclaimed.

"You should also see her in sparring practice. Her technique's excellent."

"Is she a warrior?" Tyler asked.

"Not yet, but I'm working on it." Blake beamed with pride, then added, "She also makes a great picnic lunch."

"It seems you really like Jasmine."

"Jasmine's amazing." Blake put his arm on the back of my chair. "Pretty, smart, and a badass."

"I'm surprised he's not your boyfriend, Jasmine." Tyler looked my way.

"Well, it's my fault. I'm a 'hit it and quit it' kind of guy and Jasmine's too good for that," Blake responded before I could say anything.

I looked at him, feeling my heart swell at how he had just talked me up to Tyler, hopeful that maybe I'd been wrong about his intentions this whole time. But I was still wary, especially after what had happened with Luke, and after all of Blake's friends had warned me about him. I couldn't bring myself to believe that he could actually want something more than a friends-with-benefits situation. I didn't want to get my hopes up only for them to be crushed later.

"Maybe for the right girl, you could change that about yourself."

"I like you, Tyler. Jasmine has a good brother. I hope you decide to join our pack."

"I hope so too." Jack smiled, putting his arm on the back of Tyler's chair.

After lunch, things seemed to be back to normal with Blake again. Once the sun started to set, we all took the gondola back to the parking lot and got into our individual cars. After we said goodbye to everyone, Blake drove me home.

On our way back to the pack, Blake asked, "So, what's the whole story of what happened with your family? Why did Tyler end up in a different pack?" I told him the whole story as he listened intently. When I was done, he asked, "What was the name of Katie's mate? He was from our pack?"

"I think so, Carl Miller? Do you know him?" I looked over to see that Blake's knuckles were white clutching the steering wheel.

"I know that name."

"Who is he?"

"It's the first man my father ever tortured in front of me when I was ten years old. I'll never forget him."

I looked at him, shocked. "Why did your father torture him?"

"He was a high school teacher and got caught sexually assaulting his students. I think I've told you before that rape is punishable by death in our pack. But I left out the part where my father also enjoys torturing anyone that does. That's one thing my father and I have in common. Anyway, it sounds like it worked out for the best for Katie. If she had stayed with her mate, she would have been mated to a piece of shit and would have had to live with the aftermath of her mate being put to death."

"Wow," I replied.

"See? Sometimes mate bonds are just not meant to be. Yours is not the only one." I nodded.

When Blake pulled up in front of my house, he put his hand on my chest to stop me from getting out. He leaned over and kissed me, brushing my hair back with his hand as he did. After he pulled away, he got out of the car and came around to open my door. Then he went to the trunk to grab my duffel bag and ski boots. I pulled out my skis and ski poles. I unlocked the door to my house and my dad came to the front hall to greet us.

"How was your trip?" he asked as Blake walked in and deposited my things inside.

"Good," I replied.

"Thank you for allowing Jasmine to celebrate my birthday with me." Blake put his hand out to shake my dad's. My dad took his hand, smiling, and Blake continued, "You have such an amazing daughter. I hope you'll continue to allow me to spend time with her."

"Of course, Alpha."

"Good, I'm looking forward to seeing much more of her then." Blake smiled. Before he exited, he turned and said, "Have a good night."

"Good night, Alpha," my dad replied. Then he turned to me and said, "Nice man."

Chapter 61

Jasmine

The following Wednesday, I finally returned to work. I walked in at seven thirty, ready to position myself for the morning rush. Before I could station myself to begin making drinks, Valerie pulled me in for a hug, taking me aback. There was a line of customers to serve, so she quickly let me go so I could do my job.

Once the café was empty, she came over and said, "Are you okay, Jasmine? I heard everything that happened. I've been worried. You haven't responded to any of my texts."

"I haven't been replying to anyone's texts," I replied.

"Why not?"

"It's just too much right now. I don't really want to talk about it." She nodded and moved to the back. I grabbed the spray bottle and a rag so I could clean up the café. At least I made it to work. That was progress. I just had to make it until four and then I could go back to my bed until Saturday.

I returned to behind the register after I finished cleaning, ringing in the few customers that came in. Suddenly, a familiar figure entered. I watched as the tall, muscular figure walked toward me, his piercing blue eyes staring at me. "I knew I'd find you here."

"Hi, Blake," I replied.

"You don't reply to my texts so now I really do have to start stalking you."

"Don't take it personally. I don't reply to anyone's texts. So, what can I get you today?"

"Large black coffee," he replied.

I entered his order into the register and said, "That'll be two fifty-nine."

"I wasn't done with my order."

"Oh? What else?"

"I want a date."

"A date?"

"Yes, a date with Miss Alpha." He beamed.

I took a step back, my eyes widening in surprise. "I didn't think that was your thing. I thought you just liked playing the field."

"I'm trying something new. I'll pick you up on Friday evening at six. That should give you plenty of time to mope around and not reply to my texts before you have to get ready." He smirked, pulling out his credit card and inserting it into the card reader. I quickly made his coffee and handed it to him. He took it, staring into my eyes, and said, "I look forward to it." Then he turned around to leave.

As soon as he exited, Valerie came to stand next to me and said, "Hmm, looks like Mr. Hot Sexy Alpha's back. And I don't think he wants to be your friend."

"I can't figure out what he wants."

"Seems pretty clear to me. You're too much in your head sometimes. Just enjoy your date on Friday, and tell me all the details on Saturday." she smiled, turning around to return to the back.

The next day, my mom left me a grocery list and a note to pick up my grandfather's prescription at the clinic. She came into my room before she left for work to bring me breakfast. I moaned as she handed me the paper.

She rolled her eyes and said, "You come from an alpha family. Now stop pretending you're so weak. I know you better than that. I let it go last time, but this time I won't. There better be groceries in the fridge when I get home tonight."

I skimmed the list and asked, "Why can't Grandpa get his own prescription?"

"Because it's time you got off your butt and made yourself more useful around here. I'm sick of all your brooding. That man is not worth giving up on your life. Quite frankly, it's embarrassing that I raised a daughter that would act like this." She exited. I listened as her steps disappeared down the stairs and the garage opened and closed.

I clutched my chest. The pain was still there. It made it impossible to focus on anything outside of it. Sometime closer to noon, I finally forced myself to roll over and let my feet hit the ground. I took a shower and got dressed, throwing my hair into a messy bun.

While I was in the grocery store, I kept my mind on the task at hand, refusing to let my mind go anywhere else—absolutely not about what I had witnessed the last time I was here. After my cart was full, I checked out. Almost done. Just one more errand and I could go home.

I drove past the packhouse, seeing that Blake's car was in the lot but Luke's wasn't. Then I remembered that he normally had college classes on Thursdays—something that I'd given up on. I felt a sharp pain in my chest as I drove, the thoughts of him piercing me.

I parked in the clinic parking lot and forced myself to get out of the car. The waiting room was empty, which was a relief. It was best to avoid as much human contact as possible. I went up to the front desk to ask for my grandfather's prescription. I was about to leave when Lucy and her mom exited from the back. Why did I have to keep bumping into them?

Ivy ran over to me, a big smile on her face. "Jasmine, it's so nice to see you!" My eyes were wide as she pulled me in for a hug. Lucy followed her mom, nodding at me, not saying anything. Ivy continued, "Katie and Tyler both loved meeting you. I'm so glad you were able to make it to the dinner last week."

As she spoke, I noticed something that may as well have been a bullet straight through my chest. As I looked where Lucy's neck met her collarbone, it was clear as day that she was marked. They had marked each other.

The whole world spun around me as I sprinted away from them, certain I looked crazy. I ran out of the clinic to my car. Before I got in, I doubled over and vomited, not able to hold it in. I sat in the driver's seat, and before I knew what I was doing, I sped over to the packhouse, parking my car next to Blake's. I ran to the front door and rang the doorbell.

I waited until the door opened and saw him standing in front of me. He looked down at me and said, "I think you're confused. You have the date, time, and location of the date completely wrong. I'm supposed to meet you tomorrow at six at your house. Not today at"—he looked at his cell phone—"two at my house."

"Do you have something to drink?" I asked pushing past him.

"The nightcap at my house is supposed to be after the date, not before," he shook his head. "And you think I'm the one that doesn't know how to date."

"Blake," I said, looking at him.

"Yes?" He stared into my eyes.

"They marked each other." I burst into tears.

He put his arms around me and said, "Shit, sorry. I should have told you." He led me to the couch and sat me down. He rubbed my back and said, "He had to, Jasmine. I know it hurts but he's also the beta of the pack and it's as good as guaranteed that we'll be going to war any day now. He can't be distracted. He has to do his job."

I nodded into Blake's chest. "It just hurts. I'm the only one suffering and acting pathetic. My mom told me she was embarrassed she raised a daughter like me this morning. But I can't help it. It just hurts so much."

"I know," he said, brushing his fingers through my hair.

"Are we really going to war?"

"Unfortunately, yes. That's why we implemented all these new training programs for the pack. It's almost definitely going to be fought either on or near our soil, and we need to make sure everyone's prepared because we don't know exactly how many packs will be involved."

I nodded, separating from Blake. "Sorry, you probably have work to do. I can go."

"Do you want to go for a run before you do? That always helps me feel better. I can go with you."

"Ok. But do you have an extra toothbrush or mouthwash I can use before we go?"

He laughed, shaking his head. "You're so confused. You're supposed to ask that question the morning after the date."

"It's just that I threw up, and my mouth feels gross right now."

"I think we can find something for you." He stood up and I followed. He took my hand and led me upstairs to his bedroom, into his en suite bathroom.

"Oh, you had it renovated!" I was surprised that his whole bathroom was completely different than the last time I saw it.

"I forgot that you haven't been in here since my parents still lived here. What do you think?"

"It looks great!" I looked around at the modern tiles, quartz double vanity, and huge glass walk-in shower.

"Should we, as the humans say, christen the new shower?" he smirked. "I'm starting to think that perhaps the nightcap should have happened just now."

"Uggghhh! Stop!"

He opened the cabinet under the sink and pulled out a bottle of mouthwash and handed it to me. I swished it in my mouth and spit it into the sink, turning on the water to get it all down the drain.

We went back downstairs, and Blake led me into the woods. He began stripping as soon as we stepped a few yards in. I turned my back to him, and he laughed. "It's cute how you pretend we haven't seen each other completely naked already." When I didn't turn around, he said, "I've turned around. I won't peek."

I turned my head to see that his back was to me. I then pulled off all my clothes and shifted into my wolf. I turned back around to see that he was already in his wolf form. I walked next to him. He glanced at me for a moment and then launched into a sprint. I quickly followed.

We ran together for at least an hour. It was nice not being confined to the territory. It was also nice having Blake to run with. Something about being in his presence made me feel calm and lessened the pain. When we came to a hill, Blake got down and rolled down it in his wolf form. I followed, feeling like a little kid. I stopped at the bottom on my back and Blake stood over me licking my face. It was at that moment that I could finally imagine a future without pain.

We ran back to the packhouse, and Blake turned around so I could shift back and get dressed. He then walked me to my car. Right before I got in, he pulled me against him and kissed me on my head. "See you tomorrow, six o'clock at *your* house. Hopefully that was clear enough this time."

"Bye," I replied, smiling, and got into my car. He watched as I drove away. When I got home, I pulled all the groceries out of the car, thankful that it was freezing that day. For the first time in over a week, I finally cooked dinner, a smile on my face.

Chapter 62

Blake

On Friday afternoon, Luke, my father, Alpha Antoine, and his mate, Luna Marie, were positioned around my desk as we all looked toward the conference phone. Luke gathered everyone and dialed his father's number.

"Hello? Dad?" Luke shouted into the phone.

"Hi, Luke. Who else is there?"

"We have Alpha Blake, Alpha James, Alpha Antoine, and Luna Marie."

"Ok, good. I have some unfortunate news to share. Thank you for calling me back immediately. My men have spotted a mass movement from Alpha Édouard's pack. At this point, I would advise everyone to take position. I think it's clear that they've decided to proceed with the attack, and they're definitely heading in your direction."

Alpha Antoine chimed in, "I am looking at my phone and I'm receiving the same information from my beta now."

"Let's load up the borders, and I'll call the Autumn Moon Pack in." My dad stood up.

"I'll mindlink all of the seniors now," I said.

"I'll get an email out to the pack informing them to stay home to avoid the conflict," Luke said, stationing himself in front of his laptop.

"Good luck, everyone. I'll stand by here and text you if anything changes," Alfred said as we hung up.

After I was done mindlinking, I looked down at my phone sadly and quickly typed a text message to Jasmine to let her know I'd have to take a rain check on the date. Luke and I began assigning warriors to be stationed a few miles out from the northern border in groups of two, to keep lookout in shifts. That way, they could mindlink us with a warning before the enemy packs reached us, giving everyone time to make it to the battle before the enemies began attacking. Hopefully we could keep the impending battle outside the pack territory, so it wouldn't affect our civilians. The Bois Sombre Pack was about four hours away by car, but it wasn't clear if they would proceed directly to our pack, or how far away they might park before shifting into their wolf forms to run the rest of the way.

Luke and I sat down at our desks and my father returned to the office. "I've got Alpha Marc on standby."

"Thank you, Alpha James," Luke said from his desk. My father then looked at me. I looked back at him, wondering why he was staring at me. After some time of us staring at each other, he finally shook his head and walked out. Once we heard the front door open and shut, Luke said, "Your dad hasn't been as bad lately."

"Yeah," I replied.

"How's Jasmine doing? Is she okay?" Luke looked at me.

"She'll be fine."

"I heard you took her to your birthday thing."

"Yeah."

Luke then stood up and walked over to my desk, looking down at me. "I know I don't have the right to say anything, but please, Blake, don't hurt her. She's a good girl."

"You're right, you don't have the right to say anything, so don't." I narrowed my eyes at him and pursed my lips. He nodded and walked out of the room.

I spent the rest of the day doing my rounds between patrol stations, making sure everyone was doing what they were supposed to and that they understood all the instructions. I got home close to midnight and reheated some lasagna that Connie had left in the fridge. After I ate it, I passed out in my bed, leaving my phone on the charger at full volume.

I woke to it ringing just as dawn was breaking. I looked out my window as I answered, seeing snowflakes falling. "Yeah."

"They're approaching." Mike's voice was on the other end.

"Got it," I replied and hung up. I sprinted out of bed and ran to bang on Alpha Antoine's door. Then I ran down to the beta floor and did the same on Luke's door. Both of them flew out of their rooms, along with Luna Marie. The four of us rushed outside and instantly stripped our clothes, shifted into our wolf forms, and sprinted toward the northern border. Snow fell around us as we ran, covering the ground in a sheet of white.

As we were running, I quickly mindlinked all of the seniors, informing them of the situation so that they could round up their juniors. When we got close, I felt it, a pain pulsing through my body. And I instantly knew—Mike was dead. We approached his location, about a mile out from the border, to find him lying lifeless on the ground, three darts in his shoulder, arm, and leg. I ripped one of them out with my mouth and smelled it. Wolfsbane.

Alpha Antoine's and my troops appeared, sprinting to congregate. Suddenly darts began raining on us. They were fighting dirty. It was also completely reckless. Part of the reason werewolves didn't use weapons was the risk for friendly fire was too high. Unless you were close enough to someone to smell the pack they were from, it was close to impossible to differentiate between friend and enemy, with the coloring of a wolf's fur almost never being indicative of the pack they were from. Before I could fully process the situation, sharp flashes of pain pulsed through my body, one after another. My pack members were falling. Fucking cowards couldn't even fight us the right way. I took the lead, and several darts hit my body. Luckily, I had spent years building a tolerance and was fine.

We all moved forward, and finally the cowards showed themselves, running toward us. They must have run out of darts. We all bolted toward them, attacking as we could. I quickly plunged my claws into an enemy wolf and tore out his heart, watching as he fell dead next to me. I moved forward, beheading another one. As my pack members fell, I continued to feel it pulse through my body, trying my best to move past the feeling.

Not long after the battle started, Autumn Moon Pack joined us, increasing our numbers. I continued to fight among our ally packs, taking down wolves as I could, sustaining several blows to my body. But I realized I was made for this, the energy of everyone pushing me forward.

Suddenly more darts were launched into the crowd—completely reckless. That was when Luke, who was fighting next to me, let out a loud, pained growl that pierced my bones, and fell from my peripheral vision. I turned to find he had dropped and shifted into his human form, a dart protruding from his neck. On instinct, I rapidly pulled the dart out with my teeth, spitting it onto the ground. Then I brought my face close enough to his chest so I could hear his labored breathing, confirming he was still alive. I turned my head back to battle only to be met with a wolf in midjump, claws extended and teeth bared, pouncing on me. It was as if it happened in slow motion. Before I could get into a defensive position, a huge, black, graying wolf jumped on top of me, pushing me flat against the ground. He was instantly beheaded, a debilitating pain pulsing through my body. I quickly got up and attacked the enemy wolf, plunging my paw into his chest and pulling out his heart. Then I looked next to me to see my father's human head separated from his body. My father was dead. He had sacrificed himself for me.

Before I could fully process what had happened, I realized that Luke would die if I left him where he was. He had already been injured even before the wolfsbane hit his body and wouldn't be able to heal quickly in this condition. So, I made a split-second decision to flip him onto my back into a wolfman's carry and take him away to a place where he could be safe until he recovered from the wolfsbane. I ran deep into the forest.

I didn't get too far before I came across two naked men with dart guns pointed toward me. I stood on my hind legs so that the darts would hit me instead of Luke. I felt several plunge into my torso. As I released Luke, the men shifted into wolves. At this point, I'd had so many darts shot into me that I was starting to feel my insides burning. But I powered through it, pouncing on one of the wolves, ripping out his vertebrae while the other one jumped onto my back, his claws shoving deep inside me.

I quickly flipped both of us onto our backs, using my body weight to flatten him against the ground. He kicked me off him, and I landed against a rock, my ribs cracking. He grabbed my leg in his mouth and began flinging me against the same rock, injuring me. I was eventually able to kick him off me. I could feel the final couple darts taking effect and used the last of my strength to behead the wolf.

And that was when the burning sensation finally became unbearable, the wolfsbane had fully pulsed itself into my bloodstream. That mixed with the injuries I'd sustained forced me to shift into my human form. I lay in the snow, completely immobile, unable to shift or mindlink.

I looked over at Luke who was the same. I had to hope that no one would find us here, as impossible as that was. I had barely gotten us away from the battle. It would only be a matter of time before someone finished both of us off, and our pack would no longer have an alpha or a beta. So many years of training, my father's sacrifice, and I'd still be finished off during the first battle I ever fought as an alpha. I used what little strength I had to crawl over to Luke. He looked at me, as powerless as I was, breathing heavily, holding on for his life.

"Luke," I said, feeling sadness come over me. "Luke, you have to make it. You can't die. You have a pup on the way. Just hold on until the wolfsbane's metabolized and you can heal again."

He coughed, blood flowing out of his mouth and nose, unable to speak. I lay down next to him, wondering if this was it—if my friend and beta would be taken from me. Was that my fate? Was everyone I cared about going to die, an endless cycle of pain? Would I finally become numb to it at one point or would I eventually lose my own will to live?

A huge white wolf approached us, his teeth bared, in a fighting position. And I knew it was over. Neither Luke nor I could fight anymore. I was helpless and naked, immobile against the freezing, wet snow, sure it was stained red from the cuts all over my body.

The white wolf stood over me and I realized I knew that scent. I figured out where I had smelled the scent of the mystery pack before. The wolf standing over me was Alexander Adalwolf, a man I had gone to Grey Wolf University with—a man whose life I had saved. He was the alpha of the Pine Forest Pack in Ontario. I looked up at him, wondering if he would take my life.

That was when he shifted into his human form. "Wulfric?"

I nodded.

"Fuck, man, I didn't realize this was your pack. You look like shit." His eyes darted upward, in a mindlink, then he shifted back into his wolf form. Another wolf came sprinting over—a female one. And that was when I realized that the scent of the wolf that was able to survive in cold water was this other wolf's. I couldn't believe that I hadn't realized it was a female scent at the time, too concentrated on figuring out the pack it was from.

Alexander flipped me onto his back, and the female wolf flipped Luke onto hers. They carried us away, bringing us farther into the forest, into a cave, and dropping us there.

Alexander shifted back into his human form and looked at me. "You saved my life, so I am sparing yours. Now we're even in that regard. But I am also going to do you a favor, and I expect a favor in return. I am going to withdraw my pack from this war. You will easily be able to win it without us. But it's not a completely selfless act. Your pack's much larger than the Bois Sombre Pack, and I prefer your alliance. So, when we have to fight our own war, I am going to expect your cooperation."

"Absolutely," I replied.

"Good, now you'll be safe here until you can heal."

"Who is she?" I asked, curious about the wolf he was with.

"That's my sister, Sara. She's much better at survival in the cold." He laughed, then shifted back into a wolf and turned to leave with her.

I sighed and forced myself to sit up, still weak from the wolfsbane that was burning through my body. I looked over to see that Luke was shivering. Being stuck in our human forms was not good for freezing weather, not having our fur. I moved toward him and lay my body on top of his, trying to put myself in the least intimate position possible, which was really not that possible at all. At least we could keep each other warm, as awkward as this was.

"Blake, what are you doing?" Luke asked weakly, clearly finally regaining the ability to speak.

"Let's just pretend this isn't happening. This is awkward enough as it is."

He chuckled, coughing up some blood. "Yeah, this is extremely awkward."

"Well, we can just pretend we're kids again."

"Okay, but we at least had clothes on when we were kids, and we also didn't exactly touch each other even if we shared the same bed."

"Let's talk about something else."

"Okay, why did that wolf save our lives?"

"I saved his life."

"When?"

"When I was in school. He was a year above me. I used to go for runs in my wolf form all the time to get my mind off things. His third year, he had to survive a week outside in his wolf form, and an avalanche had fallen on him. The force of the amount of snow and ice that fell on him crushed his bones and forced him into his human form. He was able to dig himself out enough to breathe, but he would have died of hypothermia if I hadn't randomly stumbled upon him. I was able to dig him out and find him shelter, where I built a fire and kept him alive until he healed."

"Damn."

"Yeah." We lay like that for at least an hour. I could feel that I had fractured several different bones in my body and the wolfsbane was still burning within me. Even if I managed to get us out of the cave, we wouldn't be able to get far. But I was relieved that the painful pulsing from the deaths of pack members had stopped. I realized then that my father had lived with that pain for years, constantly feeling every pack member's death as it occurred. He'd finally retired only to see the end of his own life just a few short months later. I sighed.

"What are you thinking about?" Luke asked.

"My father."

"What about him?"

"He's dead, Luke. Adalwolf wasn't the only one who saved my life today. I got distracted when you shifted, and the only reason I'm still alive is because my father jumped in front of the wolf that was going to kill me in my moment of distraction."

"Fuck, I'm sorry, man. Your dad wasn't a nice guy, but he's still your dad. How do you feel?"

"I don't know. It doesn't excuse everything he's done, but it's like my mom said: he wasn't all bad."

We lay in silence, reflecting. After some time, Luke suddenly uttered, "Blake, I think this is the most you've talked to me in five years. I feel like you're finally opening up to me again."

"Okay, Luke, please don't make this awkward. You're talking to me about opening up while I'm lying naked on top of you." I gave a small chuckle.

"I thought we weren't going to talk about that." He laughed.

Just then, a wolf entered the cave. I could smell that he was from the Bois Sombre Pack. I used whatever strength I had to sit up. I still couldn't shift or mindlink, but maybe I could use my alpha aura. While it wouldn't work as efficiently on stranger packs, it would at least restrain him for a few seconds until maybe I could grab him with what strength I could muster.

"Stop!" I bellowed, trying to force the alpha aura out, but it was useless. I had cheated death twice already. But, as they say, third time's a charm. He approached us slowly, his teeth bared as Luke and I stared at him, both of us completely powerless, wolfsbane burning our bodies.

"Stop!" a female voice yelled out from behind him. Suddenly he was stunned into halting, frozen and unable to move. Taking advantage of the few seconds he was motionless, I grabbed him, using my arms to restrain his mouth and hold him against my body.

My eyes widened when I saw Jasmine enter in behind him, quickly shifting into her wolf form. Springing into action, I shouted, "Jasmine!"

She turned to me, her amber eyes taking in the scene before her.

"Jasmine, you need to kill him!" I yelled.

She came closer.

"Just use your teeth to bite into his neck and separate his head from his body." The wolf was struggling against me, now having regained his ability to move. She was hesitating, I could tell. I was certain she'd never killed before. I found a regained strength in her presence, holding him more forcefully. "Jasmine, kill him!" I yelled.

"Kill him!" Luke repeated. "Before he kills us!"

She finally moved forward, opening her mouth, and bit down on his neck as I restrained him against my body, his limbs thrashing against me, trying to get free. I strengthened my grip even more, enduring the blows to my already injured body as her teeth sliced through layers of skin and his cervical spine, finally severing his head. It rolled off his body and smashed against the ground, and he fell lifeless on top of me in his human form.

"Holy fuck! You did it!" I shouted, throwing the dead corpse off me. "How the hell did you find us?"

She sat down next to me, and I patted her wolf form. I could see she was struggling to mindlink me. "I can't even receive mindlinks, Jasmine. I'm too weak right now," I explained.

She stared at me in her wolf form, lifting her nose up in a gesture.

I smirked and said, "Luke and I will close our eyes and turn around, not that we both haven't seen it all already." Luke glared at me and used the little strength he had to roll over and close his eyes. I did the same and I could feel the movement of air behind me as she shifted into her human form.

"Shit, it's cold!" she gasped behind me.

"We've definitely noticed." I chuckled. "I'm dying to know how you got here."

"When I heard you guys were missing, I got worried, and I got an idea. Since I know two people who are mated can sense the general direction where the other is at all times, I found Lucy and asked her to point me in the direction of Luke. She wanted to come too but I didn't let her, because of, well, you know, her condition. Anyway, I shifted into my wolf form and ran in that direction until I picked up your scents, which wasn't too difficult since your blood had fallen on the ground. I noticed another wolf was doing the same thing, so I stayed quiet and followed behind him, making sure he didn't notice me. After he entered the cave, I figured that's where you must be, so I ran. And then when Blake yelled for him to stop, I figured out what he was trying to do and I did the same thing. I wasn't sure if it would work, but I thought it might, and it did!"

"Hot damn, Miss Alpha!" I shouted, smiling at how amazing she was.

I felt the air move as she shifted again. I turned back around to see her in her wolf form. Her eyes darted upwards, and I could tell she was mindlinking someone. She sat and looked down at me. I looked up at her and burst into laughter. Both she and Luke looked at me, furrowing their brows in confusion.

I laughed harder, clutching my stomach at the pain it was causing and exclaimed, "Jasmine, you're so confused! Our date was supposed to be yesterday at six at your house, not today, at whatever time it is, in a fucking cave!"

Chapter 63

Blake

I woke up in a hospital bed, not knowing what day or time it was, with an IV in my arm. I could feel that my ribs were still healing, but the burning from the wolfsbane had finally subsided. After some time, Dr. Davis came in. He was the other doctor who worked at the clinic with my mom.

"Ah, Alpha, you're awake. How are you feeling?"

"Better," I replied, looking at him.

"Glad to hear it. We took some of your blood and you had at least five times the lethal amount of wolfsbane in your bloodstream. That was likely after you had already metabolized some already. To be quite honest, I am baffled that you're still alive."

"High tolerance." I smirked.

"Glad to see that we still have our alpha with us. Other than that, it seems you just need time to heal at this point."

Upon hearing what he said, a sickness came over me. "Where's my mom?" I asked.

He looked at me sadly. "Due to the circumstances, she's taking a leave of absence until she's ready to return to work. She's been in to visit you while you were sleeping, and I'm sure she'll be in again. I'm very sorry for your loss, Alpha."

I nodded at him, and fell back into my pillow, finding myself spiraling into my thoughts. I wished I could shift into my wolf so I could get rid of them, feeling trapped in my human body. Before the doctor left, I asked, "How's my beta?"

"He's almost fully recovered, Alpha."

"Good, thank you," I replied. After he left the room, I looked around to see that it was filled with flowers and cards. I found a remote and turned on the TV, hoping to find a distraction.

After some time, a nurse came in and said, "There's a visitor here to see you. Can I send her in Alpha?"

"Yes," I replied, hoping it was who I thought it was. I smiled as a familiar face walked through the door, my heart skipping a beat as she came closer and I inhaled her comforting scent.

"Hi, Blake," Jasmine greeted me, a shy smile on her face.

"Miss Alpha, my hero and the reason I'm still alive!" I smiled at her, desiring to grab her, pull her against me, and feel her body against mine.

She blushed and sat down on the chair next to my bed. "How are you feeling?"

"Like shit, but you know, it comes with the job. So, when are you joining the team?"

"You're a terrible salesperson." She laughed.

"I don't need to be good at sales. I can just force everyone to do whatever I want. And, apparently, you can too. I learn something new about you every time."

Jasmine looked at me sadly. "I heard about your dad." I turned away from her, looking up at the ceiling, and nodded my head. I could feel myself withdrawing. When I didn't say anything, she put her hand on mine and asked, "Are you okay?"

I glanced back at her and sighed. "Yeah." I didn't know what else there was to say. We stayed like that for a while, not speaking.

After some time, she said, "Okay, I should probably go and let you rest."

As she was about to withdraw her hand from where it had been placed on top of mine, I grabbed it. "Wait," I said, and looked into her eyes. "You still owe me a date." I continued speaking, "I can't give you a date, time, or place because I'm not sure when I'll finally be able to leave this place. But I will text you. And if you're still not replying to your texts then, then you'll leave me no choice but to stalk you down again." I smiled at her.

"I'm replying to texts again."

"Good. Now after seeing me suffering like this, I think I deserve a goodbye kiss before you leave."

She smiled and bent forward, placing her lips gently on mine. I brought my hands to the sides of her face as she kissed me, moving one of them upwards, weaving it through her hair. I deepened the kiss and once we started we couldn't stop. She hovered over me, supported by her forearm, her free hand tousling my hair.

Suddenly, we heard a knock interrupting us. She fell back in her chair. "Come in," I said. The door opened and my mom walked in.

"Oh, hello, Jasmine."

"Hi, Dr. Luna," she replied. "I was actually just on my way out." She got up and waved goodbye to us.

"Bye, Miss Alpha," I shouted as she walked out of the room. Then I looked at my mom whose eyes were bloodshot and filled with emotion. "Mom," I said, taking in her appearance.

She sat down in the chair that Jasmine had just abandoned and pulled one of my hands into hers. "Blake, I'm so glad you're okay. I spoke with Dr. Davis and he gave me an update on your condition. I don't know what I would have done if I'd lost you too."

"Dad saved my life," I said. "I would be dead if it weren't for Dad sacrificing himself."

She nodded and looked at me sadly. "I don't think your father ever told you this, but his father also sacrificed his life for him. I think they were much closer than the two of you were, and it was early on after your father first took the alpha position. I've spoken with Alfred in the past, and he's told me that your father changed a lot after that moment. I don't know the details of exactly what happened, but I think your father always blamed himself for the death of his own father. I think that may be part of the reason he was always so hard on you growing up. He wanted to make sure you would be a more capable alpha than he felt he was early on. But I want you to also know that your father was always very proud of you. He may have never verbalized it, but he was."

I stared at the ceiling, listening to my mom speak. Not knowing what to say. Finally, I asked, "Are you okay, Mom?"

"I will be, Blake. I'm just glad you're still alive. It gives me hope for the future, and hope is everything."

"What kind of hope?" I asked, curious.

"That one day my son will find a new mate, start a family, and be a wonderful alpha for our pack. That's all a mother wants is to see her children be successful and happy." She smiled at me, leaning forward to kiss me on the forehead. "Now, get some rest. Also, I brought you some of Connie's cookies for later." She pulled a container out of her purse and placed it on the bedside table next to me.

"Mom," I said.

"Yes?"

"I want you to know that I was not the reason the mate bond didn't work with Luke and Jasmine."

She sighed. "You know, to be honest, when I look back, the two of them didn't really have that much chemistry. But I definitely did see it between you and Jasmine." She smiled, picked up her purse, and walked to the door. "Bye, Blake," she said as she opened the door to exit.

Chapter 64

Jasmine

On Friday evening, a funeral service was held at the temple for all the fallen warriors from the battle. My parents and I arrived to pews overflowing with pack members dressed in black. It was so full that we had to take a seat near the back. I instantly spotted Blake up front, dressed in a suit and seated with his mom, Luke and his family, and Lucy. The stage was filled with flowers and framed portraits of all the lost warriors. I noted one of the former alpha in the center.

The service was at least three hours long as the priest led us through different chants and meditations. Then each warrior's family members went up to the podium to give eulogies. At the end, the priest called Blake up to speak. I felt my heart catch at the sight of him.

He pulled out a paper, which he planted onto the podium, and began speaking. "Good evening, Midnight Maple Pack. Thank you for joining me, my family, and the families of the recently fallen warriors as we honor their lives tonight. As you all know, this memorial service is especially momentous for me as I lost my own father, the former Alpha James, during the battle that ensued on Saturday. My father had a great sense of duty and loyalty to this pack and dedicated his whole life to its security and continuance. I especially witnessed this during the final moments of his life when he sacrificed himself so that I"—Blake's voice cracked—"as his heir and current alpha, could continue his legacy."

Blake paused, taking a deep breath, and then continued. "I, like my father, feel a strong sense of duty to this pack and our warriors. That's why I train and fight alongside my team. Being a warrior is a dangerous job, but it's also an honorable and noble job. It's the reason why we're able to continue our way of life and keep our loved ones safe. Everyone you see in the portraits displayed here today is a hero. They're the reason we still have our homes, our school, our temple, and our pack territory. They fought not only for what we have today, but so that our children and our children's children can continue to enjoy the amenities provided by the Midnight Maple Pack. They fought for what is most worth fighting for.

"I, as your alpha, promise to continue to honor every fallen warrior's sacrifice as I lead this pack. May future battles be few and far between. But if we must fight, we will be ready. The Midnight Maple Pack will live on!"

A round of applause erupted after Blake ended his speech. He modestly bowed his head and walked back to where he had been sitting next to his mother. She wrapped her arms around him after he sat down, and Luke leaned over and patted him on the shoulder.

After the service ended, I stayed with my parents as they mingled with everyone. I kept my eye on Blake, who walked from family to family of the fallen warriors. We eventually made it outside where around forty pyres were set up to burn all the bodies. We gathered in a large circle around them as each family lit their individual pyre. I watched as Blake stood with his own family to light his father's.

Afterward, everyone dispersed to return home. My parents fell into deep conversation with another couple at the front of the temple as we were heading to the car. I stood back, moving toward the temple steps to wait for them when Luke approached me. I clutched my chest in pain as he did, still feeling raw from the rejection and seeing him again.

"Jasmine," he said softly. "Can we talk?" I nodded, not able to speak. He took a deep breath and said, "I just want to tell you how sorry I am about everything I put you through and how much I hurt you. To be honest, I was a huge idiot, and you deserve so much better. I know there's someone else out there who will treat you really well and give you everything that I wasn't able to. After you rejected me, I was in a lot of pain, and I spent a lot of time reflecting on the past few months.

"To be totally honest, I've come to care a lot about you, and I wish things had worked out differently than they did. If I was able to live my life all over again, I would have made completely different choices. Anyway, I know that this apology probably isn't enough to make up for everything I put you through, but I hope it's at least a start. You're an amazing woman, and you're going to make someone else really happy one day. I'm not just saying that. I really believe it."

I nodded at him, feeling overcome with emotion, a prickling at the back of my throat. I did my best to hold off my tears, not wanting Luke to see how much he affected me, trying to stay strong. And then I realized, he no longer had that amazing scent anymore. He just smelled the way he had when I had first met him, long before the mate bond had taken effect. He touched my arm in a friendly gesture, and I noticed the sparks were gone. He was just Luke now, no longer my mate.

When I didn't respond to his apology, he said, "You don't have to say anything but thank you for listening to me. Take care of yourself, Jasmine. And if you ever need anything, don't hesitate to ask. After all, I owe you my life now." He then turned and walked away.

I sat down on the temple steps, my knees feeling a bit weak, reflecting on the interaction I'd just had as snowflakes began to drop from the sky. Moments later, Blake's scent entered my nose. I turned to see him sitting down next to me.

"Hey," he said.

"Hey," I replied, looking at him. "Nice speech."

"Thanks."

"Sorry again about your dad," I said, feeling emotional, touching his leg.

"Thanks." He looked down at his hands.

"I see you recovered finally."

"Yeah, I've been meaning to text you, but I got caught up in pack duty stuff. I had to visit all the families of the fallen warriors and meet with the priest. It's honestly been a lot." He sighed. We sat silently together for a bit and then he spoke again. "Do you want to do something tonight?"

"Like what?"

"Just hang out. I've missed you. I'd like to spend some time with you."

"You know how my parents are."

"One second," he said, getting up and walking toward my parents. I stood up, shocked by him approaching them so suddenly. I watched as he shook my father's hand and spoke with him. After about a minute, he returned. "You're a free woman. Let's go!"

"What did you say to him?"

"I played the whole, 'she needs to get out of the house and cheer up' card." He smiled. "Also, it helps that I'm the alpha, so no one ever says no to me." He took my hand and walked with me to the packhouse where his car was parked. He opened the passenger door and helped me in and then got into the driver's seat. Once he was seated, he turned to me and said, "Since we're already dressed up, we should go somewhere nice. Of course, there's really only one nice place around here, so looks like we're going to the casino."

I groaned. "Please don't tell me we're going to the Italian restaurant."

"I was actually going to take you to the steakhouse. What, do you not like Italian food?" He pulled out of the packhouse lot.

"Steakhouse sounds great," I replied.

"Good, because it's open late on Fridays." We drove for a while until he pulled into valet and the valet opened my door for me. Blake came around the car to take my hand and lead me inside. We walked up to the host stand where he asked for a table. The hostess clicked through her iPad when a man came over. "Mr. Wulfric! I didn't know you'd be joining us tonight!"

"It was a last-minute decision," he replied.

"Ah, well, I have the perfect table for you," he said.

"Actually, maybe something in the lounge area."

"Ah yes, even better," he said, grabbing menus. "Right this way." We followed the man to an area that was set up with couches and small tables. He brought us to one that was directly in front of the live piano player and singer duo that was putting on a live show.

After I opened my menu, Blake said, "I thought this would be more relaxing than sitting at a table."

"It's nice here," I replied.

He looked over my shoulder as I reviewed the menu. "Order whatever you want. The burgers are a personal favorite of mine, FYI. I believe they might be top-rated in Vermont. And I'm not just saying that to save some money tonight. I'd be happy to get you a steak if that's what you prefer."

"Burger sounds good to me."

"Also, don't worry about being carded when they come around to take our drink orders. Get whatever you want. Although, I'll probably take it easy and just get a beer, being the designated driver and all." He smiled at me.

The waiter came around and Blake ordered his beer and I ordered a banana nut bread martini, which sounded good. Blake also put in an order for lobster mac and cheese to start, telling me it was really good here.

After our drinks arrived, we put the order in for the burgers with parmesan truffle fries, per Blake's recommendation. We then sat back and began sipping our drinks. Blake moved in closer to me, putting his arm around me. I snuggled into him, enjoying the feeling of his body against mine.

They brought out the mac and cheese along with an assortment of other appetizers. "Compliments of the chef," the waiter said and walked away. We began picking away at the food and nursed our drinks.

When I was close to finished with my martini, I felt like I finally had the courage to say what I wanted. I turned to Blake and said, "I'm okay with us having sex."

He practically spit out his beer as he looked at me. "What?"

"I've thought about it, and I'd like to have sex with you. I understand that you don't want a commitment, and I think I can be okay with it as long as you're always honest with me. Just please don't ghost me if you decide you don't want to be with me anymore, because I think that would hurt. But I don't have a mate anymore, and I don't want to be a virgin anymore, and I trust you."

"Jasmine, stop." He looked at me, putting his hand on my lap.

"I'm not drunk. I've only had one drink, so I am cognizant of what I'm saying."

He shook his head as a busser came by to take away our empty plates. Another person came by to refill our waters, followed by the waiter who asked if we'd like more drinks. Blake nodded his head and the waiter said, "Sir, just so you're aware, there's a blizzard warning right now, and they're saying the roads are getting bad, so let me know if you'd like us to box up your meal for you."

"It's okay, I have a Wrangler," Blake replied. After the waiter nodded and left, he turned back to me and said, "Jasmine, that's not what I want."

"It's not? Why are you always saying you want to have sex with me and then every time I offer it to you, you reject me?" I started to feel dizzy. I had just completely embarrassed myself in front of Blake, and I was way too sober for this, thankful another martini was on its way. Why was I so stupid to think he was doing anything more than joking all this time? I began taking deep breaths.

He pulled me closer to him and rubbed my arm. "I do want to have sex with you, Jasmine. Very much. I think about it all the time. There's nothing I want more than to explore your entire sexy little body, Miss Alpha."

I looked into his piercing blue eyes, and asked, "Why did you say that's not what you want then?"

"Because I don't want to just hit it and quit it. I want to hit it over and over again, for as long as you'll have me. I want you to be my girlfriend, my Miss Alpha. And I most definitely don't want to quit it."

"Oh," I replied, taken aback.

"When I said you were worth fighting for, I wasn't just trying to make you feel better. I truly believed it. And I want to fight for you. Though, I'm hoping you won't put up too much of a fight, because there's literally a hotel room upstairs that I will book right now."

"I have to go home though," I replied.

"There is a pretty bad blizzard outside. It might not be safe to drive. I mean, my car would probably make it, but I am having a couple drinks so it's better safe than sorry."

"What will my parents say?"

"I will text your father right now."

"You have my father's phone number?"

"I do. We've become quite friendly recently. We have a common interest."

"What's that?"

"Seeing his daughter happy."

I stared at him, mouth wide open.

Someone deposited our burgers onto the table and then the waiter came by with our drinks, placing them in front of us. "How's your food looking?" he asked.

"Looks perfect. I can't wait to devour every bit," Blake said as he stared at me. After the waiter left, he spoke again. "So is everything sorted then? No more excuses?"

I nodded, feeling like I was in a trance.

"Ok, good, I'll be right back." He got up and I watched as he walked out of the restaurant and disappeared around the corner.

I took a sip of my new martini and picked at my fries. Blake was right—they were really good. A few minutes later, he returned and sat back down next to me, picking up his burger and taking a bite out of it. I followed his lead and did the same. After he put it back down and swallowed, he said, "I let your father know the circumstances of the blizzard and he completely understood. I let him know you'd have your own room, of course. I just didn't mention that both rooms happen to be in the same suite, but what he doesn't know can't hurt him."

When we finished our burgers, a busser came by to take our plates, and the waiter followed. "You're in luck as we have some wonderful desserts to offer tonight."

Blake cut him off and said, "It's all right. We'll take the check, please. We'll be enjoying dessert in our room tonight."

The waiter replied, "Of course, sir, completely understand," and walked away.

Blake then turned to me and said, "Sorry, that was rude. I should have made sure you didn't want any actual dessert. If you did, I'll go get him and put the order in."

"It's okay," I replied.

"We can always order room service later anyway." He smiled mischievously. "After we've built up another appetite."

Chapter 65

Jasmine

After Blake paid and signed the check, he took my hand and led me to a bank of elevators. As soon as we stepped inside an empty elevator and the door closed, he had his mouth on me, kissing me desperately. I jumped up, and he supported me as I wrapped my legs around him and he pushed me against the wall. I lost myself in the kiss, my whole body aroused with anticipation. My thighs were burning, my panties so wet I was sure Blake could feel it through my dress as his erection throbbed against me. Everything between my legs was pulsing and swollen, desperate to feel Blake inside me. I was already imagining his naked body against mine. When the elevator dinged, signaling the doors opening, we were both gasping for air. He hoisted me up over his shoulder as if I weighed nothing and practically sprinted down the hallway. Once he found the right door, he pulled a key card out of his pocket and threw the door open. I didn't even bother to look around the suite as he carried me into the bedroom.

    He gently lowered me to the floor and threw his suit jacket off onto a chair. Working quickly, he loosened his tie and undid the buttons of his dress shirt, pulling both off, revealing his amazing upper body. I took my time letting my eyes trail his massive shoulders and arms, rocklike pecs, the deep cuts that defined his Herculean abs, and the V-cuts that directed my eyes lower to where his massive erection was straining against the fabric of his pants. My legs were weak, practically shaking as he walked toward me, striding past me until he was behind me. I felt his fingertips on my shoulders, sending a shiver down my spine as he pushed my hair forward, revealing the back of my neck to him. He slowly kissed down from the nape of my neck to the zipper of my dress. Soon the only sound was that of my zipper being pulled downward, my dress loosening and falling from my body. He continued to kiss across my back, from shoulder to shoulder and down my spine, provoking me to arch my back as he unsnapped my bra. His lips slowly trailed the length of my back until he reached my ass, pulling my panties down, dropping them to the floor. I stepped out of them, the only thing left on my body being a pair of heels, the rest of me uncovered and bare.

I took a deep breath, doing my best to steady my shaking hands and not let on to how nervous I suddenly was, being completely exposed to Blake. But I was instantly put at ease when his hands slid back up my legs, the gentle graze of his palms consoling me, evoking a shiver that overtook my whole body. My leg muscles tensed under his fingertips as he slowly traced his way north until his mouth found its way back to my ass. He kissed up each cheek slowly, as if he was savoring them, his hands pulling me against his mouth, the stubble on his chin tickling the delicate skin. The sensation provoked the whole lower half of my body to throb with desire, and I couldn't help but let out soft moans in response.

He pulled away to say, "Most amazing ass." My breathing shallowed and I didn't think I'd ever been so aroused before, my whole body on fire. I turned around to face him and he got back up, putting his mouth back on mine, our tongues intertwining, hot with need. His hands slid down my back to my ass and he picked me up, throwing me onto the bed. He instantly dropped to the ground to untie and remove his shoes and socks, his hands fumbling urgently. I hurriedly unfastened my shoes at the same time, flinging them across the room. He then undid his belt and pants, hastily pulling everything off until he was completely naked standing in front of me, his erection prominent. He took in my body with a grin on his face and hunger in his eyes. I'd never felt so sexy before as I did when I was able to suddenly see myself through Blake's glistening eyes.

I held his gaze and he stepped toward me. He climbed onto the bed, positioning himself on top of me. His eyes were directly above mine as he lowered his mouth to mine, pecking my lips and kissing down my chin, down the front of my neck, kissing back up to behind my ear. I instinctively grabbed on to his arms as my muscles shuddered, holding onto them as his mouth trailed back down my neck, to my chest, to one of my breasts. He sucked my nipple into his mouth, and I let out a deep moan, completely lost in the moment. His tongue traced the circumference of my nipple, and then he kissed his way to the other breast before doing the same thing. He looked up at me, locking his eyes with mine for a split second, and then lowered his mouth back onto my body, kissing between my breasts, bringing his mouth slowly down the center of my abdomen, kissing to my belly button and past it, all the way down to my legs.

He lifted my legs and placed them over his shoulders and he planted his mouth on the inside of one of my thighs, kissing and nibbling on it, teasing me, eliciting more moans from me as I felt a desperate pulsing between my legs. He then turned his head and did the same thing to the other, spending an excruciatingly long time doing so, making me desperate to feel his mouth farther north.

His hands found my hips, pulling my body closer to his mouth, and he slowly kissed up my inner thigh and paused. When he didn't continue his journey upward, I looked down at him staring back up at me, a mischievous smile on his face. He removed his right hand from my hip, and before I could comprehend what he was doing, I felt two fingers plunge inside me, eliciting a gasp from me.

He looked back up at me and said, "My curiosity has finally been fully satisfied. Your text message was correct—you're very, very wet, and I'm very, very thirsty."

He thrust his fingers in and out of me, a loud moan escaping my lips as he added a third, building pressure. He lowered his mouth, planting it between my legs above his fingers, sucking on me, adding his tongue, finding the exact spot that gave me the most pleasure. I moaned even more loudly from the sensation of his fingers moving within me while his tongue brought me close to orgasm.

He suddenly stopped, looked up at me, and asked, "Do you really want to have sex?"

"Yes," I nodded, maybe a little too eagerly, thinking I would die if I didn't have him, my entire body desperate for him. I was already sweating, my whole body wet with desire, the bedsheets underneath me soaked with my arousal.

"Okay, good, because I am going fucking crazy not being inside you." He lowered my legs from his shoulders and crawled over to the bedside table where there was a box that he tore open and pulled out a condom.

"Where did that come from?" I asked, lifting myself up onto my forearms.

He smirked and said, "I made a request when I booked the room." My cheeks burned at the thought of whoever was involved in this request knowing what was currently happening.

"You're so cute when you're embarrassed," he said as he rolled the condom onto his massive erection. He then positioned himself directly above me, lowered his body so close to me that his body heat and scent completely engulfed me, and said, "Are you sure, Jasmine? We don't have to do this if you don't want to."

"I do want to," I replied, overwhelmed with lust, ready to beg for it.

"Thank Goddess, because I don't think I'd ever recover from the blue balls I'd have if you'd said no. I want you so fucking bad right now." He put his mouth back on mine, kissing me gently. His erection pulsed between my legs, its head right at my opening. I placed my arms on his back as he pushed inside of me slowly. I audibly gasped as my body struggled to accommodate his very generous size, feeling substantial pressure. My eyes watered as he looked down at me and asked, "Are you okay?"

"Yeah," I replied, staring into his enchanting blue eyes. He nodded, giving me a small smile, and pushed himself further in and began moving back and forth slowly. A pleasure pulsed through me at the feeling of him moving inside me, against my inner walls. His lips gently touched mine as he kissed me sweetly, and I'd never felt closer to someone before, losing myself in the shared moment.

After some time, he began to increase the speed of his movement, bringing his hand down between my legs, rubbing my most sensitive area. He continued to kiss me as he moved against my body. I savored the sensation of him being both on top of me and inside me, his lips on mine, and his fingers triggering a building sensation within my body.

My thighs trembled as I dug my nails into Blake's back and moaned against his mouth. Our kisses turned more frenzied and desperate, mimicking the urgent and accelerated movement of Blake's hips caressing the insides of my thighs. The intense feeling kept building within me until I felt an eruption course through my body, a loud moan escaping my lips. I orgasmed intensely, feeling the warmth and calm spread from the center of my body to my fingers and toes. After my release, Blake groaned loudly and collapsed on top of me, panting heavily, and lifted his head to look at me.

Not even seconds after, a trance came over me—a desire to put my mouth on Blake's neck. I felt my canines expand as I moved my head to position them in the perfect spot where his collarbone met his neck.

"Jasmine!" Blake gasped, snapping me out of my trance. I looked up at him to see that his canines were also enlarged.

"What was I doing?" I asked, pulling away from his neck.

"You were about to mark me," he replied, his words a bit muddled, from having to speak with large canines.

"Does this normally happen after sex?" I asked, my words muddled too.

"No, no it doesn't. Only when you sleep with your mate. To be honest, I've never had this happen with anyone except Ria. It's kind of freaking me out. I had the urge to mark you too."

"Oh," I replied, not knowing what to make of what he was telling me.

"Just wait it out. They'll shrink again," he said, kissing me on the forehead, getting up, and walking to the bathroom. He returned moments later, after my canines had shrunk back down to normal size, and crawled into the bed next to me, pulling the covers over us and bringing my body against his.

"What does it mean that that happened?" I asked.

"I don't know. As far as I know, if you want to mark someone who's not your mate, you have to intentionally do it. It doesn't just automatically happen like with a mate."

"Mm," I replied, thoughts swirling around my head.

"Don't worry about it too much tonight. Let's just enjoy being with each other," he said, spooning me and putting his fingers through my hair. "The night started out shitty, but ended pretty epic."

"Are you okay, Blake?" I asked, suddenly feeling terrible that we did this on the night of his father's funeral.

"I'm feeling much better now," he replied. "What better way to celebrate my father's life than to do exactly what he enjoyed the most?" He gave a soft chuckle. "Not that that's something I exactly want to think about right now."

Chapter 66

Blake

It was an amazing night. We had round two and round three after the first, barely sleeping. Then, the next morning, after we woke, we had round four. I was practically singing as I drove Jasmine home and dropped her at her parents' house.

I snuck into the packhouse and quickly showered and got dressed. Then I made my way downstairs to the office where Luke was already at his desk, concentrated on his laptop.

"What's up, what's up!" I said as I walked in, a big smile on my face.

"You're in an oddly good mood this morning." Luke looked up at me.

"Too much coffee. Maybe I should get some more," I said, getting up and heading to the kitchen. I quickly poured myself a mug. "Good morning, Connie!" I sang out, looking over at her preparing some food.

"Good morning, Alpha." She looked at me oddly. "Would you like me to make you some breakfast?"

"Yes, that would be great!" I smiled, taking my mug and heading back to the office, whistling.

"So, what's good?" I looked at Luke.

"You're acting very strange this morning," Luke replied. Then he did a double take and asked, "Did you get laid or something?" After a second, he said, "Actually, never mind, please don't answer that. I'd rather not know."

I sat down at my desk and turned on my laptop. While going through my emails, I noticed one from the priest asking me to stop by the temple that day to pick up my father's ashes. This was perfect timing as I wanted to speak with him anyway. I got up and almost bumped into Connie as I was walking out of the office.

"Your breakfast, Alpha," she said.

"I'll take it to go," I said, grabbing a couple of pieces of toast off the plate and walking away.

As I walked down the hall, I heard her say, "What's gotten into Alpha?"

I exited through the front door and walked down the street to the temple. I entered and walked to the priest's office to see he was sitting at his desk with the door open. "Good morning, Bernard," I said as I walked in.

"Good morning, Alpha. You must be here for your father's ashes?"

"Yes, I am, but I actually also have a personal question, if you don't mind."

"Of course," he replied, gesturing for me to sit. I quickly closed the door to his office and sat down.

"I hope you don't mind that this will be about a more 'adult' subject than you probably normally discuss with our pack members."

"I am happy to help however I can, Alpha. Please don't be shy."

"Okay, great. So, this is a bit of an awkward conversation, but I'm hoping you might understand it better than I do. Normally, when I, well, have relations with women who are not my mate, my canines do not extend, and I don't have the urge to mark them. However, I recently had a few encounters with a woman who, of course, is also not my mate. But, for some reason, we both had the urge to mark each other. In fact, she almost did after the first encounter until I stopped her."

He sat back in his chair, rubbing his chin, looking at me. After some time, he said, "To be honest, Alpha, this is the first I've heard of such a thing happening. It is possible that it has happened to others, but most people are not so open about their relations with me, so this particular situation has simply just never been brought to my attention."

"What do you think it means?" I asked.

"Well, I'm not certain, but if I had to make a theory, I would say that perhaps it means that the Moon Goddess approves of the match you have made with your most recent partner. And if I had to further theorize, I'd say that you, Alpha, may have been granted a second-chance mate." He smiled at me.

"Do second-chance mates exist?" I asked.

"Not officially. But Artemis is full of surprises."

"Thank you, sir," I said, getting up, then turned back around as a thought came to me. "Sir, considering the facts and circumstances, where there's a highly likely chance that this woman I speak of may be a second-chance mate, granted by Artemis herself, would you consider allowing us to marry in the temple? Even if she may have rejected her true mate?"

"Well, you're the alpha, and I can't exactly undermine your authority," he said, winking at me.

"Thank you, sir," I replied.

"Now let me go get your father's ashes, Alpha," Bernard said, getting up from his chair. I followed him down the hall where he retrieved an urn from another office and handed it to me. "Alpha, I am very sorry for your loss again. I knew your father for many years. He was a very complicated man with a difficult past. But I still remember the day he told me that your mother was expecting you. I don't believe I'd ever seen him so happy. He was always very proud of you and spoke very highly of you to me. I want you to know that. Now, go on, I'm sure you have more important things to attend to."

I smiled and said goodbye. Instead of heading back to the packhouse, I walked to my mom's house. After my parents moved out of the packhouse, they moved into a small house in the downtown area so that they would be close by if needed. I rang the doorbell, and my mom answered the door, beckoning me inside.

"I have Dad's ashes," I said, holding out the urn.

"Thank you, Blake," she said, taking the urn from me and putting it on the entryway table. "Do you want to sit down for a bit? Let me make you some tea."

"Okay," I replied, walking after her and pulling out a chair at the kitchen table. "How are you doing?"

"I'm okay, Blake. Just taking things day by day." She filled a kettle with water.

"You know, mom, I'm sorry to say this, but I'm not actually that sad about Dad's death. I know he wasn't all bad, but a lot of him was pretty terrible. He tortured both of us for years. I appreciate that he sacrificed his life for me, but it doesn't make up for everything he did. You deserved better than him. I've always thought it was messed up that the Moon Goddess mated you to him."

She came over and put her arms around me. "It's okay to feel the way you do, Blake. But if I weren't mated to your father, I wouldn't have you. For that, at least, I am thankful."

Chapter 67

Jasmine

After getting home Saturday morning, I rushed to take a shower and change into new clothes. I was extremely late for work, having completely forgotten about my shift that day. I checked my phone as soon as I walked through the door of my house to find frantic messages from Valerie. I was supposed to be there at seven thirty and I ended up walking in at eleven to come face-to-face with Lucy.

"Looks like Perfect Jasmine finally decided to grace us with her presence," Lucy taunted me as I walked past her to drop my stuff off in the back and throw on an apron.

"Where have you been?" Valerie asked, coming over to me.

"Sorry. Late night," I replied. "Got stuck far away because of the blizzard."

"Far away?" Valerie raised her eyebrow at me. "Never mind, you can tell me later. We have a line of customers. Get to work."

I went up front, taking my place to prepare orders as they came in, trying my best to avoid interaction with Lucy. I noted that she now had a proper baby bump, very clearly pregnant. Although you would never guess when she turned her back to you, still just as skinny as ever everywhere else.

After the rush ended, Valerie came out front and stood in front of Lucy. "Thanks for filling in, Lucy. You can go home now if you'd like."

"No problem," she said, walking out back to grab all her things before leaving.

Valerie crossed her arms and looked at me sternly. "I'm going to let it slide today since I know you're going through a lot right now. But it's not fair to others to have to fill in for you when you can't make it. And it's not fair on me to not even send me a text message to let me know you'll be late."

"I know. I'm sorry," I replied, sighing.

"Well, the tables need to be cleaned. You can tell me your excuse after. I'm dying to know what happened now." She playfully smiled, walking away toward the back.

I grabbed the spray bottle and a rag and made my way to the dining area to wipe down the tables. I was spraying cleaner when Lucy stepped in front of me. I looked up at her, wondering what she wanted now.

She looked at me for a second and then said, "Jasmine, I just want to say thank you for finding Luke that day. He told me the whole story of what happened and what you did, and I don't think he'd still be alive if it weren't for you." She leaned forward and wrapped her arms around me. Then just as quickly as she hugged me, she pulled away and walked out the door.

I continued cleaning the tables, wondering if we'd ever be friends again. At least Lucy didn't seem to hate me anymore. That was progress.

After I was back behind the counter and the café emptied, Valerie stepped out again. "Soooo." She looked at me. "You owe me a story now. Where were you last night? I can tell it must have been pretty interesting for you to completely forget about work. Maybe with a certain hot, sexy alpha?"

I could feel myself turning completely red.

"Thought so," she said, an amused look in her eyes.

"Okay, you caught me."

"Well, spit it out. I want to hear all the details. And don't leave any of the dirty parts out."

"Stop!" I said, laughing.

"Come on, I'm getting old! And Lucy's now betrothed. I need someone to live vicariously through."

I smiled and said, "Well, you were right. He doesn't want to be friends."

"Of course I was right. The way he looks at you is not the way a man looks at his friends." She grinned, pushing me on my arm playfully. "Well, now that you're here and the lunch rush is over, I'll be heading home. I'll try to get the story out of you next time you're in."

When I was locking up at four, I felt a presence behind me and inhaled Blake's scent. I turned around to face him, taking in his imposing presence looking down at me. "Hello, Miss Alpha. Long time no see." He broke out into a large smile, his eyes shining with happiness as they locked with mine.

"Hi, Blake," I replied, returning his smile, a warmth spreading through me at how cheery he appeared—much cheerier than he had ever seemed previously.

"I hope you weren't planning to go home because there are some issues at the packhouse that need your expertise to fix," he said in a gravelly voice, leaning close to me, his warm breath tickling my ear.

"What kind of issues?"

"Well, you see, I have a brand-new shower, and bathroom counters, and freshly tiled walls, that all need to be broken in. Oh, and then there's also the brand-new king-size bed with the same issue. And, unfortunately, there's no one else that's quite right for the job."

"I see," I replied, maintaining an even voice and keeping my cool. I was already becoming very aroused, my whole body heating with desire and a tingle traveling up the length of my legs. "I could definitely take a look."

"Wonderful, I hope you take payment in orgasms because I intend to pay you very generously for your work," he said grasping my hand, his large, calloused hand feeling nice against mine.

As he led me toward the packhouse, something came to me. "Blake?"

"Yes?" He turned to look at me, his eyes soft and attentive.

"You never told me how the battle ended."

He stopped and replied, "Well, we gained a new ally pack, the Pine Forest Pack in Ontario. After they withdrew their troops from the battle, we were easily able to overpower both the Silver Moon Pack and the Bois Sombre Pack. They withdrew their troops not long after. However, Alpha Édouard's still alive and remains a threat. Although, I'd say it'll be another few years before he tries to attack us again."

"I see."

"And, maybe, next time, you'll be fighting alongside me as my luna." He grinned, giving my hand a squeeze.

"Your luna?" I asked, taken aback by him thinking so far ahead with our relationship. But then, I realized, something about it seemed right and comforting in a way being with Luke never had.

"You would make an excellent luna, Miss Alpha." He bent down to kiss me, pulling me against his body, his muscular arms holding me tightly against him. After he withdrew, he continued. "But, let's not make any decisions today. There are some issues that need attending to at the packhouse, very urgent issues. So let's not waste any time."

THE END

To be continued: *Wolfblood*, book 2 of the *Wolfbane* series

Author's Note

Thanks for reading my debut novel *Wolfbane*!

If you enjoyed this book, please consider leaving me a review! Honest, authentic reviews and feedback, written by real readers, are invaluable to authors, especially indie ones such as myself. If you have a few moments to spare, I'd really appreciate it, even if it's only a quick sentence to say you enjoyed the book!

To stay informed of future book releases, please follow me on Instagram: @celiahartauthor

About Celia Hart

Celia Hart is a boring accountant by day and a secret paranormal romance writer by night. Much like Jasmine, she grew up with conservative parents who would likely be horrified if they ever learned about her books. Unlike Jasmine, she is a city girl who quite enjoys the company of humans. She lives just outside of Boston, MA with her two miniature schnauzers. When she's not writing, her other hobbies include traveling, eating, cooking, and indulging in her Louboutin addiction.